"Boasts a colorful cast of characters, a cool setting, and a twisty mystery." —Emma Holly

"From start to finish, *Stormwalker* is an electrifying read—hot, thrilling, tremendous fun—with characters who burn the page with so much chemistry, between themselves and the reader, that you'll be begging for more after the last word."
—Marjorie M. Liu, *New York Times* bestselling author

"James is on a hot streak as she launches an amazing new series with a book that is sexy and dynamic. This heroine has baggage galore, but also guts to spare. The mix of kick-butt action, fiery passion, and serious drama ensures readers will want to revisit this world ASAP." —*Romantic Times* (Top Pick)

"An exciting start to a new series with an electrifying blend of paranormal and real world . . . A fun read!" —*Fresh Fiction*

"Addictively compelling . . . I can't wait to read more about [Janet and Mick] when *Firewalker* comes out."
—*All Things Urban Fantasy*

"If you're looking for a book that packs romance, adventure, passion, and magic, then pick up *Stormwalker* and ride the lightning." —*Dark Wyrm Reads*

"WOW!! That was my primary reaction after turning the last page in this paranormal gem by Allyson James. *Stormwalker* grabbed me from the first page and took me on one wild and crazy roller-coaster ride." —*The Romance Dish*

"Allyson James weaves a wonderful story full of intrigue, mystery, suspense, and romance while at the same time tempting the reader with what might be next for Janet and Mick."
—*Romance Novel News*

continued . . .

Mortal Seductions

"This story will hook you from the first word to the last one . . . A very tempting read."

—*Night Owl Reviews*

"*Mortal Seductions* does an excellent job developing Demitri's story, and showing the depth of feeling between himself and Val . . . Very interesting love scenes . . . I loved watching Val and Demitri try to work out their issues. Excellent job!"

—*Romance Junkies* (five stars)

"A very modern story with lots of homages to ancient cultures and lots of hot, powerful men. Amazing characters kept me involved from beginning to end. Ms. James brings the heat, adventure, and juicy surprises that readers are demanding. The sex is smokin' hot . . . both sensual and amusing."

—*Just Erotic Romance Reviews* (five stars)

Mortal Temptations

"The balance of intrigue, romance, and unbridled sexual fantasies makes James's story of gods, demigods, and mortals a sizzling page-turner. This book is the start of a series featuring these delicious partners."

—*Romantic Times*

"Hot! Hot! Hot! It doesn't get much hotter than this one . . . If you enjoy stories full of action, both in the bedroom and out, this is one story you will want to read." —*The Romance Studio*

The Dragon Master

"Superb . . . A masterful tale."

—*Alternative Worlds*

"If you're looking for a book that's full of passion, characters who'll capture your heart, and some truly great storytelling, look no further: *The Dragon Master* is here. Get your copy today!"

—*Romance Reviews Today*

"For a fantastic romantic fantasy suspense with a delightful ethnic twist I recommend *The Dragon Master*."

—*ParaNormal Romance*

"Allyson James does an amazing job blending paranormal elements and enough heat to keep the reader turning the pages. I had a hard time putting this story down as the fiery passion that Seth and Carol have will leave you wanting more and more of these dragons! *The Dragon Master* will make you want your very own dragon to curl up with and keep you warm."

—*TwoLips Reviews*

"There are two stories going on simultaneously in this book. One is about a dragon master no one knows about and a demon god. The other is the love story between Seth and Carol. Both are good stories but together and intertwined they are fantastic. Readers can enjoy the mysteries of one and the tender love scenes of the other. The action concerning each never slows down."

—*Night Owl Reviews*

"I have loved every one of Allyson James's stories so far and have to say this one was no different. You are brought into a world just this side of reality, and you really don't want to leave. My favorite part of these books (aside from the dragons of course) is their entwining story lines and characters . . . I look forward to seeing what else is in store for us from Ms. James."

—*Fallen Angel Reviews*

The Black Dragon

"One of my favorite authors. A unique and magical urban paranormal with dragons, witches, and demons. Will keep you enthralled until the very last word!"

—Cheyenne McCray, *New York Times* bestselling author

"A fabulously delicious read."

—*Darque Reviews*

"Begins with a bang and the action never lets up, not for one single, solitary, wonderful moment. I devoured this book in just a few hours . . . So overwhelming that I couldn't even consider putting this book down. The story is unusual, wonderfully original, and filled with intriguing characters . . . Dragons, magic, and a fight to save the world—Allyson James has a winning combination that makes *The Black Dragon* a story to remember!"

—*Romance Reader at Heart*

"A book destined to leave a smile on your face and dragons in your dreams. Get your copy today." —*Romance Reviews Today*

"[Allyson James] keeps the sexual tension up to the point of boiling . . . Such an incredible talent." —*TwoLips Reviews*

Dragon Heat

"[A] delightful romantic fantasy . . . A fun tale of life between a mortal and her dragon." —*The Best Reviews*

"Ms. James's imaginative story is exceptionally intriguing . . . Highly sensual." —*The Eternal Night*

"This story has a wonderful fairy-tale feel about it. Allyson James does an outstanding job of creating and bringing these mystical creatures to life with characteristics and emotions that you can't help but fall deeply in love with; even the so-called *evil* Black Dragon with his cocky, bad-boy qualities will make the reader hum in pleasure and clamor for his story." —*TwoLips Reviews*

"A sizzling paranormal romance. Ms. James pens a riveting story that's brimming with action, sinfully sexy characters, and the beautiful gift of love. A magical and thoroughly enchanting read." —*Darque Reviews*

"A sexy, funny romantic romp . . . A truly mesmerizing read. The chemistry between Caleb and Lisa is searing and the love scenes are wonderfully entertaining." —*Romance Reader at Heart*

Firewalker

Allyson James

BERKLEY SENSATION, NEW YORK

THE BERKLEY PUBLISHING GROUP
Published by the Penguin Group
Penguin Group (USA) Inc.
375 Hudson Street, New York, New York 10014, USA

Penguin Group (Canada), 90 Eglinton Avenue East, Suite 700, Toronto, Ontario M4P 2Y3, Canada
(a division of Pearson Penguin Canada Inc.)
Penguin Books Ltd., 80 Strand, London WC2R 0RL, England
Penguin Group Ireland, 25 St. Stephen's Green, Dublin 2, Ireland (a division of Penguin Books Ltd.)
Penguin Group (Australia), 250 Camberwell Road, Camberwell, Victoria 3124, Australia
(a division of Pearson Australia Group Pty. Ltd.)
Penguin Books India Pvt. Ltd., 11 Community Centre, Panchsheel Park, New Delhi—110 017, India
Penguin Group (NZ), 67 Apollo Drive, Rosedale, North Shore 0632, New Zealand
(a division of Pearson New Zealand Ltd.)
Penguin Books (South Africa) (Pty.) Ltd., 24 Sturdee Avenue, Rosebank, Johannesburg 2196,
South Africa

Penguin Books Ltd., Registered Offices: 80 Strand, London WC2R 0RL, England

This is a work of fiction. Names, characters, places, and incidents either are the product of the author's imagination or are used fictitiously, and any resemblance to actual persons, living or dead, business establishments, events, or locales is entirely coincidental. The publisher does not have any control over and does not assume any responsibility for author or third-party websites or their content.

FIREWALKER

A Berkley Sensation Book / published by arrangement with the author

PRINTING HISTORY
Berkley Sensation mass-market edition / November 2010

Copyright © 2010 by Jennifer Ashley.
Excerpt from *Shadowwalker* by Allyson James © by Jennifer Ashley.
Cover art by Tony Mauro.
Cover design by George Long.
Interior text design by Kristin del Rosario.

ISBN: 978-0-425-23782-3

BERKLEY® SENSATION
Berkley Sensation Books are published by The Berkley Publishing Group,
a division of Penguin Group (USA) Inc.,
375 Hudson Street, New York, New York 10014.
BERKLEY® SENSATION and the "B" design are trademarks of Penguin Group (USA) Inc.

PRINTED IN THE UNITED STATES OF AMERICA

10 9 8 7 6 5 4 3 2 1

Acknowledgments

I would like to thank my editor, Kate Seaver, for supporting this series, her assistant, Katherine Pelz, for all her hard work, and the wonderful publicists at Berkley: Kathryn Tumen and Erin Galloway, for their support and behind-the-scenes greatness. Also to my readers, who took a chance on this new direction for Allyson James and encouraged me to continue.

One

I knew she was a Changer the minute she walked into my little hotel. *Wolf,* I thought from her gray white eyes, but her human features were Native American. Her dark skin and black hair made her incongruous eyes all the more terrifying. So did the fact that she was shifting even as she raced across the lobby, grabbed me by the shirt front, and slammed me against the polished reception counter.

I looked up into the face of a nightmare. Half-changed, her nose and mouth elongated into that of a wolf's, fangs coated with saliva jutting from bloodred gums.

I had no defenses. There wasn't a cloud in the sky, no storm to channel to fight her with. The wards in my walls functioned to keep evil beings like skinwalkers and Night-walkers from entering the hotel, but Changers weren't inherently evil, just arrogant. But when provoked, they tended to attack first, ask questions of the shredded corpse later.

I brought up my fist to slam her jaw, but she shook off the punch and hung on to me. I couldn't scream for Mick, because Mick had vanished into the night three weeks ago, and even the magic mirror didn't know where he was.

There was no one was in the hotel but me and my new manager, Cassandra, in her neat turquoise business suit, her blond hair in a sleek bun. The tourists were out or not yet checked in, the saloon closed. It was just us girls: a crazed Changer, a powerless Stormwalker, and a witch who stared across the reception desk in shock.

"Janet Begay," the wolf-woman said, her voice clotted with the change.

"Who wants to know?" I tried to kick her off, but she held on to me, claws poised to tear out my throat.

On the other side of the desk Cassandra crossed her arms, placed her palms on her shoulders, and started to chant. An inky cloud snaked out of her mouth, shot across the counter, and wrapped around the Changer. The Changer snarled. She shoved away from me and leapt over the counter at Cassandra.

Cassandra went down with the wolf-woman on top of her, the two grappling in a tangle of raw silk and black leather. I charged behind the counter and grabbed the Changer by the hair, her sleek black braid giving me something to grip. I pulled, but she was damn strong. She had Cassandra's head in her hands, ready to beat her skull on the Saltillo tile.

I grabbed a talisman from my pocket, clenched it in my hand, and screamed, "Stop!"

The Changer halted in mid-slam. Cassandra's head fell from her slack grip and bumped to the floor.

I waved the talisman—a bundle of rosemary bound with

wire and onyx—in the Changer's face and said in a hard voice, "Obey."

The Changer straightened up, fangs and claws receding, her face becoming human again. Her eyes remained gray, the fury in them electric.

Cassandra rose beside her in the same rigid compulsion and fixed me with a frustrated stare.

Oops. But I couldn't release Cassandra without also releasing the Changer. Mick and I had made this spell for emergencies, such as a horde of skinwalkers attacking. It was a blanket spell that wouldn't stop the attackers entirely but might at least slow them down until help arrived.

"In there," I panted, pointing at my little office behind reception. "Go in. Sit down."

The Changer marched inside, still growling softly. Cassandra followed her like a robot.

The Changer and Cassandra sat next to each other on my new sofa, both women radiating fury. They looked odd together, the sophisticated hotel manager, only a little disheveled in spite of the fight, and the Changer in black leather pants and jacket. Both struggled to break the spell, bodies swaying a little as they willed their muscles to obey. But the talisman held both Mick's dragon magic and my Stormwalker magic, a potent combination, so they'd have to put up with it.

"Who are you?" I asked the Changer.

"Pamela Grant."

"Cassandra Bryson."

"What are you doing here?"

Cassandra started telling me about whatever job she'd been doing before the Changer attacked, but Pamela said, "I was sent."

"Who sent you? To do what?"

They both started talking at once. I tuned out Cassandra and focused on Pamela. "I have a message for you, Storm-walker."

"Is that all? Then why did you attack me?"

While Cassandra protested that she had no intention of attacking me, Pamela said, "I had to, to pass on the message. Then this Wiccan bitch tried to paralyze me."

"What the hell is this message? You couldn't just tell me?"

For answer, Pamela pulled out a short-bladed knife. My eyes widened, and I shook the talisman. "Stop! Obey!"

Cassandra went rigid. Pamela came at me, her eyes fixed, as though she listened to a voice more distant than mine. I realized as she jumped me that she was under another compulsion spell, one strong enough to cancel out mine. That couldn't be good.

I fought. Cassandra remained seated, eyes fixed in agony. Pamela pinned me to the desk with her strong body and extended my left arm across the top of it.

"Cassandra, get her off me!" I shouted.

Cassandra sprang to her feet but fell back as though an invisible hand had shoved her. At the same time I smelled a bite of sulfur, hot wind, fire—the scents of dragon magic.

I stared at Pamela in shock as she nicked my palm with her knife. She flipped my hand over and squeezed a puddle of my blood onto a pristine piece of Crossroads Hotel notepaper. Dipping my forefinger in the blood, she forced me to write the words, *Help me.*

As soon as we'd formed the last "e" in "me," Pamela went limp, and her eyes rolled back in her head. I lowered her slumped body to the floor, my palm stinging where she'd cut it. As the compulsion spell released her, the Changer woman drew a peaceful breath.

I straightened up. My veins burned like fire, and my temples started pounding as the compulsion spell latched onto me. I understood now why Pamela hadn't simply relayed the message verbally or at least reached for something as conventional as a pen. She'd needed to transfer the spell through my blood.

Help me. The words screamed at me from the paper and brought my own fears boiling to the surface. I'd been worried sick about Mick, even though I'd told myself he'd simply gone off to do whatever dragon thing he needed to do. Mick came and went as he pleased, he always had, although lately he'd been nice about telling me where he was going.

Pamela's message meant that Mick was in trouble. Trapped. Ill. Maybe dying. If Mick was begging for *my* help, he was in deep shit, indeed.

My head turned of its own accord, and my gaze moved out the window to the west, where the distant mound of the San Francisco Peaks, the traditional boundary of the Navajo lands, lay in misty silhouette.

The spell made me want to race out of the hotel, leap on my Harley, and ride off toward the mountains, now, now, *now*. But Mick would want me to be smart. I needed supplies, I needed to plan, and I'd need help. The fact that the spell let me calm myself and think this through meant that I was right.

I forced my gaze back to Cassandra, who was still sitting stiffly on the sofa. I lifted the talisman, broke it, and said, "Be free."

Cassandra leapt to her feet, face dark with rage, and kicked the inert Changer in the buttocks with her Blahnik heel. "That's for calling me a bitch."

Pamela opened her eyes. The white in them had faded to human brown, and though she retained the arrogant scorn of the Changer, she no longer looked terrifying.

She pushed herself into a sitting position and smoothed back hair that had fallen from her braid. "Hey, doesn't mean I wouldn't want to sleep with you."

Cassandra flushed and folded her arms, but she didn't look as offended as she could have.

"She was under a spell," I said tightly. "And now it's gone. Right?"

The Changer woman rubbed the back of her neck. "Finally. Your boyfriend is damn strong."

"Can you give me more specific directions than 'head west'?"

Pamela shook her head. "I was on the northwest side of Death Valley when your dragon man's spell grabbed me. But there must be a memory cloud spell on the place, because I don't remember exactly where. I was doing some hunting, minding my own business, and the next thing I know, I'm digging my way through a tunnel and talking to a dragon. He couldn't talk back; he just invaded me with that damned spell. Bastard."

"When was this?" I asked.

"Middle of last night; then I rode straight here."

"Mick was alone? No other dragons around?"

"One was enough. I'd never seen a dragon before, never believed they existed." Her eyes flickered to gray and back to brown again. "Imagine my surprise."

That was Changer for "It scared the shit out of me." Changers didn't like to admit fear. Fear meant weakness, submission, and they took dominance-submission roles very seriously.

Pamela pulled herself to her feet with lithe grace. She was tall for a Native American, but most Changers were tall. She towered a good foot over me. "Compulsion spells make me hungry. Is there anything to eat in this godsforsaken town?"

"The saloon's closed until five," I said while I stared again at the clear blue of the western sky. "But there's a diner in Magellan. Two miles south."

"It'll have to do. Come with me, Wiccan?"

Cassandra gave her a withering glance. "In your dreams, wolf-girl."

Pamela gave her a half smile, shrugged, and sauntered out of the office. Cassandra followed close behind, her spiked heels on the lobby tiles a staccato contrast to the thud of Pamela's motorcycle boots. Through the window, I watched the Changer woman walk out of the hotel, mount her bike, and ride off toward Magellan.

Once she was gone, Cassandra returned to my office and shut the door. She looked none the worse for wear for the fight, except for a faint bruise on her lower lip and one strand of fair hair fallen from her bun.

"What are you going to do, Janet?" she asked. "You can't charge off looking for Mick on the word of a Changer."

"It's not just her word." I pressed my fingers to my temples where the spell throbbed mercilessly. "I have to go. I have no choice. Mick must be desperate, or he wouldn't have sent her."

"Don't go alone."

Cassandra's eyes were light blue, beautiful in her pale face. She was from Los Angeles, where she'd held a high-profile job at a luxury hotel chain. Why she'd wanted to move out to the middle of nowhere to help run my hotel, I had no idea, but I never asked. She was good with the tourists, knew the hotel business, and she put up with my magic mirror. I didn't want to lose her by asking awkward questions.

"I won't be going alone," I said. "Can you keep things together here?"

"Of course."

Of course she would. Cassandra ran this place better than I ever could.

"Keep an eye on the Changer," I said.

Cassandra gave me an odd smile. "Oh, I will." She turned and walked out of the office, smoothing her hair as she went.

I flopped into the chair behind my desk and put my head in my hands. I ached all over, would ache until the spell took me to Mick.

I glanced at the framed photo of my father that rested on the desk, a slim Navajo in a formal velvet shirt, his hair neatly braided. I'd taken the picture on my last visit to Many Farms, and he'd insisting on dressing up for it. My father didn't believe in candid shots. His wise eyes held no advice, only quiet confidence that I'd know what to do.

I did know what to do. Or rather, who to turn to. I hadn't seen Coyote, who would have been the most help, in a long time, not even in my dreams, and I had no idea how to summon him. Jamison Kee, a mountain lion Changer, was the man in Magellan I trusted the most, but he had a wife and stepdaughter to take care of, and I couldn't bring myself to put him in danger.

That left the one man I *didn't* trust, but he was powerful as all get-out. I didn't understand his power, and neither did Mick, but if I could convince him to help, I knew I'd have a potent ally.

I pulled the phone toward me and punched in the number of the sheriff's office in Flat Mesa. The deputy at the desk put me straight through. The phone made a couple of clicks, and then the sheriff's voice sounded in my ear.

"Jones," he said. Dark, biting, laconic.

"Hey, Nash. It's Janet."

There was a long silence.

"Fuck," Nash Jones said clearly, and he hung up on me.

Two

Did I mention that the sheriff of Hopi County was an asshole? Everyone cuts Nash Jones some slack because he spent time in Iraq and had battled with PTSD, but he could be the most arrogant, in-your-face bastard that ever lived.

My head still thrumming with the spell, I buckled motorcycle chaps over my jeans and left the hotel. I rolled out my Harley, a nice little twelve hundred cc Sportster, midnight blue, and took the highway north to Flat Mesa.

It was cool, the September wind chill despite the blue sky, and I was glad of my jacket. It's desert out here, but we have altitude, nearly six thousand feet, which makes for crisp autumns and cold winters. I kept looking west, yearning to turn the bike that way and ride flat out. I needed to get to Mick, needed it with my whole body, and I would have, even without the spell.

Mick and I had our differences, and he was uneasy about

the latent magic I'd inherited from my bitch-queen goddess mother, but the thought that someone held him captive worried me senseless. Mick was a strong, powerful dragon, who could wield fire magic even in his human form. Beings strong enough to imprison him would be terrifyingly powerful.

Mick had angered his dragon council this spring, and though we hadn't seen a hint of them all summer, dragons ranked up there with the kinds of beings capable of trapping Mick. And they seriously wanted to kill him.

I covered the twenty miles between Magellan and Flat Mesa quickly and pulled into the sheriff's department parking lot. Lopez grinned at me as I walked in, and he waved me through without stopping me. Lopez liked me. I think what he liked was that I stuck in Sheriff Jones's craw, and anything that could get under his boss's skin made him happy.

I did Jones the courtesy of knocking on his door. At his bitten off, "Come," I flung open the door and went inside.

Nash Jones glanced up at me with his habitual scowl, fluorescent light gleaming on his very short black hair. Nash was about thirty-two and had a hard but handsome face and gray eyes that could pierce a perp at forty paces. I'd seen criminals back down, whimpering, from that ice-cold stare. His khaki sheriff's uniform was spotless and wrinkle free, his badge shining. Even his creases had creases.

"I'm busy, Begay," he greeted me.

I leaned my fists on his desk, right over the nameplate that read "Nash Jones." "I need your help," I said in a rush. "Mick's being held against his will, out in Death Valley somewhere."

Nash didn't even blink. "Way out of my jurisdiction." He returned to the file on his desk. "Get the police up there to deal with it."

"It's not a simple kidnapping case. This is *Mick,* my giant dragon boyfriend. The police wouldn't stand a chance against anything that can snatch and hold Mick. Come on, Jones, please. I can't do this alone."

He gave me a flat stare. "You and Mick nearly got me killed, remember? You and your storms and fires and earthquakes and dragons. In fact, for the safety of everyone in Hopi County, I should haul you back to your reservation and tell the tribal police to keep you there."

Nash threatened me like this all the time and hadn't yet made good on it, but I knew that his bite really was as bad as his bark. Someday he might just arrest me and ship me back to the Navajo Nation, and the tribal police, who'd had to deal with me as a kid, would lock me up with glee.

"Believe me, if I thought I could rescue him alone, I would. If I could turn to someone else, I would. How about if I remind you that Mick once saved your ass?"

"Yes, he saved my ass from *you.* If you think I'll travel alone with you to someplace as remote as Death Valley, you're crazier than I thought."

I considered this while I hung over his desk and met the hardness in his eyes. It was true that last spring, Nash had gotten caught up in the madness when my evil goddess mother from Beneath—the shell world below this one— had possessed me and forced me to open the vortexes and let her out. She'd had nefarious plans for Nash too, because Nash, for some reason, wasn't affected by magic, any magic, no matter how powerful. My mother had wanted me to make a child with Nash, to produce a baby steeped in both my magic and Nash's ability to resist magic. Needless to say, Nash hadn't cooperated.

Nash had also taken a full blast of my mother's power,

not to mention Mick's fire, which should have obliterated any human being. But not only had Nash survived the attacks, he'd brushed them off and lived to be sarcastic about it.

Playing nice wasn't working. I needed to play dirty. "Tell you what," I said. "You help me, and I'll keep it quiet about you and Maya."

That got me a look of outrage. Maya Medina, a beautiful Latina woman who was my electrician and more or less my friend, had once had a thing going with Nash, a pretty serious one. When Nash had come home from war, they'd broken up—split at the seams was a better way of putting it. Even better, exploded into fiery fragments. What she and Jones had now couldn't be called a relationship—more a series of one-night stands—but Jones wanted it kept quiet. This hurt Maya, but she was proud and refused to acknowledge that she cared.

"Leave Maya alone," was his swift response.

"I don't think *she'd* mind if everyone knew you went to bed with her."

"Don't threaten me, Begay. No one would believe you, anyway. You're an outsider, and everyone thinks you're a little crazy." His tone said, *They're not wrong.*

"Maybe not," I said, producing my ace. "But they'd believe Fremont."

Jones jerked his head up again, and I knew I had him. Fremont Hansen, my plumber, was a nice guy, but he was also the biggest gossip in Hopi County. If I told Fremont the interesting tidbit about Jones and Maya, it would be all over Magellan and Flat Mesa by morning, and Nash knew it.

"Don't bluff me, Janet."

"I'm perfectly serious. I need you. You do this for me,

and your secret stays safe." I had no intention in the world of embarrassing Maya, but damn it, I was desperate.

"I don't have time to go traipsing through the desert," he tried.

"Not traipsing. It's a straight shot through Las Vegas, big wide freeways and highways the whole route." At least until we got to Death Valley itself. Then we'd have to search the knife-sharp mountains to find the tunnel Pamela had mentioned. I knew that once I got there, the spell would pull me to Mick's precise location, but I didn't think Nash wanted to hear that I had no idea where to start looking. "It's five or six hours there. We can be back by morning."

He gave me a severe look. "I can't leave right this minute. Maybe not until seven, or even eight. I have a job to do."

Oh, for fuck's sake. What was the use of being sheriff of the whole place if you couldn't come and go as you pleased? "There's that much crime around here that you can't take an afternoon off?"

"You want me to come with you, or not?"

I held up my hands. "Fine. Fine. You take your time."

"Go back to Magellan. I'll pick you up when I'm finished here." Nash opened his folder again and looked determinedly at it. Discussion over.

"You'll be driving?" I asked.

"I'm not riding all the way to Death Valley on the back of your motorcycle. Besides, we'll need a way to bring Mick back with us."

He was going to do it. My heart hammered in relief. I wanted to lunge across the desk and hug him, but I suspected that if I did, he'd break out the handcuffs. "Good. I'll be waiting."

I didn't miss his glare as I hurried out.

* * *

Nash showed up in front of the hotel at seven-thirty, and I was packed and ready. It was already dark, stars pricking the clear September sky. I'd been chafing with impatience and the spell, driving Cassandra crazy. She waved me off in obvious relief but told me to keep in touch—through the magic mirror if cell phones were out of range.

Nash drove his new truck, a shining black F-250 with a cab and a half and tinted windows. It looked freshly washed and polished, as though he'd readied it specifically for the trip. I tossed my duffel bag behind the front seat and climbed inside, sighing with relief that we were finally going. Nash said nothing, only waited until I'd buckled my seat belt before he drove carefully out of the parking lot, far too slowly for my taste. But at least we were off.

"Can't you go any faster?" I asked, as Nash drove up the highway at a sedate fifty miles an hour.

"No," Nash answered without looking at me.

He did the speed limit all the way to Winslow, and I was clenching my fists and biting the side of my mouth by the time we finally made it onto the I-40 heading west. Traffic picked up as we approached the Flagstaff exits, the town twinkling under the dark bulk of its volcanic mountains. The air grew chill, ponderosa pines soaring against the night sky. After Flagstaff, traffic died off again, and we rode down from green hills to rolling desert mountains.

Nash didn't talk. He didn't listen to the radio; he didn't offer conversation; he just drove. Eyes on the road, oncoming headlights glittering in his eyes, the red glow of the dashboard lighting his face. He never surpassed the speed limit—of course not—but then, he never slowed down, either.

I was a person who liked silence; my dad and I had enjoyed driving for hours through empty lands without words. But with Nash, the silence was strained. It took on its own personality—like a hostile relative who glared at a room until the happy chatter died away. It pressed on you, that silence, waited to beat you to death.

On the outskirts of Kingman, I said, "I hear that Maya's birthday is next week."

"I don't want to talk about Maya."

The answer, swift and abrupt, shut me down. Nash didn't even adjust his hands on the wheel.

He stopped for gas in Kingman and grudgingly let me use the bathroom, and then we took the highway that climbed north out of town, curving along the side of a mountain. Lights twinkled in the valley to our left, becoming sparser as we moved on. Within a few miles, the desert night was black again, the road straight and monotonous.

I folded my arms and slumped against the door, trying to grab some sleep while I could. I couldn't. My eyes stayed open, the spell pulling me onward.

After about another hour, the road began rolling through steep cuts, hard rock hammered out by dynamite long ago. To our left, beyond the hills that lined the road, was a steep drop to the Colorado River, which snaked its way southward through bone-dry land.

Orange cones gleamed ahead of us, directing us into one narrow lane that led to a checkpoint. There were only a few cars ahead of us this late, red taillights silhouetting drivers and passengers inside the cars.

I drummed my fingers on the dashboard as Nash slowed, but he had no choice. The road we took led over the massive Hoover Dam into Nevada, and a checkpoint had been set up by the nice feds to make sure we didn't do anything cute like carry explosives to the middle of the dam and set them off.

The cars in front of us moved through and drove on, but one of the officers held up his hand, signaling Nash to stop. Nash halted and rolled down the window, letting in a blast of cool night air and the acrid scent of exhaust. I folded into myself and tried not to scream in impatience.

The uniformed man strolled the few feet to us, flashlight shining. Every hair prickled on my skin, the latent Beneath magic in me screaming a warning.

"Nash, gun it," I whispered. "Get us out of here."

"Janet, if I speed out of here, every state and federal cop within range will be after us, and they won't be afraid to use deadly force."

"I'm telling you, there's something not right."

"I know that. I'm not stupid." Nash waited calmly, his hands on the wheel, as the fed approached. Gods, he drove me crazy.

"Can I see some ID?" the officer asked.

My insides crawled. I could feel the man's aura, thick, black, and inky. I had no idea what one of them was doing out here in the middle of the highway at a brightly lit checkpoint—an easy way to find victims, maybe?

The officer shone his light on the driver's license and sheriff's ID Jones handed him. The man lifted his brows and spoke in the friendly way of a patroller just doing his job. "Sheriff, eh? Official business?"

"Personal. Vacation."

The flashlight moved to me, and he smirked. "Vacation. I see. Pull over there, sir, and get out of the truck." He gestured to a pull-off just beyond the glare of the generator lights.

"Nash," I said frantically as Nash drove the few yards into the darkness. "We can't stop. This isn't what it looks like."

"I know, but I'm not running from trigger-happy feds," Nash snapped. "Besides, he still has my ID."

I seethed as Nash set the brake. The officer walked to us without fear, putting Nash's truck between himself and his fellow officers at the checkpoint. It was pitch-black out here away from the lights, only the glow of Nash's headlights and the officer's flashlight to illuminate us.

"If you'll get out of the truck, sir," he said. "You too, ma'am."

I hopped out, searching for some spark of magic within to help me out. The sky was deep, velvet black, the stars stretching across it in a ropy smudge. A Stormwalker without a storm was useless, and there wasn't a cloud in sight. I scowled at the empty sky before the officer shone his flashlight in my face.

"You have documentation on you, ma'am? Green card? Naturalization papers?"

He was either a wise-ass or just ignorant. "My ancestors have been here a hell of a lot longer than yours," I growled. "Where's *your* green card?"

"Just give him your driver's license, Janet." Nash sounded weary.

I pulled it out and handed it over. Sourly. The officer's flashlight moved across it. "Cleared for motorcycle operation, eh? You a biker, sweetie?"

"Not tonight."

The man grinned. "Funny." He had eyes of darkness, and I smelled the blood on him.

He switched the flashlight back to Nash. "Put your hands on the truck." Nash, damn him, obeyed.

"You too, ma'am."

I did it, muttering under my breath. I needed magic. Something. Anything.

The officer patted down Nash; then he reached through the passenger window to the glove compartment and fished out Nash's nine-millimeter. "You go on vacation armed?"

"I'm an officer of the law," Nash said. "I never know when I might have to help out."

The man set the gun on a boulder behind him, out of reach, then moved to me. Hands roved up and down my legs, slid between my buttocks, cupped my crotch.

"Pervert," I snarled.

Nash came to life. "Watch what you're doing."

"Oh, you'll watch me." The man took his own pistol out of its holster, cocked it, and shoved it into Nash's neck. "You'll watch while I feed off her, knowing that next, I'll do the same to you." He laughed, his unnaturally black eyes glittering. "Gods, I love the taste of mundanes in the moonlight."

Three

"Nightwalker," I grated.

"You know about Nightwalkers?" The Nightwalker sniffed me, never moving the gun from Nash. "Funny, you don't smell magical."

"What the hell is a Nightwalker?" Nash asked me. "And what does he mean, *feed off you*?"

The Nightwalker chuckled. "He doesn't know? This should be fun."

Very clever of one of the things to figure out how to work a checkpoint. He'd probably been a federal officer before he'd become a bloodsucker, likely still did his job well if he didn't make many full kills. He could only partially drain his victims and let them go, unaware of what had happened, and he'd still be able to hide his true nature from his colleagues. But bloodlust lit his eyes, and I had the feeling that this was going to be one of his kills.

I wanted to kick the thing in the balls and get the hell out of there. But Nightwalkers are strong and hard to kill, and I didn't have a handy wooden stake or sword with me. I would pack better next time. At the moment, I had no way of fighting him except with my fists, which wouldn't do anything but hurt my fists.

But something strange was happening inside me. I felt a burning sensation in my fingertips, which moved all along my veins, and it wasn't from Mick's compulsion spell. The compulsion spell was a dull ache; this was raw and cold and new.

I had a swift vision of my body growling taller, shooting up to tower over the Nightwalker, a bright whiteness glowing around me to light the night. I saw myself raising my hands, heard my mouth issuing commands in a language I didn't understand. I saw the Nightwalker screaming, his red mouth open, his body twisting in excruciating pain. He was dying but couldn't die. I was somehow holding him together, making him relive the torment of every victim he'd ever drained, over and over again. It was heady; it was exhilarating. I laughed.

Nash Jones's voice cut into my brain like a scalpel. "Don't lose it, Begay."

I blinked. The vision died, and I was standing with my hands on Nash's truck, sweating inside my leather coat. The Nightwalker was very much alive and looking at me with a tinge of fear, as though it sensed my vision but wasn't quite certain it had.

"Whatever you are," Nash was saying, "leave her alone and let her go. I'll do what you want."

What a hero. The Nightwalker would never let me go, because I'd run screaming to his fellow feds, and he'd have to abandon this sweet little setup he'd made. Nash was eyeing the other officers, but they'd surrounded a diesel pickup that had pulled up, its noise drowning out all other night sounds. Nash's truck was between us and them—the Nightwalker had perfected his methods.

But Nash's heroism gave me an idea. I didn't know whether it would work, and if not, I'd have to try to pry a blood-frenzied Nightwalker off of Nash, but it was worth a try.

"Do him first," I said, making my voice weak and whiny. "Please. Take the edge off. Then I'll make it fun when you do me."

The Nightwalker's smile returned, and I swallowed my disgust. "I think I like you, sweetheart. What did you have in mind?"

"Anything you want. I've been told I have stamina."

Nash was staring at me as though I'd lost my mind, but he kept quiet. Either he thought I *had* lost my mind, or he was trusting that I had a plan.

The Nightwalker touched my cheek, and I stood still and tried not to gag. "Sweet," he said. "If you please me, Navajo girl, I might just let you stay alive. With me."

"Sure," I said, trying to keep my voice from shaking.

The Nightwalker grabbed Nash by the neck. His mouth opened, baring fangs on both upper and lower jaw, his mouth narrow like a cat's. Nash struggled, but the Nightwalker yanked Nash's head to the side and snapped that hideous mouth over his throat.

Nash didn't go down easy. He fought, and he fought hard, smacking the guy in the head with his fists, which did about as much good as punching a building. I grabbed the Nightwalker's pistol as the feeding frenzy took him, even though I knew bullets wouldn't kill him, and stood back as he sucked down Nash's blood in greedy, wet gulps.

The Nightwalker kept feeding, and my heart pounded in terror. If my hunch was wrong, Nash could die. Words to a dozen spells ran through my head, but none would be powerful enough, especially when I didn't have a storm to draw on. The gun was pretty much useless. A Nightwalker full of bullets was just an angry Nightwalker.

And then it happened. The Nightwalker jerked, his eyes widening in sudden agony. Nightwalkers, I had the scars to prove, held fast to their victims when they were in blood frenzy, not letting go even when someone ran them through with a stake. This Nightwalker shuddered, snarling, Nash's blood running from his mouth, but he wouldn't release. Nash was white, holding on to the truck to keep to his feet.

I dropped the gun, wrapped my arms around the Nightwalker's middle, and hauled backward. At first it was like trying to move a huge boulder, but then the Nightwalker came away from Nash so suddenly that I fell, the Nightwalker landing on top of me like a wet rag. The Nightwalker keened, a sharp, piercing sound that rose to an inhuman note.

The thing crawled off me, tearing at his lips, his hands sprouting claws that raked into his own face. Nash gasped for breath, his hand clamped to his bloody neck, watching with a stunned look.

The Nightwalker, still screaming, fell apart, collapsed into steaming, stinking pieces of flesh and gore, black blood making a river in the sand. His face went last, his scream dying into a gurgle as his flesh melted into a mess of blood and veins.

Bile bubbled in my throat, and I scrambled to my feet and lunged for the truck. I heard Nash behind me, his soft, "Janet, what the fuck?"

"You killed it," I panted.

"*I* killed it? How, by standing there letting it suck me dry?"

"Can we talk about it later? We need to get the hell out of here."

I yanked open the door, but Nash's heavy hand landed on my shoulder. "Easy, Janet. Take it easy. We drive away slowly and don't attract attention."

I ground my teeth, furious that he could be so calm. I knew he was right, but my panic wanted me to dive into the truck, start it up, and peel out of there.

I made myself climb slowly into the passenger seat while Nash retrieved his gun and the Nightwalker's and got inside. He leaned over me to stow both pistols in the glove compartment, blood still staining his neck.

"You all right?" he asked me.

"Am *I* all right? You're the one bleeding to death."

"I'll take that as a yes." Nash sat up, put the truck in gear, and pulled slowly onto the highway, the same as any other vehicle that was approved to proceed. The other patrollers never even looked at us.

Not until we were well down the dark road, dipping and climbing along canyon walls, did I see that Nash's hands shook as he gripped the wheel, his face gray.

"Shit, Nash, stop and let me drive."

"No way am I letting you behind the wheel of my brand-new truck. There's a first aid kit behind the seat. Should have some gauze and antibacterial spray in it."

I dug around in the rear of the cab, found a pristine white box with a red cross on it, dragged it onto my lap, and opened it. Bandages, antibacterial, aspirin, sterile gauze, tape, and other useful items were stowed inside in neat compartments.

"This isn't a first aid kit," I said. "It's a mobile emergency room."

Nash didn't answer. I extracted a wad of gauze and scooted across the seat to wipe the blood from his neck.

I had to reach around him, because the Nightwalker had bitten the left side, and Nash grunted impatiently when I inadvertently blocked his view of the road. There was no place to pull off on this stretch, the highway moving through cuts that left maybe a foot of space on either side of the pavement. Besides, I don't think either one of us much wanted to stop.

I squirted Nash's neck with a little antibacterial and pressed more gauze over the wound, fastening it with sterile tape.

Nash returned both hands to the wheel when I sat back and started cleaning up. "What the hell was that thing?" he asked.

"A Nightwalker. In layman's terms, a vampire. Except it's real."

"A vampire." Nash digested this with a few soft swear words. "And you're saying I killed it?"

I finished putting the supplies back into the first aid kit and closed the lid. "The Nightwalker is a creature of magic, but you cancel out magic. A null, Coyote called you. The Nightwalker got enough of your magic-negative essence in it, which destroyed it." That was what I had thought would happen, and I was gut-wrenchingly relieved that I'd been right.

"I felt something change in me," Nash said. "I was losing blood, I was dying, and then it all stopped. It was as if something freezing cold formed inside me and moved to him through my blood."

"Interesting." I'd speculated with Mick over the summer how Nash had become a magic-absorber, and neither of us could figure it out. I'd never met anything like him, that was for sure.

Nash contemplated the road in silence, and I knew this was hard for him. Up until a few months ago, he had been the biggest Unbeliever in all of Hopi County. Then he'd seen dragons, watched Coyote shift from man to animal, fought skinwalkers, seen what had come out of the vortexes, and had me attack him with storm magic.

"I don't want it to be real," he said after a time. "I'm trying not to let it be real. It's not what I grew up believing."

"I know." I nodded. "Believe me, when a storm first reached out to me, it scared the shit out of me. I thought I was *chindi*, a sorceress filled with evil. The sad thing is, I wasn't far from wrong."

"What am I, then?"

"We're not sure. Coyote called you a null, a walking magic void. You've taken the brunt of some amazing power and never broken a sweat."

"Did you know for sure that I could kill that Nightwalker thing?"

I hesitated but decided to be truthful. "I figured it was worth a shot."

He shot me a scathing glance. "What the hell were you going to do if it didn't work?"

"Shoot him, maybe. Run for help."

"While I stayed behind and turned into a vampire?"

"Nightwalkers don't turn their victims," I said. "Usually. They drain them until they're dead, or they can keep them alive if they want to. Some drink only a little from each victim and then make them forget in order to not leave a trail of bodies. Some even become civilized and learn to drink animal blood, live among humans almost normally, as long as they avoid direct sunlight. The crosses and garlic thing is all a myth, though. I once met a Nightwalker who was a monk. He probably still is one."

"Damn it," Nash said when I wound down. His hands were steadier now. I'd never seen anyone heal so fast from a Nightwalker attack.

"This one bit the wrong neck, tonight," I said.

Nash banged his fists on the steering wheel. Not too hard—he wouldn't want to damage his new truck. "My life made so much more sense before you came into it. What the hell did you do to me?"

"Sorry." I really did feel sorry for him. Moving from Unbeliever to acceptance wasn't easy. "But it didn't really make sense, and you know it."

Nash had been injured in the Iraq War, when a building he'd rushed into had collapsed on him and all his men. He'd been the only one who'd made it out. He'd suffered from flashbacks and had gone through all kinds of hell.

"So, educate me," Nash said. "There are Stormwalkers like you; Nightwalkers, which are vampires; and then skinwalkers, those creatures I fought out at the vortexes. What are werewolves—dogwalkers?"

"You're hilarious, Jones. There aren't any werewolves, just Changers who can become wolves."

We were approaching the dam, the road descending sharply around hairpin curves, traffic slowing to a crawl. "I liked being an Unbeliever," Nash said. "I liked not knowing this shit was out there, on top of all the other shit. But I felt that thing die while he was drinking me, and I saw it disintegrate in a way no human could."

I said nothing but stared up at the arch of the bridge that hung against the sky. Lit up by construction lights, the man-made steel was suspended between sheer cliffs hundreds of feet above the Colorado River.

"It isn't the world I grew up in," Nash said, but I knew he'd resigned himself.

"Yes, it is," I said quietly. "But I know what you mean." My magical cherry had been broken at age eleven. Nash was thirty-two, with a lifetime of stubborn disbelief to give up. I couldn't decide which would be more difficult.

Nash fell silent again as he crossed the dam and navigated up the cliffs on the other side. Then we were heading down the highway to the glow of Las Vegas, Nash maintaining the speed limit and properly using his turn signals. The city spread out at the bottom of the valley, its line of bright colors tempting travelers to its pleasures. Nash stuck to the freeway, passing the tall hotels that reached out to us with promises of easy money, delectable food, and tantalizing glimpses of flesh of both genders.

On the other side of the city, the desert was stark and empty, lonely and cold. After more miles of endless night, Nash turned off on a narrow slice of road that headed due west.

We drove through a crease in the mountains into California and down into Death Valley itself, where moonlight danced on alkali beds that spread across the valley floor. Mountains soared around us, ten thousand feet high, cutting off moisture from this bleak gash of the land. At the same time it was cold, the hard cold of a high-desert night.

"So?" Nash asked me. "Where to?"

I looked out into all the darkness, feeling the spell pulling me northward. "Keep following this road. Pamela said she was on the northwest side of the valley."

"Who the hell is Pamela?"

If Nash had let me indulge in conversation before, I

could have told him the whole story. I gave him a truncated version now.

"We need to turn off somewhere around here," I finished.

"This is the only paved road out this way, if you hadn't noticed. I won't try to navigate unfamiliar dirt ones at night."

Which meant he didn't want to get his precious new truck dirty or, gods help us, stuck. I agreed he was probably right to be cautious; in the dark it would be easy to run off a dirt road straight into desert. Desert floors aren't necessarily hard or sandy—pockets exist under the crust that can swallow an unwary hiker's foot, or bike, or half a car. Being stranded out here when the sun came up was not a good idea.

"We'll go on foot, then," I said.

Nash grunted but pulled the truck onto the road's shoulder. "You don't have a more specific direction than 'somewhere around here?'"

"I'm lucky Pamela could tell me this much. There are probably spells all over the place to prevent people like me from finding Mick, compulsion or no compulsion. So no, I doubt she left me a detailed trail."

Nash set the brake and turned off the ignition. He got out and rummaged in the back of the cab, then began to pile stuff on his seat.

My eyes widened at the cache: a thin thermal blanket, filled canteens plus a packet of water-purifying tablets, food rations, a smaller version of his car's first aid kit, flashlights, extra batteries, waterproof matches and a couple candles, chem lights, sunscreen, a length of rope, crampons, a compass and an electronic GPS device, a pocketknife, socks and hiking boots, and a Windbreaker that would deflect the night's cold as well as tomorrow's sun. He dropped all this on his seat plus ammunition for his nine-millimeter. He retrieved both pistols from the glove compartment, adding the Nightwalker's gun to the growing pile and holstering his own.

"Shit, Nash," I said as he began stuffing all the accoutrements into a backpack. "Were you planning to invade a country?"

"It's open desert, and you don't know where we're going or how long it will take. Were you going to come out here and look around without water or light?"

I hadn't, but Nash could make an elite ops unit look underprepared. "I brought enough for you too," he said. "Can we get a move on? Dawn's at seven."

It was already two. Five hours to find Mick before daylight, when the desert floor, even in September, would become brutally hot. I'd lived my entire life in and around deserts and knew that heatstroke was swift and deadly.

I stood on the gravel waiting while Nash locked all the doors and set up a warning triangle, so that anyone driving up this road would be sure to see his precious truck.

A wash ribboned up the side of the hill a few yards from the road, rocky and treacherous, but I knew I had to ascend it. There was no other trail.

"Up there?" Nash asked in a disbelieving voice when I pointed it out. He gave me an irritated look, but he started climbing. Taking a deep breath, I scrambled up after him.

The wash was full of gravel and difficult to navigate. I slipped and slid, bloodying my hands when I grabbed boulders to steady myself, keeping a sharp eye out for snakes.

Nash reached the top of the first ridge and waited while I clambered up the last few yards, the dry limbs of creosote scratching me. Nash was in damned good shape, barely breathing hard as he stood in shadow and surveyed the landscape. Silhouetted against the sky, he looked formidable, biceps bulging, his shoulder holster and gun emphasizing the fact that he was a walking danger zone.

The truck already looked small and faraway, the valley empty and wide in the darkness. Nash flicked on his flashlight, checked his GPS, and played the light around the ridge. The mountain rose in folds around us, the narrow ridgeline running a long way north into the hills.

We walked on, following the ridge until we found another wash that led up another fold of the mountain. Nash moved swiftly along the uneven ground, me lagging farther and farther behind. It was a good thing the night remained cloudless, brilliantly clear—washes like the one we traversed would explode with water after a rain, pouring whitewater and debris down the hill, sweeping us along like so much flotsam.

A rock clicked on rock somewhere below me, and I halted, tense. It might be lizard, I reasoned, slithering to a safer shelter, or a night bird looking for a meal. I didn't sense anything down there, no auras of evil or even plain human. After a moment, I relaxed a little, and then I realized that Nash had vanished.

Shit. I looked around wildly but saw no sign of him. "Nash," I called in a whisper.

The small sound was loud in the stillness. I hurried forward, dislodging gravel in my haste, and finally, after a few yards of scrambling, I spotted him.

Wind and water had carved out a niche in the rock wall a little way up the trail, years of erosion forming a shelter. Nash had his back to the cliff, deep in shadow, his shirt a pale smudge in the darkness. As I drew closer, I saw starlight gleam softly on his drawn weapon.

"What is it?" I asked, keeping my voice soft.

Nash remained motionless.

I stepped closer before realizing my mistake. Nash was watching *me* approach, deadly purpose in his eyes. Whoever he thought was coming for him, he wasn't seeing me.

"Nash, it's Janet," I said desperately, but my words were too late.

The last thing I saw was the butt of Nash's pistol coming toward my head, and then the startled horror in his eyes when it connected with my skull.

Four

I resisted wakefulness, because waking meant pain. I didn't want pain. The darkness was so much nicer.

I heard someone calling my name, and something cold touched my forehead.

"Janet, son of a bitch, wake up." It was Nash's voice, swift, worried, urgent.

"Are you going to hit me again?" I tried to ask. No actual words came out, only a groan.

"Open your eyes, damn you."

I couldn't. I tried to make my eyelids obey, but they remained heavy and sealed shut.

I felt a hand in my hair and Nash's voice in my ear, both gentler than I'd thought possible. "Janet, I'm so, so sorry."

I floated off again, dreaming that I was in a lovely, warm bed, snuggled up to Mick, who held me against his large, sexy body. We were naked, settling down into an afterglow of lovemaking as frenzied as only Mick could make it. What Nash was doing there, I didn't know. Arresting us for having too much fun in bed? I was pretty sure that some of the things Mick liked to do were illegal in a few states.

"Janet, come on." Tender no more, the flat of Nash's palm connected with my cheek.

"Would you stop hitting me?" I growled and opened my eyes.

I lay flat on my back on hard-packed earth under a sky full of stars. Nash was silhouetted against the bright pattern of the stars until his flashlight played into my eyes. The warm dream of me in Mick's arms dissolved to mist, and a sudden headache stabbed my temples.

"Ow."

"You need to sit up. Slowly."

I felt like something was trying to bang my head into a different shape from the inside, but Nash's touch was almost tender as he helped me to sit. If he was like this as a lover, no wonder Maya had fallen for him.

"Why did you hit me?" I put my hand to my head and flinched at the pain. My fingers came away wet with blood.

Nash looked ashamed, an expression I'd never seen on him before. "I didn't mean to. I thought you were . . . No, I don't know what I thought."

"You were having a flashback." I'd understood that the second before he'd brained me. I should have hung back and talked to him before I approached. I was lucky he'd decided to disable his enemy without making noise, or I'd be dead right now, a bullet through my head. Nash's aim was accurate and sure.

"Yes," he answered, almost in a whisper.

I was sitting up now, my throbbing head making me dizzy and nauseated. "Sorry, I shouldn't have startled you."

"Don't take the blame on yourself, Janet. I'm the one who hit you."

"You shouldn't take the blame, either." I tried a smile. "It's not your fault that you're crazy."

He didn't look amused. "I haven't had a flashback in over a year. I thought I was finished with them."

"Maybe it's something you never get over."

Nash shook his head. "When Maya told me to get help, I wouldn't listen to her. I thought I was strong enough to handle it. But she was right."

"You don't want to be weak. I get that."

Jones snapped out of his self-pity. "I need to get you to an emergency room. Do you think you can make it down, or do I need to carry you?"

"Oh, no, you don't. I'm not leaving until I find Mick."

"Don't be an idiot. You're concussed. You need stitches and a doctor."

"Then patch me up with your state-of-the-art first aid kit. We find Mick, and then I promise you can drive me to the nearest ER." I couldn't leave Mick after coming this far. Even if I weren't so worried about him, the spell had me in its grip and wouldn't let me go. I felt like I was being squeezed by a giant octopus.

"I can't risk that," Nash said.

"Too bad. I can do healing spells on myself. I've done them before." So many, many times before. What did that say about my life? "They won't cure me completely, but I'll be able to go on. I have to find Mick."

Nash heard the panic in my voice; maybe he even understood it. With a growl, he returned to his first aid kit, which already lay open on the ground. He took out the antibacterial I'd used on him and cleaned my wound with gauze. It hurt like hell.

I quickly whispered the words of a healing spell, some of the minor magic I could do when there wasn't a nearby storm, but nothing happened. For a moment, fear squeezed my heart, and then I realized that Nash's body touched mine as he wiped blood from my head.

"Could you move away a little?" I asked. "I think you're killing my healing spells."

He stopped. "What?"

"You're a walking magic void, remember? My powers aren't strong enough to overcome the negative field that is you."

Nash stared at me, bloody gauze hovering. "How far?"

"I have no idea. Start walking, and I'll tell you when to stop."

No one could pin someone with a suspicious glare like Nash Jones could. Criminals who came through Magellan and Flat Mesa, thinking to hide out in small towns, ended up begging to be turned over to the feds or state police once Nash got hold of them. The times I'd been in Nash's custody, his deputies claimed Nash had gone easy on me. The thought made me shiver.

"Seriously," I said.

Nash gave me one final icy look, then unfolded to his feet and started up the ridge.

I whispered more spells to myself as he went, and finally, I felt my scalp prickle and the pain ease a little. "Far enough," I called to Nash.

He waited while I got to my feet, brushed off the gravel that had cut my skin, and packed up the first aid kit. My hands shook, and my nausea let me know the healing spells helped only so much.

Nash pushed one of the canteens into my hand when

I reached him. "Don't dehydrate. I don't want to have to carry you down this mountain."

"You have a heart of gold, Jones," I said but sucked greedily at the plastic-tasting water.

We went on. I had to stop often. My healing spell could keep my blood inside my body, but I wasn't a strong enough mage to cure myself completely. The night remained blissfully clear and quiet, the wind coming off the mountains, chilly.

"Nash," I called softly.

Nash stopped, hand on weapon. "What?"

"He wants us to go that way." I pointed to a ridge off to our left, one that this path wouldn't take us to.

Nash's eyes glittered in the beam of his flashlight. "How can you be sure?"

"I just know." I touched my temple, winced, and rubbed it. The closer I got, the more the compulsion spell hauled me to it, like a fish in a net.

"We have to backtrack about a mile to get there."

I started back down what I laughingly called our "trail." "Better than going the wrong direction the rest of the night."

Nash grunted something, but he came after me. Rocks slipped and slid under my feet, as I picked my way down the steep trail. Nash came behind, his steps slow, deliberate, the light of his flashlight bobbing behind mine. The mountains were closing around us, the occasional tree straight and stark in the moonlight.

We found the side trail that led across a saddle, folds of jagged rock tumbling away to either side of us. If I could have seen better, I'd have been nervous about the sheer drops to the right and left. As it was, we concentrated on the narrow ribbon of land beneath our feet and moved slowly.

Our makeshift trail widened when we reached the other side of the saddle, and we climbed again. I was glad of Nash's GPS device, because I'd lost track of where the hell we were.

More climbing for another mile or two. The spell grew stronger as I ascended, which increased both my hope and impatience.

Nash stopped so abruptly I almost ran into him. He stood still, saying nothing while he played flashlight over the trail.

Ahead of us, the ridge ended, dropping into a craggy morass that connected to the higher wall of mountain beyond. The gap wasn't wide—Nash's flashlight beam reached the other side—but it was wide enough. One of the bighorn sheep that populated this place might traverse it, but never two humans without rappelling gear. Flying would be another asset, but neither of us could turn into something with wings.

I was breathing hard. We'd climbed from the below-sea-level desert floor to three thousand feet according to Nash's device, and the next ridgeline was another couple thousand feet higher than that.

"What now?" Nash asked me.

I didn't know. The spell was stronger than ever, but no way in hell could I climb down those rocks with my head spinning like a merry-go-round.

Nash started exploring the top of the ridge, while I sank to a boulder and tried to feel the source of the spell. I fished a chamois bag from my backpack, carefully pulled out a shard of magic mirror, and set it on my knee.

The void inside the mirror was black, no color, no light. One big nothing.

A chill went through me. Mick also carried a piece of the broken magic mirror with him in case he needed to commu-

nicate with me. Magic mirrors beat cell phones every time.
But lately, whenever I'd tried to focus on his shard, I got this.

"Anything?" I asked it.

The blackness cleared, and the mirror reflected my anxious brown eyes in the glow of my flashlight.

"Sorry, sweetcakes," the mirror answered me in a drag-queen drawl. "Our Micky's just not answering."

"You can't tell where he is?"

"It's dark." The mirror's tone was worried, and that worried me.

"Thanks for trying," I said.

"Sure thing, sugar. Hey, tell the sheriff to come over here."

"Why? Can he help?"

"I don't know. I just want to look at his pretty ass."

I growled and stuffed the mirror back into the bag.

"Who are you talking to?" Nash stood over me, his flashlight like an interrogator's lamp.

"No one," I said. "Did you find anything?"

"There might be a cave over there. Or an old mine shaft."

Shafts dotted the land around here, left over from the days when these mountains were picked over for gold, silver, talc, and borax. No one mined up here anymore, the shafts played out and abandoned decades ago.

Nash hauled me to my feet and led me to a small hole that yawned from the base of a boulder. When Nash crouched down and shone his light inside, I saw that the hole dropped a long way below the surface. A foul-scented breeze rose from it, to be blown away by the increasing wind.

The spell wrenched me with a mighty throb. "Yes," I gasped. "Down there."

"Are you sure? Old shafts are unstable and full of poisonous gases."

I got to my hands and knees beside him and peered down the shaft. Once upon a time, wood planks had shored up the hole, but they'd rotted away, leaving a few gray slivers. The pull of the spell was damn strong.

"I'm sure. I need to go down there."

Nash moved back. "Janet, you came up here on the word of a woman you've never met, who charged into your hotel and started acting crazy. She could have lured you out here on purpose—to kill you, maybe. Have you thought of that?"

"Of course I've thought of that. It's one reason I didn't want to come alone. But I can't take the chance that Mick isn't in trouble. I have to know. I can't leave him out here without help."

Nash played the flashlight on the hole again, then on me. "You're ready to get yourself killed for him, and you don't even know if he's really down there?"

"Mick's nearly gotten himself killed for me lots of times," I said. My voice bordered on hysteria. "He's been living his whole life on the line for me."

Nash shone his light into the shaft, but he was looking at me, not the hole. "If he's risked his life for you, he'd not want you to die now. It's foolish to put yourself in danger because of guilt."

I tried a smile. "Says the man with PTSD."

"I know all about guilt. I crawled out of a pile of rubble that should have crushed me, the nine men I was supposed to lead and protect dead behind me. I lost every man, and to this day, I don't know why I lived. But I've learned the painful lesson that throwing away my life won't bring them back. Jumping into that hole and choking to death on sulfur fumes isn't going to save Mick."

"You have some better ideas?" I asked him.

"We go to the ranger station and tell them we've lost

someone up here. They'll have the equipment to get in there and find him."

"If it were that simple, don't you think Mick would be out by now? He's a *dragon* and pretty damned resilient. So, if he hasn't been able to blow himself out of this place, he's seriously trapped, magically as well as physically. No ranger station will be equipped to handle that."

"And you are?"

"No, I'm not. That's why I brought you."

"Because I'm this magic void," he said, sounding skeptical.

"That, and you're good in an emergency. Please, Nash. Anyway, if you want to talk about guilt, you've just hit me on the head with your gun. I think I'm entitled to some help for that."

Nash growled at me, but I was past caring.

He dumped his backpack on the ground and started rummaging through it. He took out a spool of twine and a candle and tied the candle securely. Leaning over the hole, he lit the candle and started unwinding the twine down into the shaft. I watched the candle burning merrily as it went down, the flame high, steady, and bright yellow.

"What happens if there's methane down there?" I asked worriedly. "Won't that explode?"

"Then we'll know it's not safe."

I backed quickly from the hole. "You're a fun date, Nash."

Nothing dire happened. The candle continued to burn, the flame looking normal and happy.

Nash brought the candle back up and blew it out. "So we know we can breathe, at least that far in. That still doesn't mean it's safe."

"I'm light and nimble, and Pamela got in and out all right."

"So she says."

While he spoke, Nash was taking out a rope and harness, so I knew he was going to help; he would just be crabby about it. Fine with me, as long as he helped.

He turned to me, held up the harness, and gave me a cold smile. "Since I'm bigger than you, you get to go down first."

Five

I was never at my best in enclosed spaces. As Nash lowered me, wrapped in the rope and harness, I secretly agreed that Nash was right. This was crazy.

I had no way of knowing whether Mick was really down here or whether this was an elaborate trap, Pamela a part of it. But the spell tugged me on, and my heart told me that Mick waited for me at the end of the line.

After what seemed a long time, my feet touched firm ground. I played my flashlight around and found that a horizontal shaft ran to my right, sloping a little downward, shored up in places with rotting timber or rough-hewn stones. Lovely. This place could collapse at any moment, and only the crushed remains of an ex-Stormwalker would be found, if anyone bothered to dig me out at all.

I called back up to Nash that I wanted to explore the

tunnel. He kept a firm hand on the rope, and I realized that if he didn't want me looking around, he'd simply haul me back up whether I liked it or not. I unhooked the harness and slid out of it.

"Janet!" he shouted down at me. "Don't be stupid."

I ignored him and started walking, the compulsion spell now too strong for me to fight.

After a long time of stepping over old timbers, rotted sacking, and fallen stones, as well as stirring up the stink of bat droppings, I felt heat. The shaft bent left, running deeper into the mountain until it ended in a wall of solid stone.

Before I could despair, my flashlight's beam found a long, vertical crack, about three inches wide, that ran from the stone's base to the rotted timbers above my head. Through that crack, something glowed.

I put my eye to the crack. It went all the way through stone about a foot thick, and beyond that, I saw a vast cavern rising high into the mountain, a spelunker's delight. The heat I felt came from a wall of flame that divided the cavern neatly in half. Behind that flame, cut off from me, lay a dragon.

"Nash!" I shouted back up the tunnel. "Get down here! I found him. I found Mick!"

I heard the fear in Nash's voice as he called down to me—after being buried in that building in Iraq, he must hate enclosed spaces even more than I did. But I could never fault Nash's courage. I heard him climbing down, cursing all the way.

"You don't have a pickax in that backpack, do you?" I asked when he reached me.

"Don't be funny."

I looked around the floor of the shaft, searching for

something, anything, that would help me break through the wall. Nash might not have a pickax, but miners did. I found one, buried under gravel. The handle had rotted away, but the head had been made of good steel. A little rusty, yes, but it would do the trick.

Nash took the pickax away from me with his gloved hands. He carefully jabbed the point of the ax into the stone and worked it until rubble started to fall. The rock wasn't solid granite, just crust that had filled the end of the shaft.

I scraped gravel aside as it trickled away until Nash and I had made a hole big enough for me to crawl through. I squeezed into the cavern, ignoring the pain of the rocks scraping my flesh.

The cavern floor sloped downward to the wall of flame. I saw a hole in the wall opposite mine, though on this side of the fire, much bigger than the one I'd just crushed through. That must be where Pamela had entered, and I wondered why the compulsion spell hadn't taken me that way. But maybe mine had been the easier route for me; after all, Pamela could change into a wolf and dig.

The dragon behind the wall of fire was folded so tightly that it turned back on itself several times, the end of a tail snaking around to touch its long snout. I couldn't see his wings, but I knew they had to be there, large and leathery, amid the pile of his body. His head was long, lips slightly pulled back from enormous, jagged teeth.

I knew that if he'd been able to shift to his human form and give himself more space, he would have. As it was, the dragon could open only one eye, a bulbous silver and black orb, and fix it on me.

"Mick," I whispered.

The spell thrummed between us, vibrating the air.

Mick's eye gleamed as he looked at me, but he was jammed in there so tightly that he could make no other move. I saw fury in the eye, plus relief, worry, and the impatience to be out of there.

As he blinked at me, his compulsion spell died away. The release sent me to my knees as did every other hurt the spell had staved off so I could get here.

Nash pressed himself into the cave and switched off his flashlight. "You all right, Janet?"

I lay still to catch my breath. "I will be."

Nash studied the motionless Mick. "He's a dragon. Why doesn't he just fly out? I doubt the fire would burn a hide that thick."

I couldn't read Mick's thoughts, but I sensed his vast irritation. He lifted his head what little he could in the tight space and shot a sudden stream of fire toward us.

I ducked instinctively, and so did Nash. The white-hot fire struck the flames, and the wall of them bulged, swelling, growing hotter. My skin burned, my hair singed, and Nash threw up his arm to ward off the brightness. Any second now, the flame would burst out; any second now, we'd be incinerated . . .

And then, we weren't. As we watched, the fire sucked Mick's dragon flame straight into it, absorbed it, inhaled it. The whole thing flared red-hot for a few seconds, then settled back down to a steady roar.

I blew out my breath. "It's magical fire," I said. "It feeds on magic, the same way Mick can siphon off my storm power. Any magic thrown at it will just make it stronger."

The dragon lowered his head with a little *whump* of breath, happy we'd figured out the obvious.

I nudged a rock that was about a foot in diameter, checking for scorpions or spiders before I hauled it into my hands. I bent, swung the rock back between my legs, and heaved it into the flames.

The fire disintegrated the rock in the blink of an eye. Nothing reached Mick's side but a trickle of dust and ash.

"Even Mick's hide wouldn't survive that," I said.

Nash studied the flame wall as though he was trying to figure out a way to arrest it. "So, did you bring a magic fire extinguisher?"

So the man had a sense of humor. "Sort of," I said in a quiet voice. "I brought you."

He turned. "And I can do what?"

"You draw off magic, like you did to the Nightwalker. Maybe you can draw off that."

Nash's brows shot up over cold gray eyes. "You want me to touch fire that burns rock to ash to see what happens? Forget it. I like my hand, not to mention the rest of my body. We'll find another way."

"There is no other way. I don't have magic without a storm, and even if I did, the fire would probably just absorb that too."

As Nash turned back to the fire, another vision hit me with the force of a hurricane. In it I was standing in this cave, my arms raised above my head, the same kind of white light I'd seen in the last vision pouring from my hands. This wasn't my storm magic—it was different, more intense, like the difference between a cheerful fire on a hearth and a stream of molten lava.

In the vision, the wall of flame bowed before me in terror. The cave shook with my power and then collapsed. The rubble buried Nash and Mick, but boulders glanced off me as I rose like the sun out of the mountain.

I heard myself screaming and then I was on my hands and knees on the bone-hard floor, Nash bending over me.

"Janet? What the hell?"

I sat down hard, my spinning head making me sick. "It's nothing. Nothing. It's just my headache."

I was such a liar. Mick's eye focused on me, the dark slit of his pupil glowing orange red. I felt his sharp interest, his worry, and not just for my physical well-being. Despite everything Mick and I had been through, despite what we had together, I knew that Mick still watched me with wariness. He loved me, protected me, shared a bed with me, yes. Had complete faith that I wasn't a danger to every living being on the planet, no.

Nash's face glistened with sweat as he contemplated the flames again. Then he quickly lowered his backpack and walked toward them.

"Wait!" I shouted. Like him, I wasn't entirely sure the fire wouldn't annihilate Nash the same as it had the boulder. As much as I wanted his help, I didn't want to witness his fiery death.

Nash ignored me. He reached toward the flame as though mesmerized, fingers extended. I scrambled to my feet, ran at him, grabbed him around the waist, and tried to yank him back.

Nash had good instincts. He grabbed me and swung me out of the way, and the momentum put him squarely into the flames.

The fire flared with glee. Nash was lost inside it, the flames covering him like a blanket. I watched in horror, and so did Mick, me cradling my arm that had come too close to the fire. Both of us knew we couldn't help him; we could only wait and see what happened.

After a few long, sickening minutes, Nash's form became a solid silhouette inside the fire, pushing the flames aside.

No, not pushing them aside. *Absorbing* them. Yellow fire outlined his body, and flames streamed from the walls and ceiling into his core. Mick and I watched in astonishment, but Nash stood still and took it; he didn't scream, and he didn't die.

As soon as the fire began pulling away from the cavern walls, Mick moved. His dragon body shrank in on itself, the sinuous curves unwinding in fast motion, his long snout flattening down to a human face. And then he was Mick, the tall man I loved with glittering dragon tattoos curling down his arms.

Mick burst out through the hole in the fire, grabbed me, shoved me back through the crack in the rock, and hauled ass back up the shaft.

For a naked man who'd just been a dragon, Mick could move. I let him half carry, half drag me down the narrow tunnel, the beam of my flashlight bouncing crazily off the walls. My arm hurt like hell, but my skin was red, not black. Nash had tossed me out of the way just in time.

"What about Nash?" I shouted.

We reached the vertical shaft. Mick grabbed the harness and snapped it around me, not listening to my breathless protests. He grabbed the rope that hung from above and started to climb out, hand over hand, feet moving on the wall, as though he was born to climb, even bare-assed naked. I had a very good view of his bare ass as he scrambled up the shaft.

Mick gained the top and started to pull me up. I braced myself against the wall and tried to help, but I was exhausted and burned, and my head throbbed like fury.

Mick mercilessly dragged me upward. Finally the rope, harness, and I went over the lip of the shaft without impediment, and then Mick ripped open the buckles with strong hands and hauled me against him.

Oh, gods, it felt so good to have him hold me again. Mick was a big man, made of muscle, his flat face and once-broken nose so damn beautiful to me. I wrapped my arms around him and held on, loving the heat of his body and the salt scent of it.

He started kissing me, lips rough, hands roving my body as though he wanted to feel all of me at once. I kissed him back, my tongue in his mouth, stroking him, tasting him. I'd never get enough of him.

The rising sun touched my face, and I finally pulled back, panting and breathless. "What about Nash?" I repeated.

Mick buried his face in my neck. "If the fire didn't get him, he'll be coming."

"If the fire didn't get him, he'll be pissed at me."

His chuckle warmed my heart. "That too." He held my face in his hands, studied me with dark blue eyes. "I missed you, baby."

We heard a grunt and a grating of rope, and Nash appeared in the shaft, clinging to the rope Mick had tossed back down. He looked unburned, his clothes in place as though nothing worse had happened to him than a hike through an old mine shaft.

"I hate to break up the happy reunion," he said, voice as dry and sarcastic as usual, "but you need to let him get dressed before we go down, Begay. I don't want his bare ass on my new seats."

I'd hoped Mick would turn back into a dragon and fly us down, but he shook his head. "The fuel for that fire was me. It siphoned off every bit of my magic, and shifting to human took the rest of it. The dragon council fixed it so I locked my own cage."

"So, it was the dragons?" I studied the night sky worriedly, expecting to see flames on the horizon any second.

"Don't worry," Mick said beside me. "They won't come back."

"How do you know?"

Instead of answering, Mick touched the white bandage on my head, his expression grave. "What happened?"

"I hit her," Nash said.

Mick might be drained of magic, but his fury when he swung on Nash would have made a lesser man back down. "What the fuck, Jones?"

Normally I'd delight in my six-foot-six biker boyfriend glaring at Nash with death-promising rage, but I was exhausted and aching and I wanted to be out of there.

"He didn't mean to," I said quickly. "He thought I was an insurgent."

"What? Shit."

"I tried to get her to go to an ER," Nash said as he stashed things in his backpack. "She refused."

"You should have tried harder," Mick growled.

Tears filled my voice. "Not and leave you out here trapped inside a mountain. Besides, I was under this compulsion spell, remember?"

Mick cupped my face in his hands again and peered into my eyes. "It was a light one; that was all I could cast. It wouldn't have let you die trying to fulfill it."

I realized the truth of it at the same time he said the words. The compulsion spell had led me to him, but it had been my own emotions that had made me so determined to get to him. "Doesn't matter. I couldn't go and leave you out here."

Mick's touch softened on my face. "Well, you're going now."

He snatched up the clothes I'd brought for him and quickly dressed, covering his naked body. I'd brought him his leather jacket as well, not knowing how cold it would be up here. Despite the rising sun, a chill wind blew fiercely along the ridge, and Mick shrugged into the jacket.

"Which way?" he asked.

Nash snapped off the flashlight. The mountains to the east cast deep shadows, but the sky above was already brightening to blue. We'd make it to lower elevations about the same time the sun did, and then we'd roast.

Nash signaled us to follow him, and we started back down the trail, me stumbling and clinging to Mick's hand.

"How do you know the dragons won't come back?" I repeated.

"Because I know the dragon council," Mick said. "Escaping was me passing a test. Putting me back would be cheating, and they'd never do anything so dishonorable."

"Passing a test?" That did not sound good.

"Sort of like me making bail, or them honoring a truce."

"But what would happen when your magic ran out?" I asked. "The fire would die?"

"No, I'd be dead," Mick said, not sounding worried. "But they wouldn't have kept me in there that long. We need to catch up to Nash."

End of conversation. Nash was marching at a swift pace, the soldier in him eating up distance. Mick propelled me along, keeping me too breathless to ask more questions, but no matter. I'd grill him later.

We caught up to Nash on the narrow saddle that led to the next chain of hills. Without thinking, I looked over the edge of the ridge, and I bit back a hysterical cry. The dawn light showed me what the darkness had hidden—to either side of the path, cliffs fell away in ripples of gray and black, down, down, down through clumps of sagebrush and creosote to the darkness at the bottom.

I saw something else down there. Eyes. Hundreds of them. Faint white light swirled at the bottom of the hill like mist. A vortex.

From the vortex, demons were crawling. The shard of mirror in my pack started shrieking, drowning out my own cry of horror.

Mick looked over the side, saw what I saw. "Aw, damn it. Up!" he shouted at Nash. "Back up!"

He started hustling me along the path back toward the mine shaft. Nash didn't waste time asking questions and sprinted with us up the trail.

The demons boiled after us. I'd fought creatures like this before, down in the dark desert of Nevada, fought for my life. That was the night I'd met Mick, but that night I'd had a good storm to help me out. This morning, the sky above remained stubbornly clear, not even a breath of wind to stir the dust.

Mick shoved me behind him and faced the onslaught. He was exhausted, I saw it in the slump of his shoulders, and he'd just said he was drained of magic. Nash passed me the gun he'd taken from the Nightwalker plus two magazines, but I knew it wouldn't do much good against a horde of crazed demons.

Nash sighted down his nine-millimeter at the beings with leathery bodies, clawed hands, and bloodred eyes. "What are they?"

"Demons," Mick answered curtly.

"Not the steal-your-soul, take-you-to-hell kind of demons," I put in. "Just the garden-variety, kill-and-eat-you demons."

Nash gave me a resigned look, sighted down his pis-

tol again, and fired. The boom of the pistol echoed into
the morning, and a roar from a hundred demon throats answered it.

Nash's bullet hit the first demon square in the chest, and
it tumbled back into its fellows in a shower of blood. The
demons came on. Nash fired again.

Flames danced in Mick's hands, but I could tell his
magic was at low ebb, very little restored yet. I aimed the
gun Nash had given me, sighting down the barrel. I hated
guns. I knew how to use one, because Mick had taught me,
but when I finally made myself pull the trigger, the kick
sent me reeling. I fell flat on my back, already off balance
from my head injury. The acrid smell of the gun, plus the
roar of it, made me want to puke, and I couldn't even tell if
I'd hit the demon.

Mick was fighting with fists, Nash shooting, and still
the things came on. At this rate, the demons would leave
our shredded bits over the mountain, and the rangers would
assume we'd been mauled by bears or a puma. I wondered
if any bits would be identifiable.

Demons boiled at Nash like a horde of cockroaches, and
he was swearing and shooting, falling to his knees. Mick
sagged, his body gleaming with sweat, his fire fading. The
demons swarmed over him, jumping on his back, dragging
him down to feast on the flesh of the man I loved.

I tossed my gun into the pack and stood up, something
wild surging inside me. I suddenly felt strong, adept, fear-
less; the surety that I could kill the demons and save the
day rising in an amalgam of white-hot heat and blinding
light. I raised my hands, and light poured out of my palms,
just as in the visions I'd had tonight.

A terrible glow lit up the mountain and flowed like a

deluge toward the demons. The white light engulfed the demons, Mick, Nash, the ridge. Rocks exploded into rubble
and rained into the crevice, and the demons screamed as they
began to fall with it. Trees on the ridge above us burst into
flame, grasses crackling in the gray morning light.

As soon as the demons fell from Mick, he sprang to
his feet, grabbed Nash, and dragged him away from the
mewling, desperate demons and the white light. I lifted my
hands higher, my laughter booming. Words came out of my
mouth, and I didn't understand one of them. I wasn't speaking Diné or any other Indian language I knew, or English,
or Latin, or Spanish.

The demons ran from me, plunging over the precipice,
screaming as they dropped. My wall of light followed them
down. It killed all of the demons, and then the light incinerated them. The magic in me killed every single demon, all
the way down into the vortex, and once they were nothing
but ash, my magic snapped the vortex closed.

I turned to face Nash and Mick, who watched from a
little way away, both of them covered with bloody bite
marks. Mick's eyes had gone black all the way across, and
the way he looked at me should have terrified the hell out
of me.

I laughed. "Hi, boys," I said, raising my hands again.
"Want to play?"

The rocks in front of them exploded. The two men
scrambled out of the way of the ensuing rain of gravel, and
Nash trained his pistol on me. "Why the hell are her eyes
green?" I heard him shout.

"Janet." Mick's voice was harsh with warning. "Stop."

I had no clue how to stop. I'd killed the demons, all of
them, completing the task I should have completed that

night six years ago. Now I wanted to crush the entire mountain, find the dragons who'd imprisoned Mick in it and imprison them too.

Mick started for me. Brave man. I knew I could stop him, enslave him, make him obey me. Mick had the ability to absorb my storm powers and not be hurt by them, but I knew good and well that he couldn't survive the magic in me now.

"I command you," I said, power boiling up inside me. "You are *mine*."

The white light wrapped around Mick, and he snarled. And then, without warning, the magic blinked out.

The light died, and with it went the last of my strength. I fell and started sliding toward the edge of the gorge, my fatal plunge stopped by a single boulder that hooked me around the waist. Beneath me, the rocks tumbled over the side, bouncing and rattling for hundreds of feet to the mists of the vortex, which faded into the rising sun.

Six

I woke up hanging facedown on Mick's back. It was damn hot, and I felt as though someone had poured cleanser into my body and scrubbed my insides with a wire brush.

As soon as I groaned, Mick stopped and laid me gently on the ground. Both Mick and Nash were breathing hard and sweating, smeared with dried blood where the demons had clawed and bitten them. Mick's wildly curly black hair hung across his face, and his blue eyes glittered behind it.

"Are you all right?" I croaked.

"We should be asking you that," Nash said in clipped tones.

Mick was watching me in a way I didn't like. His face bore the wary look of a man whose trained animal had suddenly remembered its wildness and turned on him.

"Mick, don't," I said.

"Your eyes changed color," he said. "To very light green. Like ice."

Fear kicked me in the gut and kept on kicking. "My mother isn't inside me, I swear to you. I know how that feels. We sealed her vortex, Mick, you and me. Even the cracks are sealed. She's trapped."

Nash crouched next to us, his gun out. "What the hell are you two talking about?"

Mick broke in before I could draw breath to answer. Just as well. Explaining this was beyond me.

"The entity you saw coming out of the vortex last spring," Mick said. "She is a goddess, trapped in the world Beneath. She created Janet, even though Janet was born of human parents. She is, in essence, Janet's mother. She has the ability to possess women. Or had."

Nash stared at me. "That thing was your *mother*?"

"We're not responsible for our parents," I tried to joke.

"You've always had her Beneath magic in you," Mick said. "When did you learn to channel it so well?"

His voice was quiet, dark, waiting. "I didn't," I said. "I have no idea how I used that magic, I promise you. I just did it."

Nash unfolded next to me. "Good thing you did. We wouldn't have survived that attack."

I still didn't like the way Mick watched me. He wasn't going to let it go, and I had the feeling that me busting him out of that cave and then saving his life wouldn't mitigate things. My connection to my goddess mother and the powers of Beneath were the very reasons all dragons, including, at one time, Mick, wanted me dead.

"We'll talk about it later," he said. "It's going to get hot here, quick."

It was already hot, the sun streaming over the eastern

mountains, bringing another day of heat to the valley floor. Mick carried me again, and it got hotter as we descended, the white alkali flats reflecting the sunlight in bright waves. I remembered reading a statistic that the ground temperature in Death Valley could reach two hundred degrees during the day. You could make fry bread on that. Salty, sandy fry bread. I giggled.

Mick stopped and fed me water. "She's delirious," he said.

"Not much farther," Nash promised.

Lower and lower we went, as the morning grew hotter. I hung upside down over Mick's shoulder and quietly started dying. Sun played on the pale sand dunes and dry flats, forcing my eyes shut against the brightness.

Mick finally stopped and lowered me to my feet. We stood on black pavement, a road, and my heart leapt. I never thought I'd ever be so happy to see asphalt in my life.

When the rushing sound in my ears cleared a little, I heard Nash swearing.

"What's wrong?" I tried to ask.

Nash was shouting foul and filthy words. Parallel tire tracks showed where a truck had been driven off the road, but of Nash's shiny new black pickup, there was no sign.

"Son of a *bitch*!" Nash kicked the dirt, sending up sprays of fine gravel. I knew he wasn't angry about being stranded in the middle of Death Valley with no transportation and little water—he was pissed that someone had dared to touch his beloved truck.

Mick gave me water again, and I slumped against his side to drink. "Where are we?" I heard him ask.

"About thirty miles from Stovepipe Wells," Nash said.

"We walk it, then. We can't afford to wait."

I didn't want to hear that, and I was about to argue with him, to beg him to let me lie down right here and go to sleep, when I heard the blissful sound of a car engine. It wasn't Nash's big truck but an older, dust-covered pickup with its windows down, bumping toward us along the road. Three people crowded into the cab and several more rode in the bed.

The truck stopped beside us, its engine chugging like a steamboat's. A Native American man leaned out the window and looked us over. "Hey, you folks lost?"

Mick didn't hesitate. "She needs a doctor."

A young woman peered over the driver's shoulder. "We're going into Beatty," she said. "Come on with us, if you want."

A chubby youth obligingly vacated his seat in the cab and hopped into the truck bed. The young woman remained, helping Mick slide me in next to her. Mick buckled a seat belt around me before he kissed my forehead, shut the door, and climbed into the back with Nash.

The truck had no air-conditioning, but the open windows admitted a dry breeze that still held morning cool from the mountains. My rescuers discussed something as we pulled away, using a Native American language I didn't know. If they were from Death Valley itself, they'd be Shoshone, from the tribe that lived in the southern part of the valley.

The girl turned to me. "I'm Beth," she said. "That's my dad and my good-for-nothing brothers in the back."

"Janet," I croaked. "Really, really pleased to meet you."

Beth was college age, I guessed, maybe about twenty or twenty-one. She shot me a grin. "That white guy with the gray eyes is cute. Who is he?"

"His name is Nash Jones. The sheriff of Hopi County. In Arizona," I added when she looked blank.

"Yeah?" Beth's dad said. "What's he doing out here?"

"Hiking." Well, it was partly true.

Beth looked through the back window at Nash again. "Well, he is sure cute. He have a girlfriend?"

Did Maya Medina qualify as his girlfriend? "It's hard to say. Have you seen a brand-new black Ford 250 out here? I think Nash loves it more than any girlfriend."

"Nope," Beth's dad said. "You're from Arizona, huh? What tribe?"

"Diné," I said, copying his laconic style.

He didn't make any reply to that, and neither did Beth, and my eyelids drooped. As I drifted toward sleep, my vision started to play tricks on me. Through my eyelashes I saw Beth, but I also saw a shimmering light superimposed on her and an animal shape—with feathery wings? Wings? Were they Changers?

Beth's dad glowed a little too. He was at once a black-haired Native American in dusty jeans, and a shining creature I couldn't identify. Were they aliens, maybe? I giggled.

"You okay?" Beth asked me.

I think I nodded, but the world was going dark. It occurred to me that we'd been very lucky that they'd happened by just at the time we'd made it to the road, as though they'd known we'd be in trouble and exactly where to find us.

Guardian angels?

"Did my grandmother put you up to this?" I tried to ask.

Beth gave me a worried look and touched my forehead. She whispered soothing words in Shoshone, and my eyes drifted closed again. When they opened, I was lying alone

in a hospital bed with white curtains around it, and the ride
in the pickup was fading like a dream.

I first noticed that I was cool and not thirsty, and then
I noticed that I felt no pain. Not an iota. In fact, I felt pretty
good.

"Mm," I said in satisfaction.

The curtain opened, and there was Mick, cleaned up a
little, but still in the T-shirt and jeans I'd stuffed into my
backpack for him. His arms and face were covered with
gouges from the demons, but the wounds were closed.

"Hey, Mick." I held out my hand. "Come and get into
bed with me."

Mick's smile warmed his face—gods, how I'd missed
that smile—but his eyes were still watchful.

"Sounds like you're feeling better."

I wanted to throw my arms around him and pull him down
to me, but my arms felt like rubber, and they were filled with
tubes. I also had a big bandage on my head. No pain, but the
bandage was awkward.

"She sounds high." I saw Nash Jones on a chair behind
Mick, a magazine in his hands. "What did they give her?"

I smiled. "Whatever it is, I like it."

"You had a concussion, sweetheart," Mick said. "Plus
dehydration, the beginning of sunstroke, and a third-degree
burn on your arm. Lie back and take it easy."

In other words, I was lucky my guardian angels got me
here before I keeled over. "You find your truck, Nash?"

"No." The answer was short, irritated. "I have the park
rangers and sheriffs in both Nevada and California on alert
for it."

"Must be nice to have so much power."

He gave me a noncommittal grunt.

"I want to go home," I said.

Mick smoothed my hair. "Not just yet, baby. You get better, then we'll go."

"Turn around," I said, my mind relaxing. "I want to look at your ass. I've missed your ass."

"Can you gag her?" Nash growled.

"Hey, your ass isn't so bad either," I told him.

"Please, gag her," Nash said.

Fear worked its way through the soothing drug. "Mick, why are you so certain the dragons won't come after you? What were you talking about—making bail? What the hell does that mean?"

"Janet." Mick sat on the edge of the bed and took my hands in his warm ones. With muscles and his tattoos he looked like a big, bad biker—and he was—but to me, he could be gentleness itself. Even so, there was some part of him always wary around me, and my little display on the mountain had heightened that. "Like I told you, it was a test of my resources, the equivalent of a human putting together enough money to get out on bail. They won't lock me in again, but I'm honor-bound to turn up at the trial. They know I'll show up; it's a dragon thing."

My mouth popped opened. "Trial?"

"For breaking dragon law, for letting you live." Mick's gaze held mine, that deep, ancient gaze that betrayed how nonhuman he truly was. "When they convict me at the trial, then there will be no escape from that."

The problem with good drugs is that they wear off. By the time the doctors decided I was well enough to go home the next morning, I was hungover and aching. I had meds to stave off the worst of the pain, but I was stiff and sore, my skin smarting from both the fire in the cave and the brutal sun of Death Valley.

I discovered once I was coherent that we weren't in Beatty, a small town just inside the Nevada border, but in Las Vegas.

"You made those people drive us all the way to Las Vegas?" I asked in surprise.

"They wanted to," Mick said. "They were worried about you, and I wanted you at the best possible hospital."

I remembered my conviction in the truck that Beth and her family were some kind of mystical beings, like angels or gods. Had that been real? Or pain hallucination? I'd been half-gone on sunstroke at the time, so who knew what I'd really seen.

Mick rented an SUV to get us home, but Nash insisted on driving. I wanted to grill Mick about the dragon trial, but the meds kept me too drowsy, and I slept fitfully in the backseat, my head on Mick's lap. Anytime I slid from sleep, I found Mick's comforting hand on my shoulder, heard him whispering healing spells over me. I'd drift off again, dreaming of chasing Nightwalkers and demons around Magellan, demanding that they pay their hotel bills.

When I next woke, I was in Mick's arms, being carried into the hotel through the back door. A short hall led to my bedroom and bathroom, with a door beyond my suite leading into the hotel itself. Through this entrance I could come and go when I pleased, without having to pass any of the guests or reception.

I blessed the privacy as Mick carried me in from the warm afternoon to the cool shadows of my bedroom and laid me on the bed. He quickly and competently undressed me, while I lay there and enjoyed it. What healing spells he'd done on me during the drive made me feel better, though I still had a long way to go.

Mick tucked me into bed and disappeared into the bathroom, and I heard the shower go on. I listened to him cleaning himself up and was still awake when he came out.

"Mick."

He looked down at me while he toweled his hair, in jeans but with his torso bare. He had the best body I'd ever seen, six-pack abs and muscular chest, his biceps hard and smooth. A dragon tattoo curled down each arm, their black eyes seeming to glitter with life. They kept his dragon essence, he'd once told me, holding that part of him while he walked around in human form.

"You need to tell me more about this dragon trial," I said.

Mick wrapped the towel around his neck and held on to both ends. "No, what you need is to sleep."

"I'm tired of sleeping. What did you mean when you said, *when* they convict you? Don't you mean *if*?"

"That's not how dragon trials work. Guilt is already proved. The trial is more to clear the air, but the fact that they're holding one at all gives me some hope."

How he could talk so calmly about it, I had no idea. "Hope? How can a trial in which they've already found you guilty give you hope?"

"Because even though you opened the vortexes, as they feared, we sealed them again, mitigating the threat. That act changed the order for immediate execution to one of a trial. It gives me a chance."

"This is bullshit." I wanted to leap out of bed, hunt down this damned dragon council, and tell them what I thought. "Take me to the dragons. Let me talk to them."

Wry amusement danced in Mick's eyes. "I'm not letting

you anywhere near the dragon council, or them anywhere near you. What you're going to do is stay out of it and get better."

Like hell. I didn't have the vaguest idea how to find the dragons and their council, but I'd hunt them down and wring their scaly necks if it was the last thing I did.

"Damn it, Mick," I said. "You said they know you'll show up at the trial even if they don't force you there. Why would you go? Why not fly away to Antarctica or something?"

"If I don't appear on the trial date, I'll be immediately hunted down and killed. Antarctica wouldn't help, and besides, it's too cold for me." He smiled, as though he found my human ignorance funny. "I would also be dishonored if I didn't go, and honor is everything to a dragon. Even if my sentence is execution, my honor will remain intact."

"Well, thank the gods for that."

"I know you don't understand. But there are things I can do in my defense, and I might be able to persuade them to give me a punishment I can survive."

"Shit, Mick, don't blind me with your optimism."

"You won't have to worry about this, sweetheart. When they schedule the trial, I'll go, take my punishment, and do my damndest to get back to you."

"You're not going alone. The dragons are all hot to kill you because of me, and I'm going with you."

Mick lost his smile. He turned from the bed and reached for his shirt. "No, you are not. It's far too dangerous for a human, and I don't trust that one of them won't try to kill you as soon as my back is turned. They don't like you, and your little display up on the ridge hasn't made things any better."

"My 'little display' saved your life. Which you're about to throw away when you go to this fucking trial."

"I don't have a choice," he said, words clipped.

I put my hands to my aching head. "Shit, Mick. I don't want this. I don't want any of this. Why can't we just have a normal relationship?"

Mick's face softened. "A Stormwalker and a dragon? Not in this world." He leaned to me, his body hard and warm, his fists firm on the mattress. "Janet, sweetheart, I'd a thousand times rather have what I have with you than any 'normal' relationship with anyone else."

That was more what I wanted to hear. His skin was hot and damp, his breath warm, and I'd missed him so much. I brushed my thumb over his wrist. "Stay and do some healing magic with me?"

To my vast disappointment, Mick shook his head and straightened up. "Sorry, sweetheart. I'm still pretty weak. The little healing I did on the drive back was all I had for now."

I shifted over in the bed, giving him plenty of room. "You do know that asking you to do healing magic is my subtle way of saying 'come to bed and screw my brains out'?"

Mick didn't smile. "You're tired, love. I don't want to hurt you."

"Just having you in bed with me will help me feel better. I missed you, Mick. I was so worried about you."

"Janet."

I heard the "no" in his voice. My heart ached. Never since I'd met Mick had he been anything but happy to slide between the sheets with me. I needed to reassure myself that he was back with me and unhurt.

I folded my arms. "Next time I'll leave you at the bottom of the damned shaft."

Mick leaned to me again, closer this time, his breath hot.

"What you don't understand, Janet, is that I want you so bad right now that I wouldn't be able to stop myself. The things I'd want to do to you would hurt you, maybe put you back in the hospital. Is that what you want?"

The rough note in his voice rippled agreeable heat through me. I gave him a tired smile. "I think I wouldn't mind."

Mick was strong, never mind that his magic was at a low ebb. Gods, that turned me on.

"But I'd mind." He stood up. "I'd hurt you, baby, because right now I wouldn't be able to control myself. I'm strong, and you're injured, and I'd take advantage. I don't want to have to live with that." He turned away, but not before I saw his hands shaking.

"Mick," I called before he opened the door.

He looked back, so much pain on his face that I almost relented. Almost.

"You do have the sweetest ass," I said.

He growled something, ducked out into the sunlight, and slammed the door.

I grunted and lost my smile. Mick was sexy as sin, but I still had one hell of a headache.

When I woke up again, the sun was setting, and I felt better. The healing spells Mick had done on me in the SUV had helped, and I did a few on myself while I showered, but I could have done so much more if Mick had stayed. He'd taught me the power of Tantra, and together we'd worked some brilliant magic. The wards that secured this hotel were full of it.

I still had a bandage on my head when I walked out to the reception area, though my arm felt well enough that I could leave that bandage off. It was six in the afternoon, and the hotel and lobby were quiet. Tourist season was winding down, and we weren't full, which was fine with me today.

Cassandra sat behind the reception desk at her computer. The bruise she'd sustained in the fight with Pamela was gone, probably magicked away. She wore an elegant black silk pantsuit with a rust-colored blouse, her blond hair in its usual French braid. A pair of tasteful silver and onyx earrings clasped her lobes, and she wore one silver ring with Hopi designs on her middle finger.

"Mick told me about the rescue and the demon attack," Cassandra said, flicking me a glance from her screen. "Are you all right?"

I wondered how much Mick had related about my role in it, but Cassandra only looked concerned. "I'll live." I shrugged. "Where is Mick?"

Cassandra had gotten used to the fact that I didn't always know where my boyfriend was. "He said he had errands to run in Flat Mesa."

Fine. He might believe the dragons wouldn't capture him again, but I still worried.

"Any disasters here?" I asked Cassandra.

"Depends on what you mean by disaster. Had a problem with a faucet in room six, but Fremont fixed it. I was just paying his invoice. But the magic mirror did run off one of the guests last night."

I gripped the counter, bracing myself for the worst. Normal human beings couldn't hear the mirror, but Cassandra, being magical, of course, could.

"Tell me," I said. "How did the mirror manage to run off a guest?"

"It was odd." Cassandra finished the invoice as she talked, a model of multitasking efficiency. "I didn't think the man was a supernatural. He registered as Jim Mohan, said he was from South Dakota out visiting the Southwest. His credit card checked out, and his aura looked normal—human and unthreatening. He was quiet, interested in the tourist attractions, and asked the way to the Homol'ovi ruins. I told him that the park was closed, but he said he'd come all this way to photograph them. He went up there anyway, yesterday afternoon, and showed me his pictures when he came back. Last night, when he walked into the saloon for a drink, the mirror went ballistic, shrieking and screaming and swearing like I've never heard before. I tried to shut it up, but it wouldn't listen to me. Pamela even threw her drink at it."

I lifted my brows. "Pamela's still here?"

"She decided she wanted to stay a couple of days," Cassandra said, her voice neutral. "We had a room, so she booked it. I made sure she was good for the fee."

I had no doubt. "So what was this Jim guy? A sorcerer?"

"That's just it. I don't know, but Jim could definitely hear the mirror. He went sheet white, and the mirror kept yelling at him, calling him names and spewing the filthiest language I've ever heard. Jim ran out of the saloon door to the parking lot, and I never saw him again."

"Stiffing us with the bill, you mean."

"I charged his card for the two nights he'd booked. If he wants to dispute it, fine, but he'll have to go through his credit card company."

That was Cassandra, cutting to the essentials. "Did he leave his stuff?"

"Yes; I was going to have Juana pack everything up and put it in storage, but the room's not booked for another couple of days."

"Leave his things until I have a chance to look through

them," I said. "I'd like to know what he is. Not a Night-walker?"

"Definitely not. I'd have sensed that. Plus, he ate plenty of food and went out in broad daylight. Not a Changer, either, or so Pamela says."

"What did the mirror say he was?"

"It didn't. I haven't been able to get a useful word out of it about the incident."

That didn't bode well. The mirror usually listened to Cassandra, even though technically, it was supposed to obey only me and Mick, because we'd woken it from its dormancy with one of our Tantric spells. Whenever I threatened to muzzle the thing, the mirror would burble, "Oh, honey, you wouldn't do that," and would keep right on talking, but when Cassandra told it to shut up, it did. It was in awe of Cassandra, and if she hadn't been able to make it speak, it must have been scared in a bad way.

Thanking Cassandra, I went into the saloon.

The restored saloon was all polished wood and brass, old-fashioned but not kitschy. We served light meals in here starting at breakfast and drinks well into the night.

The broken magic mirror hung over the bar. A hole had been blown in the middle of it, and spiderweb cracks radiated out to the frame. I needed to get it fixed, but there were few mages in the country who could, and I was still looking for one.

A few guests sat at a table near the window, but the bartender had ducked out somewhere. I nodded to the couple and went behind the bar, picked up the ice tongs and a glass, and helped myself to a cool drink of water.

"So what was he?" I murmured to the mirror. "The guy you scared off last night. Jim from South Dakota."

"I don't want to talk about it, sweet cheeks," the mirror said in a small voice.

I held on to my patience. "I order you to tell me."

"Oh, *honey*, that's so unfair." I heard tinkling as the mirror shuddered. "His aura—oh my *God*, it was like a tar pit. Beware him, sugar-pie. He's pure evil."

Seven

Pure evil. Terrific.

I kept my voice calm, not wanting to send the mirror into an incoherent panic. "Was he demon?"

"He's a danger to you. To all of us."

"How do you know that?"

The mirror's voice dropped to a whisper. "Because I can see the dark on the other side."

"Cut the drama. He wasn't from Beneath, was he?"

"I don't know, girlfriend. Similar feel, but different."

Very clear. I did not want to deal with any more beings from Beneath, but there was still plenty of evil up here with the rest of us. "You really don't know what he was?"

"No, hot pants. Sorry."

"Well, if you remember anything else, let me know."

"Sure thing. Tell you what, give me a little tongue, and I'll see what I can think of."

The thing never stopped. "You're a mirror," I reminded it. "You don't have body parts."

"Hey, honey, I can dream."

The bartender came back in. He was human and had no idea why I kept a broken mirror on the wall that I sometimes talked to. Like the rest of my non-magical staff, he thought I was a little crazy. I smiled at him, put my empty glass in the sink, and left without saying good-bye to the mirror.

I was itchy, and I was hungry, but I didn't want to disturb the temperamental chef who was prepping for dinner in the vast kitchen. She was an Apache woman with a gift for cuisine, who'd trained at the best restaurants in New York and Chicago. When asked why she wanted the job here, she said she wanted something near her grandchildren in Whiteriver. Elena wasn't the most pleasant woman to be around, but her sweet corn tamales were to die for.

I wanted to talk to Mick again now that I was more coherent, and I wanted Mick for other, more basic reasons as well. But he'd not returned, so I left the hotel and rode my Harley through a brilliant sunset to the diner in Magellan.

The diner was full of locals tonight, including the chief of police and his wife. The place was cramped because part of it had been barricaded by a temporary wall, an extended dining room being built behind it. The rest of the room was plenty crowded.

I took the last open seat at the diner's counter next to a man who was as tall and muscular as Mick. He wore jeans and a jeans jacket, his black cowboy boots propped on the rail under the stools. He was Native American, and his black hair hung in a thick braid down his back.

"Where the hell have you been?" I asked him.

Coyote shrugged his massive shoulders. "Around." His

liquid dark eyes took in my bandages. "Where the hell have *you* been?"

"Finding Mick. I could have used your help."

The waitress whizzed down the counter, coffeepot in hand, and asked me what I wanted. I said, "The usual," and she shouted, "Burger, extra cheese!" into the kitchen.

"I see you made it back alive," Coyote said after she'd gone.

"And almost died along the way. A big horde of demons attacked us."

"You're still in one piece, obviously."

"But if I'd have had someone along, like—I don't know—a god, to rescue Mick, I'd be happy and whole and not on medication."

Coyote shot me a grin. "Adversity builds character."

"I have plenty of character, thanks."

His smile faded, and Coyote looked at me with his god eyes, the ones that saw into every corner of my being. "Your Beneath magic came out to play, didn't it?"

I moved my water glass and traced the ring it left behind. "And how did you know that?"

"It's marked you. You need to learn to not use it, Janet. It's dangerous, and there's so much coming."

"If I live that long," I said.

"Yes. If you live that long."

Never turn to a trickster god for comfort. Before I could ask what he meant, the waitress slid my burger in front of me and slapped the check next to it. She knew I never ordered dessert.

I took a big bite of juicy burger, the cheese melted just right. I sighed in satisfaction. Hospital food had been Jell-O and crackers.

The couple who'd been sitting to my left departed, and

a woman in white coveralls slid into one of their vacated seats. She took her white cap from her head, shook out her long black curls, and fixed me with an accusing stare.

"What the hell, Janet?" she said. "Half the town was happy to tell me that you rode off with Nash in his new truck two nights ago."

I wiped burger grease from my lips. "I needed his help to rescue Mick."

Maya Medina gave me another measured stare. She'd always had the notion that Nash, her former boyfriend, was interested in me sexually. He wasn't.

"So, is Mick all right?" she asked me.

"He is now."

"Good."

I took another bite of the burger, chewed, and swallowed, savoring the warm, gooey cheese. "Nash got his truck stolen out in Death Valley."

Maya's grin broke out like sunshine after rain. "Good." She tossed her hat to the counter. "Buy me a drink, and I won't kill you."

I stopped the waitress and ordered Maya a beer. Not tequila—I knew from experience that she didn't handle it well.

As Maya tipped her head back and savored the beer, I turned back to Coyote, but the seat next to me was empty.

"I hate when he does that," I growled.

"When who does what?" Maya asked.

"Coyote. When he vanishes like that."

She gave me a confused look. "Coyote?"

"He was just here. Please don't tell me he stuck me with his bill."

Maya's frown deepened. "What are you talking about?

No one was sitting next to you, and I haven't seen Coyote in weeks."

I opened my mouth to argue; then I closed it again and touched the bandage peeking out from under my hair. "Never mind me. I got hit on the head."

I sensed another presence behind me, and Maya said, "Hey, Mick," a moment before Mick slid onto the stool where Coyote had been. He put his hand on my thigh and kissed me on my ketchup-smeared lips. "You all right?" he asked me.

"Hungry." I licked my fingers. "Did you see Coyote on your way in?"

"Coyote?" Mick looked puzzled. "No."

"I hate when he does that too," I muttered.

"Does what?"

"Makes me think I'm crazy." I knew Coyote had really been there, warning me in his cryptic way of some mysterious danger. But gods can reveal themselves to whomever they please and hide when they want to. I wondered if he'd gotten away with stiffing the diner for his meal.

Mick slid his hand up my thigh. "Ready to go?" he asked.

"Don't you want something to eat?"

"I had something in Flat Mesa. I came here to find you."

My heart beat faster. I could tell he was feeling better, his aura restored to its fiery tingle, and I was feeling better too. Mick paid for both my meal and Maya's beer, and we left the diner.

"Ride with me," Mick said when we reached the parking lot.

My excitement built as I swung onto the back of Mick's bike, settling into the familiar seat. I knew no one would bother my motorcycle if I left it here, not with the chief of police sitting inside and everyone in town knowing the little Harley belonged to me. I also knew why Mick wanted to leave it behind—wherever we were going, whatever Mick wanted to do, he didn't want the piece of magic mirror he'd had ground into my bike's mirror making smart-ass comments.

Mick rode south out of Magellan, the opposite direction from my hotel. It was dark now, the stars bright, the moon hanging on the northeastern horizon. Mick turned onto a dirt road that led back to a couple of ranches, drove down this for about half a mile, and stopped.

The road was empty, the desert dark. I smelled dust, the exhaust from Mick's bike, and Mick.

"I missed you, baby." Mick's voice was raw and dark. He pulled me from the bike and against him, his fingers biting into my arms. "I was locked away for weeks, and all I could think about was you."

"Not about food and water or freedom?"

"Funny. Dragons can go a long time without sustenance. We can exist for years curled away in the dark." He brushed back a lock of my hair. "But all this bad-ass dragon could do is crave the human woman he's fallen for."

"I missed you too," I said.

In silence, Mick kissed me. The kiss we'd shared in Death Valley after we'd crawled out of the mine shaft had been one of glad desperation. This time Mick kissed me slowly, taking his time to do it right. He pressed me to him with his palm on the back of my neck, his lips hard, the taste of his mouth dark and spicy.

Gods, I wanted him. I pried loose his belt, tugged open his waistband, finally felt him in my hand, hard and ready. He was unbuttoning my jeans as well, and then his warm hands slid to my backside.

"I want to taste you," he whispered against my mouth.

He was kissing his way downward even as I nodded. I half leaned against the bike as Mick sank to his knees, pulling my jeans and underwear down as he went. I tipped my head back as his mouth started its dance between my thighs and gazed at the stars spread out in white glory above me.

What Mick did blotted out all thought. My aching brain focused on the heat of his breath, the heady friction of his tongue, his hard fingers on my thighs. I furrowed his hair, pressing him tight to me, letting my cries ring up to the stars.

When I could think again, he was on his feet, pulling me against him. I reached into his jeans, wanting to return the favor, but he stilled my hands and kissed me again.

"Turn around and face the bike," he murmured.

Heart beating in excitement, I did as he wanted, leaning my palms on the bike's seat. His hands went to my bare waist, and I felt his kiss on my neck, his breath hot in my hair.

He made love to me right there, me bent over his bike, he lifting my hips and sliding into me. I smelled the vinyl of the bike seat, the pungent odor of dried grasses as they withered for the coming winter, and I smelled the scent of our loving. Mick stretched me gloriously, filling me with his hardness at the same time cool air touched my skin.

"I love you, Janet," Mick said, his voice thick with sex. "Love you so much, baby."

I was beyond words. He moved faster and faster, and I clung to the bike and made noises of happiness. We could be as loud as we wanted to out here, which was part of his point in bringing me here. The other part was the excitement of doing it outside, at night. He knew I'd love it.

He thrust into me, and I pushed my hips back, wanting

more and more. His hands were hard on my hips, the feel of his thighs smacking my buttocks so erotic, my breasts hot and aching with it. Mick had been my first and only lover, and he knew exactly how to make me feel the deepest kind of pleasure.

I couldn't see and couldn't think by the time I shouted my climax, but Mick went on and on, our bodies sweating even in the rapidly cooling night. He drove into me until I came again, and this time he came with me, saying my name over and over, his voice hoarse.

Then Mick turned me around and held me tight, stroking my skin, kissing my hair. I kissed his neck, feeling his pulse throb hard beneath my lips. He was so human, and yet . . .

"How do dragons do it?" I asked, out of breath.

His hands warmed my hips as he chuckled. "Carefully."

"Seriously."

"I am serious. A female dragon can turn on her lover, kill him as soon as he's done what he's there for. Females are more interested in their clutch than their mates."

"Mmm, so *that's* why you decided I was your mate. Because you don't have to worry about me going black widow on you."

Mick kissed my forehead, lips scalding. "You're pretty dangerous yourself, Janet Begay." He was laughing, but I sensed his tension despite our lovemaking.

Headlights sliced abruptly toward us out of the dark. Mick had my jeans up in two seconds flat, so that the only one caught in the light with his butt bare was himself. Mick calmly pulled up and zipped his pants as an SUV with flashing red and blue lights stopped a few yards from us.

"Damn him," I said, as Nash Jones opened the door. "Can't he give us two seconds of privacy?"

"He helped get me out of that cave and back to you," Mick said, unperturbed. "I'll cut him a lot of slack for that."

Nash approached, the SUV's headlights throwing him into stark silhouette and gleaming on his holstered gun.

"How long have you two been out here?" he asked as he reached us. He didn't ask what we'd been doing—he knew damn well what we'd been doing.

Mick coolly finished buckling his belt, not in the least embarrassed. "An hour?" he suggested. "Maybe longer."

"I have something to show you," Nash said. "You need to follow me."

Without waiting for us, he walked back to his SUV and got inside, the engine whining as he backed it until he found a place to turn around. Mick swung onto his bike and started it up.

I didn't move to join him. "You're just going to do what he says?"

Mick shrugged. "I'm curious." He pulled on his driving gloves and rested his hands on the handlebars, waiting. I heaved a sigh of exasperation and scrambled up behind him.

Mick turned the bike and headed after Nash's retreating vehicle. Nash led us out to the main highway and then turned west on a dirt service road. I coughed from the dust his SUV kicked up—it hadn't rained out here in a couple weeks.

Nash stopped about a half mile along this road, and Mick drew the bike alongside him. Nash was already climbing out, gesturing with his flashlight for us to follow him. We walked with him down the road, the SUV's spotlight blotting out the moonlight.

About ten yards along, Nash's flashlight reflected on an orange hazard cone. The cone was clean and bright, not a speck of dust or a scratch on it. Nash had probably had his deputies polish it before he came out here. He stepped off the road at the cone and led us across hard earth and clumps of bristly grass.

The stench hit me before I saw the blood. Nash didn't prepare me, didn't tell me what we were about to view. He simply played his bright light on the bloody mess stretched out on the desert floor.

"Dear gods," I whispered.

The person, whoever it had been, had been turned inside out. The bones were on top, broken and smashed, resting on a bed of blood, organs, and skin. It was a parody of a human body, deader than dead under the bright stars of the desert sky.

"Have either of you seen Coyote tonight?" Nash asked us after we'd looked at it for a while in stunned silence.

"Coyote?" I asked sharply. "Why?"

Nash gave me a grim look, eyes icy cold. "Because he's my prime suspect," he said. "Coyote was seen on this road right about the time whoever this is would have been killed. I'd like very much to talk to him."

Eight

I stared at Nash in shock. "Seen by who?" I asked.

The kill had been fairly recent, an hour or so ago at most. Whoever that poor person was, he or she hadn't lain there long.

"A reliable witness." Which meant Nash wasn't about to tell me. "This witness gave Coyote a ride from the Cross-roads Bar and dropped him off here an hour and a half ago, at his request."

"Coyote couldn't have done this," I said. He was unpredictable, cryptic, annoying, sexually blatant, and sometimes frightening, but I couldn't see him ripping someone open like this.

Then again, what did I know about him? He was a god, a powerful being who didn't necessarily follow human rules. My blood chilled.

Nash continued, "Coyote has no known address, he hangs around Magellan bothering people, and he was dropped off on this road tonight, as though he'd come out here to meet someone. That makes him a suspicious person in my book."

"But he was at the diner, sitting next to me an hour and a half ago," I said. He had been, hadn't he?

Mick didn't meet my eyes. Nash did, his gray irises like chips of ice. "Are you contradicting my reliable witness?"

I didn't know how to answer. No one had seen Coyote in the diner but me—at least, Maya and Mick hadn't. Could he be in two places at once? I had no idea.

"I don't know," I said.

Nash frowned, and Mick still wouldn't look at me.

"So, you're putting the time of death to an hour and a half ago?" I asked.

"The ME will say for certain, but I'd guess no longer than that."

"And you have no idea who it is? The victim, I mean." The bones, strings of muscle, and blood against the grass were gruesome. I doubted I'd be eating meat for a while.

"I didn't find any obvious ID. Wallet gone, no driver's license, anything like that. It will be DNA and dental records that tell us who it was."

I ran through everyone I'd seen at the diner: Maya, the McGuires, the waitress, other townspeople I recognized. They'd been safe and whole, not turned inside out on the desert floor, nor had they been out here committing murder.

But plenty of people *hadn't* been there: Jamison Kee and his wife, Naomi; Cassandra; Fremont Hansen; Assistant Chief Salas; Nash's deputies from Flat Mesa; any number of others. I'd seen Coyote, but no one else had. Why had he chosen tonight of all nights not to reveal himself to people?

"Coyote is only one possibility," Mick was saying. "This

was a pretty powerful kill, but any number of supernatural killers could have done this. A dragon, for instance."

I knew Mick spoke rhetorically, but Nash was the kind of sheriff who would arrest and interrogate in a heartbeat.

"What other kinds of supernatural killers?" Nash asked him. "These skinwalkers or Nightwalkers Janet told me about?"

I shook my head. "Skinwalkers either just kill, or they flay the corpse and steal the skin. Nightwalkers suck their victims dry. Changers would maul, in whatever animal form they change into. It would look like an animal kill." I glanced at Mick. "Wouldn't a dragon just fry someone?"

"Usually, yes," Mick said. Of the three of us, he was the calmest, looking at this with almost clinical interest. "Most often, dragons ignore humans. Not worth the trouble."

Mick spoke with easy conviction about the arrogance of his kind. I didn't know how to respond, so I asked Nash, "Why did you bring me out here to see this?"

"Because, whether I like it or not, you have the reputation for finding out the truth about weird crimes. I decided to take a shot and ask you what you thought about this one."

That Nash had even considered asking me my opinion spoke volumes as to how far he'd unbent since he'd first met me. When I'd arrived in Magellan five months ago, he'd made it clear he thought me a con artist who'd bamboozled the McGuires into believing I could find their missing daughter. It floored me that Nash was extending this small tether of trust.

I looked at the body again, at the sticky black aura surrounding it. It radiated death, but the only thing I could sense about the victim was his or her acute surprise. Whoever had killed had done so quickly, and the victim had probably been unaware it had even happened.

The magic residue from the killer was incredibly power-ful. It had a whiff of godlike power—not good, solid earth magic—but it was uncertain. It might not be god magic at all, or, indeed, Beneath magic. The fact that I couldn't see anything clearer bothered me a lot.

I rubbed my still-aching head. "Hard to say. If you're hoping I'll confirm that Coyote did this, I can't."

Nash opened his notebook and started writing. "That's it?"

"Something or someone is hiding the aura of the mur-derer. Whoever can do that would be very powerful."

"Like who?" the literal-minded Nash asked.

Coyote for one, I thought but didn't say. "A human mage, possibly. If they were powerful enough."

Nash looked at me over his notebook. "Mage?"

"A witch, you'd call them. Not necessarily Wiccan, but someone with some hard-ass magic." Someone like that, I didn't want to meet.

Nash's eyes narrowed. "Heather Hansen claims to be a witch."

Heather owned the local woo-woo store called Paradox, which sold crystals, tarot cards, incense, and other accoutre-ments for magic working. "I don't think so. Heather thor-oughly embraces the creed of doing no harm to others. She works spells of protection, leaves gifts for the wee folk, or-ganizes the Ghost Train festival. She has power, more than she knows, but she doesn't have the temperament to kill with it. Especially not like this."

Nash listened with a look of doubt, but I knew I was right. Heather's aura had no darkness. She was a truly kind person and didn't have the power I sensed here, but I watched Nash noting down Heather Hansen as a person to be questioned.

"Anyone else?"

Cassandra, I thought but didn't want to say. She was Wiccan, but I didn't know her well enough to know what she was capable of. She was strong, I knew that, and damn good at her job, but I couldn't know whether she had it in her to kill.

I was debating whether to mention her to Nash, who would probably whip her under hot lights without drawing breath, when the arrival of the rest of the police interrupted us. A car marked "City of Magellan Police" pulled up to disgorge Emilio Salas and a uniform cop. Lopez and two other deputies from the county pulled in right behind them, Lopez and Salas greeting each other like the old friends they were.

"Don't leave yet," Nash said to me. "I need statements from both of you."

"Statements? What for?"

Nash's badge winked in the light of the flares Salas was setting out. "I am still pinning my suspicions on Coyote, but either of you could have done this. You only alibi each other." He looked from me to Mick, who nodded thoughtfully.

"*I* couldn't," I said. "Not without a storm."

Mick and Nash looked at me at the same time, and I knew they were recalling what I'd done to the demons in Death Valley. Both gave me hard stares, and I didn't have to be psychic to know they thought me perfectly capable of this horrific deed.

"I don't know how I called that magic," I said irritably. "It just happened, probably because we were going to die. I can't conjure it at will."

Nash didn't believe me, but then, Nash never believed me.

He directed us to give statements to Lopez, and then he turned away to take Salas and his deputies over the scene. Lopez's lips quirked as I had to tell him exactly what time

I left the diner, who I'd seen there, and why I'd decided to ride with Mick into the middle of the desert. Everyone in town would know by tomorrow that Mick and I had been engaged in sexual activity out there in the dark, because Lopez was almost as good a gossiper as Fremont Hansen. Finally, Lopez finished with us and told me and Mick to go.

Mick stopped by the diner on the way to the hotel, where I picked up my bike. Everyone had already heard about the corpse, of course, and townspeople in the parking lot tried to get out of us what we knew. Mick and I managed to evade questions and head home.

Mick had known me long enough to understand what I needed. He pulled down the blinds and undressed me himself, and then he carried me into the bathroom and set me under a warm shower. His clothes came off, and he stepped in with me, his large body enveloping mine.

We didn't make love there as we sometimes did; we just soaked up the hot water. I closed my eyes to the feel of Mick's big hands smoothing soap over my body, opening them when he rinsed me off and lifted me out. He wrapped me in a towel, carried me into the bedroom, and laid me on the bed.

Now he made love to me, slow and easy. By the time he was done, I was pleasantly drowsy, the horror of the crime scene fading a little. As had been Mick's intention, I drifted off to sleep in his warm embrace.

Whenever I encountered Coyote in one of my dreams, I seemed to be naked. This time was no exception. We stood side by side, he in his animal form, looking down at the remains of the body, me human and naked. Turkey vultures moved in slow hops around the corpse, like hooded demons feasting on their victim. Coyotes, lured by the scent of blood, circled at a safe distance, their eyes shining in the darkness.

"Did you do this?" I asked Coyote. He sat on his haunches, a coyote as big as a wolf, except that he had the rail-thin legs and pointed nose of his species.

I am capable of such a thing.

"Don't go all cryptic on me again," I growled. "Were you really in the diner tonight?"

Were you?

"Of course I was. I was eating dinner." I glanced at the corpse. "Kind of sorry I did, now."

There is your answer.

"No one else could see you. Maya couldn't. Did you pull a glam to get free food?"

His answering laugh was full of amusement. *I wanted to talk to you without anyone knowing about it.*

"Why? You didn't say much of anything."

I didn't have time. I knew Mick was coming for you. Be careful of Mick. He's more dangerous than you know.

"You told me that before. I've seen how dangerous he is."

You know only what you've witnessed. What goes on in his mind is unfathomable to you. If he makes the decision to kill you, he will without warning. He will be swift and merciless. You love him with your human emotions, but he is not human. He never has been. His emotions are . . . complicated.

"Like yours?"

No one is as complicated as me.

"No kidding." I knew better than to ignore his warnings, but I had many immediate things to think about, like the dragons taking Mick to trial for *not* killing me and now a corpse at the edge of town. Worrying about what Mick might do in the future would have to wait.

You need to end your Beneath magic, Coyote said. *Before it ends you.*

"Easy for you to say."

You were born with the magic, but it has been biding its time, unable to grow here in this world of earth magics. Now it has been triggered by your journey Beneath.

I felt cold, but I nodded. "I figured as much. I thought maybe you could help me get rid of it."

No, Stormwalker. It is part of you. But you must control it, or it will consume you. And possibly everything else on earth.

"How could it do that? My mother is the monster, not me."

Don't worry. I'll destroy you before you can do too much damage. I love you, Janet Begay, but that doesn't mean I won't put aside my feelings and kill you.

"It is always so comforting to talk to you."

Coyote chuckled. *I could do more than comfort, if you'd let me. Sex with you would be wicked.*

"Restrain yourself." I glanced at the corpse. "Do you know who it is?"

I know. And yes, a god would make this kill if they thought it necessary.

"And you'd do that to me? If you thought it necessary?"

Yes.

I stared down at the pile of bones and gore in disquiet. The vultures moved about it unhurriedly, their wings spread for balance. The dream was mercifully free of smell, but I remembered the stench.

"Tell me one thing," I said. "Those people who gave us a ride in Death Valley, the Shoshone. They weren't what they seemed, were they? Did you send them to help us?"

Coyote's tongue lolled from his mouth as he started to pant. *For that one, you'll have to ask the lady Crow.*

The crow. I hadn't seen her in a while. "I'll give her a call."

She doesn't like to talk on the phone.

"I know. I'll ask her when I drive up again."

Coyote winced. *She's quite a woman, your grandmother. She doesn't like coyotes, and she wields a mean broom.*

I had the satisfaction of laughing. "If she went after you, I'm sure you deserved it."

Coyote didn't bother to answer that. *Time to wake up, Janet. But I have a little gift for you.*

"Don't give me anything. Really." Gifts from gods, especially trickster gods, weren't always what they seemed.

You'll like it, Janet. Trust me.

Famous last words. I noticed as we talked that the corpse had disappeared, and so had the scavengers. Thunder rumbled in the distance, followed by a waft of rain-drenched air. I inhaled, my mind calming.

The dream dissolved, and I woke up in my bed. It was early morning, the sky gray, and rain poured down outside the window. Mick was gone, but he'd left me cocooned in a nice warm bed that smelled of him.

I lifted my hand as lightning struck a few miles away and let sparks dance between my fingers. A gift indeed.

I realized as I rolled out of bed and stepped out my back door to enjoy the storm that Coyote had never answered me directly about either the identity of the victim or whether he himself had done the murder.

Nine

The storm was an autumn storm, not as wild as the monsoons that swept through during spring and summer, but one that brought steady rain and languid rumbles of thunder. I threw back my head and inhaled the clean air.

Magellan sits on a plateau that slopes slowly from the Mogollon Rim and the ten-thousand-foot White Mountains to the vistas of the Painted Desert. Wide, deep washes and gorges like Chevelon Canyon crisscross the desert floor on the east side of the old railroad bed, fissures cut by eons of flowing water. Most of the time, these washes were dry, but they'd start filling if this kept up. A shallow one ran right through Magellan, the highway curving alongside it. A few of the side streets had bridges over Magellan Wash, but many were simply cut off when it flooded. Most towns in the desert have a wash or two or three to worry about, but bridges are expensive, and mostly we just put up with it.

The storm enhanced my healing spells, and I felt much better. My bathroom mirror showed me that the wound on my head had dwindled to a yellow green bruise, and the skin on my burned arm was healthy and brown again.

I wanted to go back to the scene of the crime now that the body would be gone, to see if I could read anything, especially with my storm powers to help me. The killing had been cruel and nasty, and I needed to know what kind of being had done this and where to hunt it down.

Cassandra volunteered the information that she'd seen Mick ride away north on his bike, so I'd have to go on my own. I passed through the saloon on the way out, where my guests were whispering about the death. I wanted to reassure them that if they stayed in my heavily warded hotel, they'd be fine, but not all of them were believers.

I passed the little breakfast bar Cassandra set up every morning with the fresh breads and muffins from Magellan's bakery and took up one of the big sugar-crusted blueberry muffins. In my youth I'd listened to a university professor explain that indigenous peoples had difficulty eating simple carbohydrates, because until very recently our diet had consisted mostly of whole grains, beans, squash, nuts, and lean protein. There'd been no double cheeseburgers, milk shakes, or beer in the times of my Diné ancestors. Our metabolism hadn't evolved to tolerate processed flour, sweets, and, even more problematic, alcohol, she'd explained, which was why Native Americans had a higher risk for diabetes. The more isolated the tribe, the higher the incidence.

Therefore, I knew I shouldn't down the blueberry muffin slathered with butter and chase it with lemon poppy seed pound cake, but they were so damn good. Besides, a long road trip, nearly dying of a head wound and heatstroke, and viewing a nasty murder scene made me hungry.

Rain pelted me as I rode my motorcycle into town. The speed limit was thirty-five on the main highway through Magellan, and they weren't kidding. Magellan always needed money, and speeding tickets were lucrative. I rode slowly and pulled in at the town's one gas station.

My storm magic, too long silent, jumped along my nerves, making me wish I'd had the sense to fill up while the weather was still good. I didn't need to be sparking lightning at the gas pump.

Naomi Kee was there in her big red pickup. Naomi owned the town's plant nursery, Hansen's Garden Center, so her truck was often loaded with bags of dirt, flats of bedding plants, or whole trees as she made deliveries, but today the truck bed was empty.

"You're soaked, Janet," she greeted me. "Can I drive you somewhere?"

"Thanks, but I don't mind." I slid my credit card into the gas pump slot and started filling my small tank.

"I mind. I'm shivering just looking at you."

The rain was coming down harder. I made myself carefully finish gassing up and put the nozzle back. My powers wanted to grab the distant lightning and all this rain and play with it, but I restrained myself around the gas fumes. My Stormwalker ancestors never had to worry about gas pumps, I thought grumpily, just as they hadn't had to worry about simple carbohydrates.

"I'm heading to look at the crime scene again," I told Naomi.

"In the pouring rain?"

"Before everything gets completely washed away, yes. I didn't have time to go over it last night."

Naomi's blue green eyes narrowed. "That's it. I'm driving you. I don't want you going out there alone."

I started to argue, but lightning forked about a mile to the east, and I barely stopped myself from reaching for it. I needed to close my eyes and concentrate to keep myself under control. But I also wanted to get to the crime scene, so I took Naomi up on her offer.

Naomi used the hydraulic lift on the back of her truck to load my bike, and she covered the Sportster with a tarp. She pulled out onto the main road, also carefully driving the speed limit. Chief McGuire's boys had us trained.

Naomi asked me whether the body had been identified, and I had to say I didn't know. I doubted Nash would rush the information to me, but I suspected that he didn't know either. In the gossip mill of Hopi County, someone would have leaked a name the minute the corpse was ID'd. I wondered if it was my missing guest, Jim Mohan, but until Nash got the dental records, I had no way of knowing. I also wondered whether Jim, who'd scared the mirror so much, had done the killing. And why.

"Have you seen Coyote lately?" I asked. Naomi and her daughter Julie were friends with Coyote, as much as he could be said to have friends. Coyote had a soft spot for Julie, who'd been born with total hearing loss.

Naomi threw me a startled look. "I gave him a ride to the south edge of town last night. Dropped him off at the end of that service road where body was found."

"So *you* are Nash's reliable witness?" Well, I couldn't argue with Naomi's reliability.

"Did he call me that?" She looked amused. "I picked up Coyote outside the Crossroads Bar. I was driving back with a load of flats from Winslow, and I saw him hitchhiking. Julie was with me. He hopped in and asked me to drive him down here."

Naomi slowed the truck at the narrow dirt turnoff.

Gravel shored up the entrance to the road to keep it from being washed out, but beyond that, the ruts and holes in the hard earth were already full of water.

"Don't drive down there," I advised. "You'll get stuck."

"What are you going to do?"

"Walk."

Naomi pulled the truck off the highway and set the brake. "I'm coming with you."

"No need."

She gave me a stubborn look. "Janet, I know I don't have any magic, but I might be able to spot something with my regular human eyes. Besides, there's been one murder out here, and damned if I'll let you be a second victim."

That settled it. Naomi was nice, but not a pushover. She was coming with me.

The scene of the murder was less gruesome now that the coroner had removed the corpse and rain was washing away the blood. A lone turkey buzzard wandered around the scene checking in case the ME's team had left something behind.

The body might be gone, but the miasma of death lingered. I'd grown up in a household that held to traditional ways—when someone died in a hogan, the body was pushed out through the north wall, the way to the ancestors, and often the hogan was abandoned. Non-Diné didn't always understand why, but I'd seen firsthand how much damage a spirit in unrest could do to the living.

I smelled the stench of power that hovered over the spot and, again, sensed the victim's surprise. Whoever the person had been hadn't realized how close to death he or she was. That was comforting—he or she had died too quickly to be afraid—but then again, it meant that I was dealing with something that could strike swiftly, mercilessly, and efficiently. I gazed at the empty land around me, feeling an itch between my shoulder blades.

"This is horrible," Naomi said.

Naomi had no magic, so she saw only the rain-drenched grasses and red earth turning to mud, the lowering gray sky, the buzzard, and the leftover blood. I saw all that plus the foul darkness that coated the spot like tar, the stink of decay and hard magic.

The headache I'd finally managed to get rid of throbbed anew. Storm power tingled through my body, and I felt the Beneath magic stir in response. The Beneath magic urged me to find out who'd done this and destroy them, to kill as they had killed, except slowly, so they could experience every nuance of the unknown person's death.

All I had to do, the magic whispered to me, was send my storm power through every house in Magellan, seeking evil and destroying it. Even if I had to kill every single person, I'd be sure to get it, wouldn't I?

I closed my eyes, trying to shut off the voice, but that let me view the crime scene's aura without obstruction—dense black and shot through with red, crimson like thick blood. I popped my eyes open again, preferring the gray rain streaming into my face. Water was life. The rain would wash away the blood, cleanse the air, give life back to the earth.

But you could kill every person in this town, the magic of Beneath told me. *You know how. And no one could stop you.*

I heard a rush of wings. A big black crow sailed in to land not far from the buzzard and gave the larger bird a disapproving eye. The crow turned its head and regarded me with similar disapproval.

"I'm not going to do it," I told her. I clenched my fists

against another wave of Beneath magic that showed me how to turn the crow into a little pile of feathers. "I promise."

The crow kept her beady eye on me, the steady, watchful gaze that had been on me since babyhood. "Cross my heart." I'd said that as a child when my grandmother suspected I was up to no good. She'd usually been right. "They're my friends. I won't hurt them."

The crow either didn't believe me, or she was just a crow wondering why a human was talking to it.

Naomi watched me worriedly. "You all right, Janet?"

I turned my back and started for the road. "I'm finished here. I need to go."

Naomi fell into step beside me. "A terrible thing happened here," she said. "I'm sorry you had to see it."

She was sorry for *me*, the Stormwalker who specialized in solving magical crimes? Naomi was too sweet to be believed. "The vortexes draw the terrible. Any place magical does."

"I grew up in Magellan and never noticed." Naomi gave me a faint smile. "I thought all the vortex stuff was just a story to attract tourism. But I've seen some bad things since I stopped being an Unbeliever. I've watched a skinwalker nearly kill Jamison. Jamison had to burn the skinwalker alive to destroy it, and Jamison nearly died himself. Things like that make me wish I were an Unbeliever again."

"Trust me, Naomi, you haven't seen anything as bad as me."

"You're not evil, Janet. Not like that skinwalker."

"Looks can be deceiving."

"Nash Jones thinks Coyote did this," Naomi said, staring off into the distance. "He questioned me pretty hard about what time I'd picked up Coyote and when I dropped him off. He also wanted to know everything Coyote said to me. He even wants to interview Julie. But Coyote couldn't have done something like *this*. I know he wouldn't."

"He's a god, Naomi. If he felt justified, he would."

Naomi gave me a stubborn look. "I don't believe it for a second. You see how he is with Julie. Coyote has a lot of kindness in him, and he's saved Jamison's life—and mine—more than once."

I didn't argue. It was true that Coyote could exhibit amazing compassion, but he was dangerous, despite his affable persona. I could imagine him laughing while he killed whoever he thought he needed to kill.

We slogged through mud to Naomi's truck, which sat untouched on the side of the highway. I felt like shit, but I told Naomi I wanted to ride the bike home. I needed the wind and rain in my face to clear my brain.

She lifted the tarp from the motorcycle. I don't know why she'd felt it necessary to cover it up—I'd ridden my Harley through plenty of snow and rain and hail.

As soon as the tarp came off, the mirror on the bike cried, "Oh my God, sugar, you need to get home!"

What now? "Why?" I asked irritably.

Naomi threw me another anxious look. That's it; I'd convinced her that I was thoroughly nuts.

"Seriously, girlfriend, we are in deep doo-doo."

Damn it. I started up my bike, put on my helmet. "Go home, Naomi. Keep Julie there, and don't go anywhere without Jamison. Anywhere, all right?"

"That bad?"

"I don't know." Frustration and fear made me impatient. "Assume the worst. Ask Jamison if he's noticed anything weird around here lately—anything at all—and tell him to call me."

Naomi nodded. She'd do what I asked, being smart.

I rode back through town, the mirror urging me to hurry all the way, but I didn't dare break the speed limit. Salas or one of the uniform cops stopping me to cheerfully hand me a ticket would just slow me down.

The rain was coming down harder as I reached the Crossroads, parked the bike, and strode into the hotel. Cassandra wasn't behind the desk, but everything looked quiet. Pulling off my helmet, I headed to the saloon.

The saloon was deserted except for a large man with a hard face and long black braid who sat at one of the tables, sipping from a bottle of beer. His denim biker vest and sleeveless shirt showed that his muscular arms and neck were covered with interlocked tattoos. As I walked in, unnoticed, he moved the beer bottle from his lips and glared at the mirror.

"Hey, magic mirror," he said. "Shut the fuck up."

"You just come over here and make me, you big bully," the mirror said.

The man held up his hand, flame dancing in his palm. "Shut up, or I melt you."

The mirror made a noise like *ewp,* but I felt the thing sense me and relax. Mom was home.

"Let me guess." I put my hands on the table and leaned to study my visitor, who returned the look with eyes of chilly light blue. "Dragon?"

Ten

The dragon-man looked me up and down, then fixed a blatant gaze to my cleavage. "I get why Micky wants to keep you alive, girl. You're one fine-looking lady."

"The saloon isn't open yet," I said coldly.

"It's open for me, darling. By the end of the day, you'll open for me all the way."

In his dreams. "I own this hotel. Get out of it."

The man hooked a booted foot around a chair leg, slid out the chair, and planted both feet on it. "Not until I'm done."

I held up my hand, drawing on the lightning outside until sparks crackled and danced on my fingertips. "You're done now."

The lick of flame sprang back into his palm. "You want to play, little Stormwalker?"

I wasn't certain I could hurt him, but I'd never tell him that. The night I'd met Mick, I'd slammed him with about nine thousand volts of lightning, and he'd just laughed and sucked it in. My power, unless I was in the heart of a storm, made dragons stronger. *But Beneath magic,* the little voice whispered, *is the antithesis of all things dragon.*

Before I could figure out what the hell that meant, something moved past me with incredible speed. The chair the dragon-man sat on was scraped back and dragged around to face a furious Mick.

"Out," Mick said. "Now."

The stranger grinned, showing white, slightly pointed teeth. "Aw, come on, Micky, I came to help you. Screwing your woman will be just a bonus."

I'd seen Mick angry, but never like this. "Get away from my mate and the fuck out of my territory before I kill you."

The dragon-man lifted his hands, now free of fire. "Hey, I'm not here to cop your place. If that was my intention, it would be burned all to hell already, and you know it."

"Not through my wards it wouldn't be."

"True, you've got some good magic here. And a magic mirror. Mouthy little shit."

I broke in. "Mick, who is this guy?"

The man grinned at me. "The name's Colby. Mick's a friend in need." His grin widened. "And I'm a friend, indeed."

"Colby the dragon?" I asked in a dubious voice. "Nice name."

"It's the one humans can pronounce," Colby said. "But, hey, sweetheart, *he's* the bad guy. When the dragon council was handing out the assignment of tracking you down and offing you, I refused. Cold-blooded murder's not my thing. But Micky here volunteered. Jumped at the chance. Said he couldn't wait to break the storm bitch's sweet little neck. The storm bitch would be you, by the way."

Of course Colby would say something like that. He'd

walked in here right through our wards, scared my mirror, and challenged me and Mick. I wasn't about to whirl around and scream, *Mick, is this true?* That's what he wanted. Divide and conquer.

"Janet, go run your hotel," Mick said. Even the eyes of his dragon tattoos glittered with rage. "I need to talk to Colby."

"Forget it." I folded my arms. "I want to know who he is and what he's doing here. And I don't want to see any fire. Too many flammable things in here, and I already had to restore the place once."

"I heard about that," Colby said. "Good fight. I'm sorry I missed it."

"Talk or get out."

"She's a feisty one." Just to piss me off, Colby shot a flame skyward, but it was a small one and dissipated before it reached the tin ceiling. "She this feisty in bed?"

I let electricity dance on my fingers once again. "Have you ever seen a Stormwalker's power enhanced by a magic mirror?" I hadn't, but it might be fun to find out what would happen.

"All right, all right." Colby lifted his hands in surrender. "I really am here to help you, Micky. The dragons want to burn you to a crisp, and while I wouldn't mind seeing that, they're determined not to let you have all the rights that go with a trial, and I don't like the precedent that sets. No way do I want us all to be little slaves to the dragon council. So I'm here to take your side."

"What do you mean, not all the rights that go with a trial?" I asked in alarm.

Colby's eyes narrowed, but his anger wasn't directed at me. "The council consists of three sticks-up-their-asses dragons who have been alive since the beginning of time and think they own us. They want to control everything every dragon does. They need to learn that the times, they are a-changing."

"So, what, you came here to gang up with Mick and fight them?"

"She's precious, Micky. No, I'm going to be his defense attorney, sort of. Find precedents and stuff the rules down the elders' throats. I may need your help, honey, though you might not do well in front of the council. You're way too smart-ass."

In spite of Colby's nonchalance, I sensed his nervousness. Mick's eyes had gone black all the way across, and Colby didn't like that, in spite of the loose-limbed way he lounged in the chair. To an ordinary human, they might look like two biker buddies there to catch up on old times. But Colby's uneasiness screamed itself to me—he was like a wolf who'd wandered into another wolf's territory and had unhappily come face-to-face with the head wolf of the pack.

I pulled back a chair and sat down. "So, talk. What exactly do you have planned?"

I could tell Mick didn't want me there, but there was no way I was letting him keep me out of this. I folded my arms and waited, and finally Mick gave Colby a resigned look.

"Why the hell you are so interested in getting me free?" Mick asked him.

Colby shrugged. He leaned back and put his feet up again, and Mick sat casually on the other side of the table, but the two men might as well have been circling each other, hackles raised.

"Because this trial could make life bad for me, for all dragons. What they do to you, they can do to everyone."

"I don't plan to let them win," Mick said.

"They weren't even going to let you have a team, did you know that? I had to go to the archive, pull records, prostrate myself in front of the Mighty Three to convince them they'd get lynched if they didn't at least pretend to follow dragon law."

Mick watched him narrowly. "You don't care about the greater good; you're helping me so you can save your own ass over something. What did you do to piss off the council? This time, I mean."

Colby laughed, but the laugh was nervous. "Couple of things. Like I said, I don't want them to set a precedent of frying a dragon's hide without a defense."

"What makes you so sure you can help me?"

"I have some ideas. And I know things. Things that could give you leverage."

"And what do you want in return?"

Colby chuckled again. "You'll owe me one, Micky. And I'll call in the favor when it's the most hell for you."

"As long as that favor doesn't involve Janet."

Colby's gaze flicked to my cleavage, bared by my tight black top. "She's a tasty morsel. I'd like to lick her from neck to knees, and I don't even like humans."

"Just what I want," I said. "Dragon drool."

Colby chuckled, but Mick leaned forward. "Janet is my mate. Touch her and die." He didn't even have to raise his voice. I knew he'd do it, and so did Colby.

"Hey, you kill me, no one will be on your side at the trial."

"I won't care. So long as Janet is safe from you, I'll die happy."

Colby shook his head in amusement. "Oh, man, she's really knocked you on your ass, hasn't she?"

"More than once."

I didn't know whether to warm at Mick's fond glance or get irritated at them for talking about me as though I weren't there. "Excuse me," I said. "Can we concentrate on you surviving the trial? And I choose what dragon I end up with, not either of you."

Colby chortled. "Oh, I like her. I really do. I remember when you were all hot to kill her, Micky. You said we had to do anything to keep the Beneath-goddess's get from opening the vortexes, even if the girl had to be slaughtered. You were ready to off her without a second thought. So what happened?"

"Yes, Mick," I said in a hard voice. "What happened?"

Mick's gaze was all for me, and this time, I chose to warm to it. "I watched you fighting," he said. "You were alone, up against assholes who were ready to throw you on the floor and gangbang you. You boiled with power, but they were human, magicless. You could have wiped out every single one of them and brought the roof down to bury them." Mick's eyes went blue and hot, the hint of his smile making me remember him hard and good inside me last night. "But you didn't. You pulled your punches, tried not to hurt them."

"Stupid of you," Colby said around a sip of beer.

"I didn't have a lot of choice," I said. Mick might claim I'd been oozing power that night, and I had just come off a big storm, but I'd felt sick and weak and desperate.

"Janet was cornered. She knew she might have to kill to get away, and I saw on her face that she didn't want to."

"And this made you want to claim her as mate?" Colby sounded skeptical. "I get that she's a hot lay, but mate is forever, Micky."

I gave him a deprecating look, but Mick was still studying me with a tenderness that heated my blood. "Mate came later," he said. "After I got to know her better."

I shifted in my chair, wishing Colby far away so I could tell Mick how much I appreciated his sentiments.

Colby heaved an exaggerated sigh. "I hope you know what the hell you're doing, Micky. Mate or no, you did let her open the vortexes. The dragon council plans to screw you to the wall for that."

"And you want to keep me alive," Mick said, turning from me. "When did you fall in love with me?"

"Trust me, I don't care what happens to you, my old friend. I only care that you get a fair trial and a by-the-book defense. I don't give a demon's dick if they end up pinning one of your wings to the wall in the trophy room."

"You inspire confidence." Mick leaned across the table, putting his face close to Colby's. "But you touch Janet, and you're toast. I don't care if we're in the middle of the dragon high court."

Colby lifted his hands, tipping back in his chair. "Fine. I get it. Talons off your mate." He flashed me a grin. "Oh, girl, this is going to be fun."

Mick escorted Colby out of the hotel, saying he wanted to find Colby a place to stay, and I let them go. It was with mixed feelings that I leaned on the bar in the empty saloon watching them ride off on motorcycles toward Magellan. Colby didn't exactly inspire trust, but he'd already told me a hell of a lot more about the trial than Mick had. In spite of Mick's warm praise of me and my compassion, I didn't let that blind me to the fact that he was stubbornly trying to keep me out of all this.

"He scared me," the mirror said over my shoulder. "But, sugar, what a *bod*. I wonder if those tattoos go all the way down?"

"Why didn't you ask him to do a striptease?" I asked sourly.

"Ooh, do you think he would?"

"I think he really would melt you if you suggested it. Can you tell where they've gone?"

"Want to do a little eavesdropping, do you?"

I shrugged. "It couldn't hurt."

"Well, I don't know, sugar. Micky never takes his piece of me out of his pocket. I like it in there, but I can't see where he is. Sorry."

Of course Mick would realize I could use the magic mirror to spy and make sure he kept his shard hidden. "That's all right. Never mind."

"Tell Micky to go commando," the mirror said. "And work a little hole in his pocket . . ."

I was debating whether or not to bother with an answer when somewhere upstairs, a woman began screaming. I jumped, and the mirror shrieked response.

"Shut up!" I shouted at it and ran out to reception.

Cassandra was already halfway up the staircase. The lobby itself was mercifully free of guests at the moment, no one there to hear our maid Juana's screams die off into a string of unhappy Spanish.

The stairs went up to a railed gallery around the main lobby, the guest rooms opening onto it. The screaming had come from room nine, the very last one, which lay next to the stairs up to the third floor.

As Cassandra and I ran along the gallery, the Changer Pamela emerged from another guest room, watched us pass, and followed us.

Room nine was my most spacious. Two open shoulder bags lay on the king-sized bed next to a pile of clothing and what I knew to be an expensive camera. A pair of dusty hiking boots rested on the floor.

As soon as she saw us, Juana ran for me, her eyes wide. "It's terrible, it's evil. I don't touch it. I don't touch this room."

She ducked past us and out, and neither Cassandra nor I tried to stop her.

Pamela sniffed. "I smell blood. Dry, not fresh."

"This is Jim Mohan's room," Cassandra said. "I asked Juana to pack up his clothes. I was going to have you look over the bags and the room and then put the bags down in storage."

I approached the bed. Juana had been sorting through clothes and had folded shirts, pants, and socks into neat piles. The rest she'd dropped in an unorganized heap.

It wasn't difficult to find what had scared Juana. A T-shirt lay crumpled on the small pile of folded underwear. The logo on it read "Sedona," the town southwest of here that also boasted vortexes and mystical energies. The shirt had been dyed what was called Sedona red, the color of iron-rich earth.

I lifted the shirt and shook it out. The back of it was entirely coated with dried blood.

I dropped the shirt as the aura of it crawled up my arms and tried to invade my body. I saw movement in a mirror across the room, darkness that rose and swallowed the reflection of my blood-drained face and wild eyes.

The blackness squeezed me in a freezing embrace, my crackling storm magic trying to drive it away. The aura held me tighter, and cold lips touched my ear.

"Help me," it whispered, and then it dispersed and was gone.

"Janet? Are you all right?"

I found both Cassandra and Pamela staring down at me in concern, Pamela's eyes shifting to wolf white.

I blew out my breath. The darkness dispersed, and I was left sitting on the bed, holding a T-shirt in which a man had been murdered.

Eleven

"So, did this shirt belong to Jim?" I asked. "Or did he kill whoever was wearing it?"

The shirt in question lay on my desk in my office, bathed in sunlight that had started tearing through the clouds. Cassandra refused to touch it, but Pamela spread the cloth in back to show us the slit in it. Someone had been stabbed to death in that shirt. Maybe clawed, Pamela suggested, but if so, very neatly. A Changer, who had human intelligence and could control its strike, could do that.

"Can you smell whether the blood is Jim's?"

I pushed the shirt to her, but Pamela shook her head. "I don't need to bury my nose in it. It smells like everything else Juana was packing. That could mean it belonged to Jim or sat around his things long enough to transfer the scent. As for the blood—I wasn't paying attention to Jim closely enough. Humans smell alike to me, unless I'm focusing on a specific one."

Cassandra folded her slender arms. "If this Jim skewered someone, why not leave the shirt on the victim? Why take it off, bring it back here, and put it in the closet? And if Jim is the victim, same question."

"Maybe there was something incriminating on the T-shirt," Pamela suggested. "Like the killer's own blood or hair. A DNA test would find the difference."

I shook my head. "Then why wouldn't he go to a laundry and wash it? Or burn it?"

Pamela went on speculating. "What if Jim murdered whoever it was in his room and had to remove the shirt to take the body away without leaving a trail of blood?"

"No, Jim's room was clean," Cassandra said. "When I went up there after he didn't return that night, there was no blood, no mess. Only one towel used in the bathroom. The killer wouldn't have cleaned the place from top to bottom and then left a bloody T-shirt for us to find when we packed up. That doesn't work."

While she spoke, a voice whispered in my head. *You can find out what happened. It's easy.*

And I knew exactly how to do it.

"Reveal," I said.

Darkness poured out of my hands and engulfed the T-shirt. The darkness coalesced around the shirt like a bubble, and movement flickered inside it.

I knew right away that Pamela couldn't see the magic. She remained sitting passively on the love seat with an uninterested look. On the other hand, Cassandra's eyes widened, and she leaned forward to watch.

The darkness cleared a little, and a man I didn't recognize stood in profile to us. He had the lean, ropy build of a runner, limbs tanned from the sun, carried his state-of-the-art camera in one hand, and wore the Sedona T-shirt, walking shorts, socks, hiking boots, and a baseball hat. In the background I saw the blocks of stone that formed ancient pueblo ruins, reddish dirt, and dry desert grass.

The man's arms were out slightly, his chest thrust forward, and he had a knife buried to the hilt in his back.

As Cassandra and I watched, mesmerized, the man folded quickly and silently to the ground, the costly camera landing beside him. The man lay in a motionless heap, wind stirring the ends of his hair and the grasses around him. A hand came into view, a man's muscular hand. He yanked the bloody knife from the man's back to reveal the slit, covered in blood, that we'd found in the shirt.

I couldn't see who held the knife, but the hand and forearm was definitely a man's. The golden brown skin could belong to an Indian, but he could also be Asian, Latino, Mediterranean, or of mixed descent. The knife was plain, dull steel, nothing distinguished about it except that it had been in another man's back. The killer took it with him as he stepped back, out of sight.

The corpse lay there for a long time, but by the way the wind moved through the grass, I could tell that time had sped up, as though we were watching a film in fast motion. I was about to blink, to try to banish the vision, when Jim's eyes popped open.

Cassandra and I both jumped. Jim slowly lifted himself from the ground, limbs stiff, and then he stood up straight, blinking at the horizon. He drew a deep breath, put his hand to his back, and then stared in amazement at the blood that coated his fingers.

The image and the magic vanished the next second, leaving me breathless and staring at a T-shirt covered with blood on my desk. Pamela was on her feet.

"All right, what the hell just happened?" she demanded. "You two jerked like you saw something that scared you. What was it?"

Cassandra put her hand to her face, turning the nervous gesture into smoothing her already smooth hair. "We just witnessed a murder."

"So, who did it?" Pamela demanded.

"Someone with a knife. I couldn't see who." I pretended to be less unnerved than I was. "Not very helpful."

Cassandra studied the shirt with a bewildered look. "I don't understand. That was Jim Mohan, definitely. But I'd swear that when Jim checked into the hotel, he wasn't supernatural; he was human. I'd stake my reputation on it."

"And now he's a dead human?" Pamela asked.

"We also just witnessed him coming back to life." Cassandra's voice was faint.

"Not possible," Pamela said with conviction. "Cassandra's right; the guy was human, and he wasn't magical. He didn't smell like a sorcerer."

"Let me think." I massaged my aching temples. My mouth was dry, and I longed to suck down about a gallon of water. "I'm pretty sure that was the Homol'ovi ruins in the background. And you said the magic mirror went crazy when Jim went into the saloon, *after* he'd been out at Homol'ovi all day."

"Yes," Cassandra said. "But he was very much alive when he came back, not stabbed or covered with blood."

I looked down at the T-shirt. Jim had worn it when he died, and now the bloody shirt was in his room. When did a murderer remove a T-shirt from a corpse and throw the bloody shirt into a closet? Had Jim somehow survived and was now walking around, alive and fine and thinking he was getting away with not paying his hotel bill? The vision might not have shown me everything.

Or the magic mirror and Cassandra might have seen his ghost. Cassandra and the mirror were both very magical; they would see things that Pamela and other humans couldn't.

But in the vision, when Jim had climbed to his feet, he'd been breathing, if bloody. He'd not been a ghost but very much alive.

The next alternative on the list left me stone cold.

So, when *did* a murderer remove a T-shirt from a corpse and throw the bloody shirt into a closet? When the corpse did it himself.

"He was resurrected," I said slowly. "Jim was resurrected before he returned to the hotel. He probably didn't even know it, was surprised he'd survived, but the magic mirror knew something was wrong with him."

Cassandra looked sick. "You mean resurrected by a necromancer? Can't be. I've seen resurrected slaves before. They're zombies, animated dead. Jim was alive. Breathing, drinking, sunburned, excited, and alive."

"Then a very good resurrectionist," Pamela broke in. "Is that possible?"

"Only if he were a god," I said. *A god.*

Oh, gods.

I withdrew my hands from the T-shirt and was suddenly very, very afraid.

Cassandra and Pamela left my office together, both of them a little dazed. I must have looked the same. I folded the shirt and stashed it in the bottom drawer of my desk. I clicked through all the pictures on Jim's digital camera but saw nothing except innocent pictures of ancient ruins.

Shock and the strange surge of magic left me nauseated. I stashed the camera and left the office, heading up the stairs to the third floor and out to the roof, where I stood in the wind and the sunshine.

The storm was racing away, a few ragged clouds drifting in its wake. The air was sweet, washed clean by the rain, not charged with magic. I inhaled the freshness, letting it calm my roiling stomach.

But my worry didn't leave me. A complete resurrection could be done only by someone extremely powerful, and the vision hadn't showed me who'd done it. I remembered the fast-forward part of it—how long Jim had actually lain there, dead, I didn't know, and I'd seen no one approach him. But anyone who was strong enough to bring someone back to life would have the magic to stay out of any vision I could conjure.

The fact that I'd been able to call up such a precise vision at all bothered me. I could read auras and sense past events if they were traumatic, but never with that clarity.

I looked east past the abandoned railroad bed that marked the edge of town. The vortexes lay beyond it, swirling magnets of mystical energy, gateways to Beneath. The vortex Mick and I had sealed last spring was still there, but the energy from it was gone. Completely shut off. We made it a point to hike the mile or so to it once a week to make sure.

I wanted to blame the vortexes for the Beneath magic that had been surging in me lately, but I couldn't. What Coyote had told me in my dream I knew in my heart was right—the Beneath magic had been there since my birth, given to me by my goddess mother. But in the past, the magic had always been somewhat dormant, fighting my storm magic inside me, but doing no more damage than to give me a hangover.

Now the Beneath magic let me kill hordes of demons in one stroke and replay a man's death in living color by my simply focusing on the shirt he'd died in. It had also tried to convince me to catch a murderer by killing everyone in Magellan.

I sat down, putting my back against the wall that made up the partial third floor. The wall was warm from the sun, but I still shivered. The Beneath magic made me feel powerful, unstoppable, invincible, and that scared the shit out of me.

"You should be scared."

I shrieked, jumped halfway to my feet, and slid down the wall again. "Damn it, I wish you wouldn't *do* that."

Coyote grinned down at me. "I like to make an entrance."

At least this time we were both dressed. Coyote wore his jeans and denim jacket, as he had at the diner, turquoise buckle, and cowboy boots. "I want to keep you on your toes," he said.

"Not when I feel like this." I rubbed my temples, wishing this damn headache would go away.

Coyote crouched next to me, jeans stretching over hard thighs. "Stop using the Beneath magic, Janet."

"It uses *me*. It surges up and tells me how to do things, and I just do them." I gave him a hopeful look. "Can you teach me to control it?"

"No, I mean *stop using the Beneath magic*. I don't want you controlling it. I want you not using it."

"I can't help it . . ."

"Let me put it this way. Stop using it, or I'll destroy you.

I don't want to—I'd rather sleep with you. But I will kill you if I have to."

I looked up into the face of a god. Coyote, the affable Indian who made the tourists laugh and was friends with young Julie, had faded. His eyes were dark and hard, the power in him unmistakable. He could squash me and not break a sweat.

No, he can't, my magic whispered. *You have the strength to stop even him.*

Coyote's eyes went black.

I quickly held up my hands. "Don't. I'm trying."

"Try harder."

The way he looked at me made me want to run far and fast. "Did you resurrect Jim?" I asked him.

Coyote blinked. "Who?"

"The guy in my hotel that the mirror scared away. He got stabbed and brought back to life. I know you know who I'm talking about. Did you resurrect him?"

"No." His voice was flat. "I don't believe in that shit."

"But you could do it?"

"I could. But I didn't."

"Do you know who did?"

"Nope." He didn't look much interested. But then, Coyote wasn't always forthcoming with his feelings, except about sex.

"You've been a lot of help. As usual."

"I'm not here to help, Janet. I'm here to keep the balance."

"And screw as much as you can."

A flicker of his usual grin crossed his face. "That too." Coyote got to his feet, still the god. "Don't use the magic again."

"I don't know if I can stop it."

"If you don't, I will."

Damn it, this was so unfair. I didn't want my mother's magic to be in me, but I hadn't been given the choice.

I opened my mouth to argue some more, but a fiery presence burst onto the roof. Mick was across it in the space of three seconds, and by second number four, he had his hand around Coyote's neck and Coyote against the wall.

"Leave her alone," Mick said. His eyes were as black as Coyote's, and fire flickered on the lines of the dragon tattoos.

"Dragon," Coyote said without changing expression. "You want to tangle with me again?"

"No, I want to throw you off the roof. Leave Janet alone."

Mick radiated power, but so did Coyote. A fight between them would blow a hole in my hotel. Just what I needed, my hotel obliterated by a god and a dragon.

I got to my feet. "Would it do me any good to ask the two of you to stop it?"

"No," Coyote said. "It's sweet that he wants to protect you. Even as dangerous as you are."

"I don't care if she's queen of the damned," Mick snarled. "You won't touch her."

Coyote never lost his smile. I knew him capable of killing me and Mick both without blinking, but he just kept grinning. "I'll go through you to get to her, dragon."

"You'll have to." Mick's voice was ice-cold.

"Just make sure she doesn't use that crazy magic from the world below, and I'll leave her alone."

Mick finally eased his hand away from Coyote's throat. Coyote straightened his shirt but made no other indication that Mick had hurt him. He winked at me, turned away, and went back inside, whistling.

Mick watched him go, his eyes still hard, before he turned to me. "You all right?"

I leaned back against the sun-drenched wall. "He didn't hurt me, if that's what you're asking."

"I won't let him touch you, Janet, I promise."

"What can you possibly do against him? He's a god."

To my surprise, Mick smiled his bad-ass smile. "Remember when he told you we'd met in the past? It was a long time ago, maybe a hundred years. I won that fight, not Coyote."

I'd been curious about the encounter since the day I'd learned about it. "What happened?"

"Dragons don't stand in awe of any gods but their own. Coyote was exploring—he likes to explore and get into other people's business. He invaded my territory, and I objected. Strongly. I protected what was mine and ran him off. Gods are powerful, but you don't mess with a dragon on his territory."

I folded my arms, the air cool despite the sunshine. "Where is your territory?"

"Volcano. On a Pacific island."

I lifted a brow. "You're a Polynesian dragon?"

"Sort of. There's volcanic activity all around the Pacific Rim. There's a reason the volcanoes are named after gods."

"Because those gods are really dragons."

"No. There are gods. And dragons." He smiled at me, his eyes becoming sparkling blue again. "That was my territory—still is. But this is my territory now too. And you're my mate." He stepped in front of me, cupped my shoulders with his warm hands. "I defend you, and it, against all comers. Including Native American trickster gods and asshole dragons like Colby."

I swallowed. "Speaking of Colby, where is he?"

"Magellan Inn. I wasn't about to let him stay here."

"Because it's your territory?"

"Damn right. He's a dragon and my chief rival. It would be in his nature to try to take over if he stayed here. If he's holed up in town, less of a temptation."

Mick was firmly in front of me, the wall just as firmly behind me. "You know, Mick, this hotel actually belongs to me," I said. "I bought it with my own money."

His breath smelled of mint and was warm on my face. "Territory isn't about who owns what. You should know that."

"And we've never talked about the connotations of this 'mate' thing."

"It means I take care of you." Mick gently pried my arms apart and skimmed his hands to my wrists. "I defend you from your enemies. I keep you safe."

How nice it would be to melt into that protective warmth and let him ease my troubles. I didn't think it could be done anymore, but it was a fine fantasy.

Mick eased away from me, to my disappointment. "Coyote isn't wrong, though. You can't use the Beneath power anymore."

I blew out my breath in exasperation. "I wish the two of you would get it. I don't do it on purpose. I need to do something, and the magic just comes to me."

"But what happens when you can't stop it? When you need to fight something, and you end up destroying the entire town to do it?"

I folded my arms, suddenly cold. The magic had wanted me to destroy the entire town to prevent another person getting turned inside out. And now someone was resurrecting corpses. A being who could do that could also commit that awful murder.

"I'm trying to explain to you that I don't know how I'm

doing it. The magic comes, and then it just goes. Believe me, I haven't done half the things it's wanted me to do."

His eyes narrowed. "It talks to you?"

"Something or someone does. It's unnerving. I've resisted."

"What happens when you can't?"

"The hell if I know. That's why I keep asking for *help*, damn it."

Mick cupped my elbows, stepping against me again. "I know, baby. I'll do everything I can to keep you safe."

"From Coyote? Who keeps me safe from you?"

He hesitated. We'd gone through this, his orders to kill me and his decision to not obey those orders. Hence the dragon council putting him on trial to declare him officially guilty.

But I knew in my heart that Mick didn't think the dragons wrong for worrying about a dangerous thing like me. The dragons' ancestors hadn't come from Beneath, as mine and most of humanity's had. Dragons had been born of this earth, in fiery volcanoes. They didn't have an ounce of Beneath in them, and they liked it that way. Long ago, they'd helped Coyote trap some of the more evil gods Beneath, to keep them from emerging into this world, and it's no exaggeration to say that those gods would do anything to take their revenge.

And here I was, the daughter of one of those evil goddesses, wandering the earth alive and well. Protected by Mick, one of the dragons' own. No wonder the dragons wanted to put him to death.

But Mick wasn't any happier with Beneath goddesses and their powers than his fellow dragons were. He'd happened to start liking me—lucky me—or he'd have fried me a long time ago. I was alive because Mick had decided he admired my courage.

"Can you answer me, Mick? What happens to me when you decide I'm too dangerous for this world?"

His grip tightened on my elbows, his hands strong enough to break my bones. "That's why I want you to try, baby. So I don't have to make that decision."

"Don't rush to reassure me or anything."

Mick touched his forehead to mine, eyes troubled, breath warm on my face. "I'll do everything in my power to keep you alive, Janet. I swear to you."

I knew he would. That was Mick, protecting me from everything and everyone, even from myself. But Mick was telling me that the moment he thought the world would be better off with me dead, he'd do the deed himself, much as he hated the thought.

I pressed him away from me. "I have work to do."

Mick stepped back, and I slid out from under him and headed for the door. He was allowing me to go; I knew that. I hadn't won anything here.

His voice sounded behind me, low and deep. "I won't always let you walk away from me, Janet."

In spite of myself, a shiver ran down my spine as I continued into the hotel and shut the door behind me.

Twelve

The Magellan Inn was a single-story motel tucked into a curve of the highway right in the center of town. Assistant Chief Salas's brother, who owned and managed the motel, recognized me and was happy to let me know that my friend Colby had booked into room twenty.

I hadn't bothered to tell Mick about this errand, and I'd borrowed Fremont Hansen's truck so the magic mirror on my bike wouldn't tattle on me. I knocked on the door of room twenty, which was wrenched open after a second by Colby. He was shirtless, his hair damp, as though he'd just come out of the shower. His chest and back were as covered with tattoos as his arms. I wondered if any inch of his body wasn't.

The television blared some satellite channel, which Colby switched off with a click of the remote.

"So, did you come to your senses and leave that SOB?" he asked as I shut the door. "Course, you'd have to kill him if you have, or he'll just drag you to his lair and keep you there."

"I'm not a dragon."

"I don't think he gives a rat's ass. Not that I blame him. I wouldn't want to let you go either. Want a beer?" Colby opened the mini-fridge and took out a couple cans of Kirin, holding one out to me. I took it, and he snapped open the top of his.

"Are you a Japanese dragon?" I asked, rolling the chilled can between my hands.

"No, I'm a dragon dragon. We don't have nationalities."

"It's just that you have full-body tattoos and drink Kirin beer."

"So that makes me Japanese?" Colby chuckled. "With a name like Colby? Your name is Janet, not *Runs-With-Coyotes* or something. Not that Colby's my real one; it's just easier for humans to pronounce." He sat down on the bed, taking a gulp of beer. "I was born in Japan, though. I still like it. Thought about doing some sumo wrestling, but I couldn't put on the poundage. Flying around as a dragon keeps you lean."

"I'll bet."

He gave me an affable grin, but it held wariness. "What do you want, Stormwalker? Come to scold me about how mean I talked to Micky?"

"No, I want to know exactly how you plan to help him. Plus I want to know *why* you're willing to help him. You fed him your prepared story; now I want to know the truth."

Colby sipped his beer. He didn't reach to put on a shirt, but his body was so inked it was as though he wore living, painted fabric.

"Dragon trials are serious shit, little Stormwalker," he said. "You should stay out of it, like Micky wants you to."

"I'll be dragged into it whether I like it or not. I'd rather walk in myself, on my own terms."

Colby gave me a look of new respect. "You do have stones, girl. All right, here's the deal. The dragons will allow a defense, not of the actual crime, but of the accused. Kind of like character witnesses, to state why they don't think the accused should be executed for the crime."

"In other words, the 'trial' is more like a hearing to decide Mick's sentence?"

"Pretty much. If the defense happens to prove the accused's innocence in the process, the dragon council can reverse its verdict." He shrugged. "It's happened. Once or twice in a couple thousand years."

I opened my beer and took a casual sip. "I take it you don't hold out hope for that."

"It's obvious that Mick's guilty in this case. He agreed that he'd watch over you unless you went for the vortexes, and then he'd kill you. You did; he didn't."

"I can't be too upset about that."

"Plus he can't solve the problem by simply killing you now." Colby leaned back on his elbows on the bed, beer held negligently. "That won't negate the fact that he should have done it the minute you tried to open the vortex. No, his only chance is to make them understand why he did it, and to prove you're no longer a danger to the dragons."

"And so you rushed out to try to reason with the dragon council on his behalf? Why? Obviously Mick thinks of you as an enemy. Tell me what happened between you two."

Colby gave me another grin. "Now, for that, you'll have to ask Micky. It's old, old history, but dragons have long memories."

"Then why should Mick trust you?"

"Because this time, I'm on his side. I rushed out to help him, because the dragon council was going to have a sham trial and execute him without defense. Already decided. I figured, what they do to him, they can do to me, so I petitioned for them to give him a real, legal trial, sticking to the letter of dragon law. The whole works."

"And you don't care whether he's executed, only that he has a fair hearing."

Colby raised his beer to me and took a sip. "That's about the size of it."

I set my beer can on the table beside the television, came to him, leaned down, and got in his face. "Let me tell you something, Colby. You'd better damn well care. You'd better pull out all the stops to save his butt, or I guarantee there won't be anyone who can save yours."

"Hey, I'm not afraid of you, Stormwalker. If you throw lightning at me, I'll just lap it up. I'd love to, in fact. I'd lap anything off you, any day of the week."

I couldn't grab him by the shirt since he wasn't wearing one, so I reached behind him for his long braid. His hair was warm and thick, like coarse silk. Mick's was much the same. Nothing dragony about it.

"But I'm more than just a Stormwalker," I said. "You know that. Plus, I have some very powerful friends." I looked straight into his eyes. "Some of them are gods who don't much like dragons."

Uneasiness flickered in Colby's gaze, but he didn't drop his bravado. "You keep talking like that, and you'll condemn Mick, no matter what I try to say to the council. My line of defense was going to be that you're harmless, that Micky understood that the order to kill you was unnecessary, and besides, you helped seal up the vortexes and end the threat. Dragons hate waste, and they don't like arbitrary murder, especially not of innocents."

"How ethical of them."

"So you see, sweetheart, in order to save Micky's hide, we have to convince the dragons that you're no threat. Not to them, not to anyone."

"But I'm not a threat." I smiled. "At least, not to dragons as a whole. Just to you."

"No, darling, you are. You're bubbling with power, and sooner or later, you're going to blow. I was willing to give Micky the benefit of the doubt for not offing you, and then I met you." His smile was gone, his eyes darkening like Mick's did. "Now I think it wasn't his fault he couldn't kill you. I'm betting you wouldn't let him."

I remembered the night I'd met Mick, him and me in a seedy motel room he'd dragged me to after pulling me out of a big bar fight. Mick had dared me to try to hurt him, and I'd been angry enough and scared enough to hit him with lightning. I'd watched in shock while he absorbed my storm power like it was nothing, and then he'd laughed and taken me out to dinner.

Colby was wrong. All the decisions that night had been Mick's, not mine. The night I'd opened the vortexes, Mick had stood with me in the rain, ready to break my neck. He'd have done it; I'd felt it in him, and he'd had the strength to do it. Colby was talking out of his ass.

I released Colby's braid and straightened up. "If Mick wanted me dead, he could have killed me anytime since I met him."

"Bullshit. I see in your eyes that you would never have let him. You're a powerful being, Janet Begay, and you look down on the rest of us. I'll lie my ass off and defend Micky, because I don't want the dragon council getting too uppity. But you, girl, are another story. The dragons were right to put out a death order on you."

"You told me that when the dragons first asked you to kill me, you refused."

"Hell, yes. I'm not their puppet. Let them do their own dirty work. Plus, *then*, I didn't really believe you were a threat. What could a Stormwalker do against the might of the dragons, even if you do have a bit of goddess in you?" He looked me up and down again. "Now that I've met you, I think you could do a lot of damage, no matter how small you are."

"I don't care about any of that. I have no intention of messing with the dragons; I only want to save Mick. I'm not letting him die because of me. Understand?"

"Oh, I understand. So, help me convince the dragons that you're harmless. That's all you have to do."

I wanted to rage at him. Of course, I was harmless. Of course, I could convince them of that.

So why did I just stand there, doubts flying through my head? I had the awful feeling that if Mick's fate depended on my being a sweet and good little Stormwalker, Mick was so screwed.

I left Colby putting up his feet and skimming through the satellite channels the motel provided. He'd given me a lot to think about, ideas that hadn't occurred to me. *I'd* somehow prevented Mick from killing me? Couldn't be. My Beneath magic had always been dormant until recently, and Mick was damn powerful, whatever Colby thought about him.

Assistant Chief Salas came out of the office as I prepared to climb into Fremont's truck. "Hey, Janet. Luis told me you were here. Need to talk to you."

I was impatient to go, but I liked Emilio Salas, so I waited for him.

"What's up?" I asked. "I know this is Fremont's truck, but he let me borrow it, honest."

Salas smiled, eyes crinkling. He was good-looking, about thirty, with blue black hair and dark eyes, and did his job with quiet efficiency. "It's not about the truck. It's a personal question. You mind?"

I shrugged. I didn't really like people asking me personal questions, but Salas was a nice guy, and besides, I could always choose not to answer.

"I'm thinking of asking Maya out," he surprised me by saying. "You know her pretty well. Is it worth a shot, or is she still hung up on Jones?"

I toyed with the keys while I considered how to answer. I remembered how Nash had brushed off any question about Maya during our road trip, and the hurt in Maya's eyes when she'd approached me about it at the diner. I knew their problems were none of my business, but Nash needed a kick in the pants, and maybe Salas would give him that kick. I hated to watch Maya wasting her life waiting for Nash.

"I say go for it," I said. "Ask her. If Maya doesn't want to go out with you, she'll tell you."

"That's what I'm afraid of. Maya speaks her mind, doesn't she?"

I couldn't help smiling back. Maya had decided opinions and didn't keep them to herself. "Jones had his chance, and he blew it. There's an old Navajo saying that I think applies here: 'You snooze, you lose.'"

Salas burst out laughing. "Thanks, Janet. I'll ask her. I never know until I try, right?"

"Right."

"I'll take a chance. See you, Janet." Salas gave the truck a pat and walked away, singing under his breath. At least I'd made one person happy today.

Nash Jones himself was waiting for me at my hotel. Cassandra behind the desk looked like thunder, and I concluded that Nash had pissed her off in his usual charming way.

"Office?" Nash stalked to my cubbyhole behind reception without waiting for my reply.

"He grilled me about what kind of witchcraft I did," Cassandra muttered. "I should do a spell to make his balls fall off."

"I'd pay to see that," I said and went into my office and shut the door.

Nash waited for me on his feet like a gentleman and gestured for me to sit down. I leaned my hip against my desk and folded my arms, waiting.

Nash took his little notebook from his pocket and flipped a few pages. "Why didn't you mention that Cassandra Bryson was a witch? When I asked you at the crime scene what kind of a person could have killed the victim, you said witches. You told me you thought Heather Hansen incapable of the crime, but you never bothered to mention that you employ a woman who calls herself a witch."

"I didn't have the chance. Lopez showed up, and you shoved us off on him."

"You have the chance now. What do you know about Ms. Bryson?"

"That she's a damn good hotel manager. That's not witch-craft; that's know-how. She's good with the customers."

"If she killed the person I found out in the desert, I don't care how good she is with your customers."

"Until you have cause, Jones, could you not interrogate my employees? I have a hotel to run."

Nash's gray eyes flicked to me over the notebook. "I have a murder to solve, and my list of suspects is pretty short. You assured me that this was a magical crime, and that only certain types of people could have done it. So far I have Cassandra Bryson, Coyote with no last name, Mick Burns, and you."

"*I* could never have done that. That was awful."

His gaze sharpened. "I saw how easily you killed those things attacking us in Death Valley. For a moment, I thought you were going to turn on us."

I grew cold at the memory, not so much of killing the demons but of how I'd been tempted to test my new powers against a dragon and a man who could absorb magic.

I cleared my throat. "For one thing, they were demons, ready to eat us alive." I gestured to the red scabs on his arms. "For another, it wasn't 'easy.' Mick had to carry me down the mountain, remember? And I didn't notice you getting too upset that the demons were dead."

"I wasn't sorry to see the danger eliminated, no. But I also saw you struggle to contain yourself. The incident tells me that you have the power or magic needed to kill the person at my crime scene, and Mick admitted to me that a dragon could have done the same."

"Mick had no idea the body was out there," I said quickly. "He was with me at the time in question, remember? It's in Lopez's statement, I'm sure in lurid detail."

"So you say. But you're lovers. You'd corroborate each other."

"This is a no-win situation, isn't it?"

Nash flipped another page of his notebook. "If you or Mick did it, I'll find the evidence to prove it. Same goes for Coyote, if I can ever find him."

"Then why are you bothering Cassandra? She was here, running the hotel last night."

"At the time of the murder, Cassandra claims to have gone for a walk along the railroad bed to take a break and clear her head. No one saw her, and she met no one."

"It's three or four miles from here to the crime scene. What, she jogged there and back?"

"She could easily have driven her car and made up the story of the walk. People do tend to lie when they've committed a crime. I will be verifying the story. Meanwhile, why don't you tell me what you know about Cassandra? Besides the fact that she's good at running your hotel."

"Ask her yourself," I said.

"I did. Now I'm asking you. Don't hold out on me, Begay, or I'll ask you—and her—in an interrogation room."

Gods, he drove me crazy.

On the one hand, I didn't want to feed my manager to Jones. On the other—what did I really know about Cassandra? She'd worked for a luxury hotel chain in California, which was the main reason I'd hired her. When I'd questioned her decision to move from Los Angeles to middle-of-nowhere Magellan, she'd said she needed a break from the rat race and that she liked the energy of the vortexes. I'd taken this at face value. I liked Cassandra, needed her help, and didn't want to pry too much.

I gave Nash an abbreviated version of her work history, which he noted. "That's not much more than she said."

"It's all I know. Maybe she's coming out of a bad relationship and doesn't want the man involved to know where she is." Or woman involved, I added silently, thinking of looks passed between her and Pamela.

Nash closed his notebook. "When people move to Magellan for no apparent reason, it interests me. It's not as though Magellan is the garden spot of the world."

For *interests* I knew he meant *annoys*. Nash liked to keep his finger on the pulse of everything that went on in Hopi County. Nash had three deputies under him, and both Flat Mesa and Magellan had police departments, but Nash managed to patrol every mile of his territory. Hopi County was small, squeezed between the larger entities of Navajo and Coconino, so it wasn't difficult to drive its perimeters, but I had to wonder when the guy slept.

"Are you done grilling me?" I asked. "I have things to do."

"What about Coyote?"

I blinked. "What about him?"

"What do you know about him? Where does he go when he's not in Magellan?"

"I haven't the faintest idea. He's a god. Maybe he lives out in the desert as a coyote. Maybe he has a den."

He spared me an irritated glance. "He's Native American."

"We don't all know each other," I said. "Besides, he's not Diné. He's not any tribe specifically. He's Coyote."

"It doesn't excuse him of murder. Not in my jurisdiction."

I could imagine the Norse gods trying to have Ragnarok, and Nash lifting his hand, cop-style, and saying, "No, you don't. Not in my jurisdiction."

I said, "Well, if you do manage to find him, you can ask him whether he did it. Good luck getting a straight answer. Now, I really have things to do."

Nash didn't like being dismissed. "What things do you have to do?"

"Hotel things. I have a business to run."

Nash tucked his notebook and pen into his pocket. "Don't leave town."

"What? Why the hell not?"

"You're a suspect. Don't go anywhere until I've cleared you."

Damn the man. I wanted to go up to Homol'ovi to see if I could figure out what had happened to Jim Mohan.

Nash gave me a suspicious stare, but then, his stares were mostly suspicious, so it was difficult to decide what he was thinking. At last he left me alone, and I sat down in the desk chair and stared out the window at the wide, sunlit sky.

I knew I hadn't killed whoever had lain in the desert grasses south of town, but Nash was right; I could have. I felt the power crawling inside me, dancing with glee, wanting a way out. Likewise, I could have crushed Colby anytime I wanted to today, and he'd known it. Coyote had warned me about my magic, and so had Mick, and now Nash believed it too.

They were all waiting for me to go on a rampage, to kill everyone in my path, and the trouble was, I had no idea whether they were wrong. I squeezed my eyes shut and clenched my hands. I'd learned control over my storm powers; I could learn control over this. Couldn't I?

The best thing I could do, I reasoned, was to figure out what had happened. If the murder victim was Jim, my hotel guest, or if Jim had been the killer, I needed to find out. I could present the solution to Nash and clear myself, Mick, Coyote, and Cassandra.

If Nash didn't like the human crimes of murder and drug

dealing in his county, I didn't like unaccounted-for super-natural beings running around my territory. I left the office, told Cassandra I'd be gone the rest of the day, and fetched one of our old maps of Homol'ovi.

Thirteen

I waited forty-five minutes before I left the hotel to make sure that Jones was really gone. I wouldn't put it past him to double back to check up on me. When I figured he would be safely harassing the next person on his list, I mounted my bike and drove up the highway to Winslow.

On the north side of Winslow, I turned onto the narrow road that led the short distance to the ruins on the banks of the Little Colorado. Homol'ovi was the site of settlements dating back about eighteen hundred years, the large aboveground pueblos being built during the twelve hundreds. Archaeologists called the culture that built them the Anasazi, and they were the ancestors of the current pueblo peoples, including the Zunis and Hopis.

The state park was closed for now, but that didn't stop determined people from poking around the ruins. I parked

my motorcycle well off the road and looked around, using
the map to to orient myself to what I'd seen in the vision as
well as in the photos on Jim's discarded camera.

A green streak of vegetation on red brown land showed the
flow of the Little Colorado, which snaked across the desert
with life-giving water. I hiked that way, keeping the mounds
of the pueblo ruins in sight. Jamison had told me that those
buildings, part of a complex civilization, had contained more
than a thousand rooms.

The ruins were empty and silent, but the river teemed
with life. Birds called in the trees, and water birds waded
through the stream, an oasis in an arid land. Five steps behind me, the damp banks gave way to hard desert, but here,
the wet was a cool and welcome relief.

I found nothing, however, no clue about Jim or what had
happened to him. Once I'd ambled along the river a bit, I
climbed back to drier land and walked toward the excavation
sites. About halfway between, I stopped. Here, I thought. It
was here.

As in the vision, I saw the walls of what was called
Homol'ovi II in front of me, the river behind me. There
was nothing that told me why Jim had stopped here, but
maybe he'd wanted to take a distance shot of the ruins
against the earth and sky. The professional photographer
in me wouldn't have chosen this angle; there were better
places from which to shoot. But then, as far as I knew, Jim
had just come here to take pretty pictures, not get his fine
arts degree.

But I knew I'd found the place of his death. I smelled it
here, the acrid sweetness of decay, similar to what had been
at the murder scene south of Magellan, but this had dissipated with time. I also felt a residue of power, strong power,
again that godlike but uncertain magic I'd felt at the other

crime scene. Something evil had disturbed the sacredness of this place.

A saw a flash of movement, and I remembered that the park was closed, but people who worried about the ruins watched it closely. I hoped I wasn't about to be arrested for being a suspected looter—it was a felony to pocket so much as a potsherd or obsidian blade. Wouldn't Nash love that?

Another flash, and a man sprang from nowhere to land on his feet in front of me. He had a white and black face and a gaping red mouth, and I screamed.

The man put his hands to either side of his face and mimed my scream back. I stopped, out of breath, and then I started to laugh.

He was a clown, a Koshare, his mostly naked body painted with black-and-white stripes, two ridiculous black-and-white striped horns rising from his head. Koshares appeared with the Hopi kachina dancers, who dressed in elaborate costumes to act the parts of gods and spirits, except the Koshare weren't technically kachinas because they didn't wear masks. The dancers believed, and so did I, that the spirit of the kachina they portrayed filled them while they performed. Koshares were the clowns of the group, there to make people laugh but also to provide admonition on bad behavior through their jokes and antics.

I wondered why one was way out here. Kachina dances usually happened in the spring, during growing season, and non-Indians were not always privileged to watch. But maybe he'd just come out here to commune with the spirits in this quiet place or to keep an eye on it.

The Koshare jumped up and down on both feet, clutching his head and looking terrified. Then he did a cartwheel, whirled around, stuck out his backside, and broke wind. I laughed as hard as I had as a little kid, when I'd been happily innocent of storm magic, Beneath magic, dragons, and other terrifying things.

The painted man did a backflip with enviable athleticism. His loincloth swung wide, baring everything to me, but I was the only one around to see.

I clapped my hands like the five-year-old I'd been. "Again," I urged him.

The man spun on one leg, the other straight out like a dancer's. He put his foot down in a big stomp; then he arched forward in a sudden thrust, and I stopped laughing.

The Koshare froze, arms flung out, thrust slightly forward, exactly as Jim had done in my vision. Then, again in an identical manner, the Koshare fell to his knees and buckled onto the ground.

I ran to where he lay unmoving, the black-and-white paint on his body now covered with dust. I crouched next to the man, unsure whether I should help him up.

"You saw him, didn't you? What happened?"

The man jerked, his whole body lifting off the ground. I sprang out of the way, and he stood up, limbs stiff, looking disoriented, just as Jim had.

The Koshare had seen Jim die and come back to life.

"Tell me what happened," I said.

For answer, the man cowered away, raising his arms in a protective gesture. He looked terrified of me, eyes wide behind his paint. He backed up as I came toward him.

"I didn't kill him," I said. "I had nothing to do with it."

He put his fingers in his mouth and mimed his teeth chattering. Then he threw open his arms and spun around, pretending to be picked up by a whirlwind and slammed to the ground. The Koshare lay there in a limp heap, the dust kicked up by his body settling onto his wide and still eyes.

Oh, shit, he really looked dead. I ran to him again, sweat trickling down my face, and reached to check his pulse.

A big painted hand closed over my wrist. The guy was big, his hand enveloping my arm in a hard grip. He could snap the bone anytime he wanted to.

The Koshare pulled me up with him as he rose to his feet. He grabbed my other hand, crossed our wrists, and started pulling me around in a circle. Faster and faster we twirled, my feet dancing to keep up with him. I started to fall, but his strong hands pulled me back up. The world whirled around me, blue sky, red earth, green line of the river, pueblo ruins, empty horizon.

"Stop it," I panted. "I'm going to be sick."

He went faster, and the world spun in a blur. Panic took over. I clawed at his hands, trying to get away, but he was damn strong. He had brown eyes, Native American eyes, but he widened them so far that I started seeing only white.

The Koshare let me go. I spun around by myself and fell hard to the dirt. He was on top of me before I could gasp for breath, pinning my wrists with his hands. I looked into his terrible white eyes, and a voice rolled through my head.

We are watching you. We, the lords of the sky, will not let you win.

Oh, hell, he was no longer a man in paint; he was a god, a real one. He could annihilate me with a single thought.

As if in answer, my Beneath magic rose in me, liking the challenge. Me or a god? If I bested him, who wouldn't bow down to me?

His mouth opened wide, wider, as though he would devour me. I looked down a red gullet and a silent scream, and my own scream echoed across the valley.

I heard the pounding of paws on earth, the snarl of an animal, and the Koshare rolled off me right before a hundred and more pounds of coyote hit him. The Koshare scrambled to his feet and started running, moving in a comical lope with knees up and feet out. Coyote chased him, and the Koshare sprinted away, limbs flying.

The Koshare and Coyote disappeared under the trees that lined the river, while I sat, my arms around my knees, trying to catch my breath.

After a few minutes, Coyote trotted back alone and flopped to the ground next to me, panting. Earlier today, he'd threatened my life, but right now I was glad to see him. I threw my arms around his neck, sinking my face into his rough coat. He smelled like sunshine and dust, warm and comforting.

They will do it, Coyote's voice said in my head. *But not until I permit it.*

"Thanks. I feel so much better." I sat up and wiped my eyes. "Please don't tell me you have fleas."

Coyote scratched at his side with a back foot, and his laughter rumbled through my head.

"That Koshare witnessed Jim's murder," I said. "Correction, murder and resurrection. Or do you think *he* found Jim and brought him back to life?"

No. The clown is harmless other than being annoying. But something evil has been here. You feel it.

I did, though not as strongly as I had at the other murder site. "I do not need this on top of worrying about the dragons. What am I going to do about the dragons?"

That one I can't help you with. Dragons have their own laws, their own gods, their own hang-ups.

"Then what good are you? You give me cryptic warnings and threaten my life, but whenever I ask for advice, you brush me off."

I'm Coyote. It's what I do.

"What you really mean is, you don't know."

He chuckled. *I don't know shit about dragons; I admit it. The one you sleep with is a powerful bastard. More powerful than the dragon council wants to believe.*

"Is he? In what way?"

Coyote ignored me—of course he did. He narrowed his eyes, focusing on the trees around the river. I looked that way in alarm, and a few seconds later, the Koshare burst out of the brush, leaves flying, and started running toward the pueblo, away from us. He looked smaller somehow, and genuinely spooked.

"He's the man now," I said, realizing. "The god inhabited him, but now it's gone."

When the Koshare was halfway between us and the ruins, Coyote jerked his muzzle, and the back of the Koshare's loincloth burst into flame. He ran faster, then jumped into the air and came down on his backside, bumping up and down on the ground until the fire went out.

Coyote gave a satisfied chuckle. *I've always hated clowns,* he said.

I walked into the hotel's back entrance to be stopped by Mick's strong arm barring the way down the hall. The setting sun touched his eyes, which had changed from blue to deep black.

"Hey, Mick," I said tiredly. I tried to duck past him, but Mick stepped in front of me, wrapped his arm around my waist, and pulled me off my feet.

"I told you," he said. "I won't always let you walk away."

"I'm not trying to walk away. I'm trying to go take a shower."

Mick's human body was twice the size of mine and about ten times as strong. He lifted me with ease and carried me through the bedroom and to the bathroom, where he set me on the floor and pulled off my shirt.

"You can tell me about where the hell you've been while I wash you," he said.

"Mick . . ."

He snapped on the shower to fully hot and divested me of my clothes. I didn't resist much, because I was sweaty and mucky and wanted soap and water. Mick sat me on the lip of the tub while he tugged off my boots and socks, then my pants. Not until his big hands were pulling down my panties did I try to push him away.

"I can do that."

His eyes went darker. He batted my hands out of the way and yanked my panties down over my butt. Then he pushed my legs apart and licked between my thighs, his whiskers scraping my sensitive skin.

I leaned back, and the shower sprayed over my face. "Mick, no."

Mick raised his head, and the absolute rage in his eyes nearly stopped my heart. "Where were you that you got banged up like this?" He turned my wrists over, showing me bruises and abrasions.

"Homol'ovi."

"What the hell were you up there for? Who were you fighting, archaeologists?"

"Very funny. A Koshare."

Mick's eyes narrowed, and I told him the story of my vision and how I'd gone up to Homol'ovi to investigate the death of Jim, despite Nash trying to confine me to town, and what had happened there. I sensed Mick's anger grow as I spoke.

"I second Nash's request that you don't leave town," he growled when I finished. "Or even the hotel. I especially don't want you near Colby. You went to see him."

"Why shouldn't I have? I wanted answers."

"I don't want you involved in this."

"So you want me to stand by and watch while they kill you?" I could yell just as loud as he could. "What are you going to do, Mick? Tell them to spare you because you realized I was your soul mate?"

"Something like that."

"How unbelievably stupid."

"You let me worry about that," Mick said.

I hated this. Here I was sitting, naked, on the edge of my tub, while the shower streamed down behind me, arguing with a man I was both furious with and trying to keep alive. Mick, still dressed and half-wet, knelt in front of me.

"They're going to kill you," I repeated. "They've already decided the verdict. You'll be a sheep walking to its own slaughter."

"I'm not as weak as the dragons and Colby think I am. I know what Colby said he was up to, trying to defend me, but that doesn't mean he can be trusted."

"And yet, he turned down the dragon council's task of hunting me down and killing me."

"Because he's a fucking coward. He likes to pretend to be rebellious, so he told the dragon council to screw themselves. But only because he didn't have the balls to face you."

"And you did?" I asked.

"Yes."

I believed that. I'd only ever seen Mick afraid once, and even then he'd laughed as he got ready to die.

It should amuse me that all these bad-ass dragons were so afraid of me. I'd been exhausted and terrified the night

Mick had met me, surprised that I could muster enough magic to fight him.

But if they'd thought me anything like my hell-goddess mother, then they were right to be afraid. Lucky for them, I'd grown up with my grandmother, who probably could go toe-to-toe with my mother in a battle of sarcasm and strong wills. In a contest of magic, however, my grandmother wouldn't stand a chance. Neither would Mick, or Colby, or their dragon council.

"You said you changed your mind when you saw me fight," I said. "When I didn't try to kill those assholes in the bar."

Mick lifted me into his arms and cradled me on his lap, his jeans rough on my naked backside. "I was ready to kill you without thought. I admit that. Until I saw you standing alone against those idiots in that bar. That was the moment my world changed. You were the most amazing thing I'd ever seen."

"That's why you let me live?"

He kissed my hair, lips so gentle. "I realized that the dragon council were fools. They're arrogant and ruled by their egos and their fear. You are astonishing, Janet. You're something to be treasured, and I wanted to protect you for as long as you lived."

The hollow of his throat was right at my lips, so easy to lick. I loved the salt taste of him on my tongue. "You told me once you were afraid I'd glammed you."

"Damn right. I didn't trust myself around you." He kissed my hair again, his touch a little rougher this time.

I was going to lose him. I knew that with certainty as a tear trickled into my mouth. Not so much from the upcoming dragon trial, but because of me and what I was.

You can have him always, in any way you like.

Whatever voice whispered to me, Mick didn't hear it. He laid me down on the bathroom rug, the soft white nap tickling my back. Mick kissed me as he unfolded his big body over mine, pinning me firmly.

He kept kissing me as he slid his hands down to my bare breasts, palms rough against them. I arched to meet him, wanting to twine around him and pull him inside. I loved his body, always warm and hard and ready for mine.

You can make him do whatever you want, and you can make the dragons leave him alone.

Mick licked his way to my breasts and took one dark point between his teeth. His hair fell to my skin, the curls coarse under my fingertips.

"Mick." I pressed up into him, and he opened his mouth over my breast.

I was suddenly not afraid. Not of Mick, not of Colby, or the dragon council, or even Coyote. I had power to match them and to best them. I could do anything I pleased. No more hiding, no more shame about my origins. It didn't matter. I had more power than all of them put together.

A sudden image of the Koshare slammed into my head. His red mouth opened in his black-and-white face, and the eyes of a god burned into my brain.

I screamed. Mick jerked his mouth from my breast and peered down at me in worry. "What is it, baby? Am I hurting you?"

"No." I clutched at him, my heart pounding crazily in fear. "Do me, Mick. Now. *Please*." Maybe if I lost myself in sex with him, the visions and the whispers would stop.

Mick's answering smile ripped at my heart. He pulled off his shirt, then stood and stripped off his pants, boots, and underwear in record time. He was hard and ready, his cock dark and lifting. I sat up and took it in my mouth.

"Damn it," Mick groaned.

He hadn't seen anything yet. I slid my hand between his legs, gently playing with his balls, and stretched my mouth over him.

Mick wasn't quiet. He held on to the shower rod and started telling me, between noises of pleasure, all the dirty things he wanted to do with me. "I'm going to fuck you until you can't walk, Navajo girl. Then I'm going to tie you to the bed and do it some more."

Fine by me. I was too tired to go anywhere, anyway.

"Then I'm going to bend your ass over this bathtub and give you every inch of me."

I pretty much had every inch of him now. I played with him with my tongue and fingers for a few moments longer; then I slid my body up his, twined my arms around his neck, and kissed him.

Mick aroused was a beautiful sight. His eyes darkened to black again, his bad-boy smiles gone. I saw us in the mirror, a slim girl with black hair and a tall man with dark skin enveloping her.

He was much bigger than I was, so it was a little like climbing a tree, but I managed to work my way into his arms, my legs around his hips. Mick held me under the buttocks, his smile shining out again as he slid himself inside me.

I shouted as he went into me, hard and deep. He held me tightly and rocked with me, screwing me solidly right there in the bathroom. His back was to the mirror, and I watched over his shoulder as his ass moved, my eyes shining with the joy of it.

The only problem with the erotic picture was that the gleam under my half-closed lids wasn't my usual brown, but a light ice green.

Mick actually did all those wonderful things he'd promised me. Our sex life had never been conventional, not from day one.

I woke up as the sun rose. Mick snored softly beside me, his body keeping mine warm. The air coming through the open window had a bite to it, the promise of winter.

I drowsed, trying to summon the energy to rise and perform my morning ritual outside the back door. Every morning I scattered corn and said a prayer to the east, greeting the rising sun. It was important to me. But some days, like today, after an all-night rampage with Mick, it was difficult to get going.

I'd almost convinced myself to move when a bright flame squirted through the door lock, followed by Colby swinging open the door.

Mick was on his feet in an instant, all six-foot-six of him, his hands full of fire. I was covered, at least, but I glared at Colby over the blankets.

"Don't you knock?" I snapped.

"I figured you'd be too busy to open the door." Colby closed it before early-rising hotel guests could look down the hall and see me with my naked boyfriend. Mick let his fire recede, but he didn't move.

"What do you want?" I asked, since Mick didn't look inclined to talk. Kill, yes; talk, no.

"I heard from the dragon council this morning. They finally set a date for the trial—ten days from now as humans count time. Plus they told me what kind of sentence they'll give you." Colby looked both disturbed and slightly gleeful, a strange combination. "I'm sorry, Micky. It will be Ordeal."

Fourteen

"You are damn well going to tell me what it means,"
I snarled at Colby when the three of us shut ourselves in the
saloon, Mick and I dressed. "What kind of ordeal?"

"A deadly one," Colby said. "They always are."

Mick seemed the least disturbed by the news. He leaned
against the bar, under the magic mirror, which I knew was
listening with full attention.

"Elaborate," I said.

Colby shrugged. "Can't. The Ordeal won't be determined until we reach the trial. Even if they decide before-
hand, they won't tell us."

"Then what is the point of a defense?"

"Oh, now, sugar," the mirror drawled. "I know that one.
The defense is to convince the dragon council to give Micky
an ordeal he might possibly survive. That's why they don't
decide until he's there."

"You've got to be kidding me."

"No, honeybunch. It's what dragons do. Ferocious little beasties."

"This is bullshit." I very much wanted to get my hands around the necks of the dragon council. "So, they'll either give you a test you'll never survive or, *if* they like Colby's defense, they'll give you one you have a *slight* chance of surviving?"

"Yep," Colby said. "You got it."

"I don't believe this."

"It's their job to make it damn hard on a dragon who breaks the law," Mick said too calmly for my taste. "Dragons are powerful beings. We have to stay under control somehow."

I clenched my fists. "And your defense is going to be that I'm not really a threat to dragons? Not that I don't want to strangle the two in this room right now."

"And Janet *is* a threat," the mirror put in. "There's nothing stronger out there than her. She's a superbitch, though I love her to pieces."

I glared at the mirror. "Don't help."

"Sorry, sugar. I call them as I see them."

"The mirror's not wrong," Colby said. "You gotta control yourself, or Micky's toast."

Mick lifted his hands and let fire gather in them. "Get out."

"I'm only trying to help, old friend."

"The hell you are," Mick said. "I wouldn't put it past the council to send you here to figure out my plans, so they can prepare for contingencies."

"Aw, now I'm hurt." Colby's fingers started to burn. "I don't take orders from the frigging dragon council."

"That doesn't mean they didn't send you. For punishment maybe. What did you do?"

I wanted to break into the argument, but Colby looked so guilty, I stopped. "Wait, you mean Mick's right?"

"I didn't lie when I said I'm working to make them give you a fair trial. Yes, they sent me to suss you out, but I told you, I don't take orders from them. I'm not telling the dragon council shit."

Somehow I believed him. Even if it hadn't been Colby's completely altruistic idea to come here, he didn't seem the type to rush out and tell an authority figure everything he knew.

"So what did you do?" I repeated the question.

"Maybe I poached one of the dragon council's bit on the side for myself."

Mick shot him a look of disgust, but the mirror laughed. "Now, *this* I want to hear," it crooned.

"I want to hear it too," I said. Colby was an asshole. Here I'd hoped that there was something he could do to help Mick, and now the fingers of worry were tightening around me again.

"Is she a cute dragon?" the mirror asked. "A little red number, maybe?"

"She's human," Colby said. "She lives in Texas, and she doesn't know we're dragons. The head of the dragon council is her sugar daddy, even though he's mated. I just showed her a little fun."

"And got caught," I finished.

"Something like that. So I'm putting my ass on the line for you, Micky. They sent me to spy on you, sure, but I didn't lie when I said I don't want them offing me without a trial. So I'm helping you, not them."

"Why?" I asked Colby. "Why risk death betraying the dragons?"

Colby shrugged, his tattoos moving. "Screw them."

Mick leaned back against the bar. "You don't change, do you?"

"Hey, love me as I am."

"You know," I said, keeping my voice mild. "If I fried you now, it would save us all a lot of bother. Maybe the dragon council would spare Mick if I did."

Colby didn't look worried. "Don't bet on it. Besides, you don't know your way around a dragon council trial. I do. And if you use your goddess-from-Beneath magic on me, you can kiss your hopes of saving Micky good-bye. You can murder the entire dragon council, of course, but what would that make you?"

"Don't think I hadn't thought of it," I said.

"You'd better keep your little Stormwalker under control, Micky. She'll be the death of us all."

Mick's lips were tight with rage. "Let's talk outside, Colby."

"What for?"

"Now."

"Gods, you are still a bastard. What don't you want Janet to hear?"

"I'd like to know that too," I said.

Mick was pissed. He strode by me and caught Colby's shoulder, propelling him out. I knew he didn't want to talk to Colby in front of the mirror, because I could either listen in using my shard or command the mirror to report what they said later.

Before Mick and Colby reached the door, it opened, and Maya Medina, in her white coverall, stopped and stared at the three of us. Colby let out an appreciative whistle.

"Hey, senorita, want to throw back some margaritas with me?"

Maya gave him a scornful look as only Maya could. "Who the hell are you?"

"Your dream come true, sweetheart."

"I might puke." Maya shoved past him, her toolbox just missing his groin. "It's too early in the morning for assholes."

Mick's anger softened enough for a chuckle before he shoved Colby out the door. I closed it behind them and, just to be annoying, locked it.

"Really, who is that guy?" Maya asked me. "Mick is friends with someone like him?"

"Mick is enemies with someone like him." I still hadn't gotten one of them to tell me what had gone on between them, but I would. "I thought you'd fixed that short in here. Don't tell me there are more."

"Just checking on it. Actually, I came to talk to you."

"At six in the morning?"

"I thought you'd be outside throwing grain around. I wanted to see you before anyone else was up."

"My office," I said with one eye on the mirror.

The mirror gave me a raspberry. "Beeyotch."

Maya, not being magical, didn't hear it. I gave it the finger behind Maya's back as we left the saloon and walked through the empty lobby. Cassandra wasn't due in until six-thirty with the pastries, when early-rising guests would start checking out or looking for breakfast or both.

Maya thumped her toolbox to my desk as I shut the office door, and she plopped, cross-legged, onto my couch. Even in her body-hiding coverall with her work cap on her pinned-up hair, Maya Medina was a beautiful woman.

"Emilio Salas asked me out," she said.

Ah, girl talk. The incongruity between that and the discussion I'd just had in the saloon almost made me want to laugh. I didn't, though. Maya looked too unhappy.

I sat down next to her and rested my feet on the coffee table. "Did he?"

"I know you're not surprised, because he told me he asked you if he should."

"What did you tell him?"

"I said yes."

I smiled. "Good for you."

"I don't know. I've always liked Emilio, but . . ." Maya slammed her hat to the table and rubbed a hand through her ebony hair. "I'm lying to myself if I think there will ever be anything more between me and Nash. What we had was over a long time ago. We had a chance, and we blew it."

Maya's lower lashes were damp, but her mouth was set, as though she'd be damned if she cried over this.

"You really love him, don't you?" I asked.

"Yes." The word tore out of her. "I don't know why; Nash and I are totally incompatible. We fought all the time we were going out, and we fight now. It's what I get for falling for a white guy, I guess. At least Salas is Latino. The Joneses, they bleed white."

"Nash's whiteness never bothered you before," I said. "Besides, he has a nice tan."

"Except on his ass. He always wears shorts, even if no one can see him." A tear trickled down her cheek.

Maya wasn't the kind of woman who liked squishy girl hugs, and neither was I, so I didn't reach for her. It was one reason we were starting to get along. "Did you come to ask me whether you should go out with Salas?"

"I don't know what I came here for." Maya unfolded her legs to stand up. "Stupid idea."

"No, stay. We're going to fix this."

Maya shook her head but slumped back to the couch. "There's nothing to fix. Nash isn't interested in me. I thought we might pick up again, but he hasn't bothered to call, to stop by. He barely speaks to me when he sees me." She wiped her eyes. "Well, fuck him. I'll go out with Emilio and enjoy myself."

"Good," I said with conviction.

Maya looked crestfallen. "Bad. It's not fair to Emilio."

I stretched my arm across the back of the sofa. "You're going to have to make up your mind, Maya. If Nash doesn't realize what a beautiful woman you are and loses you to someone else, it's his own fault. You can't wait around the rest of your life for Nash to get his head out of his ass."

Another tear ran down Maya's face. "But it's a really nice ass."

True. I'd seen it. Nash had a great body, and maybe if I didn't know Mick, and Maya wasn't in love with him, and Nash didn't despise me, I might let myself grow interested.

Maya angrily wiped away her tears and slapped her hat on her head. "Forget this. I won't go out with either one of them. Tomorrow's Saturday. Let's you and me put on our party dresses and go out to this club I know in Flagstaff. Screw all men."

"Nash doesn't want me leaving town," I said glumly. I'd already left town, but I'd sneaked out and back and gone barely thirty miles. "Mick doesn't either, for that matter."

Maya gave me an incredulous look. "And you're listening to them? I thought you had more balls than that, Janet. Why let *men* push you around?"

I sat up with her, fanning my annoyance. "You're right. I didn't do anything, and it's not like I'm skipping the country. Why shouldn't I have some fun?"

Maya held up her hand, and we high-fived.

My elation lasted all of ten seconds. "Oh, wait. I don't have anything to wear." I had jeans and leather chaps for Harley riding, and while I liked my body-hugging tops, turquoise jewelry, and high-heeled boots, I'd never had the time or reason to shop for party dresses and pumps.

Maya waved this away. "Don't worry about that. I'll fix you up. You're smaller than me, but I have something perfect for you."

I got up with her, excited. I'd never had a girls' night out before, never having had a true girlfriend in my life.

Maya departed, looking much happier than when she'd come in. I knew damn well Nash would give me hell if I went to Flagstaff, and so would Mick, but I was beyond caring. Why shouldn't I snatch five minutes of fun? Or at least an evening out in a town barely an hour away? Nash could yell at me all he wanted—*after* I got back. And between my Stormwalker and Beneath magics, there wasn't a being out there who would mess with Maya and me, if he or she were smart.

Maya and I met at Fremont's house the next night, because one of Nash's cousins lived across the street from Maya, and Maya didn't want to take the risk of him reporting our activity to Nash.

We shut ourselves in Fremont's back spare bedroom, while he provided us with more chips and dip than we could ever eat. He was excited to be in on the conspiracy, and Maya had a great time fixing me up.

Maya wore a turquoise body-hugging dress and matching pumps, and she got me into a bright red tube dress that bared my shoulders, arms, and a lot of my legs. The dress was a little loose, but Maya more or less sewed me into it, and it stayed put. Maya had finagled a pair of strappy silver heels from Naomi Kee, since Naomi and I wore the same size, without, of course, telling Naomi we were sneaking out of town.

Maya put makeup on me and combed out my long black hair. When I looked at myself in the mirror I saw a comely young woman with straight black hair hanging in a shimmering swath down her back. I wished Mick could see me, but then, if he did, he'd lock me into my room in the hotel. I wanted my night out.

When we emerged into Fremont's living room, he flipped off his television. "Wow."

"Aren't we gorgeous?" Maya grinned, pivoting.

Fremont draped his arms around our shoulders. "Man, I've got two beautiful women in my house, and they want to go out without me."

"You have a girlfriend," I reminded him. Fremont had been dating a woman from Holbrook for a while now, though I'd never met her.

"True." Fremont withdrew. "She'd kill me."

"That's why you're not going to tell anyone," Maya said. "You don't tell Mick and Nash we're going out, we don't tell your girlfriend you let us change over here."

Fremont rubbed his balding head, a habit he had when concerned. "Janet, are you sure about this? There's someone killing people out there. Why not stick to the club in Flat Mesa?"

Maya snorted. "Because we want to have *fun*, Fremont. We can't do that unless we leave this entire boring county." She waved at him as we left the house. "Don't wait up."

The September night was cool and would be even colder in Flag, so I slid my leather jacket over my party dress as we walked out. We stashed my bike in Fremont's garage and drove out in Maya's red truck, under cover of darkness.

Maya and I didn't talk much until we reached Winslow, as though we had to keep the chatter down in order to sneak out of town. As soon as we pulled onto the freeway and headed west, Maya threw back her head and laughed.

"It's about time I got out of that hellhole," she shouted to the night.

"Why do you stay in Magellan?" I asked. "You're a good enough electrician to work in any of the big cities. You can go anywhere you want."

Maya shrugged and didn't answer, but I knew why. As much as she railed about Nash, Maya didn't want to live anywhere without him, and Nash would be glued to Hopi County until he died.

By eight, we were nearing Flagstaff, the city's lights spilling around the pile of mountains that thrust out of the plateau. I expected Maya to pull off, but each exit went by without her so much as turning her head.

"Where are we going?" I asked. "We're leaving Flagstaff in the dust."

"We're not going to Flagstaff," Maya announced calmly as she moved out to pass a slow-moving truck.

"Okay." I drew the word out slowly. "Where are you taking me, then?"

Maya flashed me a smile, her teeth white in the darkness. "Flagstaff is boring, Janet. We're going to Las Vegas."

Fifteen

"Maya!"

"What the hell?" Maya pressed her foot to the accelerator, and her truck leapt forward. "I said I wanted to have some fun."

I tried to be sensible Janet, well-thinking Janet, ever-mindful-of-danger Janet. Any second now, I'd talk Maya out of it, make her turn off at the next exit and drive sedately back to Magellan. Any second.

Then I burst out laughing. "What the hell?"

"The club I have in mind stays open all night," Maya said. "We'll have a good time and be back home by morning."

Convinced me. I leaned back to enjoy the ride.

I got a little nervous as we shot through Kingman, remembering the Nightwalker lying in wait on the road to the dam. He had to have been a one-off; there couldn't be a gang of them sucking people dry at the checkpoint.

Maya made the point moot by taking the turnoff to Laughlin, bypassing the dam altogether. The traffic was light by this time, and Maya's speed ate up the miles to Laughlin and across the river into Nevada. The highway shot across the flatness of a dry lake bed on the Nevada side and eventually climbed a steep hill to meet up with the main highway into town.

Maya laughed again as the city lights spread out before us. "Party time," she shouted. She cranked on the radio, letting music pour into the truck.

By the time we reached the club on the Strip and left her truck in the care of valet parking, we were both boiling over with excitement. The club was perfect, crowded and noisy and dark, with music pumping high. We were in a high-dollar hotel, and the men and women inside were dressed to kill. The retiree crowd was either in bed by now or planted at the slot machines in the casino, the hard gamblers were at the baccarat and poker tables, and the partiers like us were in the club.

After a dash to the ladies' room to freshen up, Maya and I squeezed into a tiny table and ordered drinks. Then we hit the dance floor. I hadn't let go in a long, long time. One sip of my fancy martini, and I was ready to explode.

I had fun gyrating to the music, but Maya could really dance. She raised her arms and rolled her hips, her skin-tight dress showing off her beautiful body. If I'd been a man, I'd have been all over her. As it was, it was a pleasure to watch her as she gave herself entirely to the music. I wished Nash could see her, because he'd want to sweep her into his arms and carry her off to make love. No, wait, Nash would swear at her and probably find some excuse to drag her back home. Asshole.

We attracted attention. And men. We couldn't help it.

Maya was a siren, undulating like the best harem dancer. Men flocked to her, each trying to cut in and dance with her. A few tried to dance with me as well, but it was Maya they wanted. Maya foiled them by sidestepping them all and dancing with me.

"They're going to think we're gay," I shouted at her.

"I don't care. Let the sons of bitches eat their hearts out."

I understood. She wasn't here to pick up men but to make herself remember that she could attract them anytime she wanted to.

We danced, we drank, and we danced some more. No Nightwalkers tried to pick us off, no dragons tried to burn the place down, and no gods came to admonish me. Maya and I simply had a good time.

"I'm tired," I said into her ear as I slumped into my chair after hours of dancing. I had no idea what time it was, and I didn't care. "We're too drunk to drive home."

"That's okay. I booked us a room. You're splitting the cost with me."

So much for our plan to make it back home before anyone noticed we were gone. But right now a soft bed sounded good. "I didn't bring a toothbrush." I giggled.

"The hotel sells them, and I packed clean underwear in my purse. I brought some for you."

Her purse was tiny, and I imagined the underwear was too. I started laughing, drink and exhaustion making everything hilarious.

Maya wanted to dance some more. I watched her, basking on the cushion of music, half-asleep. A guy sat down next to me and tried to pick me up, but I stonewalled him. He was good-looking, tall, obviously rich if he'd paid for that suit, but I wasn't interested. I preferred big, hard-muscled bikers who tied me to the bed.

I was in the middle of letting him down easy when Maya grabbed me by the hand and dragged me up. "Sorry," she said to the guy. "It's time for bed."

We left the man sitting there with his mouth open. I was laughing and hanging on Maya to keep myself upright as we snaked through the still-busy casino to the elevators at the back of the hotel.

"That was mean," I said.

"So? He was sleazy."

"I bet his wallet was pretty thick."

"I don't care." Bless Maya, she really didn't. While I liked bikers with wicked smiles, she liked crabby sheriffs in crisply pressed uniforms.

The elevator arrived, and we glided up alone. "Nash is going to kill us," I said.

"Serves him right. I should have slept with that guy, maybe stolen his boxers or something to show to Nash."

The idea of Maya waving her prize silk shorts in front of a furious Nash made me double over in laughter again. I'd never make it down the hallway.

The elevator spilled us out, and Maya put her arm around me to help me to our room. I shouldn't touch alcohol. I'd feel like crap in the morning, and I knew it. Oh, wait, it already was morning.

Maya was shoving her key card into the door slot when the elevator dinged softly. I heard a tread on the carpet, and then a man's voice. "*Que pasa*, ladies."

The guy who'd tried to pick me up was standing behind us. My heart thumped a little in my alcohol haze.

"Sure you want to sleep alone tonight?" he asked us.

Maya tightened her arm around me, and I failed miserably at keeping a straight face. "We're sure," Maya said.

"I don't mind watching," he said. "Tell you what, why

don't you show me a little right now? Kiss her. I'd like to see that."

"Ewwww," Maya said.

I pushed away from Maya, tried to stand upright, and ended up sagging against the wall. "Go away. I don't care how rich you are." I might have said that. The words were pretty slurred.

"Really. Kiss each other." His voice had changed from eager idiocy to something hard and nasty. "Hurry up."

"No," Maya said.

"Bitches." The man cornered Maya against the door. His hand moved, I saw the barrel of a gun pointed at Maya's gut, and my alcohol fog lifted abruptly. Maya didn't see the gun and went on cursing him.

The man shoved Maya inside the room, her calling him a son of a bitch at the top of her voice. I ran in after them, and the heavy door swung closed behind me.

"Maya," I said sharply.

"What?"

She looked down, saw the gun, and froze.

People have different reactions to guns being drawn on them. Some stare in disbelief, not believing it real. People pulling guns only happens on television. Others panic. Still others fly into a rage.

Maya chose the second reaction. She screamed. The guy pressed his hand over her mouth and shoved her into a wall.

He thought I was the lesser threat, the small Indian woman teetering in her high-heeled sandals. Too bad for him. I chose the third reaction—rage.

The Beneath magic in me surged up with the force of a tornado. One flick of my fingers twisted his pistol in half. The next sent the man flying across the room at a sickening speed until he smashed against the window. The heavy-duty window held, and he slid down it to groan in a heap on the floor.

While Maya stared in shock, I hurried to the man and leaned over him. He breathed evenly, knocked out, nothing more. I grabbed Maya's hand and dragged her out of the room.

"Wait!" she cried. "Where are we going? I'm going to puke."

"Out," I said. The elevator opened with a machine's quiet indifference. I pulled Maya inside, and we zoomed down to the lobby.

"I don't want to go back out. My feet hurt."

"Do you want to be in the room when security finds that guy? We'll be arrested for assault. I'm not sure how hard I hit him." I glanced up at a shining black half-sphere in the ceiling, behind which I knew was a spy camera, as we hurried out of the elevator and joined the crowd in the casino.

Maya stopped arguing. She let me lead her by the hand at a quick walk out the main entrance and along the line of taxis. Lucky us, we were able to jump into the back of the first one. We'd left our coats in Maya's truck, but the nights in Las Vegas were mild in September, and we slid unencumbered into the cab's backseat.

"Where to, ladies?"

"Someplace with male strippers," I said on impulse. "Not like Chippendales. Something smaller, more intimate."

The cabby grinned through his rearview. "Gotcha." He zipped smoothly down the drive and into the nearly gridlocked traffic.

"They'll charge me for the room," Maya complained. "They have my credit card; they know who I am."

"I'll pay for it." My adrenaline was high, my body

charged. "Besides," I whispered, "if they find that guy in our room, with a gun, they'll arrest *him. We* just got scared and ran off. Right? You ready to go home yet?"

Maya pushed her hair out of her face and sat up. "No. Fuck him. I want to have some fun."

I held her hand and whooped as the taxi scooted into the far lane and maneuvered down the packed Strip. He dropped us in front of a club near old downtown Vegas, the neighborhood kind of seedy, but I didn't care. I was strong and powerful. No one would mess with us.

The club was still going strong, the men on the little stage stripped down to what was legal. I went light on the drink, though Maya had another martini, but I let myself enjoy the show. I took most of the cash I'd brought with me and slid it into the G-string of a guy who looked like Mick. He rewarded me with a beautiful smile.

"This is boring," Maya yelled in my ear. "I want to dance."

A club a block away provided more dancing. It was even seedier, but by this time, Maya and I had decided we could handle anything. We danced together, attracting the same amount of attention as we had at the upscale club. The guys here were working-class and a hell of a lot more friendly than the rich ones. No one pulled a gun on us, anyway.

Then something evil entered the club.

Maya continued dancing, and two guys undulated with her. The air went thick, the music dimming, as though I watched the scene from behind textured glass. A smell came to me: death, decay.

No one noticed but me. The music ground on; the dancing continued. I scanned the crowd, tensing, waiting. I saw no skinwalker, sensed no aura of a Nightwalker. Not a dragon either, come to scoop me up and carry me off. Dragons smelled good, anyway, fiery and hot, and this thing bore the stink of rot.

He walked through the crowd toward me. People parted for him without realizing, as though their subconscious noted his presence, but their conscious minds did not. He slid through until he stopped in front of where I waited. His body was wiry, like a runner's, and his light blue eyes held no spark of evil, but I knew who he was.

"Jim?"

He was the man from my vision, the one the magic mirror had claimed was evil incarnate.

"You left your camera at my hotel," I said with a calm I didn't feel. "Nice piece. I wouldn't have run off and left that behind."

"I don't need it anymore," Jim said. "You take it."

The camera was still stashed in my desk drawer, because I felt queasy even touching it. "How did you find me here?"

"I followed you." Jim Mohan spoke in a normal voice, but I could hear him even over the music. "I sensed you were in danger, and I was right, wasn't I? That guy tried to kill you. I came to make sure you were all right."

My heart squeezed. "Why should you want to protect me?"

"Because you helped me. Your magic brought me back to life."

"What?" I stared at him. "The hell it did."

"You used the same magic tonight, when you fought the man in the hotel."

The music had dimmed to almost nothing, although people kept on dancing. It was as though Jim and I stood in a bubble surrounded by light and noise, but none of it touched us.

"What do you know about the man in the hotel?" I asked.

"I told him not to hurt you. I didn't mean to kill him."

I froze in horror. "Oh, gods."

"They're so fragile, human bodies. Even mine was." He laughed a little, his lean face so normal. "Guess it's not, anymore."

I felt sick. "You killed him?" I thought of the body out in the desert, all the blood, the smell, the terror. "Like you did that person in Magellan?"

Jim nodded. "They both were just guys. Like I used to be. I really didn't mean to do anything to the hiker. He was hurt—he'd sprained his ankle, and he didn't have a cell phone. I wanted to heal him, like you healed me."

"I had nothing to do with that," I said.

"They're looking for you. The people at the hotel. I came to warn you."

As Maya had mentioned, the hotel had her name, her address, her credit card number, all the pertinent facts about Maya Medina. I didn't know whether she'd indicated she'd be sharing the room with Janet Begay, but it didn't matter. It was one thing for two girls to run away from a man who'd shoved his way into their room with a gun, another when the girls left behind a mangled corpse. We had to go.

Jim touched me with a hand that was warm. He should have been ice-cold, dead, but he was alive. A living, breathing creature, but not right.

"They're coming," he said.

I saw red and blue lights through the open door of the club. I turned to find Maya, but she'd worked her way to the other side of the floor. "Stay here," I told Jim, and started worming my way through the crowd.

The music and noise came back with a rush. I got to

Maya and pulled her away from a Latino she'd wrapped her arms around. She swore at me.

At the same time, my midsection gave a sudden lurch, and magic flared through the building. The music died with a screech, and people started to scream.

Jim was standing in the middle of the room, his hand out, palm pressed forward. The sickening stench of magic—a mixture of death and godlike power—flowed from him to collapse the door and bury it in rubble.

People started making a dash for the emergency exit. Lights came on overhead, to be extinguished a second later, and the club plunged into darkness. I still had my hand around Maya's arm and she pulled at me, trying to get me to the emergency exit. An alarm sounded, the constant note of it lodging inside my head.

"Stop!" I screamed at Jim.

He poured more magic at the front door. I heard the crunch of cars, and plaster rained down the inside of the club. Bricks exploded inward, falling on the people trying to cram their way out.

I had to stop him. I dug for my Beneath magic and found it very close to the surface. Coyote's warnings and the Ko-share scaring me hadn't dampened it at all. My promise to try to control it was a lie, and I knew it. I couldn't control it taking me over, and right now, I didn't want to.

I didn't even need to raise my hand this time. I shot the magic around Jim, binding him and his magic into a little bubble. He stared at me and started shouting, but his sounds were muffled by the crackling magic.

His power met with mine, and the air around us expanded, unable to take the pressure. Every bottle and glass behind the bar exploded. Shards of glass sliced my face, and the smell of liquor cut sharply through the musty smell of the club.

Most of the guests had made it out of the dark club, and Maya, after one wild look at me, ran after them, the last one out. Now police officers started in through the emergency exit. I slammed up another shield over that door to keep them out of the club and safe.

"Let me go," Jim screamed.

I hadn't the faintest idea what to do with him—giving him to the police would only condemn the nice officers to a bloody and untimely death. I'd have to kill him to stop him. My insides roiled at the same time my Beneath magic rejoiced. It wanted me to be a bitch-queen goddess like my mother. It wanted me to take my mother's place.

"No," I said in a loud voice. "I won't."

You no longer have the choice.

"Coyote!" I yelled. "Help me!"

Jim turned his magic on me. My bubble expanded and burst, and the emergency lights in the club exploded. So did the flashlights the cops had brought in with them, and we were sent back into darkness. In that darkness, something inky and clutching crawled up my legs, weaving around my thighs, stretching fingers into my underpants.

I wasn't putting up with that. "Dust," I screamed, and the vinelike tentacles dissolved.

Jim was pounding me with magic like that of gods. My Stormwalker powers would have crumbled and died before it, but my Beneath magic resisted it well.

A detached part of my thoughts wondered why Jim thought I'd resurrected him. Because he sensed goddess power in me? Had he been brought back to life by another god? By my mother? I needed to find out.

Whatever had created Jim, he was currently trying to destroy me. I thought of Mick, how much I loved him, even when he drove me insane. I thought about his fire, how he could call flame without thought.

"Burn," I yelled. The magic Jim was shoving at me burst into flames. He screamed and beat at the fire that started in his hair and clothes.

I yanked down the barrier between us and smothered the flame in cold. Jim tried to fight, and he was strong, but he hadn't figured out how to control his power. I didn't know how to control mine either, but I had the advantage of years battling to keep my storm powers from killing me.

Jim withstood my magic, but the club couldn't. The walls started to fall, the ceiling to come down. Jim was already dead—my detached thoughts wondered whether he'd get up after being crushed. One thing was for certain: if the club fell on me, I wouldn't rise again. I'd be very much dead.

I sprinted for the back exit as pipes burst and fell, lights and wires tumbling down. The roof came apart slowly, piece by piece, giving me mere seconds to run for the emergency door. The police were still there, waiting on the other side of the magic barrier I'd erected.

Here was my choice: run into their arms and live out the rest of my life in prison, or stay in here and take my chances being buried alive.

Neither option excited me. A shower of bricks just missed me, kicking up a heavy cloud of dust. Jim had vanished into the darkness and rubble. I could try to climb over it, head for where the walls gaped open to the night, and get out that way.

I turned to scramble up a pile of brick, pipe, and glass when Nash Jones walked in right through my magic barrier. His body sucked the magic into it with a little *pop*, allowing Mick, his hands full of fire, to follow him in.

Nash had his gun out and trained it on me. "Stand down, Janet."

I kept scrambling for the opening in the wall. Would Nash shoot me? I could lose him in the dark, make my way to the main roads, hitch a ride somewhere. To Mexico City, maybe. Brazil was sounding good.

Mick moved between me and Nash's gun, grabbed me around the waist, and hauled me off my feet. One of Naomi's pretty sandals got left behind as the rubble wrenched it from my foot.

My Beneath magic surged to stop him. "Mick, let me go!" I cried. "I don't want to hurt you."

Flame licked his hands but didn't burn me. Mick had amazing control, and I fought to keep my flaring magic from obliterating him.

Maya waited by Nash's sheriff's SUV, huddled in Nash's coat, tears and mascara black rivulets on her cheeks. Mick put me down and took my face between his hands. "Janet, stop."

My teeth were chattering so hard I could barely speak. "I don't think I can."

I looked into blue eyes filled with anguish. Mick was scared, not for himself, but for me. "I'm sorry, baby."

It happened so quickly that my Beneath magic had no time to answer. One minute, Mick was looking at me in sorrow, the next, I had no air. I recognized the tentacles of a quick and dirty binding spell, felt Mick's hands on my neck and over my mouth, but too late. Spots crashed into my vision and then darkness.

Sixteen

I swam to wakefulness inside a moving vehicle. It was mercifully quiet, except for the occasional burst of static from a police radio. My head was cushioned against a strong thigh, and an equally strong hand smoothed my hair.

Opening my eyes didn't help much. It was daylight—I thought—but I stared at the dark, bare floorboards of someone's backseat. I groaned.

"Can you knock her out again?" Nash asked from the front.

Mick leaned over me, his touch gentle. "You okay, sweetheart?"

"No."

The word dragged out from my tight mouth. I could barely move my lips, or anything else for that matter. I lay on Mick's comfortable lap for a long time, getting my bearings and feeling absolutely shitty. The Beneath magic was gone—where, I didn't know—and it had left me with a hell of a hangover. Or maybe that was the martinis.

"I told you ten times already," Maya said from somewhere in front of me. "I don't know anything about a dead guy in the hotel room. I booked the room, but we decided not to go in. We went to a strip club instead. With male strippers. I paid a hundred bucks for a lap dance." Maya was lying—she'd never gotten near the strippers.

"I don't want to hear it," Nash said in a tight voice.

"His ass was way better than yours."

I laughed, which quickly turned into a cough. "Can I have some water?"

Mick helped me sit up against him and fed me water from a sports bottle. I almost choked on it.

He patiently wiped my mouth with a tissue, and I looked up into his worried eyes. "It's gone," I said. "The Beneath magic. I don't have a drop left."

I didn't. Outside the windows, deep banks of clouds hugged the approaching mountains, a good old-fashioned storm building. The storm tingled through my blood, but the Beneath magic had fled. Not forever; I knew that.

"Janet, Nash thinks we killed someone," Maya said. "You and me. Can you believe it?" Her voice begged me to support her in the lie.

Nash's hands tightened on the wheel. "There was a bloody corpse on the hotel room floor. The only reason you two aren't locked behind heavy bars is because I vouched for you. It looked like the guy had been turned inside out. Sound familiar?"

I leaned back against Mick. "I didn't kill him, and neither did Maya. Jim did. He killed the guy in Magellan too, a hiker. I don't know who the hiker was."

Nash gave me a furious glance in the rearview mirror. "Who the hell is Jim?"

"Jim Mohan. He was a guest at my hotel. He's dead too, stabbed up at Homol'ovi a couple days ago. Not by me," I added quickly.

"If he was stabbed a couple days ago, how the hell did he kill someone in Maya's hotel room tonight?"

"He got resurrected. I don't know who by. Now he's undead and out of control."

"Undead," Nash repeated. "Right."

"Where is he?" I asked. "Jim, I mean. He was in the club when it came down."

"They didn't pull anyone out," Mick said.

I pushed myself up into a sitting position. Outside, desert mountains rushed by, rolling Arizona mountains, not stark Nevada peaks. The motion of the SUV made my stomach unhappy, and my neck hurt too. I rubbed it, and I suddenly remembered Mick's fiercely strong hand twisting it; that plus his binding spell and his palm over my face rendering me unconscious. He could have snapped my neck right there, end of Janet problem.

I scooted away from him. "Don't touch me."

Mick didn't look contrite. I knew he wouldn't bother explaining or apologizing, and I knew he'd decided that it was the only way to stop me. I folded my arms and stared out the window. I was getting tired of being grateful to Mick for *not* killing me.

I'd grown up being distrusted by my own family, by my own people, and I'd left home as soon as I could. When I'd met Mick on the road, I'd thought I'd finally found someone for me. He'd protected me and treasured me, and I'd basked in his attention. But he'd kept so much from me, and when I'd found out why he'd really picked me up, the hurt of that had stung for a long time. I'd talked myself into putting it behind us, starting our relationship afresh.

And here was Mick, still watching me, still waiting for me to go wrong. He was my guardian and my lover but also my parole officer. When he thought I was getting dangerous, he'd step in and render me harmless. Then say, "I'm sorry, baby," kiss me, and make love to me until I forgot about it.

What the hell kind of relationship was that?

"Nash, stop," I said.

Nash continued driving at a precise seventy-five miles per hour. "Why?"

"Just stop. I want to get out."

"What for? I have airsick bags back there if you need to throw up."

"You're all heart. No, I want to get out because I don't want to be around you people. If I'm so fucking dangerous, I'll leave. I'll go to Greenland or something, and you'll never have to worry about me again."

"I'll go with you," Maya said.

"No one is going anywhere," Nash said firmly. "You, Maya, are going home to sleep it off, and you, Janet, are staying put in your hotel while you tell me everything that's really going on."

"You're a bastard," Maya said. "We went dancing. We didn't ask for some guy to pull a gun on us, or for someone to attack us in the club."

"A gun?" Nash roared. "What the hell?"

"Stop the truck," Mick said. "I'll get out."

My arms were jammed over my chest, fists buried in my sides. My throat was so tight I couldn't speak.

"We're miles from anywhere," Nash said.

"Doesn't matter. Pull off."

Nash went silent, which meant he didn't have a legiti-
mate argument for dragging Mick back to Magellan with
us. Even Maya stopped berating Nash and sat silently. At
the Ash Fork exit, Nash left the freeway, pulling over at the
bottom of the ramp.

Mick opened the door before the SUV stopped. I wanted
to be sick. I thought of the dragons waiting to make him go
through gods-knew-what ordeal. I thought of other dangers
lurking, like an undead man who couldn't control his hom-
icidal tendencies. I was scared for Mick and furious at him,
and mad at myself for caring so much.

Mick hopped from the SUV. He held the door, his body
silhouetted against the morning sky. "Janet, tell Colby that
if he brings you to the trial, I will kill him."

"Mick," I said. "It's dangerous out there."

"So am I." He slammed the door. Nash gave him an in-
quiring look out his open window, but Mick shook his head
and walked away.

Nash pulled off, and Mick started down the highway that
snaked southward to Chino Valley. I watched his lone, upright figure as long as I could, until Nash rounded a curve,
and Mick was lost to sight.

I had to explain to Naomi why I'd left her shoe behind
in Las Vegas. Nash had sent a deputy to retrieve Maya's
truck, but of course Naomi's sandal was buried under rubble. Naomi didn't care about the shoes, but she was not
happy with me for running off as we had, after I'd admon-
ished *her* to be careful. I meekly offered to buy her another
pair, but I could see that she was mad as hell at me.

If Naomi was angry, Jamison was furious. At me, not

Maya. Jamison came to the hotel the evening we got home, while I was in my office still nursing one hell of a hangover. I'd already related the entire tale to Nash, including everything I knew about the undead Jim Mohan. When Jamison started demanding explanations, I lost it.

"Mick is the gods know where," I shouted. "With dragons breathing down his neck, and a lunatic out there turning people inside out. Mick looks at me like he's scared to death of what's inside me, and unless you've had someone do that to you, you can't understand it. I'm sorry some idiot tried to rape us in Las Vegas and that Undead Jim tried to kill us. It happens to me, all right? I'm doing the best I can."

Jamison listened to me with his usual stoicism. He'd known me since high school, when he, a handsome Navajo a couple of years older than me, had helped me come to terms with my storm powers. Then, he'd been a minor shaman; now he was a Changer. It was because of Jamison that I'd moved to Magellan in the first place, and he felt responsible for me.

"None of that is why I'm angry at you," Jamison said.

"Just tell me, then. I'm not in the mood for cryptic."

Jamison folded his strong hands, the same hands that could sculpt like a god and touch Naomi with tenderness. "You're battling something, and you're doing it alone. I thought we were friends."

"If you mean the Beneath magic, it's powerful shit, Jamison. I don't want you anywhere near it. Besides, I think I can control it now."

"I'm remembering a fifteen-year-old girl, one eaten up with storm magic. So scared she was afraid to go to school, and she'd run away from home so her grandmother wouldn't make her go. She was sitting on a ledge overlooking Spider Rock and crying because she couldn't make the lightning stop."

I remembered. The storm had been a major one. Electricity had crawled all over my body, and it was coming out of me in bursts. Terrified that I'd burn down my house, the school, and everyone within reach, I'd stolen my dad's pickup and driven down to Canyon de Chelly, figuring I could direct the lightning into the chasm. The storm would keep people away, and I wouldn't hurt anyone.

Then Jamison had arrived, the young shaman out to commune with nature. The gods had been looking out for me that day. Because of Jamison, I'd finally believed I could live a somewhat normal life.

"I helped you then," Jamison said. "I can help you now."

"This is different. Storm magic is earth magic, wholesome even if it's deadly. Beneath magic isn't like that at all. It's like a living entity. It wants to destroy, and it wants to use me to do it. I hear words in my head."

"Your mother's words?"

"No. It's not her. It's me. Or some part of me I never knew existed."

"So we explore what it is. You have to look at it, Janet. You can't run away from it."

My headache gave a sharp jab, or it might have been my fear. "It's nothing you want to have anything to do with. You can't understand what this is like."

Jamison gave a short laugh. "I found out I was a Changer when my body morphed into a mountain lion's, just like that." He snapped his fingers. "I spent two years locked in a cage in Mexico while crazy people taught me how to control the change and the power. That ordeal knocked the arrogance out of me. I do think your power's dangerous, which is exactly why you need to find out what it is and how to deal with it."

I clenched my hands on my desk. My father gazed out of his picture at me, seeming to agree with Jamison.

"I hate it when you're logical," I said.

He grinned. "Get some sage. Let's do this."

We went upstairs to the roof, under the twilit sky. East of Magellan, the railroad bed made a straight border between town and desert. Beyond that, the world rolled away to the horizon. The ground looked flat, but scores of washes and arroyos cut through it, along with the wide crevice that housed Chevelon Creek. Chevelon was a place of mysteries, where ancient peoples had left petroglyphs along the walls, depicting strange-looking beings. I liked to walk there in dry weather, looking at the pictograms and trying to figure out what they meant. I was pretty sure that many of them depicted the goddesses and demons from Beneath, though some New Agers liked to believe they were aliens. But then, Beneath was another world, so maybe the New Agers aren't too far off.

Jamison and I faced each other, cross-legged, and he lit a sage stick and dropped it into a stone bowl. I'd brought a shard of the magic mirror in case it could help, though I warned it sternly to stay quiet.

Jamison took my hands and held them in the smoke. The pungent sage wafted into the cooling air, and I inhaled deeply.

Jamison spoke in the Diné language, whispering words of magic. I loved Jamison's voice, velvet and lilting. He was one hell of a good storyteller. Naomi had fallen in love with him the night he'd come to tell stories in Magellan, and I understood why.

"Let your thoughts go," he murmured to me. "Let them

drift wherever they will." His hands tightened. "And stop concentrating on sex."

How did he always know? "I was thinking about you and Naomi."

Jamison flushed but didn't look all that embarrassed. "I never thought of you as a voyeur."

"I meant that what you two have is great."

"Mmm," the shard of magic mirror said at my feet. "Please tell me *everything* you're thinking, so I can imagine it too. Don't hold back."

Jamison squeezed my hands again. "You're avoiding what we're supposed to do. Let your thoughts go. Concentrate on the smell of smoke and the sounds of the night."

What Jamison wanted me to do scared me. I could pretend that I'd already learned to direct the Beneath magic in me—hadn't I done well fighting at the club, not to mention knocking out the guy in the hotel room? But I knew Jamison was right; the magic inside me was like a beast, waiting to get out.

Jamison's low Navajo words made my Beneath magic stir. Not in fear, in anger.

The desert at our feet was also home to skinwalkers, hideous creatures of massive strength that wrapped themselves in the skins of animals or people they killed to take their form. My Beneath magic could summon them. I knew this instantly, although I'd never thought about it before.

You can summon them, control them, use them to destroy your enemies.

I didn't have enemies. I didn't have time for that.

Images of people flashed before me, everyone who'd ever hurt me. Girls at school who made fun of me. High school boys who were nice to me until they revealed they only wanted a free grope. My grandmother and her strict admonitions. Nash Jones, who liked to lock me in his jail. The dragons, vast winged creatures who wanted me to cease to exist. Mick.

You can command any of them. Skinwalkers, Nightwalkers. You summoned the one who tried to kill Nash.

Like hell I had. I opened my eyes, which had drifted shut. The sage glowed with hot sparks, orange and angry in the darkness. Jamison's voice went on, low words in Navajo that enveloped us in prayer and protection.

I'd had nothing to do with that Nightwalker at the checkpoint. How could I have? He'd been there looking for easy pickings, hadn't he?

But then, the Nightwalker had looked at me with something like fear in his eyes after I'd had the strange vision of grinding him to dust with a beam of light. What if my latent anger at Nash had manifested in me calling on a Nightwalker to finish him off? Nash's unique resistance to magic had killed it, but I'd been uncertain about that outcome.

Or maybe I'd summoned the Nightwalker to test Nash's ability to nullify its magic. Used it and let it die to satisfy my curiosity.

"No!" I said out loud.

Jamison jumped and opened his eyes.

I jerked my hands from his grasp. "This is crazy. It won't work. Leave it alone."

"What are you afraid of, Janet?"

His voice was too gentle, too understanding. It drove me crazy.

"Me." I got to my feet. "The magic telling me how evil I am, how I can make that evil work for me."

"Demons lie, Janet. They tell frightening lies to bring you under their power. That's all. You're strong enough to resist."

"It isn't demons. It's *me*. And I don't think it's wrong about me being evil."

Jamison got to his feet, boots grating. "It is wrong. I know you. You need to learn to separate yourself from it, to observe it, to not let it have power over you."

"Is this what they taught you down in Mexico?" My voice had a sneer to it I didn't like.

"No, they tried to keep me wasted on drugs down in Mexico. I learned control the hard way. But it works. Trust me."

"You can teach me to control *this*?"

The magic leapt into my hands, white light so hot that it made my hangover beat through my brain afresh. The agony in my head was so fierce I feared I was having a stroke, but at the same time, the pain was detached and faraway.

Jamison stepped back, wariness in his eyes. I scented the Changer in him, the wildcat waiting to break free in case it needed to attack.

I kicked the bowl with the sage, scattering herbs and ashes. "You don't know the first thing about me, Jamison Kee. Your arrogance never left you, no matter what you claim. They should have locked you in a stronger cage and spared all of us you coming back here."

"Janet." Jamison backed another foot or two. "This is what you need to control. Focus."

"You focus on this."

I scooped the white light into one hand, squishing it into a ball. Then I threw it, not at Jamison, but at the piece of magic mirror.

The mirror screamed, "Oh, no, girlfriend!" and then the light hit it. The mirror didn't break but reflected the light back, doubled in size and strength.

As soon as the magic left my fist, it released my body,

and I sat down hard. My head pounded like fury, and I wanted to vomit.

"No," I croaked at the light. "Stop."

Jamison's dark eyes widened in fear as the light swept his feet out from under him. I cried out, trying to get up, trying desperately to stop it. Then the magic lifted Jamison, my oldest and dearest friend, and threw him from the roof.

Seventeen

Weeping and screaming, I crawled to the edge and peered into the darkness below. The Beneath magic had dissipated and vanished, leaving me weak. Behind me, the magic mirror sobbed.

"Jamison!" I shouted.

The growl of a mountain lion answered me. I saw eyes in the dark, glowing faintly in the twilight.

I scrambled to my feet and stumbled back inside, down the stairs, around the gallery, and down to the first floor. A couple was checking in, and they stopped and stared as I ran past, my clothes filthy and my eyes wild. I heard Cassandra behind me, reassuring the guests in soothing tones. I had to wonder what excuse she was coming up with for me.

I tore out the back door and headed for the railroad bed.

A mountain lion was limping toward it, leaving a trail of Jamison's clothes behind him.

"Jamison!"

He climbed to the railroad bed and stopped, sides heaving. The rising moonlight showed me pieces of Jamison's shirt still clinging to his back.

"I'm sorry," I babbled. "It's gone. The magic has gone. Are you all right?"

Thank the gods he'd had the presence of mind to change as he fell, landing like a cat. The air shimmered, and Jamison rose on bare feet to his man shape. He moved his shirt rags to cover his privates and regarded me with a mixture of anger and fear.

"Are you all right?" I repeated.

"I'll live," he said wearily. "You were right. I am arrogant. I'm not strong enough to help you. My magics are nowhere near what yours are."

"That wasn't *me* saying that. It was the magic, whatever is inside me. I lied. I can't control it. Jamison, what the hell am I going to do?"

Jamison's angry look softened. Maybe he was remembering the scared fifteen-year-old again. Now I was twenty-six and just as scared.

"Coyote can help you. He's strong enough."

"Right. He keeps threatening to kill me if I don't stop using the magic. But I don't know how to stop it."

"Mick, then."

I hugged my arms to my chest, the evening air turning chilly. "He says the same thing. Besides, he's gone. We had a fight."

"Make up with him. You need him."

"When I said gone, I meant gone as in *I have no idea*

where he is. The last I saw him he was heading down the back roads of Arizona. He could have hitched a ride to anywhere by now."

"Nash, then. If he's this null, maybe he can help you muffle the magics."

I had thought of that but was unsure how it could work, or whether I could convince Nash to help me.

"I don't know. I'll think about it."

Jamison started to reach for me, but he thought better of it and dropped his hand.

The gesture cut my heart. Jamison had been the one person I could turn to, the one friend I could trust. Now he didn't want to touch me, and I couldn't blame him.

"I feel like shit," I said.

"You need to rest. What you're going through is . . . Well, I don't really know what you're going through, but exhaustion won't help." Jamison's tone softened. "My shaman advice to you is to go to bed. Before you do, will you call Naomi and tell her I need a ride home? If I walk home as a mountain lion in this town, I'll probably get shot. And if I do it as a naked man, I'll never live it down."

I retreated to my bedroom after I had Cassandra call Naomi, and locked the door. I sat with my back against the headboard for a long time, the thoughts in my head wringing me dry.

I'd hurt one of my best friends in the world. If Jamison hadn't been a Changer, hadn't managed to save himself from the fall, he'd be lying in a broken heap, possibly dead. I'd done that. The horror in his eyes had broken my heart.

This was the thing the dragons saw and feared, what Mick had been sent to stop. This past spring, they'd wanted to prevent me from meeting with my hell-goddess mother, but I realized now it went deeper than that. They didn't want me to *become* her.

I didn't want to either. Stupid me, thinking I had the magic under control. Just because I was now able to fight with it, to channel it to battle a threat, I thought I'd mastered it. How could I be such an idiot? This power was beyond me. It was god power, and I was a human being.

Though a goddess had brought me into existence, I'd been born of human parents, with human frailty. God power would rip me apart.

I pressed my hands between my knees, my knees to my chest. Could I be terrified now? What was I going to do? Jamison had tried to teach me to observe the magic and understand it, but I didn't think chanting and meditation was going to help this time.

I needed Mick. He'd taught me to contain my Stormwalker power, to make it part of me. His methods had been harsh at times, but they'd worked. But I had no idea where Mick had gone. I'd thought about calling him earlier today, but when I'd walked into my bedroom, I'd found his cell phone sitting square on my dresser. The sight of it had washed pain all through me.

I could use the mirror to call to Mick, but only if Mick hadn't thrown his piece away or would even take it out of his damned pocket if he heard it. I'd left the shard up on the roof, but I had another in its chamois bag in the pocket of my leather jacket. I could feel the mirror's terror from it as well as all the way from the saloon. Because I'd awakened it, it had to obey me, whether it liked it or not. Right now, it feared me, and I didn't have the heart to force it to work.

I felt so alone right then I thought I'd die.

I sat for hours while the night grew dark and the moon

floated across the sky, changing the shadows. I felt the magic wanting to come out and play, but if I held myself tightly enough, I could fend it off. Maybe.

A key turned in the lock, and the door swung inward, the bright rectangle of the doorway piercing my eyes. Maya came in, leaving the door open behind her.

"You all right, Janet?" She sat on the foot of the bed. "Everyone's worried about you, but they're afraid to come in here."

"And you aren't?"

"No." Maya wore jeans and a shirt this evening, but she managed to look as lovely in that as she had in her turquoise party dress. "The only things that frighten me are my mother's lectures about getting married and having children. She says I'm going to be fat and ugly in a few years, so I'd better have snared a man and pushed out a couple of kids by then."

I wanted to smile, but my mouth was too tight. "If you work out and take care of yourself, your looks will stay around for a while longer."

"Have you eaten anything since we got back?"

I shook my head. I'd intended to grab some lunch in the kitchen, but never got around to it.

Maya held out her hand. "Come with me. We're going to get you dinner."

"I can't."

"I'm not going to bring you a tray. Your cook is a scary bitch, and I don't want to interrupt her when she's anywhere near her knives."

"Maya, I can't. I threw Jamison off the roof. I could have killed him."

"Is that why he was standing out on the railroad bed mostly naked? You know, he's really hot. If he wasn't married . . ."

"This isn't a joke."

Maya grabbed my hand and pulled me to my feet with surprising strength. "If you're trying to get through something, not eating will just make you weaker."

Right now I felt weak as a flea. Weaker—fleas can be mean.

For some reason, I didn't try to stop Maya towing me out front and through the lobby. At least she let me bring my jacket. Cassandra watched me from the reception desk but made no move to intercept me. Pamela stood near her, arms folded, looking formidable. She was protecting Cassandra, I realized with a jolt. From me.

Maya took me out to where her own truck sat in the lot, back from its Las Vegas adventure. The Crossroads Bar was going strong, the parking lot full of motorcycles, a knot of biker men and women clustered near the door. Nash Jones liked to raid the place once in a while, looking for drugs and arms dealers. I hoped he didn't tonight, because I didn't want to see him.

I thought Maya might take me to the diner to stuff a cheeseburger and milk shake into me, but she passed the diner and turned down the road that led to her own home. The white frame house stood back from the road in a neat patch of lawn, flowers blooming in the tiny garden under the front window.

Maya let us in. "Go clean yourself up. I'll make us dinner."

I looked into the bathroom mirror and bit back a scream. My face was drained of color and streaked with dirt from crawling across the roof. My shirt was ripped and just as dirty. My eyes, though, terrified me. An ice green glint glowed out at me before receding to my usual dark brown.

My hands shook as I washed my face and dried myself with Maya's clean towels. When I walked out, Maya was

cooking something that smelled good. She pointed with a
spatula at a pile of shirts on the couch and told me to pick
one out.

"Why are you being so nice to me?" I asked her as I
stripped off my top and pulled on a black one with a span-
gled design. It was a little big for me but at least clean and
whole. "When I first moved here, you hated me."

"With good reason. You can be a true bitch, Janet. But
you also saved my ass up in Las Vegas, and you're fun to
party with."

"Good for me."

"Shut up and eat. I only know how to cook Mexican
food, so that's what you're getting. My mother wouldn't
teach me anything else."

"I like Mexican."

"That's good."

The plate she put in front of me tempted me in spite of my
mood. She hadn't made your average tacos or burritos but a
savory meat in a thick sauce ladled over a couple of fresh
corn tortillas. A corn and rice pilaf had been piled beside it.
I dug in, my eyes watering from the chiles, my mouth very
happy.

"You should open a restaurant," I said.

"No way. I like working with wiring because it doesn't
complain. People in restaurants do. All the time, about everything."

True. I'd already encountered people who couldn't be
happy with anything in my hotel, no matter how hard I
tried.

I was shoveling in the last mouthful, thinking I could
fall in love with Maya, when she glanced sharply out of the
window. "Who the hell is that?"

I whirled, nearly sending my plate to the floor. A long

black limousine had stopped in the street outside, an incongruous vehicle in this neighborhood of pickups and modest family sedans.

A dark-haired man emerged from the front passenger side and opened the back door of the limo. Another dark man got out, this one with sleek black hair in a ponytail that glittered under the streetlight. He wore a long leather coat, and I saw lines of tattoos snaking around his neck to disappear into his shirt. His aura bore sparks of fire, as did the aura of the similarly dressed men behind him.

My heart squeezed into a tiny ball. "Maya, you should get out of here."

"Why? Who are they?"

Dragons. Here to slay me? But I was under protection as Mick's mate, wasn't I? Which only lasted as long as Mick was alive, I remembered. The fine aftertaste of Maya's food turned bitter.

Had the dragons bypassed the trial and simply killed Mick? Found him walking alone and decided to take him out to get to me? And where the hell was Colby?

The two tall men in leather dusters kept coming up the walk. The Beneath magic stirred in me, ready for battle.

The first dragon stepped square into Maya's flowerbed, squashing blossoms, and she was out of the house like a shot. "Hey. Watch what you're doing!"

The man's eyes were black dark, like Mick's when the dragon in him rose to the surface. His ponytail bared his neck, and I saw that the tattoo lines were the ends of sharp wings. He must be inked all down his back, with the edges of the tatts rising up his neck.

"We're not here for you," the man said to Maya and flicked his gaze to me. The dragon-man behind him was even taller, his hair shorter, a tattoo flowing up the sides of his neck and over his ears. He looked older than the first man, more regal.

Maya regarded them coldly. "No? Who the hell are you?"

"They're here for me," I said.

I stepped out past her to face the first dragon, who was as tall as Mick. I folded my arms and gazed up at him, trying for the protective look Pamela had assumed while she'd watched over Cassandra.

Maya ducked back inside, and I saw her going for her phone. She'd call the cops, maybe Nash. The first dragon glanced in, raised his hand, and the phone burst into flame. Maya shrieked.

"Leave her alone," I said in a hard voice. "What do you want?"

"For you to come with us," the first dragon said.

"That's a line from a bad movie. Why should I?"

"We need to talk about Mick's trial."

I went cold, although some relief touched me. If they were talking about the trial, then Mick must still be alive.

"It's straightforward, isn't it?" I asked. "You've already decided that Mick's guilty. You only need to decide whether to give him a chance to survive his punishment. His Ordeal, whatever that turns out to be."

"That has yet to be determined."

"You're the dragon council, I take it."

"He is." The first man jerked a thumb over his shoulder at the taller dragon. "He wants to meet with you in private. It's perfectly within dragon law."

"I'm so relieved." Like hell I was going to get into a car with them. "We can have our little meeting right here."

"No." The taller man spoke for the first time. His voice was deep, with undertones of darkness, far richer and fuller than the first man's. He was much older, I guessed, with time to develop a timbre like that. "We will speak in a place of my choosing."

"What guarantee do I have that I'll make it back from this place of your choosing?"

His flunky answered me. "You are protected under dragon law. You are mated to a dragon, and you are a key witness. Until the trial, you are untouchable."

"And after it?"

The man raised his shoulders in a leather-clad shrug. "That remains to be seen."

"You know how to make a girl feel good."

I thought the corners of the councilman's mouth twitched, but I couldn't be sure. The flunky didn't look amused. "You can come with us voluntarily, or we can force you."

"I thought you just said I was untouchable."

He gave me a brief nod. "We are not allowed to kill you. But we can kidnap you if we later release you unharmed, especially if it might be for your own good."

"Now I know you're dragons. You have that twisted dragon logic."

Maya was on the porch again, looking scared but scowling. "You're not leaving with them, Janet."

"Yes, I am," I said, deciding. "I want to hear what they have to say."

I didn't trust them, but I did know by now that dragons fell down and worshipped dragon law and honor. I also knew that my Beneath magic was up to taking them if they got cocky. I kept that thought out of the front of my head, in case they could sense it somehow, but the magic was amused.

I was so tired of thinking of my magic as a separate entity. I wanted to conquer it or get rid of it. I didn't like it talking to me.

The councilman started walking back to the car. The flunky gestured me to precede him. I made them wait to fetch my coat, and the flunky insisted Maya bring it to me.

"Janet," Maya said as she handed me my warm leather jacket.

I shrugged it on. "Go to the Magellan Inn and ask for Colby. Tell him what I'm doing."

"Putting your trust in Colby is foolish," the flunky said.

"Yes, well, he's a dragon, and I figure at least he'll know where you've taken me. And how to find me if I don't come out."

Now the flunky looked annoyed. I didn't like going with them, but I wanted to pick their brains as much as they wanted to pick mine.

"Tell him," I said to Maya.

She nodded, and I walked down the drive ahead of the flunky. The chauffeur's assistant had the back door open, a portal to a dark, plush interior.

The councilman entered the car. The flunky stood back and waited for me to get in. Such a gentleman. I had one foot in the door when something wrapped around me from behind and yanked me out again. Not a hand, not an arm, a band of white magic that tried to squeeze me in two.

I heard shouting—the flunky, the chauffeur who'd jumped out of the car, his assistant, Maya. The band of light lifted me high and then dropped me.

I landed at the feet of Jim Mohan, who did not look good. His face and arms were covered with abrasions and bruises from the club having fallen on him. Healing abrasions—which was weird. His wounds had healed even more than mine had, and I'd done healing spells on myself.

I got speedily to my feet. The dragons rushed us, and the flunky grabbed me by the arms to haul me away from Jim.

"No!" Jim shouted. "Leave her alone!"

The flunky dragged me away. The chauffeur and his assistant pulled out pistols. I realized with a jolt that those two weren't dragons—they were as human as Maya.

I had no idea whether bullets would kill Jim or just piss him off. He'd been resurrected, but he could obviously be hurt. Could he be killed again by human weapons?

The flunky shoved me against the car and moved to Jim, hands flaming. The councilman himself came behind him.

If Jim ignored the pistols, he didn't ignore the dragon fire. He swung to face the two dragons, hands raised.

"Don't attack him!" I yelled at the dragons. "Get in your damn car, and get out of here!"

They didn't listen to me. Of course not. Stubborn, arrogant dragons. The councilman and flunky went for him, flames streaming from their hands, tattoos glowing under their clothes.

It happened so fast, I couldn't tell how he did it. One moment the two dragons were advancing, ready to burn Jim to a cinder. The next, the dragon councilman rose into the air and started to scream.

His body cracked straight down the middle. Crimson blood sprayed over me like water, the councilman's scream died to a gurgle, and his body fell, ripped inside out to land on Maya's pristine front lawn.

Eighteen

The flunky let his flame die and stared at the council-man in horror. The chauffeur and assistant started unloading their guns into Jim. Jim flinched from the impact of bullets, but he didn't fall, didn't die.

I grabbed at the magic I felt dancing in my body and hurled it at Jim. "Stop!"

"No," he said. "They'll kill you."

"Just stop!" I shouted.

The chauffeur's assistant took advantage of the distraction to plug Jim right in the head. Again, Jim flinched, but he stayed very much alive. He turned, made a slicing motion with his hand, and the chauffeur's assistant fell to the grass, dead, his body cut in half.

"No!" I screamed myself hoarse.

Jim gave me a wild look. "I'm sorry. I'm sorry." He turned and ran off into the darkness.

What was left of the councilman lay in a steaming heap, and the chauffeur was bent double, sobbing and puking. Maya had disappeared, the only smart one around here.

The flunky was standing still, his dark eyes wide, the fire under his skin red in the darkness. I grabbed his shoulders, shook him.

"Make him turn into a dragon," I panted. "Make him turn into a dragon."

I didn't even know if that would help. But whenever Mick got badly hurt as a human, he shifted to his dragon form to save himself. I had no way of knowing whether the councilman could still shift, or whether he was already dead and beyond saving.

The flunky nodded. He stripped off his coat and then his shirt, sweat pouring down his face as he hastily got rid of his clothes. Once he was naked, he raised his arms out to his sides and let fire pour out of his hands. The fire wrapped around what was left of the councilman, encasing him like a sheath.

The dragon flunky's body gleamed with sweat, the tattoo of a full dragon on his back. The tattoo wrapped all the way around his torso, the wings running down his arms; what I'd seen on his neck were the barbed spikes at the bend of the wings.

The tattoo glowed and rippled. It seemed to absorb the flunky's body into it, until a black dragon, shining in the streetlights, spread real wings and rose on them. The dragon shot into the air, expanding as he went; then he snaked one talon down and scooped up the cocoon of fire. The downdraft of his wings bombarded me with hot air, and then the dragon was rising into the night.

A second dragon swooped out of the desert to meet him, this one so fiery red it glowed with its own light. He wasn't

Mick—Mick was huge and black all over. The dragons exchanged screeches before winging off together over the empty desert. Silence settled on the street, and the breeze stirred the dead man's coat.

Sirens erupted from both sides of Magellan at once, both the town and county police responding.

I turned shakily toward Maya's house and found myself staring down the barrel of a semiautomatic. The Beneath magic had left me, vanishing as quickly as it had come. The eyes of the chauffeur over the barrel were human, terrified, and enraged.

"Get in," he said.

"What . . . ?"

"Get in the fucking car!"

I raised my hands and backed quickly into the limo, and the chauffeur slammed the door. I grabbed the handle as soon as he started for the driver's side, but he'd locked the door, and there was no button or latch to let me out. I bounced to the front of the limo, ready to crawl out that way, but thick glass separated back from front, firmly in place. They'd not wanted their prisoner to escape.

The driver slammed himself inside the car and squealed away from Maya's house just as two Magellan police cars, two sheriffs' cars, and Nash's official SUV sped toward us. The chauffeur drove through a yard to avoid them and then down Maya's street to the main highway.

One sheriff's car turned to pursue us, and I saw a flash of Lopez's face at the wheel. The other four vehicles continued their charge to Maya's lit-up house, Nash leading the way.

Meanwhile, Lopez chased the limo. The chauffeur drove through Magellan at triple the legal speed, and Lopez hung in there as we barreled out of town past my hotel and up the road toward Flat Mesa. About halfway along, the chauffeur jerked the wheel to the right, spinning us onto a road I hadn't even known existed. It was narrow and treacherous, what was known as a primitive road. That meant it hadn't even been graded, and dropped into and out of washes with jarring abruptness.

There was no way we could make it down this road in this car and not get stuck. Raised pickups with four-wheel drive could do it, but not a limousine. The recent rains had made the ground soft, and washes out here would be full of water. I didn't care how big this car was; a good whitewater wash would sweep us away in seconds.

"Where the *hell* are you going?" I shouted.

If the chauffeur heard me through the glass, he made no sign. He rocketed through the desert at an insane speed. Looking back, I saw Lopez's lights swerve wildly, and then go still. He'd hit mud or soft dirt, and his wheels would be spinning in place. I hoped he was all right.

A few moments later, the chauffeur slammed on the brakes. I went flying forward, barely stopping myself from slamming into the glass between us. Red lights blinked out of the darkness, and I heard the *thrub-thrub* of a helicopter.

The chauffeur yanked open my door, shoving his gun in my face again. I don't know where he thought I was going to run, but I let him herd me toward the helicopter.

I approached it with my heart pounding. I hated flying, and I'd heard bad things about helicopters. Yes, I had many more things to worry about right now than fear of flying, but with the machine vibrating in front of me and a gun in my back, I developed a bad case of the shakes.

With no storm to help me, and my Beneath magic hibernating again, I had no choice. I climbed onto the step, the chauffeur pushed me in, and I landed on a seat that was much like a car seat. I couldn't hear anything over the blades, couldn't see anything but the glow of cockpit lights in the front.

The chauffeur dropped into the seat next to me, gun still aimed in my direction. He jammed on a headset and started shouting something. The pilot looked over his shoulder, arguing with him, but I couldn't hear much of what they were saying. The pilot swung around to his controls, and the helicopter lifted with a slight jerk and glided up into the night.

I hunkered into the seat with my arms folded. My face was sticky, and I realized I still had the councilman's blood all over it. My jacket was spattered with it too.

We flew for a long time. I had no idea how far or how fast helicopters could go; I just knew that I was scared, uncomfortable, unhappy, and had to pee. I figured if the chauffeur had wanted me dead, he'd have shot me, so he must be under orders to take me someplace specific. Once I got there, I might be executed, but until then I was relatively safe. Such comforting thoughts.

By the clock in the cockpit, it was about two a.m. when we started to descend. I looked out the window and saw a city in the distance, far too big to be anything in northern Arizona. I had no idea which direction we'd gone, but I knew I wasn't looking at Las Vegas or the enormous sprawl of Phoenix. That left Albuquerque or Santa Fe—we couldn't have gone far enough to have reached Salt Lake City or L.A.

So by process of elimination, I was probably in New Mexico. That was confirmed as we started to land—I saw the twisty streets of old Santa Fe flash under us and the vast bulk of the Sangre de Cristo Mountains in the darkness. I'd been to Santa Fe plenty of times in my wanderings before I'd moved to Magellan, and I knew we'd headed north and west of the city.

We landed just outside a walled compound. The chauffeur had to lift me out of the helicopter, because I was too exhausted and shaky to manage on my own.

The compound turned out to be a large house surrounded by an equally large wall. The outer walls were adobe, smooth, plain, and unbroken. Inside the gate, the house itself formed another barrier, with small windows facing the approach.

Once through the next gated breezeway, I found paradise. The courtyard was a vast open space that followed the natural contours of the land, with desert mountain plants and trees in abundance. Walkways led through this lush garden, and a tiled arcade ran along all four sides of the house.

The chauffeur took me inside, still at gunpoint, and led me through cool tiled halls. The house had been built in the old Spanish style, with staircases bending upward beyond arches, rooms opening unexpectedly, and few windows except those that overlooked the courtyard. The room I was taken to, after they searched me, had a balcony, but below it was a sheer drop down the cliff face that the house had been built upon.

The chauffeur closed the door and locked me in. The balcony doors were easily opened, which meant they didn't worry that I could escape that way.

I dropped a piece of loose tile over the wrought-iron balcony rail and waited a sickeningly long time before I heard a click of rock on rock below. Unless my jailers had conveniently stashed climbing gear under the bathroom sink, I was stuck.

I explored the room, finding phone and computer jacks,

but no phones or computers. They'd taken my cell phone
when they'd rudely patted me down, but they'd left my
piece of magic mirror in its chamois bag. They probably
thought I kept it so I could check my makeup on my daring
adventures. Every person I'd seen here so far had been human, lucky me. A supernatural being would have sensed the
mirror's magic.

I sat down on the bed, which was amazingly comfortable. I'd vacation here if I wasn't being held captive.

A full-length mirror in a heavy, carved frame hung on the
wall to the left of the bed. I gazed into it for a few minutes,
noting the splotches of dried blood on my face and Maya's
pretty shirt, the black mess of my hair, my eyes wide and
brown. Brown, thankfully. No green gleam in sight. Of
course, now that I could have used magic to help me escape,
it had deserted me.

I took out the piece of magic mirror and angled it toward
the mirror on the wall.

The magic mirror purred. "Oh, girlfriend, this is *nice.*
Here I was all worried about you, and you're sitting in
splendor. So not fair."

"Locked in splendor is more like it."

I kept playing with the mirror until a white spark flashed
between the magic mirror and the mundane one. Magic
mirrors could enhance the properties of ordinary mirrors,
or so I'd heard. I hadn't taken the time to discover everything I could do with a magic mirror, being busy with the
hotel and Beneath magic and dragons and being kidnapped
and all. Plus, working with the magic mirror meant listening to it.

"Can you let me see through all mirrors in the house?" I
asked. "Channel them into this one?"

"I don't know. It depends on the mirrors and where they are."

"Well, try," I said impatiently.

"Give me a second. This is powerful magic, honey, not simple chanting and incense."

Light danced between the two pieces of glass, glinting in the way mirrors did when they caught the sunlight. It was pitch-dark beyond the windows, except for the city lights I could see in the distance. The air through the balcony doors I'd left open was crisp and cold. Winter begins early at seven thousand feet.

A key scraped in the lock. I quickly dropped the mirror to the rug and slid it under the bed with my heel. "Give me a break, sugar," the mirror said. "I can't work if I can't *see* anything."

The young man who walked in didn't hear the mirror. His aura told me he was human, one without magic. He was maybe twenty-two or so and good-looking. Very good-looking. Good thing the mirror hadn't seen him, or I'd be listening to a panegyric about his flawless face, his chocolate brown hair, his light blue eyes, his firm body, and his ass in tight jeans. He had a Taser in his belt, and the two men standing outside the door held automatic rifles.

"All that hardware for me?" I asked.

"You're dangerous," the young man said. He closed the door behind him, and someone outside locked it. "Don't bother trying to take me hostage. They wouldn't care if you killed me. I'm expendable."

I stood up. "And this doesn't bother you?"

"It's a good job, with lots of perks." The young man shook a tablecloth over a table in the corner and started laying out silverware and glasses. "I make way more money than I would in an office job; plus I get lots of time off. They don't mind if I party here when they're out, and I meet a lot of women."

"Paradise," I said.

He grinned in an un-self-conscious way. "It is for me. But really, if you killed me, they'd just hire someone else."

"I guess when you work for big reptiles, you have to expect them to be cold," I said.

He gave me a puzzled look and then shrugged as he set a covered dish on the table and opened a bottle of wine. "Yeah, I guess. I'm Todd, by the way. This is *pollo en mole*, one of the cook's specialties."

"I already ate."

"The wine's from a local vintner. It's pretty good, though I'm not really a wine guy."

"You can take all of it away when you go, Todd. I'm not about to eat and drink anything served to me by dragons who want me dead. If they can't fry me with fire, poison might work."

Todd looked blank. "They don't want to kill you; they just want to talk to you. Look, I'll eat some first." He picked up a fork and scooped a dripping bite of the chicken dish into his mouth. "Mmm. Damn good. I love poblano chiles. They're not as hot as the habaneros but still tasty. Try some."

"Maybe later," I said.

I sank down on the bed again, trying to decide what to do. I believed Todd when he said the dragons wouldn't care if I killed him. He was another flunky, a house boy, if a well-paid one. They counted on me being nice enough to not hurt an innocent. If I did hurt him, take him hostage, throw him over the balcony, or kill him, then I'd confirm to the dragons that I was the monster they believed me to be.

Todd took a sip of wine to show me that it wasn't tainted. He put the cover back over the plate to keep it warm. Very thoughtful, was Todd.

"You all right?" he asked. He came and sat beside me on the bed, switching his Taser to the side of his belt opposite me. "I'm training to be a massage therapist, so I can give you a massage if you want. Neck and shoulders or full body, clothes on or off. Or if you need sex, I'm here for that too."

I gave him an irritated look. "Do you offer that to all guests? And prisoners?"

"Sure. It's part of my job."

"What if I were a man?"

Todd laughed. "Then they'd have sent in a woman. Or a gay man."

"They really take care of their guests, don't they?"

"They do. Lie back and enjoy it. They'll talk to you and release you in a couple of days. There's clean towels in the bathroom if you want to shower, plus robes in your size. I can take your clothes down to be cleaned."

"What I really want, Todd, is a phone."

"Sorry. No can do."

"Doesn't it bother you that they're holding me here against my will?"

Todd stood up, making sure I had a good view of his behind as he looked into the mirror to smooth his hair. "No, because they told me you're their enemy, and these are some pretty cool guys. They're not drug dealers or anything like that. Just businessmen. So if they don't want you leaving before they can talk to you, they've got a good reason."

"Sure. Why don't you go away, now, Todd, so I can eat? Or shower? Or jump off the balcony, whatever I want to do?"

He grinned at me through the mirror. "You don't look

like the type who'd kill herself; you look like the type who'd try to talk her way out. That's why they're allowing you out on the balcony. It's kind of cold tonight, though. You might want to close the windows."

"Thanks for the tip."

"Sure." Todd headed for the door. "You're pretty good-looking, though, so if you change your mind about the sex, just thump on the door and tell the guard to let me back in."

"I'll think about it," I said, deadpan.

"Great. Good night."

Todd tapped on the door, it opened from the outside, and my affable jailer waltzed out. The men stationed in the hall didn't bother to look in or give me an evil glare or anything else villainous before one of them shut the door and locked it again.

I snatched the mirror out from under the bed. "I assume you heard all that."

"Yes. Please tell him you want sex, and please let me watch. He sounds *divine.*"

I held the shard up in front of the other mirror. "Concentrate."

"Oh, you're no fun."

I didn't want to be fun; I wanted to get free. "Show me what's going on in this damn house. And while you're at it, yell at Mick. I need to find him."

"Well, which do you want first, sugar? I'm not powerful enough to do both. Especially since Micky *hates* to pull me out of his pocket. I like it in there, as I said, but I can never see him."

"Show me the house, first." I'd have more information to impart to Mick if I did reconnaissance, and besides, Mick might have tossed away his mirror shard. The look in his eyes when he'd left us on the highway had been bleak and empty.

"Got something," the mirror said. "Oh, nice."

The big mirror clouded as though shower steam coated it. Then it cleared, showing me a picture of a bathroom. Todd had just opened his pants to take a leak and preen himself in the mirror at the same time.

"Something a little more important," I said in irritation.

"Can't help it, sweetie. I'm fixing on him because he was in here, and he's easiest to follow. He'll go somewhere else in a minute."

Todd took his time at the toilet; then he moved to wash his hands and preen some more. He didn't look self-absorbed, just anxious to present the best possible picture to the world when he left the bathroom again.

Finally, after he'd combed his hair, anxiously scrutinized it, and combed it again, Todd left the room. The image of the bathroom dissolved, and I caught a glimpse of Todd striding down a long, tiled hall. I guessed I was looking at the corridor from an ornamental mirror on the wall.

"He's out of range," the mirror said. "Want me to keep following him?"

"Stay here for a while. Let's see if we can see someone else."

We waited for the longest time while the hall remained boringly empty. I ducked into the bathroom after twenty minutes and washed my face, hands, and arms clean of blood, but I refused to discard my clothes.

To give myself something to do I took a few bites of the food Todd had left. It was lukewarm now but quite good as promised. I liked mole, which was a smooth sauce of chiles and unsweetened chocolate, with various vegetables and other ingredients, depending on what the cook had handy. This one had the bite of hazelnuts in it. I wondered if the chef was also like Todd, working here for high pay but knowing he or she was expendable.

I didn't have the appetite or the time to appreciate the food. After my second bite, the mirror said, "Who's that?"

I glanced at the mirror and let my fork clatter to the plate. The dragon flunky was striding down the hall away from us, his leather duster moving, his ponytail in place.

"Him," I said. "Focus on him." I moved to the mirror to watch the flunky disappear around the corner. "Follow him!"

"All right, keep your pants on. Or not, if you're wearing that cute little black satin number."

I didn't bother to tell the mirror to shut up. It never listened anyway.

The big mirror clouded again, and when it cleared I saw the flunky entering a long, dark room. The end was lit by a fireplace—no, it was the cocoon of fire the flunky had wrapped around the councilman. So he'd made it here.

The room was dark, the windows high in the ceiling and covered with wooden shutters. The only light came from the fiery cocoon.

Another man, a dragon, stepped from the shadows beside it. He was as tall as the councilman, tattoos covering his neck and reaching up to his cheekbones. "Draconilingius," he said.

The word appeared to be the flunky's name, because he stopped and bowed. "Sir."

"The Stormwalker did this, didn't she?" the new dragon said. His voice was deep like the councilman's, though a little more gravelly.

"No, sir. Another creature did. He looked human, but he stank of powerful magic."

"In league with her, then."

"I'm not certain," Draconil—whatever his name was said. I'd have to call him Drake. "She joined in the attempt to fight him off."

"If he had any Beneath magic, then she was the cause of it. She should be killed now. Where is she?"

Drake hesitated. He glanced at the fire as though asking for guidance from the flames. "I don't know, sir. We lost her in the darkness."

I sat back in surprise. Drake must know I was here, must have been the one to give the order for me to be brought here. Why was he lying?

The other dragon snarled. "Find her. I don't give a damn if she is Micalerianicum's mate; she's not a dragon. I want her obliterated. End of problem."

Drake bowed again, his entire body deferential. "Yes, sir. Will you be staying here, sir? I can have accommodation readied for you."

"No, I have a mate to return to. I'll see you at the trial."

The flunky looked startled. "That's still going through? Even though . . ." He glanced again at the cocoon of fire.

"You assured me he'd recover. We'll elect another to the council if we have to, but I hope that it won't be necessary."

"Yes, sir."

The second dragon turned away and strode off into darkness without saying good-bye. I heard a door clang, and I wondered if it opened right out into the cliffs. Dragons wouldn't need to worry about sheer drops.

The flunky, Drake, turned away from his master and stared directly into the mirror. His eyes met mine, although I knew there was no way he could see me. Drake's face set, and he strode past the mirror on his way out the door.

"He sensed you," I said.

"I can't help that. He's magical and very powerful." The mirror hummed. "And cute."

The lock rattled again, and the door swung open. The two men with guns pointed their weapons at me. One wore an earpiece, through which Drake downstairs could easily give him orders.

"You are to come with me," he said.

I dropped the mirror shard onto the bed. "Keep trying to find Mick," I whispered to it, covering by pretending to straighten my shirt.

I followed the earpiece guy down the staircase, fully aware of the other man with an equally large gun coming behind me. We went through another hall to a large dining room. A wide wooden table with heavily carved legs ran the length of it, surrounded by equally heavily carved chairs. The table was bare.

Drake the flunky stood at one end of the room, waiting. The men with rifles walked me to him, then closed in behind me while I faced him.

Drake looked unhappy. Lines tightened around his black eyes, strands of hair had come out of his ponytail, and his breathing was uneven. He folded his arms, closing himself off to me while he scrutinized me.

"Stormwalker," he said. "Is His Honor right? Should I just obliterate you while I have the chance?"

"No," I said, trying for a confidence I was far from feeling. "Because I'm the only one who can save your master. Will you let me try?"

Nineteen

Drake's mouth tightened, but his eyes took on uncertainty. "Let you near my master with your hell-magic? What sort of fool do you think I am? What is to stop you from killing him, and me, and everyone else in this place?"

"He's still alive, then?" I hadn't been able to tell.

"Only just."

"I can heal him." I didn't know how I knew that. But I could—if I could channel the Beneath magic, and if it would wake up and answer my bidding. "If you don't let me, he will die. Not great choices, I know."

"You are asking me to trust you."

"Yeah, I am."

Drake watched me a moment. "Why?"

"Why didn't you tell the other dragon I was here?" I hoped the hired men behind me were loyal to Drake and wouldn't rush off and blab to the other dragon about me the moment they left the room.

Drake didn't seem concerned. "You are my responsibility. My councilman wanted to see you before the trial, apart from the others. He wants to assess the situation for himself. The others now know he was hurt, but not how it happened or why you were near. It is his wish."

"Then honor his wish. Let me try, at least. You know he'll die otherwise, don't you?"

"We have healers . . ."

"I've learned things about dragons living with Mick," I interrupted. "Shifting to dragon helps you heal from human-induced wounds—gunshots, for instance. Magically induced wounds are different. Dragon healers are powerful, Mick tells me, but they're earth-magic creatures. The person who did this has magic given to him by a god. I think. I do too."

Drake looked anguished, poor guy. He didn't trust me an inch, but I could see that he desperately wanted to save his master. Finally he jerked a nod at me and gestured the gunmen to lead me out.

The room he took me to deep in the bowels of the complex was the size of a small hangar. The room was furnished for comfort, I could see, but was also a big enough to house a full-sized dragon if necessary. A tight fit, if I went by Mick's size, but a dragon could shift here.

I looked into the big mirror that hung near the door. "Ready?" I asked it.

Dimly, as though from a radio playing in another room, came my magic mirror's voice. "Ready anytime you are, girlfriend."

A muscle moved on Drake's jaw. "They should have searched you better."

"That's what happens when you employ humans," I

said. "They don't know a magical implement from a piece of glass."

His eyes glittered. "They should have confiscated everything."

"Should have, but didn't. Good thing. My knowledge and my connection to the mirror can help you."

"They had better."

I had no doubt that Drake would order his men to open fire on me the minute I did anything wrong. Sweat trickled down my back, and my hands ached from me clenching them so hard. I was all bluff, and I knew it.

The heat increased as I approached the living flame at the end of the big room. I'd never seen anything like this. Mick might be able to explain what was happening beneath the fiery casing, maybe even tell me what to do. Drake stood silently, watching me like the menace he was.

I asked the mirror, "Did you find him yet?"

"No, honey. Sorry. He likes to play hard to get."

"If something happens to me here, I bequeath you to Cassandra."

Magic mirrors could be owned by one mage at a time—two in our case, because Mick and I had wakened it together. When a mage left a mirror to another mage upon his or her death, the mirror automatically obeyed the inheritor, no matter what other magical creature was lying in wait to enslave it. Bequeathing it to Cassandra meant that Drake couldn't grab the shard and start using it the minute I was dead.

"Cassandra hates me," the mirror complained.

"She has strong earth magics, and she'll take care of you. And you'll still be loyal to Mick."

"If I can ever find his sweet ass."

I turned to Drake, who'd been watching me narrowly.

"Do you have any sage, or incense? Sticks are better in this case."

"That's witch magic."

"Can you stop being all superior-race for five minutes and see if you have any?"

Drake looked annoyed, but he picked up an earpiece, put it on, and gave orders. I imagined Todd scrambling around the kitchen searching for sage. I wondered if he even knew what it looked like.

While we waited, I closed my eyes and tried to still my mind, but that was a waste of time. My thoughts couldn't settle. Coyote would know that I'd called on the Beneath magic—he always did. In fact, I was surprised he wasn't already here, ready to stop me.

But if I didn't try to save the dragon councilman's life, the dragons would certainly kill me. Todd might have been told that the councilman had brought me here to talk, but Drake had murder in his eyes. He'd sent away the other dragon, yes, but probably because he wanted first dibs on ripping me apart.

The incense sticks came at last, brought not by Todd but by a young woman. She was blond and as beautiful in the feminine way as Todd was in the masculine. I assumed her job was to wait on the male guests. She handed Drake a box of incense sticks, gave him a quick bow, and left the room. She never once looked at me or showed any interest. Her gaze had been only for Drake.

I held up three sticks of incense and asked Drake to light them. He did so with a flick of dragon fire, though I could tell he was irritated at my request. I propped the sticks in a copper bowl on one of the tables, and he looked even more irritated. Likely the bowl was a priceless antique.

The ends of the sticks started to glow. I thought about

sitting on my rooftop with Jamison—had it been only this afternoon?—and how I'd awakened the Beneath magic by watching sparks on the lit sage.

No, I'd awakened it by thinking about how powerful I was, how easily I could summon beings to do my bidding: skinwalkers, Nightwalkers. Dragons.

Dragons were huge creatures, born of fire and rock. No one had created the dragons, Mick told me—they'd come from the volcanoes themselves. Dragons answered to the earth alone, not to magic of the gods of this world or to magic from Beneath.

Jamison called dragons *Firewalkers*, beings that could summon and control fire, make it do their bidding as I used storms to do mine. There was no storm tonight, but a strength inside told me that I no longer needed one.

With Jamison this afternoon, I'd used the mirror to enhance the Beneath magic, that time to push my best friend off the roof. I'd acted in anger. Could I heal this dragon in desperation to save my own life, or would my Beneath magic take over and try to kill?

If I killed the councilman, Drake would signal his men to unload their guns into me. Could I stop them before I fell dead at their feet? The magic inside me chuckled, thinking it a nice challenge.

Shit.

I focused on the incense, trying to calm myself by observing the shape and intensity of the orange glow at the end of each stick. The dragon fire around the councilman raged on, preserving him and keeping him alive. I'd have to remove the fire, which was powerful earth magic, before I could use the Beneath magic on him. I could do it myself, but I decided it was a good idea to let the dragons think I couldn't negate their power.

"Shut it off," I said to Drake, gesturing to the fire.

"He'll die," Drake snapped.

"You have to take that chance."

I stepped back and waited. Drake's face shone with per-
spiration and anger, and his eyes, to my surprise, were wet
with tears.

Giving me a final warning stare, Drake lifted his hand
over the fire. The flames streamed upward into his palm,
much as the fiery barrier had into Nash when we'd rescued
Mick. Drake's tattoos glowed where they peeked from beneath his clothes, and his eyes took on a red tinge.

The fire came away to reveal the bloody mess that was
the councilman's body. I flinched when I saw it, and I heard
one of the gunmen swear under his breath. I had no idea
how the councilman could still be alive, but I sensed his red
and black aura, still smelling of heat and ash but laced with
the stench of death.

"Ish," the magic mirror said in the distance. "He doesn't
look good."

I made myself touch the councilman's aura. It was cold,
death so close. I let the aura wrap around my hand, shivering as the death-chill touched my skin. With my other
hand, I tried to summon a white ball of Beneath magic,
similar to the one I'd thrown at Jamison.

It wouldn't come, of course. I swallowed hard, tried
again. Nothing.

I glanced wildly at the mirror, but it didn't help me. The
mirror reflected me, a slender Navajo woman in dirty jeans,
her hair disheveled, with one hand held out to her side, the
other in front of her.

Drake started to growl. I'd heard growling like that before, from Mick whenever he got ready to fight something.

Come on.

Make the dragons bow to you, my inner self whispered. *Hold the elder's life in your hand, and make the dragons worship you for saving him. Demand it of them, or they'll never respect you.*

I don't want their damned respect, I snarled in return. *I want them to let me go home and to leave Mick alone.*

And they will, when you command them.

"I'm sick of people telling me what to do!" I shouted out loud.

Drake blinked, wondering who the hell I was talking to. There was a restless noise behind me and the small metallic sound of guns cocking. Guns made me so damn nervous.

"Tell them to back off," I said to Drake. "Tell them to put the weapons down—in another room preferably—or he dies."

Drake hated me. I saw the hatred deep inside him, in his fire, and in his aura. He wanted me to drop dead at his feet.

"Do it," he said to his lackeys. "Leave the room. Do not return until I summon you."

In the mirror, I saw the two gunmen's reluctance to obey. Drake kept his glare on them, until one of them said a resigned, "Yes, sir," and led the other one out.

I relaxed a fraction. "I don't like guns."

"Neither do I." Drake called flame to dance in his hand. "Save him or you fry."

I willed the magic again. *He can't resist you,* it said. *You can snuff his puny fire with the flick of your finger.*

I could. And I did.

Drake took several hasty steps back as the flames in his hand died. He opened his mouth to shout for the guards again, but I said, "Wait."

A white ball rose above my hand. I tossed it, almost casually, toward the mirror.

The ball shot down the length of the room as though I were a pro baseball player. It hit the mirror and returned like a beacon, arrowing toward the councilman's torn-apart body.

The light surrounded the body, encasing it in whiteness the same way it had been encased in fire. I still held the councilman's aura, and now I directed the white light to it. Holding both the dying aura and the light, I found the compassion inside myself that my crazy mother hadn't managed to crush.

"Live," I whispered.

The light brightened. The councilman's aura grew hot, hotter, so searing hot I wanted to fling it from me. I gritted my teeth and held on in spite of the pain, knowing that if I let go now, the dragon would die. Finally and completely.

Drake's eyes widened behind the white glow as the councilman's muscles began to knit. As we watched, the bloody pulp of his body started to close, healthy skin growing to replace that which had been torn apart. I could now see the real shape of the councilman's human body instead of a pile of bones and muscle. His face solidified, became recognizable as that of the stern man who'd approached Maya's house with the intent of kidnapping me.

You can still destroy him. You're plenty strong enough.

But I was also strong enough to save him.

I kept the magic going. Drake had clenched his fists, his tension and worry palpable. I felt invincible, power surging through me until I knew I could sprint around the world and never get tired. If I jumped from the cliffs behind the house, I would soar into the air like the dragons.

The sensible Stormwalker in me told me that the magic said this because it wanted me to try jumping off the cliff. The Beneath magic would think it funny if I didn't succeed.

That makes no sense, I thought in annoyance. *If I'm dead, it is too.*

Beneath magic is the magic of gods. It doesn't understand mortality.

And that, another little thought said to me, might be what saved me.

"Gods," Drake whispered. "He's alive."

The councilman lay on his bier, whole and unbloody, surrounded by my light. I released his aura, which wrapped around his body like loving hands. I closed both my fists, and the beacon shot back into the mirror, like a film in reverse, kicking the original ball of light around back to me.

As soon as the light hit me, the magic winked out and released me. I fell to the ground like a wrung-out rag, my strength gone. Either I banged my head on the floor, or Drake kicked the hell of out me, because my head filled with stunning pain, and then there was nothing.

Twenty

I woke to a warm, bare body at my back. I thought I was home, snuggled down under the covers with Mick spooned up behind me, his large hand cupping my hip. Lips grazed the back of my neck, so warm, so loving.

I opened my eyes to an unfamiliar room with priceless artwork on the walls and faint light coming through balcony windows. A mirror in a heavy frame reflected me under thick quilts with a man lying behind me.

"Todd?" I said in alarm. I jumped away to find Mick next to me, watching me with bad-boy blue eyes.

"Todd? Who the hell is Todd?"

"A house boy with a wide range of responsibilities." I pressed a shaking hand to my hair. "Mick, what are you doing here?"

"The mirror told me where you were."

"I mean, what are you doing here giving yourself up to the dragons?"

"Who says I'm giving myself up? The outside doors aren't locked, and I can fly."

I sat up straight. "Then why didn't you grab me and haul me out of here? We could be having this conversation back at my hotel."

Mick shrugged. "I want to hear what Bancroft has to say."

"Bancroft?"

"Bancroft is the dragon council member whose life you happened to save. I want to know why he's so interested in talking to you."

"Couldn't you call him instead? I want out of this place."

Mick's hand on my arm was warm, caressing. "Janet, love, if you play by their rules, the dragons will be civilized. They won't imprison me here. I'm honor-bound to appear at my trial, and they're honor-bound to let me get there unimpeded. Honor means a hell of a lot to dragons."

I didn't feel better. "They might be honor-bound to you, but not to me. The dragon who visited Drake last night talked about obliterating me. What's to say this Bancroft hasn't decided the same thing? What if he orders you to obliterate me for him?"

"Then I'll disobey, and they'll have to go through me to get to you."

I flopped back down on the mattress, still drained and sick in spite of my heavy sleep. I also had a tender spot on my head, which I was pretty sure had been put there by Drake's boot.

"What guarantee do I have that you don't agree with them?" I asked tiredly. "I saw your face when I crawled out of the club, Mick. It's unnerving to know that the man you love thinks the world might be better off with you dead."

Mick touched my face, and I was too exhausted to roll away from him. "I've spent a lot of time thinking since I last saw you, Janet. Walking and thinking. You have some crazy magic inside you, but you did when I met you too. You learned to deal with that, and you'll learn to deal with this." The touch turned to a caress, his fingers on my lips. "And I want to be here to watch you grow."

His words warmed me, but I couldn't relax. "You suddenly have a lot of faith in me."

"Not suddenly. The magics are part of you, no matter how frightening they are. They are what make you uniquely you."

"Lucky me."

Mick rose on his elbow to gaze down at me. "You're a beautiful woman, Janet Begay. You have amazing strength but amazing gentleness too. I saw that when I first met you— you tempered your strength to keep from hurting others. This Beneath magic isn't better than you. It's strong, but you're stronger."

I thought of the way the little voice talked to me whenever the Beneath magic woke up, the terrible knowledge that the voice belonged to me, not something outside of me.

"The magic's voice is mine, but it's her words," I said worriedly. "Mick, I'm so afraid of turning into her."

"Into your mother?"

My mother, in her realm Beneath, was a woman of astonishing beauty and cold cruelty. She was powerful—there. Above, she could barely function and had to possess others to do it. She was sealed in now, but she wasn't dead. I anticipated she'd find a way out again someday.

"You're nothing like her," Mick said. "I met her, remember?"

"You weren't there the entire time. I was *just* like her. We can't ever really get away from our genetics, can we?"

Mick twined his fingers through mine. "When we're finished here, I'm taking you to Many Farms."

I wanted to laugh. "What for? My grandmother won't have anything good to say to me, especially not after I've been using my mother's magic."

"I want to remind you what else you inherited through your genetics. Your father is a kind and gentle man, and your grandmother has some powerfully strong earth magic. They're a part of you, and you're a part of them. You're also a part of the land, the Dinetah. Both natures are you, both are equally important."

I unwound enough to smile. "When did you become such a philosopher?"

"Walking down that road all the way to Prescott. It's a long way on foot, through incredible country. All that beauty reminded me of you, and why I needed you to stay alive. The world would *not* be a better place without you in it, Janet, and it will just have to learn to live with you."

Again, the warmth, accompanied by heat in his damn gorgeous blue eyes. Mick always knew what to say. "Even if I'm a dangerous killer?" I asked.

"Are you?" Mick sat up, proving that he was mother-naked under the covers. "You stopped Undead Jim from killing people in the club. You stopped him before he could destroy the dragons who came for you, and you healed Bancroft."

"One man died." I thought of the chauffeur's assistant, whose name I'd never learned, lying dead on Maya's front lawn. His only crime had been to open the car door for me.

"More would have if you hadn't intervened."

"No, he wouldn't be dead *at all* if not for me. Jim rushed out there to prevent the dragons from taking me."

Mick frowned. "Why?"

"Good question. Hell if I know. Maybe he senses my Beneath magic when I use it, like Coyote does, and comes to find me."

"Do you think your mother was the one who resurrected him?"

"I don't know. The vortex is sealed. I haven't sensed her come out, and she hasn't tried to find me. If—when—she can get out again, I think I'd be the first person she hunted down. I'd know if she were free."

"Another god from Beneath, then?"

"Could be. That's what I'm gambling on. But there are plenty of gods above too, aren't there? Coyote for one. Spider Woman. The kachinas. They can be benevolent but also scary. And powerful."

"Coyote doesn't admit to it?" Mick asked.

"He says no, but does Coyote never lie? He's a trickster god. He does what he pleases, for his own reasons."

Outside, the sunlight began to dim as clouds gathered on the mountains. They were black, dense clouds, full of water and lightning. The storm magic in me reached out to the thickening storm like an old friend, and a spark of lightning danced between my fingers.

Mick's eyes started to darken. "Want me to draw it off?" he asked in a low voice.

Mick knew how to heat my blood with only a look. He'd done that to me the night I'd met him, over a meal in a Las Vegas restaurant. Within an hour, I'd been in bed with him, surrendering my virginity to a man with wicked eyes.

"Mick," I said slowly, "I'm not sure I've forgiven you. For not trusting me."

"I know." He laid his hand on my belly and eased the sheet down so he could toy with the tiny stud at my navel.

"And I think you're right to not trust me," I said.

"I don't agree." He moved to play with the stud with his tongue.

His hot breath on my skin made me go warm and pliant in spite of myself. "Mick, why do you always do this to me?"

"Because I love you. And because I want to feast on you whenever I see you."

He proceeded to feast. I could have stopped him, I suppose, could have told him to get out, or, better still, to fly me out of here with him. But no, I leaned back against the pillows and moaned softly as he licked his way from my navel, taking his time, until his mouth closed over my cleft.

Mick did things to me with his tongue that no man should know how to do. My hips moved as he licked me, his mouth sending gritty heat all up and down my body. Outside, the storm built, cold wind driving the clouds from the towering mountains. Lightning sparkled in my fingertips, and Mick raised his head and sucked that out of me too.

Mick's eyes were now black all the way across. He lowered his head again and devoured me until I was holding on to the headboard, crying my ecstasy to the ceiling. He kept on until I'd come once, twice. Right before the third time, Mick shoved the rest of the covers from the bed and climbed over me, his body hot and hard with wanting. I caught his shaft in my hand to stroke him, to return the pleasure he'd given me, but he shoved my hand away, pressed me down, and entered me.

Gods, it felt so good to have him inside me. I'd feared I'd never feel that again. I arched to meet Mick's thrusts, my nails raking down his back. The tattoo that snaked across the small of his back, from hip to hip, was hot under my touch, my dragon-man barely containing his fire. Thoughts of what would happen when he decided to let go excited the hell out of me.

He rode me until he spilled his seed, both of us groaning in release. But I knew he wasn't finished. Mick could sex me all night and well into the next day if he wanted to, and he'd only stop for my sake.

He wasn't one for unadventurous sex, and the things we did on that bed—not to mention the use we made of the headboard, the chair across the room, and the balcony railing—created more hot memories I could savor when I was old and gray.

When Mick finally finished, hours later, and laid me gently on the bed, covering me with the tumbled quilts, my head had stopped hurting, my scoured body refreshed. Mick had healed me as he'd loved me, and I hadn't even noticed.

Drake sent his gunmen for us about ten minutes into our afterglow. I wondered if Drake had the room monitored, and then I decided I didn't care. They'd kidnapped me and held me captive; they could eat their hearts out watching my boyfriend enjoy me.

When the nice men with automatic rifles walked into the room, the one who seemed to be in charge told us to get dressed and accompany them to Drake. No offer of breakfast, no Todd breezing in with a tray and fresh towels.

I got out of bed and put on my clothes right in front of

the gunmen, figuring it would save them from searching me later. I left the shard of mirror where it was next to the bed. Drake already knew about it, and it had keyed into all the mirrors in the house by now. If things got bad, it could send a message to Cassandra, who might be able to find Coyote, who might get off his butt and save us.

Might, might, might. Nothing was certain.

As we were marched through the house, I wondered about Jim. I'd told Mick that I thought Jim was sensing when I used my Beneath magic, and I'd used it big-time to heal Bancroft last night. I wondered if Jim were somewhere around here or whether Bancroft's men shooting him full of holes had slowed him down any.

I felt sorry for Jim. He hadn't asked to be resurrected, and he couldn't handle the power that ran through his body. But although he didn't mean to kill people, he still did it. He had to be found and stopped.

The room the gunmen took us to opened onto the court-yard, where a fountain played, its water soothing music. Rain pattered into the courtyard, thunder rumbled in the distance, and the breeze brought us the fine scents of rain and wind.

Bancroft the councilman, now wearing a black suit similar to the one I'd first seen him in, stood by the open window with his back to us. Drake, waiting near him, said nothing when we entered, only motioned with a flick of his fingers for the gunmen to leave us.

"Micalerianicum," Bancroft said. "I'm surprised to see you here."

"Not surprising at all. Janet is my mate."

"You always told me your name was Mick," I said under my breath.

Mick gave me a smile. "I didn't want to scare you away."

Drake snorted. "Humans have difficulty with names that are longer than a few syllables."

"You haven't met some Native Americans I know," I said. "But I agree that Mick's full name is a little ridiculous. So is yours."

"And yours is so brief it is finished before one takes in its meaning," Drake returned. "What does it mean, this Janet Begay?"

"Just Janet." I had another name, in fact, the spirit name my father had given me the day of my birth, but no one was allowed to know it. Names could be tricky things. If you gave someone your true name, they could use it to gain power over you.

"These words are not our real names," Mick said, as though he read my thoughts. "Our true names are like musical notes, sung to us before we're hatched. They're part of the magic that makes dragons what they are."

Drake scowled. "You would give this knowledge to a being like her?"

"The being like her saved your master's ass."

Bancroft finally turned around. "I was told what happened, and your magic mirror replayed the incident for me." Bancroft gave me a stiff bow. "I am grateful for your assistance."

"She healed you," Mick said. "Pure and simple."

"She shouldn't have been able to," Drake said.

"No one can be stronger than the mighty dragons?" I asked. "That's what this is all about, isn't it?"

Drake went a fine shade of purple. He'd recovered well from last night, his dark suit pristine, his ponytail sleek, every hair in place. "You've known of the existence of dragons for what, four months? How can you even begin to know what being a dragon is?"

"I know you were terrified I'd open the vortexes and release a goddess from Beneath, endangering the dragons."

"Endangering everyone," Bancroft said. "Humans as well."

"Oh, you're finally getting around to mentioning humans, are you?" I asked. "All I ever hear is that the *dragons* fear the magic, that releasing it will be the end of the *dragons*. You don't give a rat's ass about the rest of humanity. There are plenty of dangers to humans, but I don't see you running around trying to put a stop to them. But when the dragons are in trouble, suddenly people have to die, and Mick gets put on trial for *not* doing murder."

Bancroft gave me a frosty look. "You know nothing, girl."

"She's not wrong," Mick said. "You two know very little about humans. You don't walk among them. Janet has far more compassion than any dragon I know."

"We walk among them," Drake said. "We live here, outside a human city. We employ humans."

"Outside the city," Mick answered. "Employ them. You don't *live* with them. You don't go to their bars and play pool with them and listen to what they have to say. You've locked yourselves in your fortresses so long you don't know what goes on outside them."

Bancroft broke in. "She might have compassion as you say, but the magic from Beneath will consume her if she does not learn to suppress it. But that is a separate issue. You, Mick, will stand trial for breaking your word to the council and disobeying dragon law. I've tried to find some way around it, but I can't. The other councilors are adamant."

"That's fine," Mick said in a mild voice. "I'll be there."

"It's ridiculous," I said.

"That doesn't matter." Bancroft's tone was hard. "Whether

a human girl thinks our laws are right or wrong is irrelevant. He has broken his pledge, and he must answer for it."

Damn but they were stubborn. Mick wasn't much better, simply answering with a nod. He was going to let them conduct their sham trial and decide what kind of ordeal he had to withstand for the crime of sparing my life.

"Why did you bring me here?" I asked. "Before Jim went on his killing rampage, you planned to kidnap me and drag me off here for some reason. You've never gotten around to telling me what."

Bancroft surprised me with a little smile. He really was a good-looking man when he did that. So was Drake, though I doubted I'd ever catch Drake smiling.

"I brought you here to interrogate you about what Mick's defense would be."

My brows shot up. "Really? And you expected me to tell you?"

"I expected to pry it out of you using whatever methods I had at hand. So that I can prepare."

"Well, forget it." I let lightning crackle through my fingers. I knew this wouldn't scare dragons, who could eat storm power and enjoy it, but the sparks dancing in my hands made a nice show. "Why didn't you kidnap Colby and interrogate him? Or have you already?"

Bancroft shook his head. "That is forbidden."

"But interrogating me isn't?"

"You're human."

I growled, tossed the lightning around the room, and smiled when Drake and Bancroft jumped. The electricity dissipated harmlessly, but the air smelled of ozone and power. "I'd have disappointed you even if you did torture me. I really don't know what Colby is planning."

Shouts outside the door interrupted us. I heard the head gunman yell, "Stand down! Stand down!" and a snarled response. A third man out there was trying to apologize at the top of his voice.

Bancroft jerked a hand at Drake, but Drake was already moving, a pistol coming out from under his coat as he flung open the door.

"You send her out here, unhurt, and I'll go away," a sharp voice said. "*With* her."

"Oh, for the gods' sake," I whispered.

"Mr. Bancroft, I am so sorry," another man was saying. "I told him we couldn't burst in here, that you were a prominent citizen in your private home, not a criminal."

"Where is she?"

I peered over Drake's shoulder. Nash stood there with his nine-millimeter pointed at the lead gunman's head, his hand unwavering. Behind Nash was another man in a sheriff's deputy's uniform, looking red, apologetic, and out of breath.

"I'm all right, Nash," I said. "We were just chatting."

Nash's gun didn't move. "Let her walk out here."

"Explain this," Bancroft snapped at them.

"I'm sorry, sir," the head gunman said. "He charged the front door and shoved his way in."

"He shouldn't have been able to," Bancroft said. "Not through my wards."

I knew damn well how Nash had walked in through the dragon's heavy spells, but I wasn't about to volunteer the information.

"Mick got in through your wards," I pointed out.

"We allowed him in," Drake said. "And knew when he arrived."

"Let her walk out of here and get into my truck," Nash said, ignoring us. "If you do that, I won't charge you with kidnapping and assault."

"Mick too," I said.

Nash didn't betray any surprise to see Mick other than a minute flicker of his gray eyes. "Mick too."

"Stand down," Bancroft said to his gunmen. "Let her go."

The gunmen lowered their weapons without arguing. I knew they didn't give a shit whether Bancroft showered me with gifts or ordered me shot. They were like Todd—either way, they got paid.

Drake, with great reluctance, lowered his gun as well. I lost no time stepping around him and Nash, putting myself out of the line of fire. Mick was right behind me, his hand on my back to guide me.

We didn't stop walking until we'd reached Nash's familiar SUV, parked just outside the open gates of the compound. I was glad I'd grabbed my coat when I'd gone down to see Bancroft, but I'd left the shard of mirror in the bedroom. No matter. The mirror couldn't obey them if I ordered it not to, but it was free to shower them with snarky comments. I smiled.

Nash came out with Drake and Bancroft. He'd holstered his weapon, but he was clearly in charge. The deputy followed, continuing to apologize. I wondered how much Bancroft paid him.

Mick had already helped me into Nash's front seat and taken a place in the back by the time Nash climbed into his SUV. He said nothing to us as he drove down the winding road that led to a highway. Nash picked up his sunglasses from the dashboard and shoved them on, one-handed, but not before I saw the dark smudges under his eyes.

"He do anything to you?" he asked me as he pulled onto the freeway.

"Nothing dire," I said. "You didn't have to come all the way out here, you know."

"It's my job. Maya told me that you'd been kidnapped at gunpoint, and Lopez lost you out in the desert."

Mick spoke from the backseat, sounding tired. "I think she means you could have reported the abduction and let the Santa Fe police take care of it."

"I did. Lopez saw the number of the helicopter, and the Sante Fe County sheriff's department recognized it as belonging to one Mr. Bancroft, reclusive billionaire. The entire department refused to bother him and make sure you were all right, so I decided to bother him for them. Thank Maya. She was hysterical about what happened, adamant that I go after you."

I could imagine. Maya could be loud and resolute and didn't tire easily. Likely Nash had come to find me to get her to shut up.

"I'll be sure to thank her when we get back to Magellan. Maybe you should go see her too, to tell her what happened."

Nash gave me a flat stare from behind his sunglasses. "I'm not taking you to Magellan yet."

"No?" I really wanted to see my own bed. "Where, then?"

"Flat Mesa. I have in my custody a man who has confessed to killing your hotel guest, Jim Mohan."

Twenty-one

A Native American man sat across the metal-topped table from me in the interrogation room in the Hopi County jail. Mick, surprisingly, agreed to wait outside when Nash told us that the man refused to speak to anyone but Janet Begay. Nash wasn't about to let me stay alone in here with the suspect, so he took an intimidating seat at the end of the table.

The suspect was a Hopi, large and muscular, and he sat with his head bowed. His black hair was brushed with dust but pulled neatly back into a braid. He wore nondescript clothes—jeans and a loose shirt—and his large hands were scarred.

When he looked up at me his dark eyes were filled with sorrow and shame, his mouth pulled down at the corners. I'd rarely seen a more miserable-looking human being.

And he was completely human. No aura of the supernatural hung anywhere about him.

"This is Ben Kavena," Nash said. "Early this morning, he walked into a tribal police station and confessed to killing a white tourist at the Homol'ovi ruins. The police knew I'd been looking into Jim Mohan's disappearance and death and called me. I showed Mr. Kavena a picture of Jim Mohan, and he confirmed it was the same man."

I looked at Ben, not Nash. "Why?" I asked him.

"I was very angry," Ben said. "He violated a sacred place, and I became crazy with anger." Tears stood in his eyes. "But I committed a worse violation. I have lived with the knowledge ever since."

"What did Jim do?" I asked.

For answer, Nash shoved a lidless cardboard box at me. "We found Mr. Kavena with these."

Ben made a noise of protest. "I was not stealing them. I want them put back where they belong."

I looked inside at several substantial chunks of clay pots. They looked old, very old, and had yellow and black designs on them.

"Jim was pot hunting," I said. "The asshole. The photography story was just a cover."

Pot hunters—looters—grazed out-of-the-way places for ancient pottery, which could fetch large prices in museums whose curators might not pay much attention to laws or ethics. The pottery in the Homol'ovi area belonged to the pueblo peoples and dated back a thousand years and more, and these artifacts could be sold for high dollar to collectors.

But the same pots that people prized for intrinsic value were sacred to the pueblo tribes. The pottery had belonged

to their ancestors, used both for everyday tasks and in buri-
als. Someone digging a pot out of a grave was like someone
removing your great-grandmother's tombstone and flog-
ging it to a collector.

I could imagine Ben witnessing this rape of his ancestors and growing furious. If he considered himself a de-
scendant of the people of Homol'ovi, he'd be even more
enraged.

Studying his face, I realized that his anger went even
deeper than that.

"You're the Koshare," I said, realizing. "The one who
scared me up there the other day. At least, you were his
channel."

Ben nodded. "I had gone up there to look around, to
keep an eye on the place. There is no one now to keep the
stealers of the sacred away. And I saw this Mr. Mohan next
to the river, putting pieces of pots into a box. When he left
the box and went back up the hill to look for more, I followed him. He laughed at me when I demanded he return
what he was stealing, thinking I was just a stupid Hopi.
Why should I worry about a few pieces of broken pottery? I
had a knife with me. When he turned around, I struck out."

I remembered my vision, Jim falling forward with the
knife in his back and a man's muscular hand grasping the
hilt. The hand hadn't been covered in the Koshare's black-
and-white paint. Ben had done the killing, not the Koshare
that sometimes inhabited him.

"I have taken a life." Tears spilled down Ben's leathery
cheeks. "I have destroyed myself."

"After you killed Jim, what did you do?" I asked.

"Ran away. I was a coward. I grabbed the potsherds and
went home. I couldn't risk lingering to put the pots back. I
was going to do it later."

"I mean before that." I mulled over how to put it. "Did the Koshare—the spirit that fills you—did he come to you? Maybe tried to heal Jim?"

Ben didn't change expression as he shook his head. "The Koshare didn't dare come to me. I was unworthy of him."

"But he came to you when I went up to Homol'ovi to investigate. He was in you when he frightened me."

"I don't know why he came back. Yes, I was there when you came. I'd put on my paint, hoping he would come to me in that sacred place and forgive me, but when he entered me, he was so angry. He was angry at you too, and afraid. After that day, he has left me and not returned."

He finished, silently weeping.

Damn Jim, anyway. If he hadn't gone out looking for what he thought was easy money, Ben wouldn't have been driven to murder, and we wouldn't be stuck with an undead maniac turning people inside out.

But then, Ben should have simply reported Jim to the police, not taken it upon himself to seek retribution. Pot theft was a crime, and Jim could have done time for it. Now Ben would do time for murder.

"What's going to happen to him?" I asked Nash.

"I'm not sure. You and I both have seen Jim Mohan alive and well, after he was supposed to have been killed."

Ben looked up, puzzled. "The man was dead. I've seen death; I know what it looks like."

"He isn't alive," I said softly. "He was resurrected."

Ben's tears ceased, and his eyes widened in horror. "No." He moaned it, rocking slightly back and forth. "No."

"Did the Koshare resurrect him?" I asked.

"No. No. He would not do such a thing."

"Does he know who did?"

Ben shook his head. "I don't know. I don't know."

Nash pulled the box of potsherds back toward him and stood up. "Ben Kavena, I'm going to hold you until I can find this Jim Mohan and figure out what really happened. I'll tell you now that the least you'll be charged with is assault and attempted murder."

I sprang to my feet. "Nash, don't try to find Undead Jim yourself. Don't send your deputies out to hunt him either. He's a killer. He'll destroy whoever tries to approach him."

Nash gave me an annoyed look. "I can't very well tell a judge that I want to press charges against Ben for murder, but sorry, I can't produce the body because it's been resurrected."

"I bet a judge who was raised in Magellan would believe you."

Nash scowled, not finding me funny. "I still need to find this Jim. He killed the man in Maya's front yard, not to mention the hiker south of town and your assailant in Las Vegas."

Ben looked terrified. "If such a one finds me, he will kill me. He will tear me open."

"Can you put a good guard on him?" I asked Nash. "Or at least let Mick ward his cell?"

"Yes," Ben said. "Please, I will stay here under your protection."

Nash wanted to argue some more, but I walked out before he could and went to find Mick. Ben Kavena was smart to be afraid. I needed to find Undead Jim, sooner rather than later. He responded to me—fine, I'd let him come to me.

What I'd do with him after that, and how I'd stop him, I didn't know. I very much feared I'd have to kill him, and I wasn't at all certain I was strong enough for that. What worried me even more was that something out there was powerful enough to resurrect a human being, and I still hadn't figured out who.

Nash wouldn't let me go until I'd signed forms and promised to not discuss what I'd heard with the press. Not that Magellan or Flat Mesa had much press, and it didn't matter anyway, because the rumor mill was far quicker and more accurate. But I signed the papers to make him happy.

"How is Maya?" I asked.

"Fine when I left her," was Nash's abrupt answer. Nash looked awful, running on adrenaline and pure stubbornness. I doubted he'd slept in the last twenty-four or so hours.

"Which was?"

"Last night. I asked Lopez to make sure she didn't need any medical attention or counseling."

"You are such a romantic, Nash," I said.

"I followed procedure. Get the hell out of here and let me keep following it."

I gave up and left him. I did tell Mick everything I'd learned from Ben Kavena, and Mick agreed to set wards on the cell. He stayed behind to do that, and one of the deputies ran me back to the Crossroads Hotel.

Cassandra was relieved to see me, although Pamela gave me a steady look and said nothing. I wondered how long the Changer woman was going to stay. Until she conquered Cassandra? Looking at the two of them, I couldn't tell whether that had happened or not.

"Dragons can't be trusted," Cassandra told me in a low voice after I'd showered and changed my filthy clothes. "They talk a lot about honor, but they don't extend that honor to humans. Don't trust them."

"I don't, much."

"Good. Then maybe you could persuade Colby to leave the saloon and return to his hotel. He sets the wrong tone."

Cassandra turned away to greet a couple checking in with a courteous smile on her face. As I moved to the saloon, I wondered how Cassandra knew so much about dragons. Mick had told me they preferred to remain hidden from humans, and yet Cassandra spoke her opinions about them with conviction. I wondered where she'd encountered them before and what had happened.

Both Colby and Mick sat at a table in the saloon, Mick having returned from Flat Mesa while I'd been in the shower. I'd been a little disappointed he hadn't come in to wash me again, but now I was glad to see him in here keeping an eye on Colby.

As I sat down, Mick flashed me a warning look and said, "The magic mirror showed him everything."

"Everything." Colby's grin became a leer. "You have stamina in the sack, girl. It was stimulating, even if I had to watch through a lot of cracks."

My face heated. "I swear I'm melting that thing."

"Don't be embarrassed. It was beautiful. Way better than any porn I can find on that motel TV."

Mick, damn him, didn't look ashamed at all, or even angry at Colby for having seen me in my naked glory. Maybe it was a dragon thing—having Colby watch Mick making such hard love to me reinforced the idea that I was Mick's mate.

"Interesting, though," Colby said, taking another sip of beer. "I mean about Bancroft wanting to grill you. Sounds like the dragon council is not at all united in their opinions about Micky or this trial. We can use that to our advantage."

"How?"

Colby shrugged. "Trust me, darling."

"Your defense was going to be that I was harmless," I said. "But that's out. Bancroft and Drake have seen what I can do. Even if I saved Bancroft's life."

"True. You fucked that up. Doesn't matter. I have a few other things up my sleeves."

"Like what?"

Colby gave me another shrug. "Have to think about what I can do."

I glanced at Mick, but he and Colby exchanged a look. I grasped that the two of them knew exactly what Colby had in mind, and neither would bother to tell me.

Irritated, I stood up. "Fine. While you're plotting together, try to think of a way I can find Undead Jim. One that won't hurt anyone."

I stalked out and nearly ran into Pamela at the door coming in. She looked me up and down, and for the first time, she smiled at me, even if it was a predatory smile.

"I heard what Colby said." Her eyes smoldered. "He's right. You're hot, Janet."

Boiling water couldn't have made me any more uncomfortable. "I'm surprised the mirror didn't sell tickets and serve popcorn."

"It was a good show, believe me."

"I thought you liked Cassandra," I said.

"I do." Pamela grinned. "But I still have eyes." She walked on inside the saloon, and I hauled myself out of there.

Cassandra had no more guests at her counter. She was typing up something, her fingers skimming across the computer keyboard with ease and grace. She flicked her light blue gaze to me as I approached.

"You need to find Jim Mohan," she told me.

"I do." I wondered if she too had seen the show through the mirror, but if she had, I knew she'd never mention it.

"He's attracted to my magic, but I used it plenty in Santa Fe and never heard a peep from him."

A small pucker appeared between Cassandra's brows, and she lightly caressed the lip of the counter. "Perhaps because you weren't in danger."

"But I was in danger. I'd been kidnapped and held against my will."

"If I understand what happened correctly, the dragons captured you to talk to you about Mick's trial. They had no plans to kill you. Perhaps Jim sensed that."

"The other dragon councilor wanted me dead. He said so, most emphatically."

"But Draconilingius protected you. He didn't let on that they had you in custody, which means they had no intention of letting you be hurt."

"Gods, you can even pronounce their names."

Cassandra's shrug was elegant. "I studied up on dragons."

"I never knew they existed until a few months ago."

"You're not a witch, and I was a diligent student. Dragons can be useful to witches, if the witch is powerful enough."

First I'd heard of it. "My immediate problem is to find and stop Jim. If I can get him in front of a magistrate, a Hopi man might be spared a life sentence. Then again, Jim is unstable, and if he's hauled into court, he might just kill the magistrate, the Hopi man, Nash, and me."

"We can try to bind him."

"His magic is pretty damn powerful, Cassandra. I can barely slap him."

"I know some spells that are pretty damn powerful too."

I leaned casually on the counter. "Is that why you're working at a tiny hotel in a backwater town in the middle of nowhere?"

Cassandra gave me the tiniest of smiles. "I made some mistakes. But I enjoy working here. I like the quiet."

"With horny dragons, attacking Changers, and an undead man filled with destructive magic wreaking havoc? Sure, I can see where that would be restful."

Her smile widened. "I enjoy a challenge."

I tamped down my curiosity and returned to the problem at hand. "I could find a place out in the desert, work a little magic, see if he comes. Someplace far from town, far from the vortexes, far from people. If we can do a binding spell, great. It would have to be a very powerful one." I remembered the binding spell Mick had used on me to stop me in Las Vegas. That spell had been decently strong, but if I'd seen it coming, I knew I'd have been able to resist it. We needed something more powerful for Jim.

"I can do it," Cassandra said. "Give me a little time to prepare. But will you be able to take away what's animating him? If you can do that, he'll die of his own accord, his body responding to the natural force of death."

I grimaced. "I don't know. I don't know if Mick can either, or even whether Mick and I combined can do anything. My magic doesn't always come at will."

I wondered whether I could combine my storm magic with the Beneath magic to defeat Jim. Whether I could or not, that process would be contingent on having a powerful storm raging at the time. I couldn't count on the weather cooperating, and I couldn't count on my Beneath magic working perfectly either.

I pushed away from the counter. "I'm going to go scout a location."

Cassandra gave me a warning look. "Don't try *anything* until I can perfect a binding spell."

I agreed and left the hotel. I didn't bother telling Mick where I was going. I had picked up another shard of magic mirror from my bedroom nightstand, this one a little larger than the others. I reflected that maybe I shouldn't bother getting the mirror repaired at all. Having pieces of it to carry around was too useful.

I climbed the railroad bed and headed east of town, to the vortexes. Magellan had been built on an ancient crossroads, and the vanished tribes that had once populated this place had left petroglyphs that indicated its mystical energy. It had been no coincidence, Jamison had told me, that the railroad had been laid where it had, along a line of mystical energy, and no coincidence that the railway had gone broke and shut down.

The ties and rails had been stripped away decades ago, to leave a long, flat trail from Flat Mesa all the way to the southern end of town. I had no idea how far the bed went, not having explored that far yet.

On the other side of the railroad bed lay the vortexes. I had no intention of luring Jim out here. If he had godlike magic in him, I didn't want him throwing it around and maybe unlocking one of the gateways; no telling what would come out of one.

I'd come here for a different reason. I made my way down the other side of the railroad bed and climbed to the top of a rise. From here I had a good view of Magellan, the town strung out along the curving highway. Behind me, the desert stretched its emptiness to the horizon. A wash had once flowed at the bottom of the little hill I stood on, but no more. The sides of it had collapsed, and fallen trees lay encased in baked earth where the mud from a terrible storm had dried.

Mick and I had done this, destroyed the wash and sealed the vortex beneath it. I closed my eyes, calmed my mind, letting nothing but the sounds, scents, and feel of the place touch me.

I breathed clean air that bore only the scent of drying grasses and the pungent odor of juniper. Nothing more. No tingle of magic, no shiver of danger.

When I opened my eyes, I saw a crow hopping near my feet. It stopped and cocked a black eye at me.

"She's still trapped, isn't she?" I asked it.

The crow didn't answer. It half hopped, half walked in its ungainly way to the middle of the now-closed wash and pecked the ground with a haughty manner.

"Still trapped," I said with certainty. Whoever or whatever had brought Undead Jim back to life, it hadn't been my mother. That relieved me, but it also left open far too many possibilities.

When I turned around, Coyote was standing right behind me.

"Damn it, will you please stop doing that?"

Coyote regarded me with glittering dark eyes, no trace of his usual humor anywhere. "I told you, Janet, not to use the Beneath magic, ever again. Not for any reason."

Twenty-two

My smart-ass retort died in my mouth. Coyote had made me nervous before, but right now he looked terrifying. There was nothing in his eyes of the Coyote I knew, nothing but deep rage and vast power.

"I had to," I began. "The dragon—Bancroft—would have died. He couldn't heal himself."

"Then he should have died. It's the natural order of things. Dragons are mortal—they're hurt, they bleed, and they die."

"I didn't have a choice. First of all, I couldn't stand to see a creature die because of me; second, I needed to do something to keep Drake from killing me; and third, Bancroft seems more reasonable about this trial than the others. I couldn't risk not having him there."

"I see. You healed the dragon to save your boyfriend."

"Not just that. I saved Bancroft's life to save his life."

"Even when I told you not to use the magic?"

I regarded him with a courage I didn't have. "It was necessary."

"No, it wasn't. You don't get to choose who lives and who dies, Janet Begay."

"And you do?"

"I'm a god. One of the first gods. I've existed since the first world. Some consider me the embodiment of all that is evil, but I'm not. I'm just a god, and gods can be capricious."

No kidding. "I made the best decision I could given the circumstances."

"You went with your emotions, and you thought me far away, where I'd never know."

"But you did know."

A hint of a wicked glimmer returned to his eyes. "Your mirror put on a good show."

"Hell," I said.

"You're a beautiful woman, Janet. You're passionate, and you're in love. But you're human. Leave the god forces alone."

"But *am* I truly human? I was conceived by a woman possessed by a goddess, born to a man with Stormwalker magic in his family. My grandmother is powerful enough to project herself as a crow a couple hundred miles from home. I didn't ask to inherit both powers. I'd have been happy being plain Janet, one with a real mother and father, who found simple joy in walking the land."

"I once told you that we don't choose what we are," Coyote said. "We only choose what we do with what we've been given."

"And I chose to save the dragon's life. And to help Mick, and those people in Las Vegas. And I'll choose again to find that undead menace and stop him before he hurts anyone else."

Coyote gave me a thoughtful look. "You know, Janet, I feel about you the way you feel about Jim."

"No, there's one thing different," I said. "I don't want to have sex with Jim."

"Touché."

"Damn it, I wish you'd stop threatening me and *help* me. We've got to find this guy. Do you know where he is?"

"No. You plan to take away his life?"

"What choice do we have? If I thought he could control the magic in him, then it would be different, but I don't think there's much chance of that."

"Exactly."

The way he said the word made my heart squeeze in fear. But I knew that if I ran, Coyote would just catch me. He'd tumble me to the ground, and with one flick of his big paw, he'd kill me. Janet would be dust, floating away on the wind.

"Are you saying that if I give Jim a chance, you'll give me one?" I asked.

"I'm saying that I'm watching you, and that you don't have that many chances left."

I knew he meant it. Coyote held my life between his fingers, and all he had to do was snap them, and I'd be gone.

I closed my eyes. I thought of the voice that spoke within me every time the magic stirred, the evil it urged me to do. Could I stop the whispers? Could I somehow kill that part of my power and channel the rest to do what I bade it? Or would the Beneath magic simply consume me in the end? My mother was evil, and that evil was in me. Coyote, the dragons, my grandmother—none of them were wrong about that.

I heard voices, human ones, and opened my eyes, exhaling in relief. Naomi Kee and Jamison, with Julie between them, were climbing down the railroad bed to make their way toward us. Julie broke from her mother and started running with the long-legged, coltish lope of an eleven-year-old. She reached Coyote and threw her arms around him, and he spun her off her feet.

"Hello, Julie." Coyote's voice was gentleness itself as he set her down.

"Hello, Coyote." Julie both spoke and signed at the same time. "What are you doing way out here? Are you and Janet walking to Chevelon Canyon? That's where we're going. Can we come with you?"

I didn't really want to see Jamison, but he gave me a not-unfriendly nod when he and Naomi reached us. I wanted to hug him, to apologize over and over for what I'd done.

Coyote gave me a look over Julie's head that told me I'd passed some kind of test. "Sure, Julie," he said. "I'll come with you. But Janet, she has things she needs to do."

I took the hint. I stood back and watched as the three adults and Julie walked off into the desert, the sun haloing Julie as though she were a sacred being.

Mick was still with Colby when I reached the hotel again. I didn't want to listen to Colby going on about my prowess in bed, so I got on my bike and told Cassandra I was running errands. I really did have errands to run—I was behind on so much—but I used them as an excuse to get away from the things that unnerved me.

I had to either convince Coyote that I was in full control of my magic and would use it only when entirely necessary, or give in to what he wanted and stop using it altogether. I wasn't certain I could do either.

I stopped at the tourist board to arrange to have my new brochures displayed there. The office was about to close, the sun already setting, but I got in just in time. Then I visited the tiny suite behind the post office where a woman who printed cute maps for the tourists accepted my money to list my hotel on one of the maps. Advertising was a never-ending game.

I decided to grab some food at the diner, and that's where Assistant Chief Salas found me. Still in his police uniform, he slid into the booth with me and ordered coffee when the waitress brought my usual cheeseburger.

"So what's up with Maya?" he asked.

I lifted my brows and my cheeseburger at the same time. "She turned you down?"

"Yes."

"Sorry." I did feel bad for him, because Emilio was a nice guy. "She's still hung up on Nash. Give her time."

"No, I mean, I went to see her this afternoon, and she barely opened the door. She just said through the crack that she appreciated me asking her out, but she didn't want to go." Salas thanked the waitress for the coffee but toyed with the cup instead of drinking. "I only went over there to see if she was all right. You know, after the shit that went down last night."

"You mean when I got abducted? I'm fine; thanks for asking."

Salas's cheekbones stained red. "I know you're okay, Janet. Lopez told me Nash brought you home; plus you're pretty tough, and you have Mick looking out for you. Maya . . ."

"Is a delicate flower?" I grinned at him. "You have it bad, Emilio."

"I'm just worried about her. She looked like she hadn't slept at all, almost like she was sick. And she slammed the door in my face without even saying good-bye."

"She saw someone be sliced in half on her front lawn," I said. "Nash said she was pretty hysterical."

"I know." Salas leaned forward and spoke in a low voice. "And I hate to say this, but it kind of smelled in there. Like rotting food or something. That's not like Maya. She's usually so . . . *prolijo*. What is it in English? Fastidious."

I dropped my burger. Ketchup and grease splashed out and hit Salas's coffee cup, and he jumped. "You all right, Janet?"

"Yes, fine. I just remembered something I have to do. Finish the burger if you want it."

I slapped ten bucks on the table and hustled out of the diner, leaving Salas staring after me in concern.

Maya didn't live far from the diner, but I rode my bike the block or so through the darkening streets, making a lot of noise so she'd know I'd arrived. The shades were down over her front windows, though a light glowed behind one, the flowers in her little garden still smashed where Drake had stepped on them.

I went to the porch and knocked on the door. Maya didn't answer until I'd started knocking the third time. She switched on the porch light, opened the door about two inches, and looked out at me.

I saw what Salas had meant. Maya's face was pale and drawn, her dark eyes burning in sunken hollows. Her hair was a mess, her T-shirt stained with coffee. I couldn't see beyond her, but Salas had been right about the smell. It was not the stench of death, as I'd feared, but more like someone hadn't taken out the garbage in a while.

"Janet," she said in a clipped voice.

"Hey, Maya. I came to see if . . . if you still wanted to go shopping with me tomorrow."

Maya didn't blink. "No. Sorry, I'm too busy. I have a lot of cleaning up to do."

She opened the door another inch until I could see the kitchen sink piled with dishes. Far too many dishes for one person, even if she'd gone on a cooking spree.

Without turning her head, Maya flicked her gaze down the hall. She had two bedrooms back there, her own and one she used as a den and guest room. Both doors were closed.

"That's all right," I said loudly. "How about if you call me later?"

"My phone's still broken."

"Oh, yeah. Well, come over when you have time."

"Sure."

She started closing the door. I wished I could tell her something to reassure her, to make some gesture that I understood, but her life hung on a breath, and I didn't want to say or do the wrong thing.

I let her close the door, and I made myself walk calmly to my bike, put on my helmet, start the engine, and ride away. I rode steadily as I passed the diner, in case Salas was looking out the window. I didn't want him getting worried and hurrying down to Maya's house again.

Around the next curve was the gas station and Hansen's Garden Center. I pulled into the empty lot of the garden center and took out my cell phone. When I reached the Hopi County Sheriff's Department, Lopez told me, amazingly, that Nash had gone home to sleep.

"Anything I can do for you, Janet?" Lopez asked.

My heart hammered as I dithered. If I behaved as though this was the emergency it was, Lopez would send cars down and alert the Magellan police. If that happened, who knew what kind of chaos would erupt? One thing was certain—Maya would be the first to die. This had to be dealt with quietly.

"No," I said. "I just wanted to ask him a question."

"All right, good night." Lopez hung up.

I parked and walked around the garden center and through Naomi's backyard, which abutted it. Jamison's studio was locked, Jamison nowhere in sight. Julie answered the back door with delight, and Naomi greeted me from the kitchen. Jamison was there, leaning on the breakfast bar, watching Naomi cook. If I hadn't been so panicked, I would have enjoyed soaking up the coziness.

Julie started telling me about the walk they'd taken with Coyote and the petroglyphs he'd showed them: whirling stars, strange-looking men, and what he'd said were coyotes. Naomi sensed my hurry and told Julie to save the stories until I could stay longer. She didn't have Nash's number, she said, but she gave me directions to his house in Flat Mesa.

I could tell that Naomi and Jamison were curious, but my dear friends didn't ask. For that I'd return and let Julie talk to me for hours about anything she wanted.

My hands sweated inside my gloves as I drove through the rest of Magellan at precisely thirty-five miles per hour. The stars were out by the time I hit the town limits, and I opened it up on the road to Flat Mesa.

Sheriff Jones lived in a modest neighborhood in a house built about a century ago. It was one-story, long and low, with a porch that ran the length of the front of the house. The peaked roof had been built to let the winter snow slide from it and also to cast deep shade over the porch in summer.

Nash's sheriff's SUV was parked in the driveway, and

I remembered that he'd not yet recovered his new pickup stolen in Death Valley. It was probably in Mexico by now, and unrecognizable.

Nash came to the door in sweatpants and a sweat-soaked gray T-shirt. He had a bottle of water in one hand and a towel in the other, and did not look happy to see me.

"Let me in," I said in a calm voice. "Close the door, and keep your voice down."

Nash's lips pinched, but he did as I asked. Even Nash could be perceptive.

He closed the door behind me and locked it. Nash's house was very much a bachelor's—his living room held an all-in-one weight machine and not much else, and one stool was drawn up to a breakfast bar. His reading material, stacked neatly on the breakfast bar, was magazines, mostly about guns. Nash's own gun was nowhere in sight; being Nash, I had no doubt he kept it responsibly locked away.

Nash drank some water and wiped his face with the end of the towel. "What?"

"I know where Jim Mohan is."

Nash froze, the towel at his face. "Where? Tell me now."

"He's at Maya's."

Nash stared at me for a stunned moment, his pupils dilating to darken his light gray eyes. Then he exploded past me, and it was all I could do to get to the door before he did.

Twenty-three

Nash was damn strong, but I was desperate enough to jam my hands against the doorframe and resist his attempts to charge out of the house.

"Nash, no! If you go running in there, he'll kill her. He will even if he doesn't mean to."

Nash stared at me in fury, but I saw his instinctive rage recede and terrible fear take over. He swung back into his living room and slammed his fist onto his exercise machine. Metal cracked.

Shaking out his hand, Nash strode swiftly down a long hallway that ran behind his living room. I caught up to him in a small, dark room with a gun safe. Nash removed his nine-millimeter from it and slapped in a magazine.

"Nash!"

"He won't hurt her if I kill him first."

I blocked his exit. "Jim is already dead. If two men

pummeling him with bullets didn't take him down, that little gun won't either. I don't care how accurate you are."

From the look Nash gave me, I was surprised he didn't shoot me then and there. He'd happily step over my dying body and race off to save the woman he loved.

"All right," he said, his jaw rigid. "All right. Damn it." Nash snatched up a shoulder holster and buckled it on, jamming the gun inside it. "I have to believe you. This guy can rip people inside out; I've seen that. What can we do against him?"

"*We* can't. I can. But there's a reason I came to get you."

"Because I can absorb and negate magic."

I nodded. "You are the only one who might be able to take his attack and survive."

Nash's mouth tightened. "And he's in there with Maya."

I no longer needed to ask whether Nash cared for Maya. It was in his eyes and in every line of him, the terror that she'd be hurt, killed, no longer in his life.

He pulled out and loaded another pistol and tucked it into a second shoulder holster. Nash's gun cabinet held about ten handguns, all neatly lined up in their cases. He didn't offer one to me.

Nash locked the cabinet, and we left his house for his SUV. His radio crackled when he turned it on, a deputy calling in from a remote area of the county to report not much of anything. Nash didn't answer. I think he understood as much as I did why he and I were the only ones who could go to Maya's rescue. Anyone else was a potential casualty and would increase the risk to Maya's life.

We rode in silence through the darkened back streets of Flat Mesa, avoiding the sheriff's department. Nash floored it on the highway between the towns, the first time I'd ever seen him break the speed limit. It was fifty-five on this narrow road, and Nash pushed it to eighty and ninety, eating up the miles in a matter of minutes.

He slowed to legal speed as we passed my hotel, not wanting to draw attention, and continued this way all the way to Maya's. Nash drove through the alley behind the houses and parked in front of a vacant lot.

Maya's street was dark, the back neighborhoods of Magellan having few streetlights. Nash and I crept quietly through Maya's unfenced yard, going slowly in the darkness. Maya had a little porch in the back with lawn chairs for warm days. Hummingbird feeders hung at intervals, all filled.

French doors led to Maya's bedroom, but they were locked, the blinds drawn so we couldn't see in. I didn't sense any wards around the windows—but then, Jim was human; he wouldn't know how to ward a house. He counted on his god magic to keep Maya penned in and others out. The moment I tried to use magic to unlock the doors, Jim would know it.

I was pondering how we'd get in without alerting Jim or Maya, when Nash pulled out a key.

I filed that fact away to think about later. Nash quietly slipped the key in the lock and turned it. He had his gun out, ready, as he quickly pushed open the door and stepped sideways into the room. I copied his movements, ducking in behind him.

The room was empty. If a magic barrier *had* existed to keep out the magically inclined, Nash would have just negated it.

Nash moved soundlessly to the closed bedroom door, listened, and eased the door open.

"Maya!" a man called from the second bedroom. "Bring me more coffee."

"I'm all out," Maya said. "I have to go get some."

"You are not leaving this house." Jim's voice took on a note of panic, and he flung open the second bedroom's door.

Jim looked the same as he ever had, tall and thin, a face neither handsome nor ugly, brown hair and brown eyes. A plain, ordinary man. He stepped out of the room and found himself facing the barrel of Nash's gun.

Jim stopped. For one frozen, soundless moment Jim stared at Nash and me, and we stared back at Jim. Then he threw magic at us.

Jim had grown in strength and skill. His ball of magic hit Nash full in the chest, the impact sending Nash crashing into the wall. But Nash didn't fall down dead, as he was supposed to. A wave of magic emerged from Nash's back as he staggered upright; then the magic slammed back into him, dissipated, and was gone.

Jim's eyes widened. "Holy shit. How'd he do that?"

Maya appeared at the end of the hallway. "Nash? What the hell?"

I stepped past Nash and shoved Maya back into the living room. "Get out," I said. I fumbled with the locks of the front door, pushed it open. "Run."

"This is my *house*!"

"If you want to live in it some more, run now. Go!"

Maya cast an anguished look down the hall. "Nash," she cried. "I love you!" Tears on her face, she ran out the door.

"No!" Jim shouted. He tried to blast Maya with a wave of magic, but Nash got in his way. Once again Nash's body absorbed the magic, but Nash drew a sharp breath with the impact. I wondered how much of Jim's power he'd be able to take before he was spent.

"You don't deserve her," Jim snarled at him. "A fine girl like that, and you ignore her."

Nash's lips were white. "If you touched her, I will twist your head from your body and kick it down the street."

"She's hung up on you, man. I tried to persuade her to drop you, but she won't."

"What do you want?" I asked Jim.

Nash wouldn't put down his damn gun. I knew bullets wouldn't hurt Jim, but Nash probably felt more comfortable with the heaviness of a weapon in his hands.

Jim faced me. "What do you mean, what do *I* want?"

Magic burned inside me, needing release. The magic urged me to crush Jim, end of problem.

But Coyote was right—if I did that, I'd be no different from Jim. I realized that Coyote could have killed me long ago, when the Beneath magic first manifested in me—no, he could have killed me at birth, or whenever he'd realized that my mother had successfully made a child. But Coyote had given me a chance, many chances. I had to step back and do the same with Jim.

"When you came here, you were looking to get rich," I said. "You'd steal a few old pots, sell them for big money on the black market. But that got you killed, and you aren't interested in pot hunting anymore. So, what are you interested in?"

Jim shrugged. "Figuring out what happened to me."

"Then why take Maya hostage?"

"I didn't take her hostage. I just needed a place to crash where no one was trying to shoot me. You all ran off and left her alone last night, and I needed to heal."

"You've killed three people," I pointed out.

"I didn't mean to."

"But you did it," Nash said. "And you'll answer for it."

"What about the guy who killed *me*? Will he answer for it?"

"Yes," Nash said in a steady voice.

"What about whoever brought me back to life? Made me a killing machine? What happens to her? It's not my fault."

"Her?" I asked. "Why do you say *her*?"

"Because it was a her. I thought it was you."

Not me, not my mother. Then who? Cassandra? I chilled. No, couldn't be. She'd been as amazed as I was when she'd seen the vision of Jim's resurrection.

"Well, it wasn't me." I buried my speculations, but I would remember the clue. "You have to control this magic. You're hurting people who never did anything to you."

"What about the man who tried to shove you into that limo at gunpoint? I was trying to save you. And that guy in the hotel in Las Vegas—he wanted to rape you and Maya. Was I supposed to let that go? You're my only friends."

The fact that he described me and Maya as his friends made me slightly sick. "We'd already gotten away from the guy in Las Vegas. Security would have found him and taken care of him."

"He tried to hurt you," Jim argued. "I couldn't let that go."

"Damn it, why are you so determined to be my avenging angel?"

"Avenging angel. I like that. Because you're like me, and they're trying to kill you too. I thought you made me . . ."

"At the time of your death and resurrection in Homol'ovi, I was in Death Valley with Nash and Mick. Nowhere near you."

He didn't look convinced. "Maybe I was brought back for a reason."

"No," I said. "It was a mistake."

Jim's face darkened. "How the hell do you know that?"

"Because no human can handle the magic that was dumped into you. I don't know why whoever it was, whatever god it was, decided to bring you back to life, but they should never have. You're not even bothering to control yourself."

"I did at first. It scared me, and I'm sorry about the hiker. I really was trying to help him. The others—they deserved it."

"No one deserves that."

"No?" Jim lifted his brows. "So what are you going to do about it?"

"If you can control the magic, if you stop hurting people with it, maybe I can help you." Coyote might not let him off so easy, but Jim didn't need to know that. I just wanted him out of Maya's house.

"While he's in prison," Nash said tightly. "He's killed three people."

Jim smiled. "I'm not going to prison, Sheriff. I'm staying here with Maya. She'll come back. She likes me."

Nash's finger moved on the trigger.

"Take some advice," I said quickly to Jim. "If you want to live a peaceful, happy life, don't piss off Nash Jones."

"Screw Nash Jones," Jim said, and he blasted both of us with magic.

Nash shot him. The bullet went right into Jim's brain, and he flinched, but he didn't fall or stop. Nothing showed he'd been shot but a small, red hole in the side of his head.

You don't have to take this.

At the same time my little voice spoke, I raised a shield of white light between me and Jim. I could kill him. I had the power. Days ago, at the club in Las Vegas, I could barely fend him off. Today, I knew exactly what to do.

"Jim," I said. "Stop."

Jim's eyes widened when his power couldn't break through my barrier. He stared at me through it for a second, and then he swung around and ran for his bedroom window.

Nash shot him again, plugging him at the base of the spine. Jim threw open the window and dove through it as though he didn't feel a thing.

Swearing, Nash ran back through Maya's bedroom and out the French doors. I rushed to the window in Jim's bedroom and slid my slim body through it.

Jim found himself caught between the two of us. He gave us a wild look before bolting through the neighbors' side yard. Nash went right after him, me coming behind. Jim ran between houses, dodging garden sheds, kids' toys, and barking dogs. He hit the edge of the neighborhood and kept running out into the desert.

His runner's body made him fast, and the magic made him strong. But Nash had stamina. He kept a flat-out pace, as tired as he must be. I felt like crap, but my magic was awake and excited and propelled me along.

Jim scrambled over the railroad bed and headed for the vortexes. Shit. If he started using god-magic around them, he might open one and let out who knew what. The last thing the world needed was my mother emerging to go on a rampage.

The sky was beautifully clear, the moon so bright it was like an incandescent light. The moonlight outlined Jim against the dark desert, and Nash took a few more shots at him. Not that it did any good.

Jim kept running. I was panting, lagging, realizing I needed to get into better shape. I saw Jim disappear into the earth, Nash after him. Heart hammering, I made it to where they'd vanished and realized they'd jumped not into a vortex but down into the canyon that housed Chevelon Creek. The walls were steep, the bottom wide and rocky, the flat edges of the creek itself thick with scrub seeking water.

Nash had Jim cornered against the rock wall on the other side of the canyon. I jogged through weeds and water until I caught up to them.

"Leave me alone," Jim said. His face was wan in the moonlight, his body full of bullet holes, sagging against the rock. "I'll go somewhere else, never bother you again."

"We can't let you go." I rested my hands on my thighs, trying to catch my breath. "You know we can't. You're too dangerous. You have to learn control."

"Like you do?" Jim asked with a sneer. "You can't control your magic either."

I shook my head, straightening up. "But I'm willing to learn. Willing not to use it at all."

"But you have to use it, if you're going to stop me. A dilemma, isn't it?"

At that moment, I hated Jim, hated Coyote for making me so scared of him and myself, and hated my mother for bestowing this magic on me at all. The Beneath magic had given me nothing but trouble since the moment I'd first felt it stir.

Just kill him, my voice said.

"No. I won't. I'll find another way."

"You can't." Jim sounded smug. "No one is strong enough to kill me but you. I'm going."

"Like hell you are," Nash said.

"And how do you intend to stop me?"

Nash glanced upward. "With them."

I jerked my gaze to where he pointed. Four giant beasts

filled the sky, and they were angling toward our position. Four jets of dragon flame burst into the night, the dragons winging in to solve the problem.

I breathed a sigh of relief. I would be spared the decision. Coyote couldn't blame *me* if Mick led three dragons in formation to eliminate the deadly undead. I suddenly loved Mick very, very much.

The dragons came on, the black bulk of Mick in front. Streams of dragon fire met and meshed, becoming one single flame that arrowed toward Jim. I watched the bright fire, mesmerized, until Nash grabbed me and yanked me out of the way.

We landed ankle-deep in the creek as all four flames shot into Jim. Jim shouted and flailed, looking like a man made of fire, his screams horrible. I watched, unable to look away, as Jim's skin melted, draining away to the earth.

Nash still held me, the butt of his gun pressed into my stomach. I knew even then that I could have saved Jim. I was powerful enough to do it. I could have damped the dragon fire and let him live, but I chose to stand with Nash and watch Jim die.

Except that he didn't die. The flames started to dim, although the dragons continued to pour them on. The fire and smoke dampened more and more until I could see that Jim was grabbing the flames into his own hands, squishing them down into a smaller and smaller ball. The thing glowed like a dwarf star that longed to be a supernova.

I shouted. I fought my away out of Nash's hold and charged at Jim just as he released the fire back into the air.

The dragons shrieked and broke apart. Mick streamed past me, his black hide gleaming in the moonlight as the four dragons regrouped and re-formed. They streaked again toward Jim, faster and faster, flaming him a split second before they reached him.

This time, Jim was ready for them. The dragon flames burst against a wall of nothing, while Jim, burned and blackened, hid behind the wall and sucked the dispersed dragon fire into his hands. As the dragons rolled away and climbed to the sky again, Jim hurled the fire back at them.

The flames caught a red dragon on the tail. He screeched and sailed downward, landing somewhere out in the darkness. Mick soared over the spot where his comrade had fallen, and then he turned back to the canyon and came at Jim like a bullet from a gun.

Mick was furious. I read it in the tight line of his huge body, in his intense speed, in the red of his eyes as he zoomed between the canyon walls. He went for Jim with his mouth open, ready to finish this in the dragon way—with one bite.

Jim gathered every bit of god-magic in him and threw it at Mick.

Nash tried to jump in the way, to take it, but Mick was coming too fast. Mick's talon batted Nash out of the way, and the white light grabbed Mick full force. The magic carried Mick up and up, higher and higher. Desperately, I threw my own magic at him, and Jim and I had a wrestling match for Mick's dragon body while it hung in midair.

The forces of our fight rippled through the darkness, expanding the air until a sonic boom floated over the desert. Mick was being torn apart. He was screaming and writhing, trying to escape the both of us. I had to let go, but if I did . . .

Gasping, I snapped my magic from Mick and threw it directly at Jim. Jim collapsed.

But the second before his magic winked out, Jim gave

a twist of his hand. Mick's body wrenched in two different directions at once. I heard the crunch of bones and cartilage, two hundred feet above me. Then Jim's magic vanished, and Mick plummeted to the ground.

I tried to grab Mick, to cushion his fall, but he hit hard. The ground shook as Mick's huge dragon body landed at the top of the canyon wall, the impact cascading boulders and gravel into the creek.

I was racing to Mick, scrambling up the side of the canyon, stumbling and falling, racked with sobs. Dragons touched down around me as I reached the top, became human. The smaller red that had gotten burned was Colby; the other black, Drake, the large red orange, Bancroft. They converged around Mick as he lay motionless in the darkness. Mick opened one huge silver and black eye, which flickered with flame and then started to film over.

The dragons surrounded him. Air shimmered. Mick shifted from dragon into the naked and limp human body of the man I loved and sought me with eyes that could no longer see. I threw myself on my knees next to him, where I could touch his hair, kiss his face, let him know I was there.

His smiled at me with a hint of his bad-boy smile. "Sorry, baby," he whispered.

"Mick." My voice grated, barely working.

The other dragons circled around us. Colby was inked all over, only his hands, feet, and face free of tattoos. Drake's dragon tattoo covered his back with a wing down each arm. Bancroft, older, had more modest tattoos, like Mick, dragons encircling his biceps and flowing upward around his neck. I gazed at them all through my tears.

"Help him," I said.

Bancroft put a gentle hand on my back. "He's too far gone. There's nothing to be done."

"He can turn back into a dragon. That will save him, right?"

Colby answered, his gravelly voice somber. "It's too late, Janet. If that would have helped, he'd have stayed dragon."

"You don't want to help him," I said. "You all want him dead."

They didn't contradict me, and my anger flowed anew. I was about to scream at them when I saw movement out of the corner of my eye. A large coyote was bounding toward us, his body surrounded by a blue nimbus.

He became the man Coyote as he stopped and looked down at Mick with profound sorrow.

"Janet," he said, his dark eyes filled with sadness. For me, for Mick. "I'm so sorry."

"Don't be sorry. Help him! You can bring him back to life. I've seen you do it."

"Mick is mortal," Coyote said. "I told you. You can't change someone's time to die."

I couldn't believe this. My lover was dying, and the most powerful men I'd ever met were standing around shaking their heads and feeling sorry for me. I flung myself away from Coyote just as I heard more shots in the canyon.

Don't let him get away, my voice said.

I sprinted for the edge of the canyon. Coyote in coyote form bounded after me, planted himself in front of me, and snarled.

"Fuck you!" I screamed. I shoved Coyote aside. It didn't even hurt.

As I scrambled to the bottom, Nash was shooting frantically at Jim, who was racing down the creek, splashing water as he ran. I reached out with my magic, lassoed Jim around the middle, and jerked him to a halt.

Jim looked horrible, half his skin burned away, his body a bloody mess. Bone poked through his melted flesh, and still he faced me, his burned mouth forming a parody of a smile.

Never piss off a Stormwalker who's been filled with the power of the gods.

"Jim," I said. I held up my hand. A small ball of white light hovered above my palm.

"Janet, no," Coyote, human again, growled. The command was clear.

"This is your life," I said to Jim, pointing at the silver white ball. "And now, it's over."

I pinched the ball between my thumb and forefinger. It went out like a spark, and Undead Jim died.

Twenty-four

Coyote blasted me with magic. I should have died on the spot, but Nash stepped between him and me and took the brunt of Coyote's power.

Damned if Nash didn't absorb it all, the full magic of a powerful god like Coyote. Coyote's eyes widened in surprise as Nash sucked the blue light into his body until the magic flickered out and disappeared.

At least Nash was breathing hard this time. "Is that all you've got?" he asked.

"Well, fuck me," Coyote whispered.

Jim was dead. Unmistakably, irrevocably dead. The pile of his bones lay motionlessly in a few inches of water, his skin half-rotted, the decomposition that should have started days ago finally catching up to him.

I'd killed him. And if I had to do it all over again, I would.

Still, I kept Nash between myself and Coyote, just in case. I glared at Coyote. "Save Mick."

"Janet . . ."

I knew my eyes were ice green without looking into a mirror. "Save him. All-powerful god, can't you even heal a dragon?"

"It's too late." Coyote's voice was so damn calm it made me livid.

"No, it isn't. And if you can't, I will."

Coyote took a step toward me, but Nash remained planted in his way, a firm, protective wall.

"Look at him." Coyote pointed an angry finger at Jim's remains. "Mick would become as Jim was. Is that what you want?"

"Whoever resurrected Jim didn't know what they were doing," I said. "They gave him life, animation, but not a soul. I know how to restore Mick completely."

Coyote's eyes narrowed. "No mortal knows how to bestow a soul. Only the gods can do that."

"You'd better start learning what mortals can do, Trickster. Especially *this* mortal. I'm the daughter of a goddess; why shouldn't I have a goddess's power?"

"Because if you use it, she will have won."

Something cold burned in my stomach, fear churning with dread. "It's worth it. Worth it to save Mick."

"Janet," Nash said. "You know that you're acting more crazy than you normally do, right?"

I switched my green gaze to Nash. "My mother wanted me to mate with you. To create a child that combined my power and yours, because she said that such a child would be unstoppable. I understand what she meant now. You're infused with more power than any of us put together."

"Good." Nash clearly didn't know what the hell I was

talking about, but that didn't matter. "Then let's go help Mick."

He took my hand, and we started climbing out of the canyon. Coyote watched us go, neither interfering nor helping. Just watching. He was letting me make my choice.

Nash and I pulled each other through dirt and rock. I was so tired I could barely move, and Nash was shaky also. When we scrambled over the top, we walked to the dragons who encircled Mick's motionless body.

When I saw Mick, my heart broke all over again. His human limbs were askew, his chest no longer rising with breath. He stared at nothing, his black hair flowing over his lifeless face.

I dropped to my knees beside him and lifted his head into my lap. I smoothed his wild hair from the face I loved so much, the mouth I'd kissed so many times. "Mick, do you trust me?"

Colby moved behind me, his voice subdued for the first time since I'd met him. "Janet, he's dead."

"He will have a dragon funeral," Bancroft said. "With full honors."

"Screw that," I said. "He's coming home with me."

"Stop her," Drake growled. I flung the smallest amount of magic at him, and Drake froze in his tracks.

I touched Mick's face again. What I had to do was complicated, requiring great stillness within myself. My thoughts had to be orderly and straight. One wrong word, one wrong syllable, and Mick would be lost, beyond saving, or else messed up like Jim.

Nash knelt on Mick's other side. He'd holstered both his pistols, and he looked at me in grave sympathy. "What do you want me to do?"

"Keep them off me."

Nash got to his feet and walked toward the three dragons, arms out, like a police officer keeping a crowd from a crime scene. "Stand back, gentlemen. Let her work."

"What she's doing violates every law of life and death," Bancroft said. "This is why we sent Mick to kill her in the first place."

"Mick is my friend," Nash answered. "I have to let her help him."

I was touched by Nash's compassion. I also didn't know what the hell I was doing. I closed my eyes and tried to look inside myself, as Jamison had wanted me to. He'd wanted me to find my two natures, to observe them, to learn about them, to make them play nicely together.

I wished I was better at meditation. I knew I needed to focus on something specific—a sound, a string of words, my breathing. But all I heard was buzzing in my ears, I couldn't think of a mantra to say to myself, and my breathing was all over the place.

It's simple, the magic said. *Push the puny Stormwalker power out, and let this one take over. You can do anything. Remember what it felt like when you were Beneath.*

That experience had been heady. When I'd been Beneath and wanted something to happen, it just happened. I had but to say a word.

And you don't even really need the word.

Being a Stormwalker is what I am. The storms drive me crazy, but if I couldn't ride them, who would I be?

A damn powerful hell-goddess, the magic answered.

A hell-goddess who has arguments with herself. Both magics are part of me. I'm not all one or the other.

You can't save Mick with the storm magic.

Why not? Storm magic makes dragons even stronger.

Because there's no storm, you simple-minded bitch!

Well, that was true. The night was cloudless, cold, crisp.

Watch who you're calling a bitch, I thought grumpily. *You want to rule me, to take over and use me to work your own will. Well, I'm not letting you. Wimpy Janet doesn't live here anymore.*

You must embrace the goddess power entirely, or you'll never be able to save Mick.

Wanna bet?

For just an instant, I felt the other voice waver. Then it went on.

Forget about Mick. He's weak. The other dragon, Drake, has a nice body, and he'd make a good slave. Or the human, Nash. You know you want him in bed with you. Just to see what it would be like.

A vision took me. Mick gone, ashes scattered, Nash consoling me. His mouth on mine. Me on top of him on the exercise machine in his long, low house.

Then I thought of the way he usually looked at me—in vast irritation. I thought about Maya, the look on her face when she'd called down the hall tonight: *Nash, I love you.*

The vision fled. *Not likely.*

You won't be able to save Mick. Not by yourself.

I had the feeling the voice was right. But talking to it let me start to separate it from the Stormwalker within me. The feeling of each magic was different. The Beneath power was bright, sharp, brittle. The storm power smelled like damp, clean earth; it was thick, substantial, solid, and strong. The Beneath power came and went, but the Stormwalker power was always there, centering me.

I touched both, marveling at the difference. If I wound them together, grounding myself with the Stormwalker magic while wielding the Beneath magic like a sword, I could do this. I could do anything.

I drew a breath. With my feet I reached for the earth, for the core that bound the world together. With my hands I reached for the Beneath magic. I twined the darkness of the storm power with the brightness of Beneath, and twisted it into something that sparkled like black onyx.

Beneath my fingers, Mick twitched.

At the same time, all the breath was abruptly squeezed out of me. My storm power and the Beneath power squeaked like the magic mirror when it was scared, and both vanished. I opened my eyes, weak, sick, and suddenly magicless.

Cassandra stood not far from me, protected by Drake and Colby. She wore a business skirt suit, which looked ridiculous out here in the middle of dust, rocks, and scrub. Pamela stood behind her, arms folded.

Cassandra's glowing hands were pressed together while she chanted words I didn't understand. I knelt beside Mick, rigid, unable to move.

The binding spell. Cassandra had been working on one to weave around Jim, except now she'd decided to work it on me. And it was so damned powerful that my own magic, both Stormwalker and Beneath, hid behind me and whimpered.

The dragons stood back and let her work. I saw Coyote at the lip of the canyon in his coyote form, simply watching.

Beyond the dragons, Maya Medina's red truck threw up dirt as it spun to a halt, and Maya leapt out of it. She ran toward us, slipping and stumbling on gravel. Nash met her halfway, and she flung her arms around his neck.

It should have been a beautiful moment. Nash held Maya tight, tight, lifting her from her feet, holding her close. When Maya raised her head to look at him, he cupped one hand around her face and kissed her.

My attention was dragged from them by the sound of

wings. Not leather dragon wings, but feathered wings. I expected the crow, but there was too much noise for just one bird.

I couldn't look around, couldn't speak. The binding spell certainly wouldn't allow me to talk. So many mages commanded words of power, could destroy their enemies in two or three syllables. A smart witch would include speech suppression in her binding spell, and Cassandra was so very smart.

When the winged beings surrounded me, I nearly screamed in spite of the spell. I couldn't, of course, and so the sound plunged back down my gullet and rested like a rock in my stomach.

They were men with masks painted in patterns of red, turquoise, white, black, and yellow. They wore loincloths and soft boots, and their winged bodies were painted as well. These were the kachinas, the real ones, gods not very happy with one small Navajo woman.

They surrounded me, cutting off my vision from my friends, my enemies, and my lover. I couldn't tell whether the shudder I'd felt in Mick was the magic working or just a residual spark of his own life force.

I'd never know. The kachinas whirled around me until I could see nothing but feathery wings, and then the desert and the night vanished. I found myself in a small, enclosed space, in the dark, and utterly alone.

There's nothing like being walled in a living tomb to make you appreciate the small things in life.

I sat on cold stone, and cold stone surrounded me. I could stand up and walk a few feet from wall to wall, but sharp pebbles littered the floor, making footing treacherous. After I'd fallen and cut my hands a few times, I decided it was safer to just sit.

I wiped my hands on my shirt and toyed with the pebble I'd picked up. It was light but sharp—lava rock. My tired mind told me that the kachinas dwelled in the San Francisco mountains, which Navajo call the *Diichilí Dzil* and the Hopi call *Navatekiaoui*. The San Francisco Peaks were extinct volcanoes, the cinder cone of Sunset Crater and the lava tubes around it reminders of that fact.

Was I there, under those mountains? Or in another world entirely? Would the kachinas have risked taking me to their spirit world? Or had they simply walled me in here and left me to starve to death?

Strangely, I didn't panic. The room was dark and cool but not freezing, and I had air. I couldn't feel any breeze, but the air wasn't stale and I didn't struggle to breathe, so I figured oxygen got to me from somewhere.

It was calm here after the crazy fight with Jim, after fighting, terrified, against the stasis spell. In here I was alone, dirty, sore, tired, and trapped—but at least I was safe.

Needless to say, my cell phone didn't work, not even to tell me the time. I was surprised it had survived intact. I had the habit of being hard on cell phones.

I pulled out the chamois bag I kept the mirror in and pulled out the shard. Even in the absolute darkness, the mirror glinted with a spark of its own.

"So, where am I?" I asked it.

"Haven't the faintest idea, sugar. It's dark."

"Well, thank the gods you were here to tell me that. Your best guess, then? How far am I from Magellan?"

"I don't know. Distance means nothing to me."

I refrained from putting the shard under my boot heel and grinding it to powder. "Will you at least give me some light?"

"That I *can* do. Coming right up, sweetie."

The mirror glowed, the white light stabbing into my dark-accustomed eyes. I snapped my eyelids shut and then opened them a fraction of an inch at a time.

The pale light revealed what I'd guessed—I was in a small, cavelike room with no entrance anywhere to be seen. The floor was littered with black lava rock and glittering Apache tears, which were translucent obsidian stones. I picked up one of the Apache tears, liking how I could hold it to my eye and see the light through it.

"Where is everyone?" I asked the mirror. "What is happening at the hotel?" I avoided the question I most wanted to ask, but the mirror caught on.

"I don't know whether Micky's all right, honey. If he were the only mage I answered to, I'd know, because I'd go dark if he were dead. But I answer to you too, so I'm still here, and I can't tell."

Pain lanced my heart. "Can you just show me the hotel?" I asked.

The shard of mirror clouded for a few seconds, and when it cleared, I looked through a spiderweb of cracks into the saloon of my hotel. The room was dark, the chairs up on the tables, the place closed.

I was about to tell the mirror not to bother when Cassandra walked in, took down a chair, and sank into it, resting her head in her hands. Cassandra, whose damned binding spell had landed me here.

Another figure followed her: Pamela, tall and strong in jeans and sleeveless shirt. She stood behind Cassandra and put her hands on her shoulders.

"It wasn't your fault, sweetheart," Pamela said. "You were trying to help."

"No, I was trying to stop her from using the magic. I

didn't know they were going to take her. How do I know she's even alive? My locator spells haven't worked. They're being blocked." She laughed a little. "Gods can do that, you know."

Pamela softly kneaded Cassandra's shoulders. "I didn't realize Janet was that special to you."

"She gave me a chance without question, never pries about my past. She's given me what I need, a place to lick my wounds and be alone."

"Is that what you need? To be alone?"

"I thought so when I first came here." Cassandra laid her hand over one of Pamela's. "Not so sure now."

Pamela leaned down, sliding her arms all the way around Cassandra. "We'll find her. That was some damn powerful magic you did out there. You'll work some more."

Cassandra looked miserable. "I don't know if I can. I'm so tired."

I'd never seen Cassandra anything but calm and cool, always knowing exactly what to do. Now she raised a tear-streaked face to Pamela, and Pamela bent and kissed her lips.

"Turn it off," I told the mirror. "Leave them alone."

"No way, sugar pie. Those two ladies are *hot*."

I put my hand over the glass. "What is it with your obsession with sex?"

"I'm a mirror. I can only be a voyeur, so I have to go for it."

"Will you get their attention? When they're ready; don't rush."

"Hang on, they're coming up for air."

When Cassandra's face filled the broken mirror, I let go of my anger at her. Her eyes were red and anxious, her usually sleek hair in tangles, her makeup smeared by tears.

"Janet? Where are you?" She peered into the mirror, but I could tell she saw only her own reflection, not me.

She was magical enough to hear me, though. "I was hoping you could tell me," I said.

"My locator spells won't work. They fizzle out. Sheriff Jones tried to activate the GPS on your phone, but that didn't work either."

"I'm somewhere underground. Probably too deep for satellites or phone signals. It's lava, though. An old volcano. That should narrow it down to a few hundred places in the world."

"Keep the mirror going," Cassandra suggested. "Maybe my spells will work through that."

"Worth a try." My matter-of-fact, brave tone faltered. "Mick?"

The lines on Cassandra's face deepened. "I don't know. The dragons took him away. Janet, I'm sorry. I think he's gone."

I thought he was too. I remembered the film over his eyes, the last breath he drew when he smiled at me and said, *Sorry, baby.* I put my hand over my mouth, stifling a sob.

"Janet?" Cassandra kept trying to find me in the mirror. "You all right?"

I wiped my eyes. "I'll keep the mirror out, and you keep trying those spells."

"I will." She turned away and started talking rapidly to Pamela as the two of them moved out of sight.

I drew my feet up and hugged my knees. I couldn't concentrate anymore on trying to figure out where I was; I didn't try to wake up my magic that seemed to have gone dormant; I stopped worrying about how I was going to get out.

I could only think about Mick.

Memories are most vivid when there is nothing else to interfere with them. Perhaps that's why the very old remember their younger years so well while forgetting the monotonous drone of their current, day-to-day existence.

I remembered the first night I'd made love with Mick, how he'd surprised me with his gentleness. He'd been patient with an inexperienced young woman, never hurrying me, never laughing at me. He'd introduced me to the astonishing pleasure that could be found in bed, and I'd fallen hard and fast in love with him.

I thought of his smile, the one that said he was a wicked man who wanted to do naughty things with me. I thought of his blue eyes that could turn black when he was angry or aroused, his crazy hair that would never stay put. Any suggestion he cut his shoulder-length hair so he wouldn't have to bother with it was met with an amazed stare. Maybe when he switched from dragon, that's just the way his hair went. I'd noted that the other dragons—Colby, Bancroft, Drake—wore their hair long too.

My mind dredged up the halcyon days after we'd first met, when Mick and I traveled up and down the country. They'd been the happiest of my life. I remembered standing on a rocky promontory overlooking the northern Pacific, wind buffeting my body while Mick stood rock-solid behind me. He'd held on to me, and I'd basked in his warmth while we watched the beauty of the cold sea. We'd gone from there up and down the country, gradually making our way across. We rode for miles during the day, stayed in motels at night. We laughed, talked, fought, made up, and made love.

I remembered my astonishment when I found out Mick was a dragon. I'd been blind to it before that, because I

hadn't known that dragons existed at all. Skinwalkers,
Nightwalkers, magic mirrors, yes. Dragons, no.

My world had changed that night, and it had changed
again tonight. I'd walked away from Mick a little over five
years ago because I'd been young and afraid, but somehow
I'd never thought of him as completely out of my life. And
he hadn't been; I just hadn't been able to see him.

The memories flew at me faster and faster, until my
emotions were all twisted around, and I couldn't stop crying. Who gave a damn about the magic inside me, when
Mick was dead because of it?

I heard a tiny noise, the barest click of rock on rock. I
opened my eyes, and through my tears saw the Koshare sitting on a boulder opposite me, the light of the magic mirror
between us.

Twenty-five

"Haven't you tortured me enough?" My voice came out a harsh croak. "I thought clowns were supposed to make people laugh."

He sat still, his god power filling the room with crackling intensity. I might get a shock just touching the air. The Koshare's dark eyes fixed on me, but his red mouth was closed, without smiles.

"Do you speak English?" I asked. "I only know a few words in Hopi, and all of them are dirty."

I speak all languages. Including that of the Diné.

The kachinas were benevolent gods, coming to the Hopi people to help them find the bounty of the land. As a kid, I'd loved watching the stately kachina dances, and the clowns and their antics. So why was I so afraid of them now?

Then it struck me: because, in this story, they were the

good guys, and I was the evil being. My mother had bestowed upon me her powers, her ruthlessness, and her evil. I could pretend all I wanted to that my storm power mitigated the effects of the Beneath magic, that I could handle both. But as I looked into the Koshare's eyes, I knew it for the lie it was.

"So now what?" I asked. "Are you going to leave me here? Or kill me? I suppose it doesn't make much difference, but killing me outright will be quicker than leaving me here to starve."

Is that what you want? Death?

"No, but it's what you're going to give me."

It is your choice, Stormwalker. You choose the path.

"Now, see, this is what I don't like about gods. I ask a straight question, and you give me some cryptic answer."

You can die. Or we can take the magic from you.

I stared, shocked. "You can take away the magic?"

We can. Your Stormwalker magic is natural, inherited from your Diné ancestors. It is a part of your world. The other magic is not. We can take it from you, return it to the world to which it belongs.

I opened my mouth to bellow, *Yes!* Without the Beneath magic vying for mastery inside me, I could go back to being only half-crazy. I could use only the storm magic as I'd learned to, knowing I controlled it, not the other way around. Maybe I could get rid of the hangovers I got after a storm—I'd discovered that they came from the Beneath magic fighting my Stormwalker power. I'd be able to sleep better, and Coyote and all the dragons would cease talking about killing me.

But then a truth hit me, and I closed my mouth again. If the Stormwalker magic was a natural part of me, so was my mother's magic. It might have lain quietly inside me until I'd awakened it traveling Beneath, but it had always been there.

I didn't want to be evil. I was tired of gods and dragons following me around, watching my every move. I wanted to be plain old Janet, who'd spent a few years wandering the country photographing the remotest parts of it, and who now was taking on the challenge of running a small hotel in the middle of nowhere. But on the other hand, if something so deeply ingrained in me was ripped out, what would happen to me?

"You're afraid that the Beneath magic will take me over," I said. "That I'll be too great a threat to you. Coyote fears that too. But that's because none of you understand what it is to be human. We make mistakes, and then we fix them."

The Koshare watched me in silence. He was supposed to be comical with his striped paint and knobby horns, but his grave stillness gave him dignity.

"If I didn't have this magic, Undead Jim would have killed so many more people," I said. "You can't blame his existence on me. I didn't bring him back to life."

Humans like to argue. To justify their deeds.

"When my life depends on it, hell yes."

It was easy to be in touch with my earth magic in this place—the earth was all around me. I'd managed to twine the two magics together when I was trying to save Mick, and looking inside myself, the interwoven magic was still there, warm and quiet. Part of me.

I knew right then I couldn't separate them, that if the Koshare and the kachinas or Coyote tried to remove the Beneath magic from me, I'd cease to exist. The two magics would fight to remain twined into my psyche, as they had always been, and I would end up empty, dead, nothing.

Before this awful day started, my Beneath magic would have told me that I could best this puny god and then goad me into doing it. Now I knew that I couldn't best him—the attempt would be the death of me—but I also knew that I wasn't as powerless as I feared.

I gathered the woven magic and let my senses reach through the heavy rock above me, up, up, and up until I found the open air. It smelled pungent with humidity and greenery, the air sharp and cool.

"A storm outside." I smiled. "I like storms."

The Koshare just watched me.

"You don't want to kill me, you know," I said. "You didn't even want to kill Jim, and he was a walking destructive force."

The Koshare's eyes widened in surprise. I knew the clown, for his talk, did not really want to do murder. His job was to make people laugh, or to admonish them by making fun of them. I wasn't so certain about the kachinas, some of whom were pretty damn powerful, but he had been sent to me because he'd try every method he could before he had to give up and kill me. Because he had compassion.

But his compassion meant that he might keep me stuck in here the rest of my natural life if I didn't cooperate with him. I reached with my mind through the hundreds of feet of rock and touched water, wind, lightning.

I was a Stormwalker, a strong one. Lightning struck the earth where I guided it, tearing a hole in the rock. The Koshare jumped, but he made no attempt to stop me. Either he wanted to see what I'd do, or he was waiting for his brethren to drag me out and crush me into little pieces.

The mountain rumbled, and dust and pebbles rained down. I snapped off my magic current in alarm. Bringing the cave down on my head was not what I had in mind.

The rumbling didn't cease. The Koshare looked up in alarm, and the magic mirror said, "Oh, honey bun, this does *not* look good."

I snatched up the mirror and thrust it into its bag. The cave plunged into darkness.

I don't know whether the Koshare stayed or vanished, but I was on my feet, trying to divert the storm elsewhere. Maybe trying to have it dig me out had been a bad idea.

More dirt rained on me, and I heard a loud *boom*. I screamed as half the ceiling crashed down, and I fell. I expected to land on the Koshare, but he wasn't there. He'd left me to my fate.

Above me the rocks were ripped aside, and dirt started to smother me. I didn't want to die like this. I grabbed my magic and forced it into a bubble shape, with me inside. What good it would do me in the long run I didn't know, but I needed to breathe *now*.

Something ripped at my bubble, and the air burned red with fire. Great, just great. I was inside a live volcano that had decided to erupt. I'd never see my father again. Or my grandmother. Or the moon rising over the stark hill at Many Farms. Or my hotel and my new friends. I whimpered like a baby.

Or . . . not a volcano. My protective shell was torn apart, not by the forces of an eruption, but by a huge talon. A dragon talon.

My name is Janet Begay, and dragons want to slay me.

Now that Mick was dead and no longer protected me as his mate, there was no dragon law to stop them finding me and flaming me out of existence.

I fought. The trouble with figuring out how to serenely blend my magics was that each one grew a little less powerful as it combined with the other. The whole was stronger than its parts, but dragons, creatures of air and fire, could absorb my storm magic. They ate lightning for breakfast. So they'd swallow half my magic, and the other half would no longer be strong enough to best them.

That's what I'd wanted, wasn't it? A Stormwalker who could use her Beneath powers for benevolence and goodness?

The dragon who pulled me out of the mountain wasn't interested in benevolence or goodness. He yanked me straight through a dragon-sized hole, wings beating the air to gain height. It was a black dragon, a big one, but not Mick. It was Drake, the flunky to Bancroft of the dragon council, the flunky who really didn't like me.

Once we hit the starry night, I saw flames high in the sky, bright streams like comets. Dragons, dozens of them, were fighting winged beings who darted and dodged the fires.

My stomach lurched as Drake dove swiftly down and sideways, avoiding a fireball that erupted in the exact place we'd been. What the hell?

Then I realized I wasn't seeing a simple battle out here. Dragons were flaming dragons. The winged creatures, the kachinas, zapped dragons with white magic, but not all the dragons. I couldn't work out who was on whose side, and Drake dipping and whirling didn't help. All I could do was hang on and pray.

A dragon took the brunt of another's fire. He screamed on the way down, until he met a kachina's white light and disappeared. Dead? Or sent somewhere? Alive? Or incinerated?

"Why are they fighting?" I shouted. "What do they want?"

The wind tore away my words. Either Drake didn't hear, or he had no interest in answering.

The battle heated, fire lashing the night, white heat answering. I didn't understand how it happened, but a formation of dragons suddenly cut high, roaring in triumph. The dragons below them began streaking for the horizon. The kachinas chased those dragons, the gods' huge, feathery wings flashing in the sunrise. Then dragons and kachinas alike were swallowed into the coming dawn.

The formation, about a dozen dragons in a perfect phalanx, headed our way. Drake's wings whooshed, and we shot backward at least a couple thousand feet. I screamed, then snapped my mouth shut as bile boiled up from my stomach.

I had no idea who'd won the battle, or whether the phalanx of dragons forming behind one screaming leader was on Drake's side or not. I got my answer as the formation streamed past us, the dragons a winged blur, and Drake took his place at the end of one of the lines.

Who led them, I wondered. Bancroft? Or a dragon interested in killing off an interfering Stormwalker?

Drake carried me through graying light at the end of the dragon line. I decided against trying to hit him with magic, because if he dropped me, it was a long way down. Could Beneath magic keep me from splatting on the ground? I didn't want to find out.

The dragons angled away from city lights I could see to the south of us and out across the blackness of desert. If I'd been right about being inside the San Francisco Peaks, then the town we were speeding north and west from was Flagstaff. Which meant if Drake dropped me now, I'd fall about a mile and a half or more to the bottom of the Grand Canyon.

The wind was freezing. I hunkered behind the dragon talon to keep warm the best I could.

"Couldn't bother to bring me a sweater?" I asked between chattering teeth. Drake didn't answer, but I hadn't really thought he would.

We flew a long way, over another city of lights and off again into darkness. The dragons began to circle, and as we descended, the rising sun outlined sharp, high mountains and glittered on white alkali flats.

A good place to die: Death Valley.

The dragons flew over mountains from which I'd rescued Mick not many days ago to land in the very center of a dry lake bed. Drake set me on my feet with a thump, and when my head stopped spinning, I understood where we were.

They call it the Racetrack. Not because there are any races on it, or even pavement on which to race. The dry lake bed was an oval two and a half miles long, and its floor consisted of flat, baked, cracked earth. Boulders stood like sentinels at one end; behind each of them was a long, pale smear in the dirt.

The boulders moved by themselves when no one was looking—no one knew how or why, although there were plenty of theories. It was eerie to see the trails each had taken stretching out behind them, like stone creatures who glided across the lake bed and then froze the moment someone looked at them.

Dragons touched down around us, still in formation, changing from beast to human as they landed. There were tall women among the equally tall men, and all were well tattooed.

My eyes riveted to the leader of the phalanx, the dragon who'd been the point of the formation. Not Bancroft, as I'd thought, or the second dragon councilor, as I'd feared.

The phalanx's leader had dragon tattoos winding down his arms and a flame tattoo across the small of his back, wildly curly black hair, and amazing blue eyes. Drake tried to hold me back, but I shook him off and was running, running, kicking up a choking white cloud of dust as I sprinted across the lake bed.

I launched myself at Mick so hard he stumbled as he caught me, and we went down, tangled together, to the parched, cracked earth.

Twenty-six

I kissed Mick's lips, his face, his neck, his lips again, tears of relief and joy streaming down my cheeks. Mick cupped my face and returned the kisses, his own eyes wet. I drew a deep, choking breath, swallowing the dust I'd kicked up.

"Damn you," I cried. "Why aren't you dead?"

Mick wrapped me in arms that were whole and unbroken. "It was a close-run thing, sweetheart. But you gave me the spark that kept me alive."

I splayed one hand against his chest, feeling his heart beating hard and strong. "You're not *un*dead, are you?" I asked, worried.

He smiled his bad-boy smile. "No. You jump-started me and my healing magic. Kind of like CPR—or a shock to a battery. Colby and Drake took me off and helped me heal. Don't be too hard on them."

"I'll love them to pieces if they brought you back to me."

Hands seized my shoulders. I fought as they tried to pull me off of Mick. Mick climbed to his feet and lifted me with him. "It's all right," he told the other dragon, one I didn't know. "She's not attacking me."

"Not yet," I promised, my smile hot.

Mick turned me around and gave me a long kiss. His skin was covered with white dust, which stuck to him like powder, and my skin was covered with black volcanic dust. I'm sure we looked hilarious.

The other dragons remained in place, as though they were waiting for Mick to tell them what to do. Drake had maintained his position, and Colby was there, naked, inked, and grinning.

None of the dragons had clothes, I noticed, and none of them seemed bothered by it. If a park ranger happened along, what would he or she think of a group of people standing in naked formation in the middle of the lake?

Only one person was clothed, Nash Jones, who stood next to Colby. He must have been carried here as well—I wondered how he'd fared.

"Why did you bring us here?" I asked Mick. "You were fighting kachinas and other dragons. Weren't you? What the hell is going on?"

"We're here because this is where my trial will take place."

"Your trial?" I sought out Colby, who nodded confirmation. "Why? You almost died. Isn't that good enough for them?"

Mick smoothed a lock of hair from my face. "It's dragon law. I still have to face the charges, no matter what else has happened."

"What else did happen? Besides Drake rescuing me? Should I be thanking him?"

"Cassandra found me through the mirror. She said you'd told her you thought you were inside a volcano. We flew to the one sacred to the kachinas, and then a lightning bolt struck the mountain, pointing the way. I knew you'd called it to you."

"So you had Drake dig me out?"

"Yes. There are other dragons who want you dead—they thought me dead and gone, so they decided to go for you. I and my dragons got there first."

"Then who were the kachinas fighting?"

"The other dragons. The kachinas were trying to protect you."

"Protect me," I repeated. "Not kill me?"

"They don't want the other dragons to get their hands on your power. I know their leader; if he thought he could control and use you, he'd keep you alive and do just that."

"Control me?"

Mick smoothed my hair again. "I said he'd try. When he didn't succeed, he'd kill you. But don't worry. I'll never let that happen." This was the man I loved. Cryptic, evasive, hiding things from me until he thought I needed to know.

"The kachinas are fine with you having me?" I asked.

"You seemed to make a good impression on them."

I thought about my debate in the cave with the Koshare. I didn't remember winning the argument, but maybe it had made him think. Good gods, did that mean someone had actually *listened* to me?

I had other worries at the moment.

"Why is the dragon trial *now*?" I asked. "I thought it was in a week—not that I know what day it is."

"The dragon council called an emergency session. First order of business, my trial."

I looked around at the dragons who'd broken formation

and stood talking together in clumps like people waiting at an airport.

"What are *they* going to do?"

"They're here to observe. Not much else they can do. The council of three will preside, and only they and my defense can do any talking."

"What about you? The defendant? Do you get to talk?"

Mick shook his head. "The prisoner is mute, because the council can't trust that he won't lie to save himself. A neutral defense will tell the truth."

"And Colby is your defense. I wouldn't call him neutral. Why don't we fly away now and go to Australia?"

"Then we'd have the trial in Australia. There are dragons there too."

I touched the magic inside myself, the beautiful, solid, hard core of it. "What do you want me to do? I can take out the dragon council if you want. I can do it, you know. They need to understand that."

"They do understand it." He brushed my skin with his thumbs. "Tell me something. When Drake snatched you, why didn't you, as you say, 'take him out'?"

"I didn't want him to drop me."

"You could have hurt him before he snatched you. Why didn't you?"

I shrugged. I loved Mick's hands on my shoulders, warm through the chill of the desert night. "I didn't know who he was at first, or which side he was on."

Mick touched his forehead to mine, breath on my face. "And that's why I believe in you. You could wipe away anyone you want with the sweep of your hand, but you wait, in case they turn out to be innocent."

"Not always smart."

"But you'd rather take the consequences on yourself than destroy someone who doesn't deserve it. Jim couldn't make that distinction."

I gave him a shaky smile. "Is that why you'd rather go to bed with me than him?"

Mick's wicked grin answered. "That, and so many other reasons."

I felt someone breathing down my neck. Colby. "This is very sweet," he said. "But the council is arriving."

Three dragons landed a little way away from our group and changed to human form. One was Bancroft; another was the man I'd seen Drake talking to at Bancroft's stronghold in Santa Fe. The third was a woman, tall and broad-shouldered with white hair sweeping to her waist.

The dragons that had followed Mick started moving away from the three, retreating a distance, arranging themselves to watch.

Except for Nash Jones, who had walked over with Colby. "What are you doing here?" I asked him.

He looked incongruous, the only man dressed and not tattooed. He wore his sheriff's uniform, the star-shaped badge glinting in the morning sunlight.

"The dragons wanted a neutral human observer, since there was another human involved. Colby asked, I volunteered."

"Another human . . . meaning me?"

"Yes."

I glanced at Colby. "I'm magical."

"But mortal human," Colby said. "And you're what this trial is all about. You're entitled to representation by a human."

"Besides, I didn't trust them to return you safely." Nash

spoke matter-of-factly, as though being carried hundreds of miles by a dragon to the middle of Death Valley was part of his job. "Neither did Maya or Cassandra."

I imagined both ladies had given him hell. "You know, Nash, you're a good guy, underneath it all."

Nash frowned at me and returned to watching the dragon council. "Don't push it, Begay."

I didn't want to wait through the damned trial. I had no way of knowing how long it would take. Twenty minutes? Twenty days? I wanted to grab Mick and take off with him somewhere, to hole up with him and make love for a week. I'd grieved for him; now I needed to reassure myself that he was here, alive, not a dream. I wanted to touch and taste him, to hold him and reconnect with him. And yes, I most of all I wanted to have hard, heavy, and sweat-soaked sex with him.

The dragons didn't do anything so formal as call the meeting to order. The dragon council simply stood in place, and Mick and Colby led me and Nash to stand before them.

The female councilor had fine-lined tattoos down her arms and legs plus one snaking across her perfect belly. Her aura told me she was older than the other two, but I'd never know it from her lineless body and face.

"That's Aine," Colby said in my ear. "At least that's the shortened version of her name. She's who we have to watch out for. She's old, experienced, smart, and doesn't have an ounce of compassion in her ice-cold body."

"Comforting," I said. "Worse than the other guy? The one who wants me obliterated?"

"Farrell. He's got a nasty temper, but he can be reasonable—if the stars are aligned. He's the senior."

"The one whose—what did you call it—'bit on the side' you stole?"

Colby grinned. "Yep. The man hates me."

Bancroft was the third of the council. "Will it make any difference that I saved Bancroft's life?" I whispered to Colby.

"Nope. The dragon council likes to believe that they're blind justice, impartial judges. Huh."

"This trial will be fair, won't it?" Nash asked him.

"In dragon terms, sure," Colby said. "In human terms, not so much."

Mick said nothing. He stood a little apart from us, his stance calm, the wind from the mountains stirring his hair. His eyes were dragon-black, and the jagged tattoo that snaked across his lower back glowed with fire.

The woman, Aine, spoke. "Micalerianicum has been charged with disobeying a direct order from the dragon council to kill the Stormwalker Janet Begay when she committed an act that could have brought danger to all dragon-kind. Mick had pledged his life to be contingent upon the Stormwalker's good behavior, which she then violated by opening a vortex. However, Mick still insisted she be kept alive even after that, and took her as mate to protect her under dragon law. How does he plead?"

Colby stepped forward. White dust clung to his tattooed body, making him look a little like the Koshare.

"He pleads guilty," Colby said.

"Damn it, Colby." I knew Mick had already been found guilty, but it was another thing to hear Colby so gleefully say it.

"Please advise the Stormwalker that she may not speak until recognized," Aine said.

"Fuck you, lady," I muttered, but Nash put his lips close to my ear.

"It's a trial, Janet, rife with rules we don't understand. For once in your life, shut up."

I closed my mouth, knowing he had a point, but this was Mick's fate we were talking about. Losing him last night had nearly destroyed me, and I didn't want to go through that again.

Mick said nothing and didn't move, a man awaiting his fate. He'd told me he had ideas on how to get out of his sentence, but he hadn't shared them with me. Besides, what could he possibly do if he was not allowed to say anything?

Farrell spoke. "Does the defense counsel have anything to say before sentence is passed?"

"Oh, I have plenty to say." Colby walked forward a pace. "But I'll keep it brief. My first idea was to claim that Micky was insane, which was why he chose to believe that the Stormwalker was harmless, but I think that won't wash."

"No," Aine agreed.

"The second was to prove that the Stormwalker really is harmless, and it was all right that Micky didn't kill her. But after everything that's happened, everything the council has seen her do, that won't wash either."

Obviously not. All three council members nodded.

"So my third and final idea is to let the Stormwalker herself plead for Mick's life," Colby continued. "To tell you why he was justified in sparing her. Therefore I give you the Stormwalker, Janet Begay."

All eyes turned expectantly to me.

"Colby, when I get you alone . . ." I said under my breath.

Colby rubbed his hands. "I can't wait."

I stepped forward, putting myself under the scrutinizing stare of three tall dragons. Bancroft and Farrell had let their eyes become dragon-black; Aine's were a chill light gray.

The magic inside me was calm, serene, like the sheet of water that must have covered this lake eons ago. I imagined a pool of clear, deep blue that had reflected the sky. I felt my magic waiting, ready for my command. The dawn sky was empty of clouds—no more storms—but that no longer mattered. The Beneath magic would pull what it needed from the storm magic and vice versa.

My mouth was dry, but no one had bothered to bring any water. I cleared my throat.

"Mick sacrificed everything when he decided nearly six years ago not to kill me," I said. "I didn't know it at the time, but letting me live went against everything he sincerely believed in. Dragon law and dragon honor are very important to him—I know this because he wouldn't have showed up at this stupid trial if they weren't."

Farrell's eyes narrowed. "You are insolent."

"I know I am. I think that's why Colby wants me to speak, so he can see your faces when I say what I've got to say." Colby's smirk confirmed my suspicion. "I didn't coerce Mick or glam him into keeping me alive. When I met him I had no idea he was a dragon—no idea that dragons even existed—and no idea what he'd come to do. I only saw him as a man who'd come to my rescue, a man who seemed to like me, a man who could take my Stormwalker magic and live. Mick's had to make some tough decisions regarding me, decisions that none of you people could have made. You follow your rules and never stop to think about the consequences."

Aine's lip curled. "Are you finished?"

"Not quite." I was warming up, beginning to enjoy myself. "You feared me because I might open the way to Beneath. Well, if Mick had followed his rules and killed me, my goddess mother would still be wandering around up here, trying to create another daughter to help her, one who would have done whatever my mother wanted. And if Mick had stuck to his pledge *after* I opened the vortex and killed me, I wouldn't have been around when Undead Jim, who couldn't control his magic, started destroying people. He could have killed every single person in Magellan and gone on a murdering rampage. *You* couldn't have stopped him." I still hadn't figured out who'd resurrected Jim, but that was a worry for another time.

"However," Farrell broke in, "if not for you, and if not for Bancroft going behind our backs, this undead person would have come nowhere near dragons. The point is moot."

"Gee, what compassion you have," I said. "Maybe Jim wouldn't have gone near any dragons if Bancroft had stayed home, but he was still killing human beings. No wonder dragons like to stay hidden from humans—you'd be locked up for being sociopaths. Mick's act kept a lot of people alive and even saved Bancroft's ass."

"But this destructive human would not have been walking about at all, had it not been for magic like yours," Farrell said.

"Magic *like* mine," I returned. "Not mine. At the time Jim Mohan was getting himself resurrected, I was pulling Mick out of a jail of your making, in a mountain ridge not far from this one. Nash Jones is witness to that. I know you want to pin Jim's second life on me, but you can't. And I bet that pisses you off."

"Easy, Janet," Colby warned. "Don't let them get you for contempt of court."

"But I have every contempt for this court."

Aine spoke. "We acknowledge that you did not create the creature you refer to as Undead Jim. But you must know who did."

"I haven't the foggiest who resurrected him. A god with an agenda, maybe? Someone trying to help him and screw-

ing up? The power didn't come from my mother. I made
sure of that." All this bugged me. If I hadn't done it, and
my mother hadn't done it, and Coyote hadn't done it—that
meant that some other god or goddess from Beneath must
have brought Jim back to life and given him Beneath powers. But I'd have to concentrate on figuring out who made
Jim after I got Mick out of this.

Bancroft, who hadn't spoken at all yet, raised his hand
for silence. "The gist of your argument is, therefore, that
Mick's decision to disobey an order from the dragon council resulted, in the long run, in a few benevolent acts from
you. However, many of the situations in which your benevolent acts were performed would not have occurred at
all had you been terminated at once."

"Yes, things do tend to happen around me," I said. "I'm
a Stormwalker, and I have a lot of magic in me. People tend
to ask me to help them because of it." I felt as though I'd
swallowed half the dry lake's dust and cleared my throat
again. "My argument is that Mick is more farsighted and
compassionate than you give him credit for. He disobeyed
because he's smarter than any of you. No, let me rephrase
that—smarter than all of you put together."

Aine's lips thinned. "You do know that the penalty for
contempt of court is instant death?"

I hadn't known that, but why was I not surprised?

"Try it." I was angry and exhausted, scared and unhappy. "I wouldn't mind a little workout."

"No, you wouldn't," Colby said. Even Mick shot a warning look at me.

Aine drew herself up. "Do not toy with the rage of dragons, little Stormwalker. You are very small compared to us."

"Then why are you so afraid of me?" I bravely met her
cold gaze. "This is what this trial is really about, isn't it?

Fear. You don't want to acknowledge that any force in the world might be more powerful than the mighty dragons. That someone might not allow you to get away with whatever you want to get away with. Such as holding a trial for someone when you've already decided he's guilty. Such as ordering a hit on a young woman who might be your only defense against whatever might come out of the vortexes. Did you ever stop to think of that? That you might need me? Or are you too afraid to need anyone? Why, because I might call in the favor someday?"

"I think that's enough," Farrell said in a hard voice.

"I agree," Bancroft said. Aine's eyes were narrow in rage, but she kept silent.

"Not quite," I said. "Would you like to tell the dragons gathered here that you'd rather me be dead than alive to help when you need it? Or do you not want them to realize that you're not strong enough to defend them from certain forces?"

"Okay, now even I think that's enough," Colby said. "Shut up before you get me fried too."

Aine's lips barely moved. "You die, Stormwalker. Right now."

She raised her hands. For one awful second I imagined red-hot dragon fire ripping through me before I could even bring my magic to bear, when both Nash and Mick stepped in front of me.

I was sure Mick had just broken all kinds of dragon rules doing so, but he remained a solid wall of muscle, the tattoo on his back glowing red. He didn't say a word, just let the council know by his stance that they sure as hell weren't killing me without going through him. I prayed that it would be a huge dragon gaffe if they fried him in the middle of his own trial.

Nash was just as formidable, and just as much in the way. "Mick tried to explain a little about a dragon's perception of honor," he said to the dragons. "Killing a witness before a trial is over doesn't seem very honorable to me."

Farrell stared at him in disbelief. "What do you know of dragon honor, human man?"

"I don't know much about dragons—hell, I didn't even believe in them until I saw Mick turn into one—but I know about honor. If a person thinks an order is wrong and harmful, that person has the obligation to question the order and disobey if necessary. Mick made a decision based on the best intelligence he had at the time, and it turned out to be a correct one."

"Why do you defend her?" Bancroft looked puzzled. "From our observations, you don't regard the witness with much warmth."

"I agree that Janet Begay is a pain in the ass, has a smart mouth, and seems to attract trouble wherever she goes," Nash said.

"Thanks," I murmured.

"She also shows great courage under pressure and has saved the lives of several people I care about. I keep extensive records on her activities and discovered that before she came to live in Magellan she helped numerous people with serious problems. She found missing persons and solved puzzles that eluded others. If she hadn't been available to do that, the wrong people would have been punished for those crimes, or the missing would still be lost and in danger."

My heart warmed. I'd never heard Nash be so eloquent. I knew better than to think he spoke out of great liking for me—Nash was keenly aware of right and wrong, of harm versus good. He'd thought about this logically and applied his unique knowledge to it.

Still, I wanted to hug him.

"We will take that into consideration." Aine's voice was frosty. "Defense counsel, do you have anything to add?"

Nash remained in front of me, as did Mick, to absorb any dragon fire that might come my way. I wasn't foolish enough to leave the relative protection of their bodies.

Colby took another step forward. Strange, I'd stopped noticing that everyone was without clothes except me and Nash. The dragons were so comfortable with their bodies, just as Mick had always been. They didn't see the need to attach shame to bare skin.

"The defense has one more thing to add." Colby glanced at Mick, and his grin grew broad.

Mick tensed, opened his mouth as if to speak, then snapped it shut again. Damned dragon trial rules.

"Micalerianicum came here today because honor mandated it," Colby said. "He'd never skip out on a trial called by the dragon council. But you know damn well he's here only to be courteous to you, and not because you can command him. He never uses his status for personal privilege."

Colby turned to Mick again. Mick's alarmed look had vanished to be replaced with mixed annoyance and anger.

"Micky was the dragon who won the battle for you against demons two hundred years ago, one that happened not fifty miles from here. If not for him, two of you good council members—Aine and Farrell—would be little dragon smears on rocks in the middle of the Sierras. Mick was decorated for valor and given the highest status a dragon can achieve: lord and general. One of the perks of this status is that it can be used to lessen any penalties levied against him by the dragon council. As humans would say, a Get Out of Jail Free card. Or almost free. The reason for this relative immunity from the dragon council ruling is that it's thought a dragon lord wouldn't be stupid enough to go against the council without a damn good reason. Or else, he wouldn't be a dragon lord. Circular logic, but I don't make up the rules."

I stared at Colby with my mouth open. "A dragon lord?"

Colby winked at me. "One of the highest. Damned arrogant bastard."

"This is your defense?" Aine asked in a freezing voice.

"Sure thing, your ladyship. If Micky decided that the dragon council was a triumvirate of idiots for wanting to kill Janet Begay, then he was privileged to make that choice. You can still punish him for doing it, of course, but you have to take his status into account when you pass your sentence."

Colby gave them a bow and stepped back, finished.

"That's it?" I asked. "They will still find him guilty, but because he's a dragon lord they can pass a lesser sentence? So instead of certain death, it will be *almost* certain death?"

"Best I can do," Colby said.

"Damn it." I released the magic I'd been holding back, letting it ripple to the edges of the lake bed.

I was in the mood for destruction, but I wasn't going to give the dragon council the satisfaction of confirming that I was the bad-ass evil being they thought I was. Instead, I brought all the boulders that littered the lake bed sliding rapidly to surround the three arrogant dragons.

"I'm not here to change your laws," I said as they stared at me. "As stupid as they are. But as much as I am Mick's mate, by your terms—so he is mine. If he dies, you answer to me. Is that what you really want?"

I had the satisfaction of seeing the three dragons look worried. I sensed their deep-seated fear that somehow I would destroy them, not to mention their power, their world, and everything they were.

And maybe I could. The magic in me was pretty damned strong, and I didn't know yet what I could do with it. Dragons were powerful, but I was now more than the naïve Stormwalker that Mick had met all those years ago. I'd learned to master my storm powers, and I'd helped many people, as Nash had said. I'd grown stronger, more capable, less afraid.

Mick had been responsible for some of my growth, but much of it had been because of me, myself. I was Navajo, tied to this earth, but my spirit soared into the storms and tapped the magic of the world that created us.

I folded my arms and stepped away from Nash and Mick. Yes, I still believed the dragons could burn me to a crisp, but I was finished with being frightened of them. I was filthy, bruised, cut, and so tired I could barely stand, yet the dragons watched *me* in trepidation.

"Decide," I said. "And hurry up. I want to go home, and I'm tired of being messed with."

Bancroft gave me a nod, though his look was anything but approving. "We will deliberate."

He and the other two turned their backs on me, and I could tell that it scared the piss out of them to do so.

Twenty-seven

"Great assist, Janet," Colby growled at me half an hour later. "I was hoping to go the hell home. But no, I'm stuck surviving Mick's stupid sentence with him. Walking out of this place with you, no magic and no shape-shifting allowed."

I wasn't much happier, being already hot and thirsty. Mick's arms came around me from behind, his body hard and warm and oh-so-good. "Janet just saved all our asses, Colby. As Ordeals go, it's not a bad one, so suck it up. Besides, wasn't it worth it to watch her embarrass the dragon council?" He chuckled and pressed a blood-tingling kiss to my neck. "I never thought I'd live to see that."

Colby's face relaxed, even as he wiped sweat from it. "Yeah, that was pretty good. Janet, sweetie, want to be my defense if I have to go to trial?"

"No," I said.

Nash snatched sunglasses out of his pocket and shoved them on. "If you're all finished with self-congratulations, we need to get going. That sun's going to be pretty fierce." He looked once at the glare coming over the mountains and then started walking.

The dragon council's sentence, passed after about twenty minutes of heated argument, was for Mick and his counsel for the defense—Colby, me, and Nash—to walk out of the Racetrack and make it back to civilization the best we could. No shape-shifting and flying out, no magic. Just us, the merciless sun, and no water. One dragon trusted by the council was to accompany us to act as our watcher: Drake. To say he wasn't happy about it is a severe understatement.

On a relative scale, it was a light sentence, a slap on the wrist. Mick, Nash, Colby, and Drake were in good shape, and we might well run into someone driving around out here. I held out faint hope, however, that the council would let us have it that easy. Remembering Bancroft's horde of devoted lackeys, including his county sheriff, I imagined the council could ensure, by devious methods, that no one drove up these back roads. It was a twenty-five-or-so-mile walk across the desert and over steep hills on a dirt road. We could still die of dehydration and heatstroke, not a terrific prospect.

Nash led the way. He removed his button-down shirt and draped it over his head, the white T-shirt he wore beneath bright in the sunlight. He had sunglasses, but I had nothing with which to shield my eyes, and the sun beat down on me without mercy.

I trudged behind Nash, with Mick and Colby behind me, and Drake bringing up the rear. Drake was angry as hell, but with his stoic loyalty, I knew he wouldn't simply say, *Screw this,* and fly off. He'd stay and die with us if that was what he had to do. It was that dragon honor thing again. I also knew Mick would obey the edict of no magic and no shape-shifting, and he'd make damn sure Colby obeyed it too. Mick must be one hell of a dragon lord. I was still adjusting to that.

I couldn't use my cell phone, and neither could Nash, because both of ours were inexplicably dead. I had my piece of magic mirror, but using it to communicate with the outside was forbidden—that would violate the rule of no magic. The dragons had thought of everything.

I caught up to Nash, who was setting a swift pace. "Thanks for the things you said about me back there."

"They were true." His voice held no inflection.

"It was real sweet." I couldn't resist saying that. "I didn't know you loved me so much."

Nash's glance, even through sunglasses, could have crumbled boulders into dust. "What I said about you being a pain in the ass with a smart mouth was true too. That and the fact that you cause trouble."

"I can't deny it." I shrugged as I strode next to him. "So, how are things between you and Maya? I saw the passionate kiss you gave her."

"None of your business."

I gave him a dry-lipped smile. "That's all right. I'll just ask her."

Nash scowled. He picked up his pace to a quick-time march, his long legs eating distance. If I wanted to keep up with him, I'd have to trot, panting, at his side.

I dropped back to walk with Mick and Colby. Mick slanted me a smile that made me hot, even under the burning sun, and took my hand. I looked forward, in more ways than one, to getting home again.

Drake also gave me a look, but one of undisguised fury. I knew he blamed me for his being chosen to carry out the sentence with us. Would I have problems with Drake in the future? Probably. I didn't have the energy to contemplate it right now.

Already I needed water, having drunk nothing since sometime the day before. I was going to be half-dead before we even reached the edge of the lake bed. The boulders stood innocently behind us, where I'd left them. I could imagine the geologists scratching their heads at the pattern they'd left, drawn from the edges of the lake to a circle in the center. It would give my ghost something amusing to watch when I was a pile of dried bones in the dust.

When we finally reached the narrow dirt road that led into a pass between the hills, there were no vehicles in sight. Any approaching truck or SUV would kick a thin spiral of dust high into the air behind it, but the sky remained a clear and bright blue. No one would come. It would be just the five of us traipsing across open desert under the blinding sun.

Colby said behind me, "If you get hot, Janet, feel free to take off your top."

I ignored him, too tired to banter.

For the first mile or so after that, I was fine. The dragons had made it too easy, I thought. I finished the next two miles drenched in sweat, feeling a sunburn. What little shade the sides of the mountains had made in the pass vanished as the sun climbed overhead.

By mile seven, I was stumbling. My tongue was glued to the roof of my mouth, and my breathing was labored. We rested, taking our time, but it didn't help much.

At mile ten, or at least I think it was mile ten, Mick picked me up and carried me. We'd seen no cars, trucks, SUVs, park rangers, hikers, campers, or anyone. The place was deserted, eerily so. I wondered how much Bancroft had paid off the park employees.

Mick carried me without complaint, his strong arms never faltering. But even Nash was slowing—twenty miles was likely not that far for him, but being without water, while the temperature climbed past one hundred degrees, took its toll. Talk had ceased, each of us saving breath and moisture for the journey.

A carrion crow glided overhead, on the lookout for fresh kill. I waved to it.

"Over here," I croaked.

"Don't invite it," Colby said behind Mick. "It might want to get an early start on picking meat off us."

The crow didn't seem to see us. I dug into my pocket, and Mick had to put me down. Barely able to stand, I pulled out the piece of magic mirror. I couldn't use it magically, but I could use it for what it was—a mirror, a piece of silvered glass. I moved it until it caught the sun, flashing a bright white star of light.

The crow saw it. It wheeled over us once, head cocked to investigate, then flew away into searing blue sky.

"What the hell was that about?" Nash asked.

"You never know," I said.

"A harbinger," Colby said, and then we all fell silent again.

Mick carried me again as we moved up another hill and walked down into the trough on the other side. I heard rattling like a metal shed in a windstorm, and I started to laugh.

"I knew she wouldn't let me down."

My words were unintelligible, even to me. Mick leaned to me. "What, baby?"

I didn't answer. A battered white pickup crested the rise ahead of us, banging and clattering down the rutted road. It was full of people, three in the cab, a couple in the bed. Nash stopped, hands on hips, and waited.

The pickup pulled to a halt next to Nash, and a Native American man with a lined face leaned out and called to Mick, "Hey, what happened to your clothes?" He chortled. "Must have been some windstorm."

Two grinning young men jumped out of the back, tossing pants and shirts at Mick, Colby, and Drake.

Colby caught them with an amazed look. "You carry extra sets of clothes, in case you meet naked men on the road?"

Inside the cab, the young woman—Beth, I remembered her name was—leaned around her father. "The crow, she told us what you'd need. She said Firewalkers didn't have any sense of decency."

That was my grandmother. Colby chuckled as he pulled on the worn pair of jeans. "She's right. Whoever she is."

Mick didn't move to pick up the clothes or cover himself. He carried me around the other side of the truck and waited for Beth to open the door. "Do you have water?" he asked. "She's dehydrated."

"Sure thing." As Mick set me gently on the seat next to her, Beth produced a thermos, poured out a trickle of beautiful water, and handed me the cup. She had to help me raise it to my swollen lips.

Sweet, clear, cool liquid filled my mouth. I wanted to savor it, but my needy body sucked it down, and I nearly choked as I swallowed.

"Easy," Beth said. She poured me another cup.

I felt the truck list as the others climbed into the back. In my half-dazed state, I once again saw other beings superimposed on Beth and her father. White swirling lights, a hint of feather.

"Are you kachinas too?" I asked.

Beth's father chuckled. "Nah. We're similar, but we use a different term. Where you need to go?"

"Home," I said. "Although, anyplace with a phone is fine."

"That's easy." Beth's father put the truck in gear and started to drive.

Beth glanced through the open back window at Mick, Colby, Drake, and Nash. "Hey, cute white sheriff," she called. "I think we found your truck."

Nash was at the window, ripping off his sunglasses. "Did you? Black? Ford 250? Arizona plates?" He rattled off the license number.

"Yeah, I think that's it," Beth's father said. "Want me to take you to it?"

"Please." Nash sat back. "Yes. Thank you."

I drank more water. "He's happier to find his truck than he is to get out of here alive."

"Men and their cars," Beth agreed. "But he still is cute."

We banged and bounced over the dirt road for a very long time. Then Beth's father turned a corner, and the road eased into the smoothness of pavement. The truck's horrible jouncing died into sudden calm.

I closed my eyes as we glided down the restful highway. Before we'd gone far, Beth's father turned off on another dirt road, this one wider and better graded than the one from the Racetrack.

We stopped, and I peeled open my eyes. We were on top of a little bridge that had been constructed over an arroyo, the bridge just high enough so that a mild rainstorm wouldn't wash it out. Anything stronger, and this road would be flooded.

An intense rain had obviously come and gone. The bottom of the arroyo was filled with silt and loose brush, though much of it had piled over an obstacle upstream of the bridge. From this jetsam protruded a dust-covered black cab. Nash's beautiful, shiny new pickup in which I'd ridden out here to search for Mick was now half-buried in white sand.

Tension drained, and a sudden wave of sleep hit me. The last thing I heard before I drifted away, smiling, against Beth's comfortable shoulder was Nash Jones swearing and swearing hard.

Two mornings later I wandered out of my bedroom and sank into a leather couch in my lobby. It was quiet—guests had breakfasted and either checked out or gone off sightseeing. We had a few hours' respite before lunch.

Mick came out of the back, hair wet from his shower, and sat next to me, our bodies touching. He twined his fingers through mine.

"How are you doing?" he asked me.

"Better."

He was silent for a while, just holding my hand. He'd done this a lot since we'd gotten home. The Shoshone had driven us to Furnace Creek, and Mick had somehow booked the two of us into the luxury inn there. Cool sheets, air-conditioning, gourmet food . . . It reinforced my belief that there is nowhere in the world so remote that someone won't try to build a resort in it.

I'd slept for a long time, and Mick left me to it. I had no idea what had become of Drake, Colby, and Nash, but when Mick returned to take me to dinner, he told me that Nash had gotten park rangers plus the California Highway

Patrol to help him rescue his truck. Apparently, joy riders had taken it while we'd been running around the mountains and then abandoned it in the wash. It had been hot-wired, the underside of the dash broken, and a nice torrent of rain had done the rest. Poor Nash.

"So what did Colby do to you all those years ago?" I asked Mick over a quiet table in the restaurant. "To make him your enemy, I mean?"

Mick looked uncomfortable. "Long story."

"We have time," I said, sipping my cool wine. No martinis.

Mick toyed with the frosted glass of his beer mug for a while. I waited. I wasn't going anywhere, not while I was cool and fed and hydrated.

Finally Mick took a sip of beer and sat back. "He stole my mate."

I blinked in surprise. "Wait, I thought I was your mate."

"A long time ago. She was a dragon. I shouldn't strictly say she was my mate—I was courting her, in the dragon way, and Colby decided to cut in. We fought. He won."

"*Colby* won? But why is he so afraid of you?"

"Because he fought dirty, and he knows it. I stupidly clung to honor and the rules, while he went behind my back. He destroyed my lair, stole everything I had—and it turns out that this lady was looking for a mate based on his worth. I was young enough to think it was me she wanted. When I discovered her true colors, I withdrew from the contest and let Colby have her."

"What happened to the lady dragon? Is she still with Colby?"

"She died."

"Oh." Though I'd already labeled the dragon as a she-bitch, that was sad. "How?"

"Battle with another dragon faction. We're not all best friends."

I remembered the fight when Drake had pulled me out of the mountain. "So I gathered." I toyed with the stem of my wineglass. "I'm sorry. About the lady dragon, I mean."

"She and Colby hadn't mated yet. No bond there. But still it was hard on him."

"And you?"

He nodded. "And on me too."

It gave me something to think about later while he held me so tenderly in bed. Mick fighting Colby for a lady dragon. I remembered him telling me that female dragons could turn on their mates and try to kill them. If female dragons were all like Aine, I believed it. I wondered how Mick viewed me in comparison.

Fast-forward two days to the cool lobby of my hotel, me sitting comfortably with Mick and watching day-to-day business commence. Fremont came in to check a leak in the kitchen, his cheerful affability soothing. Pamela leaned over the counter to talk to Cassandra. I didn't see Maya, but I would visit her later and grill her about her and Nash. Nash had damn well better have gone to see her by this time.

I hadn't seen Coyote since the big fight in the wash. Had he forgiven me, eased his strictures, and let me go? I needed to know.

I also wanted to twist his fur to help me figure out who had made Undead Jim in the first place. Now that the dragon trial was over, I'd take more time to pursue the question. If some other goddess with the same kind of powers as my mother was walking around up here, I'd need to know. I also wanted to know why they'd brought Jim back

to life and given him Beneath powers. And, more important, would they try again?

I didn't *think* Coyote had done it, but he needed to help
me track this person down. We could start at the vortexes
and work our way from there.

Worrying about all this was a strain, so I told Mick I
needed to take a walk.

Mick didn't want to let me out of his sight—he had that
look.

"To the railroad bed, that's all," I said. "You won against
the dragons, and the kachinas will keep away the dragons
who still want to kill me. So you told me."

Mick didn't like it, but he'd learned something about
me—that if he tried to tether me, I'd struggle that much
harder to break free. I gave him a smile that said that when
I got back, he could tether me in a more fun way. I kissed
him and left.

The sun was well up in a blue sky, but the air was cool.
The brutal heat of Death Valley had no place here in the
mile-high elevation of my desert. I climbed to the top of
the railroad bed and breathed in clean scents of scrub and
grasses, cedar and juniper, fresh earth, dust, and wind. The
vortexes lay out there under the sun, closed, quiet.

The crow flew to the juniper it liked and gave me the
eye. I smiled at it. "Thanks, Grandmother."

She gave me her "humph" look, but I swore I saw affec-
tion in the glittering black orb.

"Janet Begay?"

At the woman's voice, the crow gave a hoarse caw and
flapped into the air. I turned to face a young woman who
was my age, perhaps a few years younger.

She was Native American, but I didn't think Navajo.
She was about an inch shorter than me, and her face was

rounder than mine. She wore her hair in a straight ponytail and had on ordinary clothes—jeans and a tight-fitting
black top. The only thing out of the ordinary was the lovely
silver necklace around her neck, heavy disks decorated
with swirls and animal symbols. If it was artisan-created, it
would be worth a thousand or so.

"Yes?" I answered.

"I've been wanting to meet you." She stuck her hands
in her pockets as I sometimes did, and grinned at me. "My
name's Gabrielle Massey. From Whiteriver."

"My chef is from Whiteriver," I said. I wondered if
this was one of the Apache woman's daughters or grand-
daughters.

"I heard." Gabrielle smiled at me again, the smile wrin-
kling her nose. She looked friendly, but in a standoffish
way, if that made any sense. As though she waited to see
how I reacted to her and was prepared to find the reaction
amusing.

"Are you looking for a room?" I asked politely. It never
hurt to be nice to a potential guest.

"Not this time." Her smile broadened. "You don't know
who I am, do you? And you think you're so good at reading auras."

I looked at hers—no, I looked *for* hers and didn't sense
one. That was weird. The only being whose aura I couldn't
always sense was Coyote's, because he knew how to suppress it. That's how he always snuck up on me.

She laughed. "I learned the trick. You should too. Your
aura is messy. Black and white, like smoke in sunshine. Two
natures struggling against each other so hard. I'm lucky. I
only have one kind of magic."

I stared at her, confused as hell and getting nervous. I

wasn't ready to experiment with my newly mixed magic, but I started imagining a nice, impervious barrier rising between her and me.

"I'm not here to hurt you," she said, as though she sensed what I wanted to do. "I just wanted to meet you, really. And for you to meet me. It's been a long time coming."

I gave up on politeness. "Well, since I don't know who the hell you are, I can't say I've been waiting."

"I want us to be friends," Gabrielle said, "which is why I've done it this way. But if you want to see . . ."

She dropped whatever shields she'd been using, and I got the full blast of her aura. It was white, glittering, hard as ice and just as cold. I swallowed a scream, and it nearly choked me. I'd felt this kind of aura before, and I knew exactly where. It had happened not a mile from this place about four months ago, on a powerfully stormy night.

The swift glimpse was all I got. By the time I'd drawn a single breath, Gabrielle's shields were back in place.

"I learned to hide," she said. "Because there are things out there that are so easily frightened."

Me being one of them. I swallowed on dryness. "You can't be . . . She said I was the only one that survived."

Gabrielle's eyes crinkled in the corners. "The thing about Mother, Janet, is that she lies. She's very, very good at it."

I felt as though one of the locomotives that used to traverse this track had just slammed into me. My mother, the goddess from Beneath, had made it a habit to possess women, get them with child through unsuspecting males, then withdraw. The resulting child, like me, often had too much magic in her for the innocent woman to carry. The mother most often died, taking the baby with her. The goddess had told me that in all the years she'd been trying, there had only been me.

The young woman who stood before me, half-Apache, half-goddess, was another.

Another me.

Another Janet.

The world just got very, very complicated.

"You made Undead Jim," I said, knowing I was right.

"Very good. I felt sorry for the guy, lying there stabbed to death, and all he'd done was dig up a few pots. I knew I could bring him back before he was too far gone, so I did. I didn't realize he'd go on a killing rampage."

I understood now why Jim thought I'd resurrected him, why the kachinas had thought I'd made him. They'd sensed Beneath magic, Gabrielle's magic, and thought it was mine.

"You didn't *realize?*" I repeated. "Three people dead, and you didn't realize?"

Gabrielle shrugged. "I'd never resurrected anyone before. Don't go all moralizing on me, Janet. I made a mistake. You fixed it. Everything's fine now."

"*After* I got buried alive by kachinas, nearly fried by dragons, and threatened with death by Coyote. Sure, everything's fine."

"Overreact, why don't you? I came here as a courtesy, because I wanted to meet my sister." Gabrielle grinned. "So I'm meeting you. I'll go away now, so you don't keep getting beat up for what I do."

"Go away where?" I asked in alarm.

"I don't know. Somewhere. Don't worry, I'll come back to visit." Gabrielle took her hands out of her pockets and smiled, sunshine glistening on her black hair. "See you, Janet."

And she vanished.

Not in a puff of smoke or anything dramatic like that. She was simply there, and then she wasn't.

I stood there for a stunned, frozen moment, and then I scrambled back down the railroad bed and sprinted back to the hotel, shouting for Mick.

Twenty-eight

Gabrielle didn't make a reappearance, but I had Mick and Cassandra help me put extra wards all over the hotel. I spent the next several days looking for my "sister," checking up on my friends to make sure she hadn't come near them, and warding their houses as well.

Coyote didn't come to me to make good on his promise to kill me for using the Beneath magic to kill Jim and save Mick, but the crow started hanging around a lot.

My grandmother was pissed as hell about Gabrielle and let me know it. The fact that Grandmother called me on the phone about her, voluntarily, the afternoon after I'd encountered Gabrielle, told me how upset she was. Grandmother had not been thrilled about *my* existence, but at least I was part of her blood and carried her earth magic. This Gabrielle—I hadn't sensed any other magic in her but that of Beneath, which meant her biological father and mother must have been ordinary humans. I drove home to Many Farms, taking Mick with me, to try to reassure Grandmother plus strengthen the wards on my family home. My mother had never been able to reach as far as Many Farms, but Gabrielle, born of this earth, could go anywhere she wanted.

In spite of my worries, I went through weeks of nothing very traumatic happening at my hotel. Guests came and went, I sold some of my art photos, Pamela started renting an apartment in town, and Cassandra moved in with her. The only excitement came when a soft-spoken Nightwalker appeared at my heavily warded door and asked if he could spend the night. He had the hollow look of one of the tame ones, so I let him, provided he was watched. He kept to himself, didn't make any trouble, didn't try to suck the other guests dry, and so I put the stakes back into my desk drawer.

Coyote finally did come to me, in a dream of course.

We stood in the cut of Chevelon Canyon, the petroglyphs on its steep walls glowing with their own light. The strange creatures in the pictures seemed to writhe and whirl, dancing in their own little frenzy. The creek flowed down the middle, quiet in the moonlight.

As usual, I was naked. So was Coyote, in his man shape this time.

"You did good, Janet," Coyote said, looking me up and down. "I'm proud of you."

"Is that why I'm still alive and walking around?"

Coyote gave me a grin. "Yep."

"How did I do good?" I asked, fed up. "You were ready to blast me into atoms the last time I saw you. You did try, and only Nash jumping in front of me saved me."

"I wasn't going to kill you, sweetie, just slow you down a little, but Nash misunderstood and got in the way. You see, you passed my test."

"Your test?" I glared at him, folding my arms over my bare breasts. "What do you mean, your *test*?"

"I needed to know what you'd do once you realized how powerful you were. Though I wasn't lying when I said I'd kill you if you screwed up. But you didn't. You chose to show compassion, even for someone as mindlessly evil as Undead Jim. I get that you had to destroy him in the end. He was wrong, and he had to be stopped."

Damn him. He regarded me with calm, dark eyes, still powerful, still a god. Still Coyote.

I glared back at him in rage. "Would it kill you to *tell* me these things at the time? I've been losing sleep worrying about what you were going to do to me."

"Poor baby. Staying awake so Mick can help relax you. Damn, I should have been looking in the window."

"Bastard," I said.

"Hey, it was for your own good, and you know it. You needed to learn how to silence that voice in your head."

The little voice had gone away. I think. I hadn't heard it in a while anyway, not since I'd learned to braid the Beneath magic and the storm magic into one entity. The good, the bad, and the ugly, coming together to make a useful whole.

"You learned, you grew," Coyote said. "I had faith that you would, my Stormwalker."

"And if I hadn't, you would have killed me?"

"Yep." Coyote put his strong arm around me. "But you showed your true colors. I love you, Janet."

"Thanks," I said drily. "But I'm still not having sex with you."

"Hey, a god's gotta try."

A lizard scurried by, scattering gravel as it scrambled for its next spot of cover. "I need to tell you something," I said slowly.

"About your sister?"

I made an exasperated noise. "How long have you known about that? Will it do me any good to ask why you didn't bother to tell me about her?"

"Relax. I didn't know until she came to you. I was lurking at the bottom of the wash, watching you. I heard when you heard."

"You're telling me you didn't know she existed? You knew all about *me*."

"That's because you blundered around burning down buildings as soon as your storm magic manifested. You sure know how to attract attention, Janet. And then your Beneath magic flared up all sparkly once you met your mother. Stealth was never your strength. This Gabrielle, now, she's learned somehow to hide what she is and hide it damn well. She must have been raised by someone powerful and very smart. We'll have to keep our eye on our Gabrielle."

"No kidding."

"Don't worry, sweetie. You have a lot of friends ready to protect you. Me, for one. Him, for another."

Him was the Koshare cartwheeling down the wash. He did a final cartwheel in front of us, misjudged, and fell on his backside. He gazed up at me with a look so comical I had to laugh.

This wasn't Ben Kavena; it was the real Koshare, who'd come to me in the cave. I noticed he'd left off the loincloth. What was it about naked flesh in Coyote-instigated dreams?

"My friend?" I asked the Koshare. "The one who buried me inside a volcano?"

The Koshare mimed grievous weeping. He fell on his back and kicked his heels like a kid in a crying tantrum.

"Yes, a friend," Coyote said. "You passed his test too."

"I'm glad I was such a star student."

"You should be."

The Koshare stopped kicking, arched back, and leapt forward to his feet. He grabbed my hands and spun me around, but only once this time before letting me go.

You are powerful, he said in my head. *You have the magic of the storms—good magic of this earth—and the magic from the place of origin. You have proved that you are strong enough to contain both. You have earned the great respect of my brothers and sisters.*

"Glad to hear it."

If you have need, ever, you call on me.

"Thank you." I was grateful for that, in truth. Kachinas were powerful entities, and I'd much, much rather they regarded me as a friend than an enemy.

"We're good to go, then?" Coyote asked me. "How about some celebratory nookie?"

I laughed, finally relaxing. "You never stop, do you?"

Coyote winked. "Okay, then. How about a beer at the Crossroads Bar?"

"Now, that I can do. Can I bring Mick?"

"Sure. You know I'm always up for a threesome."

The Koshare made a snorting noise. He studied Coyote in mock disgust and shook his hips so that his penis rocked back and forth.

Coyote's grin vanished. "Oh, yeah?"

He morphed into his coyote form, a blue nimbus surrounding his lanky body, and leapt at the Koshare.

The Koshare sprang into the air and started running for the shallow creek, Coyote right behind him. Halfway there, the Koshare spun around and pointed at Coyote, and Coyote's long tail burst into flames.

Coyote's high-pitched yowls echoed up and down the canyon, and he ran flat out for the creek. I heard a heavy splash and the hiss of steam.

The Koshare mimed sidesplitting laughter, sprang into the air, and vanished. I ran to the bank as Coyote climbed from the water, his limbs stiff, tail sodden. He shook himself out, glaring at the air where the Koshare had been, and snarled.

I fucking hate *clowns*.

One

Nothing quite makes your night like falling two hundred feet into a sinkhole.

My motorcycle spun as the solid pavement of the highway opened up under me, and then I was falling down, down, down, into the bowels of the earth. An avalanche of rocks, dirt, trees, and the speeding sheriff's SUV followed me into the abyss.

My bike and I separated, and it smashed against the side of the hole and broke into many pieces. I tried to stop my fall, to grab on to the roots that protruded from the breaking wall, but I fell so fast, my hands could close on nothing. The SUV ground its way down with the boulders, metal groaning, glass flying to mix with the shower of dirt and gravel.

I'd been wearing padded leather against the January cold, which protected me somewhat, but all my padding wouldn't help me if Nash Jones's SUV fell on top of me. I tried to reach into myself and draw on my magic, but I'm foremost a Stormwalker, which means I can channel the power of a storm, but I need a storm to be present to work the magic. The night, though raw with cold, was stubbornly clear.

I also had Beneath magic in me from the world below this one, but I had to be in a steady frame of mind to temper it with my Stormwalker magic, or I'd simply blow up the sinkhole and me and Nash with it.

Falling a couple hundred feet down a sheer drop with an SUV did nothing to put me into a calm frame of mind. I could only flail and claw, gasping for breath as dirt leaked under my helmet and threatened to suffocate me.

I don't know why I didn't die. Maybe the gods and the universe had other plans for me. I tumbled over and over, and at last came to rest on an upthrust boulder, while mud, roots, grass, and gravel poured on around me. A bone in my arm snapped, the pain sharp and numbing.

The sinkhole proved to be a wide one, and the SUV landed about five feet from me, wedged on its side between two colossal boulders. I sprawled like a bug on top of the mud-coated boulder, amazed that my heart still beat.

The landslide ceased but sent up a choking cloud of dust that cut off all air and light. The SUV went silent except for the creaks and hisses of engine parts.

I pulled off my helmet with my good hand—which sounds easy. What I really did was fruitlessly claw at it, crying with fear, until it at last unstuck from my head.

I thanked every god and goddess who might care that I'd bothered with the helmet at all. Sometimes I rode bareheaded, which was perfectly legal in this state, but I'd been traveling back from Chinle, and I didn't like to ride on the interstate without my helmet, especially at night. If I hadn't bothered with it, my brains would now be wet smears on the rocks around me.

It was pitch-black down here, the moonlight blotted out by the dust. Coughing, I crawled to the SUV, hissing through my teeth when I touched the hot metal of the engine. The vehicle was wedged in tight, the passenger door facing upward. I climbed onto the door, my hurt arm clenched against my side, my legs clumsy. The window glass had broken away, leaving a gap in the darkness.

"Jones," I croaked. It didn't even sound like a word, just a guttural sound.

Nothing moved. Everything inside was dark, the sheriff's radio and computer interface dead. The SUV was nothing but a silent hunk of metal, plastic, and fiberglass. I groped for Nash, half falling into the slanted cab.

Sheriff Nash Jones had been chasing me out on that lonely highway, because when I'd taken the turnoff to Flat Mesa, I'd driven right through his speed trap. I hadn't been paying attention, thinking about the nice day I'd spent at Canyon de Chelly snapping photos after an equally nice visit to my father in Many Farms. I'd flown past the clump of cedars on the deserted road, and Nash had burst out from behind them, lights flaring, to pursue me like a hungry lion.

Damn you, Jones, don't you have anything better to do with your nights than to park behind a tree with a radar gun? You seriously need to get laid.

I touched a warm body, Nash Jones in an unmoving huddle against the far door. I tugged off my glove and found his face, his neck, but I couldn't feel a pulse. I put my fingers under his nose and exhaled in relief when I felt a tiny breath touch my skin. He was alive.

Now what?

No radio, no cell phone, because I'd left mine behind at my hotel and Nash's, once I dug it from his belt, didn't work. The piece of magic mirror, which had been ground into the mirror on my motorcycle, must have been smashed along with every bit of my bike. The mirror was why I hadn't been carrying my cell phone—magic mirrors were more reliable.

The full magic mirror, which hung over the bar in my hotel, would know that its slice had fallen into the sinkhole—if, that was, the damned thing was awake. It liked to nod off at the worst of times. I hoped it was screaming at the top of its obnoxious voice that something was wrong, alerting Mick, my dragon shifter boyfriend, and Cassandra, my Wiccan hotel manager. Only the magical could hear the mirror, and I wanted them to hear it now.

Without being able to see past the dense cloud of dust, I had no way of knowing how far down we were. Or whether we'd continue to fall if the rocks shifted. Had we hit bottom, or had the rubble built a shelf that would stabilize awhile before again breaking apart?

I'd read somewhere that sinkholes were formed when groundwater finished eating away at the roof of gigantic caverns far below the surface. Once the layer is gone, the up to a thousand or so feet of rock above it collapses straight down, dragging everything on the surface with it and leaving a sheer-faced sink for everyone to ponder. The upland deserts are riddled with the things. They're very interesting when you read about them in a book, but not so much when one forms right beneath your feet.

Was this SUV rigged to send out a distress signal if it crashed? Nash's deputies would notice that they'd lost radio contact with him—wouldn't they? I had no idea where police technology stood these days, or whether Hopi County had enough money to keep up with the rest of the world. All I knew was that every communication device in the SUV was dead and silent. Nash himself still wasn't moving.

"Come on, Mick," I whispered. "Cassandra. Someone."

The truck shifted and my heart raced, my adrenaline off the scale. I felt my raw Beneath magic wanting to strike out in response, to get me the hell out of there. It tensed like a coiled rattlesnake and was just as deadly.

I closed my eyes to try to still my mind, but my heart was pounding so hard it made me sick. The Beneath magic responded, bright and white and strong enough to destroy the world. I didn't want to destroy the world: I just wanted to get out of this damned hole.

Light flickered through my closed lids, and I popped my eyes open, hope flaring. Was it the moonlight filtering through dust, or the flashlights of rescue workers?

Neither. The glow didn't come from the surface, but from the rocks around me. As I watched, thin lines of light began moving across the boulders. The lines looked like petroglyphs, pictures left from the ancient people of this land, but these glowed with phosphorescent-like light.

The lines thickened, multiplied, still glowing faintly, and then, under my watching gaze, they sprouted skeletal hands. I went utterly still. Bony fingers started flowing across rocks, making no sound, groping, searching.

I gripped the seat of Nash's truck and swallowed bile. I'd never seen anything like them before. Were they the gods of Beneath, trying to get out through a vortex down here? Or was this some new horror?

I touched my Beneath magic again, my only weapon. Using it without being able to twine it with my storm magic might either rip a hole in reality or make my brain implode. I wasn't sure which. But I knew with ever-increasing certainty that I didn't want those skeletal fingers touching me.

The hands multiplied as they poured across the surface of the boulders, sliding through them like fish through water. The sickly light increased until it lit up the whole inside of the cab, illuminating the blood that was black on Nash's head and face. His skin was pasty, his lips bloodless. He'd die if I didn't get him out of here.

Mentally, I closed my fist around a ball of Beneath magic and drew it to the surface. Oh, it hurt. It hurt like holy hell, as though someone had thrust a lit firework into my chest. I held on to the magic as hard as I could, knowing that if I lost control of it, it might kill me, Nash, and every living creature within a mile. But at least I could try to send up a signal, like a magical flare.

I opened my imaginary fingers, releasing a bit of light. The skeletal hands stopped, fingers moving slightly, each hand pulsing in exact time with the other. Like a heartbeat, I realized. *My* heartbeat.

In panic, I let out more of my magic, and the moment I did that, the hands oriented sharply on me.

The scream that came out of my mouth was more of a croak. I closed my mind over the Beneath magic, frantically shutting it down. As soon as my magic retreated below the surface, the hands stopped, stilling, waiting.

Shit, shit, shit. If the Beneath magic excited them, and I had no storm, then I was seriously screwed. All I could do was sit here with the dying sheriff and watch the hands fill the sinkhole to the right and left, above us and below. They started moving again, enclosing the SUV in a bubble of light, and I was so scared I wanted to puke.

A face appeared in the middle of the unnatural glow,

an animal face, long-nosed and pointed-eared. It looked
more like a glyph of an animal rather than a real one, but I
grasped the hope.

"Coyote? Damn it, help us!"

The animal faded, but the bony fingers didn't. They
were touching the SUV now, sliding through the metal and
fiberglass, and the whole truck began to groan.

I grabbed Nash and lifted him the best I could, cradling him against my chest. I feared to move him, but I
feared those hands even more. Nash himself was a walking
magic void—which meant that his body somehow negated
all magic thrown his way, even the most powerful stuff.
Whether he could negate these evil hands, I didn't know,
but I had to take what I could get. They were all around us
now, crawling across the hood toward the broken windows.

I couldn't just sit here and do nothing. The hands had
homed in on my Beneath magic, but maybe, if I were fast
enough, I could take them out before they could touch me.

I reached into myself for the ball of white magic again.
Coyote had told me he didn't want me to use my Beneath
magic unless I tempered it with storm magic, but Coyote
wasn't here, was he? And it wasn't my fault there was no
raging storm overhead. I was stuck in a sinkhole with weird
petroglyphs coming for me, and I wanted to go *home*.

I had to let go of Nash—I knew from experience that he
could negate my magic, even the strongest of it. I laid him
gently against the far door and braced myself on the dash to
push up through the broken passenger window.

I screamed as I threw the snake of Beneath magic at the
hands on the truck. Screams echoed through the sinkhole—
my screams—absorbed by the hands and thrown back at
me. The hood of the SUV melted, hoses breaking and fluid
erupting. And the hands kept coming.

I drew back for another strike when red light and sudden heat burst high above me. Hot orange light poured down the hole like a thousand bonfires strung together, burning the dust into little yellow sparks.

The skeletal hands froze, and as I held my breath, clenching the Beneath magic, they retreated. In the distance, I heard the bellow of a gigantic beast and then felt a downdraft as a huge dragon flapped his wings.

I started to laugh, tears streaming down my face. "Mick," I tried to shout, but all I could manage was a clogged whisper.

"Mick," I whispered again. "Down here."

NEW FROM NATIONAL BESTSELLING AUTHOR
ALLYSON JAMES

Stormwalker

"*Stormwalker* boasts a colorful cast of characters,
a cool setting, and a twisty mystery!
A fresh new take on paranormal romance!"

—Emma Holly

Janet Begay is a Stormwalker, capable of wielding the raw elemental power of nature, a power that threatens to overwhelm her. Only her lover, Mick, is able to calm the storm within her—even as their passion reaches unimaginable heights of ecstasy.

But when an Arizona police chief's daughter is taken by a paranormal evil, they find themselves venturing where no human can survive alone—and only together can they overcome the greatest danger they've ever faced.

M645T0210

THE NEW VICTORIAN HISTORICAL
ROMANCE NOVEL FROM
USA TODAY BESTSELLING AUTHOR

JENNIFER ASHLEY

~

Lady Isabella's Scandalous Marriage

Lady Isabella Scranton scandalized London by leaving her husband, notorious artist Lord Mac Mackenzie, after only three turbulent years of marriage. But Mac has a few tricks to get the lady back in his life, and more importantly, back into his bed.

"I adore this novel."

—Eloisa James, *New York Times* bestselling author

penguin.com